DETONATOR

PART ONE

1

'Nick . . .'

Voices.

'Nick . . .'

Women's voices. One of them sounds . . . Russian . . .

'You stupid little—'

Not that one. That's my mate Gaz's mum. I'd know her anywhere. She'd caught us throwing condoms full of tomato sauce off the roof of his block of flats . . .

Fuck, my head hurts.

Gunfire.

I can hear gunfire.

And screaming.

Not human screams. The scream of twisted, tortured metal.

I'm hiding in a storm drain. Darker than a shit pit down here. And colder than the grave. I've tabbed across the desert for ever, under fire. If I curl up tight, maybe they won't find me.

The steel plates above me creak and groan.

'I need your help, Nick . . .' A man's voice, now. 'I need your help . . .'

I hear breaking glass.

I'm moving. Shards of gleaming light. Blindingly bright.

I'm being dragged into the sun.

Wait a minute . . .

Glass breaking in a storm drain?

Where the fuck am I?

My eyelids flicker.

I'm right about the daylight, at least. But I can't see a thing.

I try to open them wide. The left one seems to work. The other's been glued shut. I wipe it with the back of my hand, smearing my knuckles with crimson.

My stomach clenches. Bile floods through my chest. I can feel it burning its way up to the back of my throat. I can't stop myself gagging. Whatever I had for breakfast fills my mouth. I try to control it. And fail.

Breakfast . . . ?

Lunch . . . ?

Dinner . . . ?

Whatever . . . It's all over the fucking place now.

I blink. Twice, I think. Maybe more.

A face looks back at me through the haze. A man's face. Fucked up. Blood leaking from a gash on his forehead. Spiky hair. Vomit clinging to the stubble around his lips.

I open my mouth to speak.

So does he.

A strand of yellowy green mucus stretches between his top and bottom teeth, like a bar on a cage.

I'm staring into a mirror. A rear-view mirror.

I glance down.

There's a wheel in front of me. A steering-wheel. At its centre, a silver badge.

Letters.

A word.

Nissan.

I'm pretty sure I don't drive a Nissan.

More creaks and groans. I lurch forward. A strap bites into my left shoulder.

Left shoulder . . .

What the fuck am I doing on this side of the wagon?

I grip the wheel hard. Both hands. Try to focus on the road ahead. But the windscreen is a starburst, a glass mosaic, impossible to see through.

I ram my foot down on the pedal. The middle one. The brake. It seems to make things worse, not better.

A digital display glows on a console to the right of the dashboard. An arrow at the bottom edge of a patch of green. Along the top, a thin orange line. Nothing else. Nothing to tell me where in the world I am. I scrabble at the knob on the right of the screen. Start to zoom out, maybe get some sense of my surroundings.

A crack. Then another. And another.

Not gunshots. Snapping wood.

Grinding. From below me, and each side.

I freeze.

Straighten my back, so slowly I can't even see myself move.

Then silence. Except for the whisper of a fan.

I reach for the air-con button, a millimetre at a time, and switch it off. Air-con. Somewhere hot? Desert? Maybe just summer.

I turn towards the passenger seat, where I guess the first of the voices must have come from.

The seat starts to spin.

No. Not the seat. My head. It's my head spinning.

I close my eyes. More vomit rushes up to invade my mouth. This time I manage to swallow it back.

When I open my eyes again I see there is no one there.

Which is fucking good news, because a very shiny black-and-white-striped steel rod has rammed itself through the windscreen and into the backrest.

Beneath it, where my passenger's arse would have been, lies a cigarette pack. I pick it up. Examine it closely. Marlboro. With a picture of a pair of charred, weeping lungs, and some kind of warning I can't read. Cyrillic, maybe. Whatever, the message is clear. These things aren't good for you.

I run my tongue around the inside of my mouth, blow into my hand. I smell like a sewer. I can't tell if I'm a smoker. I examine the index and middle fingers of my right hand. No nicotine stains. I don't think the cigarettes belong to me. So whose are they?

I slide the pack into the left-hand pocket of my bomber jacket. There's something in there already. Cold. Compact. A loaded mag for a pistol. Brass casing. Ten rounds. No. Thirteen?

Who cares?

Me. I should. You can't just spray these things around without knowing how many you've fired. How many you've got left.

How do I know that?

What was the brand again?

I can't fucking remember.

My hand retraces its journey into my pocket. It seems to know more than I do. Closes around a cardboard box. Brings it out.

Oh, yeah. Marlboro.

With a picture of a pair of charred, weeping lungs, and some kind of warning I can't read. Cyrillic, maybe. Whatever, the message is clear. These things aren't good for you . . .

I've been here before. I'm caught in a loop.

Pictures . . . words . . .

The same pictures, the same words, echoing in my head . . .

Then sliding away. Sliding beyond my grasp.

There's a day sack in the passenger foot well. Still in slow-mo, I release the safety-belt and lean towards it, clutch its handle, drag it on to the seat.

I see an eagle, wings and talons outstretched.

A manufacturer's logo, almost obscured by a smear of blood, stamped on to the stripy steel missile a hand's width from where it has punctured the skin of the wagon's grey leather upholstery. My blood, I reckon. I give it a wipe. There's a string of letters and numbers beneath.

Adler . . .

Adler Gesellschaft.

I repeat the words aloud. I have no idea whether they'll be of any use to me, but try to fix them in my mental databank. I need something to grab hold of. Something solid.

It isn't happening.

Above and beyond the missile: branches. Branches, covered with dark green needles. Pressed against the window. I swivel my head and shoulders to the left. Same on my side.

I'm in a malfunctioning dark green car wash. I need to get the fuck out of here.

I lean back. Bend my knee. Raise my foot above the dash. The wagon starts to tilt with me as I push at the screen with my boot. The safety-film balloons outwards, then bursts. A few fragments of glass lose their grip on the laminate and sprinkle across the bonnet. The rest cling on, but now I have a porthole to look through.

Cool air rushes in, heavy with the scent of pine.

More branches, left and right.

At the centre, sky.

A lot of sky. Sky of the brightest blue. A canopy of blue, rising from a distant jagged grey snow-topped mountain ridge.

That grinding sound again. The nose of the wagon dips far enough for me to see what's directly in front of me.

Nothing.

A break in the trees.

A sheer drop.

Rock.

Rock.

And more rock.

Pasture.

A river snaking through a valley.

Maybe four hundred below. Maybe more. My eyes aren't focusing too well.

Someone – fuck knows who – once told me it takes about five seconds for a falling body to reach terminal velocity. So how long before I hit the dirt? I have a feeling I once knew how to work out shit like that.

Now all I know is that it's the distance between living to fight another day and being totally fucked, once and for all.

I try the door.

No joy there. My palm slips off the handle. Jammed solid. Bent panel.

And the window won't power down.

I take a deep breath. Sit absolutely still. For fuck's sake, I need to get a grip here.

I wipe away the sweat on my jeans and feel something solid under my right thigh. The shape seems familiar. I bring it out into the open. A pistol.

I know about pistols. Not sure why.

I remove the mag, eject the round from the chamber; realize I can run through this drill blindfolded.

I close my palm over the top slide, so that enough of the muzzle protrudes from the bottom of my fist to smash it against the corner of the side window, immediately above where the part number is etched. I don't need to do it twice. There's a crack and a pop, a shower of sparkly bits and a whole lot more fresh air where the glass had been.

I unzip the day sack, then shove the mag and the weapon inside. Looping its strap over my right arm, I brush away the remnants of the glass from the edge of the frame with my left sleeve, get my arse off the seat and start to lean out.

With a noise like tyres on gravel, the pointy end of the wagon drops even further and its tail comes up. The trees on both sides do their best to hang on to it, but they're losing the battle. I grab the nearest branch, bend my knees, kick hard and launch myself out of the cockpit as it gives a final lurch and disappears over the edge.

I manage to hang on, but my hands are on fire. As they slide down the branch, pulled by the weight of my body, needles and splinters of bark tear into my flesh. I search for some kind of purchase with my toecaps but that just makes things worse. From the waist down I'm hanging into space.

I tighten my grip. Work my way back towards the trunk, hand over hand. It's not just my palms that are burning now. My shoulder muscles are too. I somehow manage to swing one knee on to firm ground, then pull up the other.

The dull crump of an explosion echoes across the valley. The wagon's fuel tank must have ruptured as it bounced off the rock face. The first spark would have ignited the fumes.

I don't look down. I can't.

The world's biggest fireworks display sparks up inside my head. A wave of molten lava forces its way up from the pit of my stomach, setting my chest on fire as it goes.

A jet of weapons-grade vomit spews out of my mouth.

I can't remember the last time I vomited.

I can feel myself frowning as I look at the sticky, brightly coloured stream that seems to be connecting my face to the bed of brown needles below it.

Then the pool of vomit rises up and smacks me between the eyes and the darkness rushes in again.

2

I don't know how long I lay there.

I thought I was drowning, to start with. Drowning in a mountain lake. No. Drowning in a pool of vomit. My own vomit.

'Nick . . .'

A man's voice.

Clipped. Precise. Eastern European.

'I need your help, Nick . . .'

You need *my* help?

That can't be right. I can't even help myself.

'I need your help . . . I don't know who else I can trust . . .

'Don't know who else I can trust . . .

'Can trust . . .

'Can trust . . .'

My head was an echo chamber.

Somewhere deep inside what was left of my brain, a drumbeat sounded.

Pounding.

Insistent.

'This is not a drill . . .'

More drums. A guitar, maybe.

'This shit is for real . . .'

I raised my head.

Fuck, my face stank. It was coated with puke. I was lying beside some trees, fir trees, on a bed of dank brown and yellow pine needles. I grabbed a fistful of them and wiped away as much of the puke as I could.

Then something made me rake over the needles so that there was no trace of it on show there either, and cover my tracks as I scrambled beneath the trees.

I felt my right arm jerk back. The strap of my day sack was looped around a low-hanging branch. I unhooked the thing and deposited it on the far side of the largest trunk I could reach, then crawled after it.

Took a couple of slow, deep breaths. A couple more.

I rolled over and lay on my back. Struggled to slow everything down. I knew I was in the shit. Physically and mentally. But I had no idea why.

I shut my eyes tight, opened them and looked up through the trees. Brown. Green. Little diamonds of blue. Sky, maybe? Fragments of colour, like fragments of memory. They seemed to make sense for a moment, until I lost my grip on them again.

To try to get my thinking straight, I decided to count backwards from a hundred. I was vaguely aware that that was what a doctor would ask me to do. What I would ask someone to do if I thought they'd taken a blow to the head and lost a few marbles.

Did that mean I was a doctor?

I knew I'd given my brain stem enough of a rattle to fuck up my short-term memory.

And I knew some other medical shit.

Morphine syrettes . . .

Field dressings . . .

Tourniquets . . .

I knew that when you took a round in the thigh you sometimes had to dig around and grip the soggy end of your femoral artery between thumb and forefinger to stop yourself bleeding out.

I filled my lungs with air and began.

'One hundred . . .

'Ninety-nine . . .

'Ninety-eight . . .

'One hundred . . .

'Ninety-nine . . .'

I was getting nowhere fast.

I didn't think I'd forgotten how to count. I just kept forgetting where I was in the sequence.

Maybe because questions kept echoing inside my head.

The same questions, probably.

Who am I?

Where am I?

'I need your help, Nick . . .'

I'm not a doctor. So not that kind of help.

No. I'm on a task.

I'd been briefed. By a man in a room. I couldn't remember who. But the room was green. A green room. A green room without windows.

'Nick . . .'

I'm Nick. I must be. I've heard that name before. People keep calling that name.

I patted the front of my bomber. Then felt inside. A wallet. Battered brown leather. I rifled through it. Euros. Not pounds. Not dollars. Not roubles. Euros. Hundreds. Fifties. Twenties. And a bunch of Swiss francs. A plain black card with no markings, just a magnetic strip on the back. And that was it.

I pulled up my right sleeve. A watch. Green face. Black LCD display. Multifunction Suunto Vector.

Time: 11:16.

Altitude: 1,987 metres. 1,987 metres? Shit . . .

Compass? South was the way to oblivion. I needed to go north.

Barometric pressure? I'd never understood barometric pressure.

A load of information. But nothing to help me ID the owner.

I reached into the neck of my T-shirt. No dog tags.

Look at my fingers, one by one. No rings. No bling.

I'm sterile.

What was I expecting?

'Nicholas . . .'

The Russian girl again.

Fuck, my head hurt.

Other voices.

Faraway voices.

Maybe I was imagining them as well.

No, I wasn't. They were coming closer.

That was why I was lying up. That was why I'd brushed over my tracks.

I rolled on to my belt buckle, raised my head and scanned my immediate surroundings. I was at the lower edge of a stretch of densely planted firs. I couldn't tell how far they ran uphill. To my immediate left there was a break: a path or track through the trees.

I grabbed the day sack and crawled deeper into cover. I lifted the waistband of my bomber jacket and reached for my pistol. It wasn't there.

Had I dropped the fucker?

A mag in my pocket, but no weapon in my belt.

Concentrate, for fuck's sake.

No, relax.

Breathe.

And don't lose control.

I peeled back the zipper of the day sack and slid my hand inside. It came out holding a matt black compact Sphinx 9mm. The Swiss might be neutral, but they knew a thing or two about stuff that goes bang. I pulled the top slide back along its rails until it locked. Next came the mag. I checked that the rounds were correctly bedded and slid it slowly into the pistol grip until I heard a gentle click.

I needed to keep noise to a minimum, so instead of allowing the top-slide spring to snap into place I released it with the side lever and eased the working parts over the mag. Then I pulled it back a couple of mills. The glint of brass in the ejection opening told me a round was in the chamber. I examined it closely, wondering why I knew this shit, then pushed it home again.

The weapon was ready. I hoped I was. For what, I hadn't a clue. These guys might have been coming to admire the view, but if there was a drama, I didn't want to take any chances.

The voices were louder now. I could also hear footsteps. Two voices. Two sets of boots on the ground. Getting closer.

I had no idea what they were saying to each other. Their waffle was low and guttural, one of those languages that makes even kids having fun in the playground sound like they're pissed off with each other.

Something else stirred in the depths of my mental databank. Then it was gone.

My eyes followed two pairs of legs coming down the track. One in shiny black tracksuit bottoms. One in khaki combats. They slowed to a halt some distance from the edge of the mountain. Turned towards me.

Acid attacked my sinuses as I lowered my nose into the pine litter. Unless you've caked it with cam cream, the shape of your face can give you away, and skin shines in the dark. If I knew stuff like that, maybe I wasn't completely fucked.

I felt my gut heave and vomit flooded over my tongue. To me, it sounded like an earthquake. Had it to them? I tightened my hold on the pistol grip. Fought to swallow as I slowly raised my head.

But they didn't move in. They bent to examine a trail of torn branches and scarred bark.

Were those lads on my side? Had they come to see if I was OK?

I kept eyes on them, hoping to catch sight of anything distinctive that might trigger some form of recognition. All I got to start with was footwear – hiking boots beneath the khaki, gleaming red and white trainers beneath the tracksuit. Then the occasional hand. The ones closest to me the colour of ebony. The furthest away tanned, white, a mat of dark hair sprouting from the backs of them, all the way down to the knuckles.

Nothing above the waist.

I followed the hands, looking out for a distinctive watch, a ring, a bracelet, a wristband . . . Though fuck knew how I'd hang on to the information if I did. No matter how hard I tried to focus on incoming sights and sounds, I could still feel them disappearing through the cracks in my brain.

No luck with the hands. These lads were bling free.

Then they stepped into the sunlight and looked over the precipice. I could see now that the shiny black tracksuit bottoms were topped off with a sleeveless Puffa jacket that matched the red of the trainers. The khaki combats went with a khaki shirt.

I could still see only bits of them, and from behind, but I could tell they liked whatever it was they saw. There was a lot of nodding and grunting and one clapping the other between the shoulder blades.

Wait a second . . .

A glint of silver. Khaki Combats did have a ring. A silver device in a red setting. A double eagle, maybe, but I couldn't be sure. Albania is the land of the eagles. Why did I know that? An Albanian eagle?

I began to make out the odd word among the grunts. It wasn't tourist chat. It was satisfaction at a job well done. It was how you reacted when you'd pushed a guy off a mountain, then confirmed the kill.

The lad closest to me – with the flash trainers and Puffa – was a very big unit. He was the one with hands the colour of ebony. And a headful of dreads.

A chunky gold bracelet slid out of his sleeve and hung around his wrist as they gave each other a huge high-five.

I could almost hear the cogs whirring inside my skull. I'd seen that boy in action before. But the where, when and how remained beyond my reach.

His mate was shorter and squarer. Not just dressed like a Hesco barrier. Built like one too. Something about his body language said he was the boss. He brought out his mobile, jabbed the speed dial and waffled into the mouthpiece. Either he was ordering himself a takeaway or he was sharing the good news.

Then, out of nowhere, words I recognized.

'Yeah. You're right. Fuck him. He got what he deserved.'

He cut the call, waved an arm then they both turned and tabbed back up the slope.

I never saw their faces.

3

As soon as they were out of sight I opened my mouth and listened. I needed to make sure they were well clear before I carried on trying to work out how the fuck I'd got into this shit.

I didn't count backwards again. I couldn't be arsed. When I could no longer hear voices and footsteps I started counting forwards instead. Much easier. And it helped me measure time and distance. I couldn't move on until they were well gone.

I got to thirty. I was pretty sure I hadn't missed any numbers out.

I moved on to sixty. It was slow work, but I was ridiculously pleased with myself. I felt a stupid smile spread across my cheeks.

I reached a ton and felt like cheering. I wasn't firing on every single cylinder yet, but maybe my brain wasn't terminally fucked after all.

I grabbed the day sack to check out what else was in there. Had I done that before? Probably. But there was only one way of finding out. I was about to put the Sphinx on the ground beside me when I heard another of those voices. 'Pistols are always attached, you knob-head. On the body, or in the hand. You must keep control . . .' No Russian accent. Jock, maybe. An instructor somewhere.

Control. Fuck. If that voice could see me now . . .

I hauled myself to my feet and tucked the barrel of the weapon into the front of my jeans, polymer grip within easy reach in case

I had to draw down. These things don't have a safety any more. They're double action, so unless I did something really fucking stupid I wasn't going to lose my bollocks as well as my marbles.

I peeled off my bomber jacket, spread it out on the ground and emptied the contents of the day sack on to the lining.

Clean shirt and boxers. Socks.

Compact Pentax 10x50 binoculars on a strap.

Titanium pen. UZI stamped on the barrel. It looked like you could use it to hijack an aircraft or fire it from a Rarden cannon. The top end, above the clip, had been designed to punch holes through toughened glass.

Disposable lighter.

Clear plastic Silva compass. Not a bombproof prismatic number with folding sights, one that you could put flat on a map.

Small bottle of mineral water.

A couple of second-hand Nokia mobiles, ten SIM cards and four battery packs.

But no ID.

I was getting the strong impression I was the Invisible Man, but this was fucking outrageous. Even if I was on the holiday of a lifetime, I'd need ID.

And if I was on the holiday of a lifetime, I wouldn't need a 9mm Sphinx and a spare mag.

I gave the day sack a good shake, then felt around in the lining and found a zipped compartment. Tucked inside was a wad of euros, a UK passport and photocard driving licence, both in the name of Nicholas Head. The Nick bit made sense. The Head bit made me frown. Nickhead. Was that my real name or some kind of joke?

I unscrewed the top of the mineral water. Got the lot down my neck. I couldn't remember the last time I'd rehydrated. And the inside of my mouth needed all the help it could get.

I threw everything back into the sack, including the empty bottle, and slung it over my shoulder, then moved towards the track.

I did a three-sixty before stepping out beyond the treeline. My head was spinning a bit, but maybe that was because of the sunlight. Pretty much everything stayed in focus as I looked right, up the hill. No sign of anything moving except the gentle sway of the firs as they reached for the ribbon of sky.

There was a trail of snapped branches and gouges in their trunks, some flecked with blue vehicle paint, on both sides of the track. The turf between them had been chewed up by tyres. Parallel furrows slalomed about eight metres to my left, ending with a short stretch of churned earth and rock where the funnel narrowed. Then nothing.

I walked to the edge of what must have been a four-hundred-metre drop.

A buzzard rode the thermals below me.

Then rock.

More rock.

Pasture.

A river snaking through a valley.

Smoke billowed from a chunk of burning wreckage. I narrowed my eyes. Shielded them with my hand. Some kind of wagon. Smashed beyond recognition. But I knew with sudden certainty that it was a Nissan. A 4WD. And that Hesco and his black side-kick thought I was still behind the wheel.

Good. Perhaps they'd relax now and leave it at that. Perhaps they'd get careless. But that didn't mean *I* could.

I turned back and followed the scars the Nissan's tyres had ripped into the grass that carpeted the break between the trees. The gradient steepened as I went. Thank fuck I hadn't a clue about my journey down. Was I even conscious? It must have been one hell of a ride.

I stopped short of the open ground and ducked into cover. I needed to check out the next tactical bound before making it. I knew that. Just like I knew the rules of concealment. Shape, shine, shadow, silhouette, spacing and movement are the shit that give you away. Two more lessons that must have been driven into me so deep they had become second nature.

I wove my way twenty or thirty paces through the wood, until I found a vantage-point with a clear view of the next three hundred and fifty metres of slope.

My eyes swept right to left and back again. Outcrops of bare rock, bald baby's heads, were scattered randomly across the turf. A small furry creature appeared briefly beside one, sniffed the air, then made itself scarce.

No other bodies, no other sign of life in the territory that separated me from the place the tyre marks seemed to begin. Black-and-white-striped rods, spaced at regular intervals, stood proud of the crest to either side of it.

I guessed that was where the road must be.

I waited, listened and looked.

Still nothing.

I set off, running at the crouch. My head bounced around on my shoulders, like my neck had turned into a Slinky.

About fifty up, I doubled over and puked my guts out again. There was hardly anything there, but it seemed to take for ever to come out. Not good in open ground.

Once I'd stopped retching, I waited for my vision to clear. The splashes of watery puke by my boots were a world away from the multi-coloured explosions you see outside pubs and kebab shops: they were clear and shiny and flecked with brown. I kicked over the traces anyway.

About a hundred up, I had a clearer picture of my objective. A stretch of retaining wall to my half-left; thickly mortared stone, constructed to stop the tarmac throwing itself downhill. I paralleled the tyre tracks then veered left towards it. As I drew closer, I could see it was waist high, enough to give me cover. I stooped beside it and listened for vehicle engines and the crunch of boots on gravel and allowed my stomach to settle.

All I could hear was a siren. Somewhere behind me, a few Ks further down the valley. It wasn't getting any louder.

I raised my head fractionally above the parapet and scanned beneath the safety barrier. There was no one in my field of vision in either direction. A two-lane blacktop that had been carved out of the rock face which towered above me. I was at the apex of a curve. Fragments of shattered glass glittered in the sunlight on the far side of it.

I skirted the stonework for a metre or two, then clambered on top of it. To my right, violent skid marks swerved across the white centre line, leading to a point, short of the barrier and beside another clump of trees, where the edge of the metalled surface had crumbled on to the turf.

This was where my rollercoaster had kicked off.

A sudden flashback . . .

I'm leading a two-car convoy. A shiny black SUV with darkened windows is behind me. I can see it in the rear-view. Then red lights fill the screen inside my head. A big fuck-off flatbed artic slamming on the anchors with zero warning.

A big fuck-off flatbed artic with a company name on the rear panel and an eagle logo on each mudguard.

The kind you'd expect to see clutching at a swastika.

I can hear the screech of tyres, see the smoke pouring out of the wheel arches. I can smell the burning brake fluid and bubbling rubber on the tarmac . . .

I could feel the sweat prickle in my armpits and groin and on the gash below my hairline. I could feel my shoulder muscles clench. But I tried to hang on to the image.

I needed to know what happened next.

4

The artic's brake-lights faded, bleached by the sunlight. I hadn't a clue where the SUV had gone.

But I could see another skid pattern on the tarmac now. Twin sets of parallel tracks – a wide-wheel-base monster – starting behind the first traces of the smaller vehicle's attempt to avoid collision, and ending after its side exit from the highway.

I took a closer look at the nearest of the striped poles that lined the roadside, designed to keep winter drivers from taking the quickest route – my route – down the mountain. There was an ID code stamped on its paintwork, about a hand's width from where it had been sunk into the verge. Then the manufacturer's name: Adler Gesellschaft.

And a graphic of an eagle, with wings and talons outstretched.

I'd seen this shit before.

I fished the UZI pen out of my day sack and rolled back my left sleeve. I saw a pattern of raised, bite-sized scars just below my elbow. Guard dog. German Shepherd? Rottweiler? I had the vaguest recollection of one not liking me in another life.

Painfully slowly, I scrawled 'Adler Gesellschaft' on my skin, then did my best to draw the logo as well. The drawing was shit: it looked nothing like an eagle. But the cogs in my brain seemed to be moving up a gear. I knew that one of these missiles had been buried in my passenger seat.

I looked along the line of rods standing to attention at the roadside. There didn't seem to be one missing. And even if it had been, there was no way it would have jumped up and hurled itself through my windscreen just for the hell of it. It had been launched off the flatbed. And some fucker must have helped it on its way.

I needed to find out who.

I needed to find out why.

And if I got half a chance, I'd plant the pointy end of one of those things – or something similar – in the middle of his fucking forehead.

I walked to the place my downhill adventure must have begun.

The ground fell away big-time from there. Going right or straight ahead, you'd leave the grass sharpish and the odd bit of shrubbery clinging to the rock couldn't stop a wagon launching itself off the precipice. That must have been the reason they'd chosen to force me off at this point. The wooded strip bottom-left offered the only safety barrier once you'd left the tarmac. And it didn't look as big from here as I'd thought it was when I was hidden in it.

So what had happened to the SUV once it had melted away from my rear-view?

I turned back to the road. As far as I could see, it was still deserted. Both ways. It continued beyond the curve, heading up the mountain through a corridor of trees. There was no sign of the artic. Of course there wasn't. After fucking me over, it would have kept on going.

I walked about fifty paces in the direction I must have driven from. To my left, the road hugged the hillside. To my right, there was another stretch of safety barrier. In the distance, the mouth of a tunnel bored into the mountain. I retraced my steps past the skid marks and carried on round the curve.

From there the tarmac snaked towards the trees. A hundred-metre length of heavy-duty wire mesh lined the scar that was left where it had been blasted out of the granite.

A signpost came into view, warning of a P half a K ahead. It didn't tell me where the fuck I was, but it told me what language they spoke here. Beneath a graphic of a big white tyre with snow chains in a blue circle were the words 'AIRE DE CHAÎNAGE'. So,

France or Switzerland. Not Belgium. No mountains in Belgium.

Almost immediately, the bank of firs sheltered the left side of the main. I could see a gravelled area to my right, tucked into a fold in the rock. And another tunnel a half-K beyond it.

As I got closer to the turn-off I heard the sound of rushing water. I left the verge and took to the trees. It was slower going here because of the steepness of the slope and the uneven footing, but I didn't want to be caught in the open. I dropped down below the level of the road.

I stopped for a moment to draw breath. My head wasn't pounding any more, but my heart was, and my gut ached. Fuck it, I'd worry about that later if I needed to. Right now I had to keep going. I did my best to avoid the tangle of roots and dead branches that littered the slope, but slid from time to time on loose scree.

Water spewed from a concrete pipe running under the road ten metres in front of me and splashed down the mountainside. I got close enough to scoop some handfuls of it over my face and into my mouth. It was cold and clear, washed away the acid in my throat and tasted fucking wonderful. I got as much as I could down my neck. I had no idea when I'd last rehydrated. Did I have a bottle in my day sack? Did I drink it? Maybe. But who knew when I'd have another chance? I rinsed as much as I could of the vomit off the front of my gear.

Built over the mouth of the pipe, a small metal gantry bridged the stream. Using it as a platform, I raised my head gradually above the verge.

A wooden hut, shutters down, stood by the entrance to the layby. Nothing special. Just somewhere for the snow-chain police to take a break from the winter-sports traffic and have a brew. A row of slatted tables and benches were anchored to a patch of concrete alongside it. This place obviously doubled as a picnic spot for anyone who didn't fancy an Alpine view.

The waterfall cascaded down the rock face at the back of the gravelled area, throwing up a curtain of spray. Nosy-parked a safe distance away from it was a shiny black SUV with darkened rear windows and a showroom shine. Armoured, probably, judging by how low it sat on its suspension.

My missing SUV.

A flash model that looked like someone with the world's biggest arse had sat on the roof and squashed it. A black Range Rover Evoque. I knew that was what it was because it said so on the tailgate.

It had French plates. I took out my magic pen and scribbled the registration on my wrist.

The wagon was completely still. No vapour spilling out of the gleaming twin exhaust pipes. I scanned the entire area for any sign of the big lads or their mates. Hesco had been talking to somebody at the top of the precipice. Somebody up here?

The place seemed deserted. Unless they were using the brew hut as cover.

I heard an engine. Lights blazed in the darkness of the tunnel. I stayed where I was long enough to check that they were just bog-standard headlamps, not blue and flashing, then dipped out of sight.

It slowed as it drew alongside the layby, and for a moment I thought it was going to pull in. Why? Reinforcements for Hesco and Dreads? Or holidaymakers stopping for a pig roll and a piss? I hoped neither. I didn't want to spend all day there.

Seconds later the engine note changed and the vehicle accelerated away towards my bend.

I grabbed the nearest trunk and hauled myself back up. The second vehicle was nowhere in sight. The brew hut was directly between me and the Evoque. Keeping low, I scooted across the tarmac and sheltered behind it. Right up close to the woodwork. Not good. Especially on a dodgy gut. It had recently been given a coat of preservative. The stench caught at the back of my throat.

I worked my way round to the far corner, keeping eyes and ears open for movement on the dead side of the hut. Not that I'd have heard anything above the roar of the waterfall. A fine mist hung in the air as it crashed against a pile of boulders before draining away under the road.

I was now invisible both from the Evoque and any passing traffic. I put down my day sack, took a deep breath and leant out.

It was a five-door model. I couldn't see through the darkened rear windows: they just reflected whatever happened to be opposite them. The front ones were tinted, but transparent enough to let me check the driver and passenger seats for movement or shadow.

They looked clear.

And if I was wrong about that, so what? Mincing about wasn't going to change anything.

The nearest door was on the passenger side and I expected it to be locked, but I strode across to it like I was the owner.

It opened with a soft clunk. And, fuck, was it heavy. Armoured, for sure. The window glass was laminated, and as thick as my thumb.

As I slid on to the seat the screen inside my head kicked off again. I'm in the Nissan, shortly before it loses its grip on the mountain. And I know that if I hadn't swerved left when the artic rammed on its brakes, the stripy steel missile would have gone right through me.

I was now in a world of cream leather and dark-wood veneer. No sign of ignition keys. A small medallion – the patron saint of travellers – swung gently from the rear-view in the air I'd managed to disturb.

Air that smelt faintly but unmistakably of cordite and blood.

5

I raised my eyes to the mirror. The St Christopher hadn't worked its magic for the body that was sprawled across the bench seat behind me. I swivelled and squinted past the headrest.

A small man, lying on his stomach, frozen in the act of diving sideways, arms outstretched, making for the door.

He was wearing designer jeans with a carefully ironed crease and a cashmere pullover. The pattern on the cashmere matched the one on the upholstery: cream, with two big splashes of crimson. I couldn't see his chest, but the two exit wounds in his back were the size and consistency of a Starbucks Strawberry Frappuccino.

It would take more than a quick wipe to fix the leather too. The rounds that had killed the passenger had ripped straight through it.

He had a big fuck-off platinum watch on his left wrist. I took a closer look. A Zenith Class Traveller. No jewels, no glitter, but loads of little dials. It had probably cost even more than the wagon.

I didn't need to go to the trouble of checking his pulse.

I heard an engine.

I glanced up as another car appeared from the direction of the tunnel. It whipped past, right to left, without showing the slightest interest in this little drama. I did a three-sixty around the immediate area for good measure. The place was still deserted.

I could see only the side of the victim's face – chiselled out of stone; precisely trimmed, swept-back hair, greying at the temples – but when I looked down again, something triggered the thought that this wasn't the first time we'd met.

I reached through the gap between the seats and tried to lift his head. And realized that I wasn't sharing this wagon with one corpse. I was sharing it with two.

I reversed out of the front passenger seat at warp speed and pulled open the rear door.

I wasn't wrong. Hidden under Mr Cashmere there was another body.

A small one.

From this angle I could see a child's head buried beneath the man's torso. He hadn't been trying to escape. In the final seconds of his own life, the man had tried to save the boy. Who would do that? He wasn't a BG. Not with those clothes and that watch. He must have been his father.

The killer had been inside the wagon. Nothing short of an RPG would have given the outside of it more than a scratch. And there was no sign of forced entry, no scarring on the skin of the Evoque.

I tried to roll Dad back far enough to allow me to separate them. The kid was six or seven years old, max. He was wearing trainers and some kind of football strip. His torso was covered with so much blood I couldn't tell what had killed him. I couldn't even tell what club he supported.

I was about to turn my attention back to his dad when I saw a small red bubble form at the corner of the boy's mouth, then burst. I gripped his arms and dragged his limp body from the car. It was still warm.

I carried him across the gravel and laid him down on a strip of turf behind the brew hut. More bubbles. I wiped the gore and snot away from his nose and mouth and cleared his airway. Then I gave him a rapid once-over to make sure he wasn't doing any leaking of his own. He wasn't. It wasn't his blood. It was his dad's. My palms were slippery with the stuff.

He grimaced and his eyelids fluttered. Then they opened wide.

He smacked my hand away.

'Nick . . . ?'

It wasn't the first time today I'd been called that.

'How do you . . . ?' I didn't bother finishing the question. It could wait. 'Stefan?' The name crept out of the muddle in my brain before I even knew it was there.

He gave the smallest of nods, but didn't utter a word. Then his hand shot out and clung to me, like a limpet. I murmured some reassuring waffle and managed to unclamp his fingers.

My top priority now was to stop him going into shock. I knew this kid. There were things he could tell me. And if I lost him, we were both fucked. I had to make sure he didn't go down.

I pulled off my bomber and wrapped it around his upper half. Then I opened my mouth and listened, scanning as much as I could see of the road in both directions.

All clear.

I wiped my hands clean on the grass and went back to the Range Rover. We needed to make distance from it. But there was some shit I needed to do before we got out of here.

My first instinct had been to bundle the kid back into the wagon, try to start it and drive somewhere safer where I could sort out my options. But hot-wiring those things was virtually impossible now, and most of them had trackers. I also couldn't go through either tunnel without running the risk of being caught on camera. And moving the thing would leave whoever had done this in no doubt that I was still alive.

My memory was shot to pieces, but I could still do the procedural stuff, if I didn't think about it too hard. I shut the rear door so the corpse was out of sight and slid back on to the passenger seat. The clock on the dash read 13:27. The same as my Suunto.

I flipped open the glovebox. A bunch of CDs, a French chocolate bar. A pack of cigarettes. Marlboro. A picture of a guy in an oxygen mask. A health warning in Cyrillic lettering. A slim box of matches. Brown. Gold lettering. Five stars. Hotel Le Strato, Courchevel.

Beneath them, two spiral-bound map books. France and Italy. I chucked both into my day sack, along with the chocolate bar and the matches. I pressed the tailgate release. As the hydraulics worked their magic, I stepped out of the passenger door, closed it, and checked out the contents of the boot.

A neatly folded suede jacket was draped across two matching cases. They smelt of money. Gold and brown, with a repeating pattern of Vs and Ls. And a couple of big holes where the rounds had blasted through the back of the seat.

There was also a kid-size rucksack, containing a change of clothes, a washbag and a hand towel. I frisked the jacket and found two passports in crocodile-skin covers and a bunch of crisp euro and rouble notes in a gold clip. This guy obviously didn't do credit cards any more than I did.

The passports were both dark blue with gold lettering and some kind of shield. The first bearer was from Ukraine. His name was Francis Timis. And he had short-stay visas for France, Italy and Switzerland.

Some more useful stuff clicked into place.

Ukraine.

Francis Timis.

Frank Timis.

Frank.

I did know him.

He had a job for me.

He needed my help.

He didn't know who he could trust.

That was why I was there.

The second passport belonged to the boy, Stefan Timis.

I replaced the cash and refolded the jacket. I pocketed both passports, and undid the cases. Nothing useful. Just clothes, and in the smaller one, some books that looked more like homework than fun. One of the spent rounds had gone most of the way through a maths instruction manual. I closed them again, grabbed the rucksack and pressed the button to shut the tailgate.

I legged it back to the boy. He hadn't moved a millimetre. He wasn't even blinking. Just staring up into space. The lights were on, but nobody was home.

I was tempted to fuck off out of there and leave him where he was. But I knew that wasn't an option. I had to find out why I was in this shit, and right now he was the only one who could help. For starters, he'd know who'd killed his dad.

He could also ID me. And being IDed was the last thing I needed. I had to stay dead for as long as possible.

I raised him to a sitting position against the brew hut, slung my day sack and his rucksack over my right shoulder and lifted the boy on to my back. I didn't need to tell him to hang on. He'd locked his arms around me, his blood-wet arms soaking my hair, before I threaded my wrists under his knees.

I stayed in the shadow of the hut as a tour bus thundered past, left to right. Thank fuck none of the passengers was in the mood for a piss or a picnic. I gave it a count of five, then stumbled across the road and into the trees.

Small, bony arms slid up and tightened around my throat as the hill steepened and I hit a patch of scree. I grabbed the nearest trunk to steady myself and wrenched them down on to my chest again. I got some air back into my lungs. 'Stefan, you're going to fucking throttle me if you keep doing that . . .'

I carried on down, paralleling the stream. I had no idea whether I was heading for some *Sound of Music* mountain pasture or another fucking great precipice, but even with temporary oxygen starvation, I seemed to be capable of a bit of joined-up thinking.

After about thirty slips and slides and one tumble, the ground levelled out. I glanced back. I could no longer see the road. I couldn't even see the stripy rods that told me where it was. The stream was flowing quite gently there. I moved to my half-right and crouched beside it. The boy's arms unlocked and I helped him find his feet.

I plunged my hands into the cold, clear spring water and gave them a good rub, then rinsed Frank's blood off my head. I dried them on the front of my jeans, opened Stefan's rucksack and told him to get his kit off.

He gave me a look that was still part zombie, but I got the impression he wasn't completely out of it.

I pulled off my jacket and grabbed a handful of his football shirt and mimed what I wanted him to do. 'Off! The blood . . .'

All I got back was a blank stare. Maybe he didn't speak much English.

No. He definitely spoke English.

And I'd seen that stare before.

It was the stare of a kid who's no stranger to pain. Top-of-the-range wagons and designer luggage and the shiny watch I could now see on his wrist hadn't sheltered him from some severe dramas in his young life.

And not just today.

Another image took shape inside my head.

A bearded mullah. Flashing eyes. Knife raised. His other arm around the boy's throat.

We're in a madrasa.

Afghan? No, Somali.

I feel my right index finger curl and take first pressure on the trigger of my Makarov. My target grabs a fistful of his captive's hair and prepares to plunge the blade into his chest.

My foresight, ramrod straight, locks on to a bead of sweat a centimetre above the mullah's left eye.

Second pressure.

Then everything above the beard turns to mist, and I'm back beside an Alpine stream with a lad whose life I've saved before.

I took my bomber out of my day sack. Did my best to rinse the blood and vomit off the front and sleeves. Swapped my T-shirt for the clean one.

He finally got the message: pulled off his outer gear and his trainers. He had some kind of medallion on a chain around his neck. A St Christopher. It bounced around in the sunlight as he washed himself. Pretty soon the stream turned red.

I handed him the towel from his rucksack, then the spare shirt, a maroon polo with a crocodile logo, and khaki shorts. I filled the water bottle while he dressed himself and fastened the Velcro strips on his trainers. They each had a crocodile too. So did his socks.

I shrugged on my bomber. No crocodiles anywhere near it. It still had a pink patch about halfway down, beside the zip, but I reckoned it wouldn't stand out once it was dry. It started to steam. I hoped the warmth of the day would sort it out before too long.

I picked up his football kit. The shirt was still covered with blood but I could now see a white badge on the front of it – a set of antlers, two pillars and a crown, and the words '*Città di Brindisi*'.

'*Don't leave a thing that betrays your presence . . .*' The Jock voice again. I wrapped it in my T-shirt and shoved it in the side compartment of my day sack. Then I put a hand on each of his shoulders and looked into his troubled eyes.

'Stefan?' I gestured back towards the road. 'The car . . . Your dad, right?'

His face crumpled.

I gripped him more firmly. 'What about me? You know my name. Why am I here?'

I wasn't getting anything back.

I showed him the Hotel Le Strato matchbox. 'Have we been to this place? Did we stay at this hotel?'

I finally got something. A shake of the head.

I felt my teeth chew at my bottom lip.

In the movies, this is where the hero slaps the kid to bring him to his senses. It doesn't work. Why did I know that? I knew that because when I was his age my stepdad did the slapping. It either triggered a major meltdown or just prolonged the silence.

I realized I'd asked the wrong question. The Le Strato had rung another bell because I'd driven past it. Not last night, maybe, but some time, on his dad's business. I needed to broaden my target area.

'So, not the hotel. But Courchevel, yeah? You've got a place in Courchevel? A chalet with a green room? A green room with no windows?'

A green room with a desk. And monitors. And photographs.

A green room where Frank had told me what was on his mind.

Stefan's mouth stayed shut but I saw his jaw start to work like he was chewing something he didn't fancy before swallowing it.

I was beginning to think I should go the slapping route after all when it opened.

'Cour-che-vel . . .'

For a moment, I thought he might be correcting my pronunciation. Then a strobe sparked up in my head. I pictured, in rapid succession, the sign for 'Centre Village', the Verdons ski lift, the entrance to Frank's chalet.

We were in France.

Something else sprang at me, fuck knew where from. 'And a pool, yeah? An indoor swimming-pool?'

For a moment, the tension seemed to leave his body.

'I love . . . to swim . . .'

I sat him down and took out the French map and the Silva compass. After a few false starts and a bit of head scratching, I zeroed in on the Haute Savoie, then the stretch of road that seemed to match the reference points – tunnels, curve, waterfall, layby – of the killing zone. It would have taken us to Turin.

I reckoned Courchevel was fifteen Ks or so as the crow flew. But I wasn't about to bring out the crampons and karabiners, even if I'd had some with me. So maybe three times that, if we went round the peaks instead of over them.

I was about to fold the corner of the page when the Jock voice came back into my head. *'Never mark a map. Why tell the enemy where you're going and what you're doing?'* I buried the matchbook and put the map and compass back into my day sack. The passports went in there too. I looped the binoculars strap around my neck.

'Right. We're sorted.' I kept it simple. 'I'm going to get you home.'

6

I planned to tab as far as we could down the valley, then we'd make our way to Courchevel. After what had happened to his dad, I wasn't expecting it to be a place of safety, but I needed answers to the questions that were buzzing around in my head, and I had nowhere else to start.

'Do you think you can walk?'

Another nod.

I loaded myself up again with my day sack and his rucksack, and he reached for my free hand. His palm was cold and a little bit clammy. I gripped it and aimed us at the point where the stream looked like it exited the trees.

The gradient was still steep, but the ground was solid and we made steady progress. Every so often he grabbed a low-hanging branch to help him keep his footing.

There was a sheer drop at the edge of the treeline, but only for a couple of metres. I lowered the bags, transferred the pistol to the back of my waistband, then got down on my belt buckle and slid over the edge feet first.

He followed the same drill and wriggled after me. As soon as my Timberland boots touched the ground, I put the Sphinx back where it belonged and reached up for him.

The next stretch wasn't pasture, exactly, but the slope was no longer forty-five degrees. We zigzagged down it, ramming our heels firmly into the turf with every step.

About two hundred further on I had a clearer view of the valley floor. I could see our stream gather momentum with a series of leaps and falls, on its way to join the river. I could see the still smoking wreckage of my wagon. And I could see blue lights flashing in the distance, making their way along the road towards it.

A cluster of farm buildings were dug into the hill another four or five hundred below us. I brought up the binos and took a closer look. Stone bases; wood cladding; shallow-raked slate roofs. Barns, cowsheds, all that sort of shit. Movement. A couple of carrot-crunchers in dungarees and wellies loading stuff on to their quad bikes.

We weren't kitted out as hikers, and Stefan's crocodiles looked like they'd be more at home in a five-star hotel than yomping across the hillside, so we had to stay out of sight as much as possible. I steered him to the right, towards a fold in the ground that would give us cover and allow us to skirt around them.

He stepped into a rut or a rabbit hole as he changed direction and fell heavily, twisting his foot. He immediately heaved himself up and stumbled on.

After a few paces I could see he was hurting. His teeth were gritted – he was determined to stick at it – but his cheeks and forehead had lost their colour and his eyes were starting to leak. It wasn't just the injury: the nightmare in the Range Rover was going to fuck him up too.

I grabbed his hand again to help him along, and made encouraging noises about home, but it made no difference, so I sat him down and took a closer look at his injury. The ankle wasn't broken, but the flesh around it was ballooning fast.

I took out my T-shirt and tore a clean four- or five-centimetre-wide strip off the bottom of it. I unlaced his trainer and bound the swelling in a figure of eight, starting under his arch and finishing halfway up his calf.

Then I carried him the rest of the way to the gully our stream had cut into the hill. It was only about a metre wide and a metre deep to start with, but enough to give us both some cover. I sat him down again, took off his trainer and shoved his injured foot in the stream. He tried to remove it almost immediately, but I didn't let him. I knew that the water was bitingly cold, but it would reduce the swelling and ease the throbbing. I handed him the water bottle and the chocolate bar to try to take his mind off it.

As he got munching I had another look at the map. I wasn't wrong: no shortcuts. That settled it. I couldn't leave the kid in a stable and pretend it was Christmas. And carrying him all the way to his dad's front door would take for ever. 'Mate . . .'

Stefan looked up.

'We need to find us some transport.'

We went into piggy-back mode again. The gully widened and deepened as we went. After a hundred metres I put him and the luggage down, crawled up on to the turf and, keeping low, eased myself forwards until I could take a closer look at the out-buildings.

A track ran through the property below me. One of the carrot-crunchers was bouncing his quad bike towards a barn that stood at the far end of it, beside a low wooden bridge spanning our gully. Beyond it, a bunch of cows grazed at the edge of the pasture, beside a stand of firs.

I ducked back into the gully and loaded myself up again. It broadened and deepened as it headed downhill. I had no idea whether the lad I hoped was about to become my new best mate was on his way to do a bit of routine maintenance or to have a chat with the livestock, but I had to start somewhere, and I figured this was our best chance of a result.

I reached the bridge before he crossed it. It was a sturdily built, slatted hardwood affair. I deposited Stefan underneath it, with his ankle back in the stream and the bags alongside him, and put a finger to my lips. His eyes were glassy and there were beads of sweat on his forehead, but he was on receive. I handed him the water bottle again and motioned for him to drink.

I stayed under the bridge with him and listened. I could no longer hear the engine, so the driver had either taken a detour or parked up. After a moment or two a hinge creaked, a can rattled and – judging by the sudden flurry of grunts and groans – some heavy-duty equipment was being moved close by.

I grabbed hold of the nearest post and hauled myself up until my eyes were level with the top of the bank. The side of the barn was about five metres away. The quad bike was parked out front. The grunting and groaning continued, but there were no bodies in sight.

I brought up the binos and had a good look along the track. When I was satisfied that no one else was approaching from the main farmyard, I scrambled into the cover of the wall, stopped and listened again. More grunts and groans and sounds of heavy lifting, then silence. I moved round to the front of the building and took up position beside the open door. It was one of a pair. The other was bolted shut. A padlock the size of a landmine hung from a staple not far from my elbow.

The quad's engine was ticking. It was a red Honda 300 4x4 All-Terrain Vehicle. It said so on the cowling, underneath the odd splash of cow shit. It had front and rear racks and a key in the ignition. But I couldn't just leap on to the saddle and fuck off. The owner was probably fit as a butcher's dog and I didn't fancy my chances of hoisting Stefan and our stuff out of the ditch and scooting into the trees before a couple of big lads in dungarees jumped on us and fucked us over. I needed to buy us some time.

Sunlight flooded through the entrance into the barn. I looked inside, as far as I could without making myself visible. From where I was standing I could see a big fuck-off workbench with a circular saw. Behind it were shelves of farm kit, fuel cans and well-maintained hand tools, rolls of gaffer tape and baling twine, all in their proper place.

The trick was going to be to gain entry without presenting a target. The only advantage to being backlit was that my face would be in shadow. I didn't want to have it imprinted on anyone's memory if I could avoid it.

I heard movement inside. I opened my mouth to deaden the sound of the blood pumping through my head, and listened more closely. Whatever Mr Dungarees was up to, he was doing it at the back of the building, as far as I could tell. Fuck it. I couldn't play guessing games all day. I needed to get in there.

I gripped the Sphinx and removed it from my waistband. I

didn't want to use it unless I had to, but it would go a long way towards persuading my target to keep quiet while I constrained him. And if I had to make it go bang, it would guarantee his full attention.

I took a couple of deep breaths, flexed my knees, bent low and aimed for the shelter of the workbench. There was no sawdust anywhere near it. Either this guy was the tidiest carpenter in the universe or this was what he'd just been relocating.

I stayed in the crouch and scanned the space beyond it. The sunlight picked out some bits and pieces of agricultural machinery and a couple of galvanized-metal feeding troughs. After that, the whole place was in shadow.

I reached for a roll of tape, shoved it over my forearm, and crept past the workbench and the troughs. I didn't have time for my eyes to adjust to the darkness, but I immediately felt safer in it. As long as I didn't collide with anything noisy, it was the best protection I had.

I heard movement again at the back, to my half-right.

And voices.

Fuck.

With my brain not yet firing on all cylinders, getting to grips with one body was never going to be easy. Sorting out two – and without being pinged – was pretty much out of the question. That was where the Sphinx came in. I somehow knew I didn't kill real people. I also knew that when you're staring down a muzzle and it's a new experience you tend to do exactly what you're told.

Then I heard a slap and a gasp and a giggle, and some of the grunting I'd caught earlier made more sense. This lad hadn't just been rearranging the furniture.

The giggles and gasps were coming from the far corner of the barn, but I followed the line of the wall rather than heading across the middle of the floor. The sounds got louder as I drew nearer. They were coming from a storage room, whose door wasn't quite closed. I eased it the last couple of centimetres into its frame and quietly fastened both bolts. They were big old-fashioned cast-iron rods, and wouldn't go anywhere in a hurry.

Whatever, I reckoned it would be a while before the lad inside got his dungarees back on, and with any luck he'd then assume that his mate was taking the piss by shutting him and his girlfriend in. Who knew? I was just pleased I didn't have to give him the good news with the weapon, after all, and risk compromising myself. I tucked it back under my jacket and, keeping to the shadows, began to retrace my route.

My next priorities were to help myself to a pair of bungee cords off the storage shelf, then to push the ATV to the bridge before firing it up. The couple I'd locked up were already making quite a bit of noise of their own, and an extra bit of distance would help to draw less attention to mine.

As I skirted the largest of the feeding troughs I sensed movement in the darkness behind me and to my right.

I turned, but wasn't quick enough to see whoever smashed me across the back with the world's biggest lump of wood.

7

The roll of gaffer tape flew off my arm and skittered across the deck as I dropped to my hands and knees, fighting for breath. I toppled forward, hoping the lip of the trough would get between me and the next blow.

My kidneys felt like they'd been belted with a railway sleeper and my lungs weren't too happy either, but by the time I hit the ground I'd got some air into them and pulled up the front of my jacket to clear the pistol grip. I stayed face down for a moment, curling my body to take the pain and free the weapon. My right hand went into autopilot and whipped it out of my belt as I rotated to face whoever had taken me down.

All I could see above me was a mass of dungarees and wellington boot. My head spun as the Sphinx swung up and into the aim, almost as if it had a mind of its own. A chunky moulded rubber sole, caked in cow shit, steamed towards me and connected with my knuckles. The Sphinx flew out of my hand, clanked against the galvanized-metal side of the trough and spun into the darkness.

I rolled and turned, then scrabbled after it. The boots were crunching in the same direction, a metre in front of me. My only option was to try to climb aboard him, try to control him before he reached the weapon. Fighting to maintain my focus, I threw my hands around his legs to slow him or bring him down. He kicked me away with one but I managed to hang on to the other.

I was a dead weight, clamped to his ankle like a ball and chain, but he was a very big lad. He took another couple of paces, dragging my body with him, and started to bend down. I glimpsed a giant paw brush the concrete ahead of me. There was nothing I could do to stop him.

I let go of his leg and made a grab for his forearm as the pistol grip disappeared into his right hand. I put every ounce of strength into trying to stop the business end of it pointing my way. It wasn't enough. His grip was like a vice. Slowly but surely, the muzzle came round towards me.

I grabbed the barrel. He grunted as he struggled to shake me off. His knuckles turned white as his right fist tightened around the grip. His left banged down on the top of my skull, then pounded against the back of my neck. I felt something dribble down my right temple.

I jerked and twisted, and somehow managed to dodge the full weight of his blows. Then I felt the cold gunmetal pressed against my cheek and went very still indeed.

From this angle, there was a chance the round would go straight through my oral cavity, just fucking up some of my teeth, gum and upper jaw before it exited.

If I carried on jerking around, I might dislodge the muzzle, but I might also end up with a 9-mill ripping a hole in my brain.

Everything went into slow-mo.

I could hear him clear his throat.

I could smell the garlic on his breath.

I could feel the sweat dripping off his palm and running down my chin.

I could almost feel his finger squeeze the trigger.

If this was where the story ended, then fuck it: that had always been part of the deal.

The hammer reached its tipping point and rocketed the firing pin towards the round's percussion cap.

But instead of losing a big chunk of my face, I heard the unmistakable sound of the dead man's click.

Every second I was alive after that was a bonus.

Reaching up, I grabbed two clumps of damp and greasy hair and wrenched his face down hard on to the top of my skull. He tried to resist, so I cannoned upwards until we connected and he gave a yell. I didn't know where I'd hit him and it didn't really matter. I tightened my grip and butted him once more. I saw starbursts, but I was expecting them. That's the shit that happens.

It bought me enough time to struggle to my feet but not to aim my first kick. It didn't matter. Finesse wasn't the order of the day. Anything to slow him down. I went for his centre mass for starters, then moved on up. I didn't want to permanently damage him. On the other hand, I wasn't messing about. I needed to stop him thinking, and doing anything I didn't want him to do.

He stayed on his feet, but started to droop.

I got a couple of blows into the side of his head and that was enough to make him come out with the white flag. He dropped like a sack of shit.

The locked door at the back of the barn was taking a hammering from the inside. The first carrot-cruncher sounded very concerned. He shouted, 'Claude,' once or twice, then hollered a stream of profanities. It didn't take a UN interpreter to help me catch his drift. *Fucking let me out of here, you bastard . . .*

I didn't mind. Nobody was going to hear. And as long as he was shouting, he wasn't on a mobile phone to the police.

Claude wasn't going anywhere fast. I let him lie where he'd fallen while I reclaimed the gaffer tape and the pistol from beside a pallet loaded with fence posts. The pistol went into my waistband.

Claude stirred when I got back alongside him. Maybe he'd heard the rasp as I pulled a length of tape off the roll. Maybe the door banging and his mate yelling had forced its way into the depths of his consciousness. Whatever, I had to kick into him a couple more times. I didn't know if I was hurting him and I didn't care. I needed him to be in no doubt that I was the top dog round here at the moment, so I could secure him. That boy could pack a punch, and if he regained control there was no telling what he might do.

The profanity kept echoing around the back of the barn as I rolled Claude on to his stomach, pulled his wrists together behind his back and wrapped the tape around them. I made it tight, very tight, so his hands would soon start to swell. I wanted him to focus on the pain instead of raising the alarm.

I tugged off his wellies and did the same to his ankles, then bent his legs back so I could connect the two sets of binding. He lay with his cheek on the floor, eyes closed, even when I plastered the sticky stuff across his mouth and looped it twice around the back of his neck. I wasn't sure if he was unconscious by then or in denial. It didn't matter much either way.

Finally, I fastened him to one of the legs of the feeding trough.

I stepped over the fence post he'd dropped me with and grabbed the bungee cords off the shelf on my way out. I padlocked the main door for good measure and threw away the key.

There was no need to push the Honda anywhere now. The shouts had mostly turned into whines, and as soon as I hit the starter button the engine noise drowned them out completely. I pulled up beside the bridge and clambered into the gully.

Stefan had finished the chocolate and most of the water by the time I got back to him. Other than that he hadn't moved an inch. Either he trusted me completely, or he was still so traumatized he was frozen to the spot. His foot was obviously giving him some grief, but he'd kept it in the stream. As for the rest, only time would tell.

He took one look at me, opened his mouth and pointed at my temple. I touched it with my fingertips, still hoping that Claude might just have gobbed on me. They came away sticky and crimson.

I shrugged. 'No time now. I'll sort it later.'

He still didn't say anything, but I saw a ghost of a smile when I carried him up the bank and he spotted the Honda. I settled him on the front of the saddle and strapped our bags to the rear rack with the bungee cords. I didn't bother refilling the water bottle. Now that we had wheels, dying of thirst wasn't an issue.

I climbed on behind him, and told him to hang on to my arms. When I turned the ignition key, even the cows took no notice. I aimed the machine directly across the slope towards the trees. The incline wasn't too steep, but I didn't go into Red Bull Extreme mode. Rolling it would really fuck us up.

Once we were twenty metres or so in cover I spotted a track, which was probably a ski run in the winter. I turned on to it and opened up the throttle whenever the gradient allowed. I knew this wasn't the first time today I'd travelled downhill at speed through trees, but now I could see our route stretching ahead of us, and the further we got, the more confident I became that we weren't going to launch ourselves into space.

I stopped every so often to scan the open ground below us, and to check the compass and the map. I wasn't worried about taking a wrong turning: I needed to keep fixing the bearings of our journey in my head. It wasn't leaking so badly now.

Shit from my past had started to bubble up through my brain. Maybe the drama in the barn had triggered something way beneath the waterline.

I knew I was ex-Special Forces.

I knew Frank Timis was a Ukrainian oligarch.

I knew I'd rescued his son in Somalia, back in the day.

I knew he had needed my help again.

I knew that whoever had killed him wanted me dead too.

But I didn't know why. Maybe the Timis house in Courchevel would give me some answers.

The mountain air made everything ahead of me pin sharp. I was still a long way short of total recall, but the breeze against my face seemed to be blowing away some of my confusion. It was also drying off the bomber nicely.

Once we'd got well away from the body on the mountain and the flashing lights around what was left of my wagon, I brought the ATV to a halt. I lifted Stefan off and told him to take a piss while I unhooked the bungees and took my stained T-shirt out of my day sack, emptied the rest of the water bottle on to it and dabbed as much of the blood off my head as I could manage. There was fuck-all I could do about the wound itself right now, but at least I'd look a bit tidier.

Then I had a closer look at the contents of his rucksack. Under the hand towel and washbag there was a paperback the size of a small breezeblock. 'You're kidding me, right?' My Russian wasn't anything to shout about, but I recognized Dostoevsky's *Crime and*

Punishment when I saw it. Fuck, he was only seven. I hadn't even managed *Jack and Jill* by the time I was his age.

He gave me the kind of look that suddenly reminded me of his dad. No, he wasn't kidding.

I carried my bloodstained T-shirt and his Brindisi strip ten metres in from the track, scraped back some loose earth and leaf litter behind a tree and buried it. Being caught with Frank's son would compromise me big-time. Having the dead man's blood on my clothing and his would be even more difficult to explain.

8

We made it to the outskirts of Courchevel 1850 an hour or so before last light. The ATV had done what it said on the cowling; I'd managed to go the whole way without spending any more time on tarmac than we had to.

I pulled up beneath an empty chairlift on the high ground. We were still sheltered by trees, but had a clear view of the layout of the resort. Hotels and apartment blocks rubbed shoulders with cable-car stations and overpriced restaurants.

Further up the valley, the dying rays of the sun glinted off the canopy of a Bell Jetranger coming in to land at the Altiport, the airfield of choice for the super-rich that popped out there for the weekend. Snow still dusted the peaks that dominated the skyline behind it.

I'd seen Frank's place before. But from the front, not the back. I asked Stefan to ID it and he pointed at the middle building in a row of massive fairy-tale chalets with gently sloping roofs and wide eaves a few hundred metres to our left.

I could see that he was straining to get in there, like a puppy on a lead. I steadied him with a hand on the shoulder. 'Mate, we can't rush this. Whoever fucked up your dad on the mountain might be paying it a visit . . .'

I swept the binos across the rear of the property. Massive picture windows on the top floor reflected knock-out views of the upper slopes. Most of the shutters on those below were closed, either against the sunlight or because nobody was home.

A party-size Jacuzzi took pride of place in a walled terrace that separated the back door from the granite hillside. The whole set-up had been built to repel boarders, but you could obviously ski straight in there during the winter, through a steel security gate set into an archway.

I couldn't see any sign of movement, inside or out.

I'd definitely been to this three-storey slice of paradise, though I still couldn't remember exactly when. Whatever, poor people obviously weren't allowed in this part of town: we were looking at Oligarch Central.

Before hitting Frank's place, I had to hide my day sack. If everything went to rat-shit in there I needed to have travel docs and cash securely in a place I could get back to. I tucked it behind the bright orange padding that surrounded the base of the nearest chairlift pylon, then parked the ATV behind the one fifty metres below. It wasn't completely out of sight, but you'd have to be right on top of the thing before you pinged it.

I swung Stefan off the saddle. 'How's that ankle? Do you think you can walk?'

He nodded, and gave me the gritty, determined look I'd seen on the hillside. But after a couple of paces I knew it still wasn't working. I picked him up and carried him back to our original vantage-point. He started to shiver. The temperature was dropping now. I hadn't noticed.

I sat him down beside me and brought up the binos again. Nothing had changed. No big lads had emerged to enjoy an early-evening vodka on the balcony. I checked out the various approaches to the rear entrance for concealment and ease of access. A four-metre-wide alleyway separated it from the palaces on either side. They seemed to be empty too.

I wondered about leaping from the slope on to the top of the wall, but binned the idea almost immediately. A keypad was set into the stonework beside the security gate, with a camera above it. Two more cameras were mounted at each end of the rear elevation. Short of shooting them off the walls, all I could do was hope that if anyone unfriendly was inside they weren't watching the monitors.

I turned to Stefan. He was following my every move, eyes like saucers. 'We can get in through the back, yeah?'

He nodded.

'Will there be anyone there? A maid, maybe? A cook? A bodyguard?'

He gave me something halfway between a shake of the head and a shrug.

'Do you know the entry code?'

He nodded again.

I brought out the UZI pen and lifted my left hand.

He flinched like I was about to hit him. I went down on one knee, so we could get eye to eye. 'Steady, mate. I just want you to write it here . . .' I tapped my palm.

Concentrating hard, his tongue jutting out a fraction between his teeth, he drew a nine-square grid on my very grimy skin. Then he touched six of them in sequence and wrote the numbers below it.

'Is there an alarm system?'

Another nod. The tongue stayed where it was as he added a second set of figures.

'OK. Let's do it.'

I lifted him on to my back. He wrapped his arms around my chest and I threaded my wrists under his knees; this was starting to feel more like teamwork. I shifted the pistol in my waistband so I could still draw down with my right hand.

We were able to stay inside the treeline most of the way, and drop down on to the ski track at the last moment. I kept eyes on the three buildings every step of the way, only stopping a couple of times to glance backwards and forwards along the path.

I put Stefan down and tapped in the code. The locking mechanism clicked. I pushed open the gate, then hid him behind the Jacuzzi before repeating the process at the back entrance. This time the door swung back automatically, on some kind of hydraulic arm.

I stepped across the threshold into a room lined with top-of-the-range skis in a variety of sizes, bright quilted jackets and matching helmets on a row of wooden hooks. The alarm panel was alongside one of those boot-driers with stalks that breathed warm air into your liners after a day on the *piste*. I brought up my left palm, read the numbers and disarmed it.

I fetched Stefan and pressed the button to shut the door.

We moved through into an entrance hall that was more Manhattan penthouse than rustic mountain lodge. Frank had had a whole lot of fingers in a whole lot of pies, and judging by what was on display there, he'd cornered the market in grey marble as well. I wondered how much of this I'd paid for. He had once laundered a big chunk of money I'd stolen from a Mexican drug baron, and taken twenty-five cents on the dollar.

I felt a big stupid grin spread across my face. If I still knew that, there was hope for me yet.

I stopped and listened. The fact that the alarm had been set meant that no one was likely to be inside, but old habits die hard, even when you're struggling. That was the whole point of them, after all.

Once I was sure no one was there, I could comb the place for clues to what the fuck was going on, and why I was in the shit.

I walked across the shiniest floor I'd ever seen and Stefan hobbled after me. The huge wooden front door ahead of us was firmly shut. I wanted to keep it that way. Another to our right was far enough ajar for me to get a glimpse of the corner of a brushed-aluminium four-poster bed. No surprises there. Most of these mountain homes were designed to save the best views for the living areas, not waste them on the bits where you shut your eyes.

The room was enormous but minimally furnished – mostly in suede and metal. The bed and a formal portrait of Frank with a dark-haired beauty above it told me this was where the master of the house got his head down. The bed was made, but the slight dip in the mattress told me that for a while only one person had slept in it.

There were two more bedrooms across the hall. One was pink and fluffy and untouched; the other was a shrine to Brindisi football club and Spider-Man. A couple of dinosaurs acted as bookends for yet more homework. There was no mess anywhere. It reminded me of Frank's love of precision – and the seriousness with which he had been schooling Stefan to take over his empire. I told the boy to wait there until I came back.

A wide glass and steel staircase ran up the centre of the building.

I climbed it soundlessly. The first floor was similarly sleek and minimalist. Immediately ahead there was a panoramic view of lush greenery and snow-capped mountains. A maroon Bentley Continental swept past the front driveway, heading for the centre of town. I kept well back from the window.

A set of huge double doors led right, into a high-ceilinged family room. A very tidy high-ceilinged family room. Tall panelled windows overlooked a lone dog-walker making her way up the path we'd taken through the trees. A corridor opposite led into yet more rooms with views of mountains or trees. One was a dining room, complete with dumb waiter.

The floor above had a couple of giant Velux skylights that opened on to the roof, and an attic filled with the kind of stuff everyone leaves in an attic. Frank probably didn't even know it existed.

There was a glass and steel lift at the far end. It had been the highlight of the guided tour he'd given me when he'd bought the place. As I drew closer to it I heard his voice: *'Italian design, German hydraulics. Precision-built houses and Swiss watches – they are very nice things to have, Nick. But there is always someone in more control than you are . . .'*

Keep talking, Frank. Don't just go on about the fucking lift. Tell me what this shit is all about. Once I know that, I can work out what to do about it – and how to keep me and your boy safe . . .

As we'd moved smoothly downwards his jaw had tightened, and he'd given me a rare insight into his relationship with the big dog immediately above him in the food chain. *'Vladimir Vladimirovich Putin. Prime minister of the Russian Federation, chairman of both United Russia and the Council of Ministers of the Union of Russia and Belarus. A truly powerful man . . .'*

I'd asked him who Putin's boss was.

'People like me who buy chalets in this village.' He wasn't smiling. *'If he wants to be elected president again.'*

I hoped he was right about that.

I wasn't going to take the lift this time. I preferred the stairs. They gave me the illusion of control.

There were two more storeys below ground. The bottom one contained a swimming-pool, which filled the entire footprint of the building. So I hadn't been imagining it. Carved out of the mountainside, it looked like a South Pacific rock-pool. The water was crystal clear. I was glad something around here was.

Above it, a two-car garage housed another gleaming black Range Rover alongside a workbench complete with vices and all the tools you could need to keep the motor running and your skis edged and waxed. At one end, there was a neat little Dremel rotary tool and a set of silicone carbide grinders. Alongside them was an empty Marlboro packet. Cyrillic script. Bad-news photograph. I fished around in my pocket and brought out its identical twin. I wondered who was in charge of the DIY around here. I had the feeling it had been some time since Frank had got his hands dirty.

Next came a gym, a sauna and a massage room. Then a state-of-the-art kitchen, whose centrepiece was a coffee machine the size of a nuclear reactor. Frank did love a brew. The fridge was like a stainless-steel shipping container. An empty stainless-steel shipping container. And the matching pedal bin was empty too. So no clues there either.

I had more luck with the dishwasher. It had reached the end of its cycle and been switched off, but no one had bothered to empty it. There was dinner and breakfast stuff in there. Four of everything. I reckoned that meant Frank, Stefan, me and a BG.

Close by were four box rooms, each with a single bed, a wardrobe, a chest of drawers, and an en-suite shower and toilet. This was where the hired help hung out. I'd give them a closer look later.

At the far end of the corridor, next to his precious lift, was the place I really wanted to explore: Frank's hideaway. I went and fetched Stefan from his room. Trauma or not, it was time for him to make himself useful.

9

Mr T's enthusiasm for metal, suede and gleaming coffee machines was as obvious here as it had been everywhere else, but three walls were painted the green of an English gentlemen's club. The fourth was bare granite, coated with some kind of sealant. The only thing missing was a pool full of piranhas.

'A pool full of piranhas . . . ?' Frank had frowned when I'd cracked that funny.

I could see his expression now. Eyes narrowed as he sat down behind a desk the size of a championship snooker table. This desk. In this room.

He hadn't understood the Blofeld joke. But he'd gone on to make a bad one of his own. *'There are enough piranhas out there in the world, Nick. I don't need them in here as well.'*

Frank never had been much of a stand-up.

The wall to the left of it was lined with shelves, mostly displaying portraits and photos of the dead man and his family. I pointed to one. 'Your dad . . .'

Stefan nodded.

'My friend Frank . . .'

He nodded again.

I'd had a blow to the head, but I hadn't completely lost it. I'd been Frank's gun for hire. He'd sorted some finances for me. But he and I had never been friends. The boy seemed to like the idea, though, so I was happy to stick with it.

I stopped in front of an informal snapshot of father and son. A couple of heavies were standing on either side of them. On the left, a chunky Asiatic, who looked like Genghis Khan. Hesco? I didn't think so. On the right, with a cigarette in his left hand and his right protectively on the boy's shoulder, a huge Nigerian with dreads brushing his shoulders.

I leant in closer. I couldn't see what brand of smoke he liked, but the chunky gold bracelet around his wrist was impossible to miss. He was wearing blindingly white trainers with a red flash. And his dreads seemed to have a life of their own.

I'd seen this lad before. He was one of Frank's most trusted BGs. I'd spent time with him and Genghis in Somalia. And, a handful of hours ago, I'd watched his back as he and Hesco admired the wreckage of my wagon on the mountain.

I'd never known his name. I'd always called him Mr Lover Man. I hadn't a clue why. I knew he would have sacrificed himself to save Stefan. He'd once warned me that he'd kill me if I harmed one hair on the boy's head.

Stefan reached up and placed the tips of his fingers against the glass, almost as if he was trying to touch his BG. For the first time since I'd dragged him out of the Evoque, he started to cry.

I left him to it. Getting emotional was not on my agenda. It got in the way. I didn't need that right now. I needed answers.

I knelt down beside him. 'I've been here before, haven't I? Last night?'

Another nod.

'And this morning?'

I suddenly didn't need his confirmation. I remembered Frank bringing me here. Telling me he needed my help. Telling me his and his son's life were under threat.

I'd immediately thought of the fuckers who'd kidnapped Stefan in Somalia. *'Who from? Those fucking Georgians?'*

Frank had had no idea. Insiders, maybe. A takeover bid. Some shit was happening in a couple of his companies that was causing him dramas. The four of us had to go on a journey. Because he no longer knew who else to trust.

My eyes moved back to the picture of Mr Lover Man and the

boy. Who to trust? I knew that was where I came in. And I knew his briefing hadn't stopped there. But the deeper I tried to dig in my memory, the less I could recall.

I pointed at the beautiful dark-haired woman in the pictures. 'Where's your mum?'

The boy's face clouded again. Wrong question. The light went out of his eyes. He retreated further into himself. What was that about?

I put both my hands on his arms and gripped him. Fuck it, I didn't have time to piss around. And he was his father's son. 'Stefan, I need you to help me. I need to know who killed your dad . . .'

Now he was in real pain. His face went rigid, then looked like it was starting to melt. He opened and closed his mouth, but still no sound came out.

He pointed at the photo again.

Pointed straight at Mr Lover Man.

'The black guy? Are you sure?'

Another stupid question, but it had to be asked. Maybe his memory had been fucked, a bit like mine. Maybe it was playing tricks. The more I looked at that big protective clasp on Stefan's shoulder, the more clearly I could picture the Nigerian constantly putting himself in harm's way to save Frank's son.

But the shots that had killed Frank had come from inside the wagon.

By a body in the driving seat.

Mr Lover Man wasn't right-handed. He held his cigarette in his left. Which meant he would have been able to just turn and fire.

Stefan's mouth opened again. This time a word spilt out. 'Yes.'

I picked him up and put him on a designer wing chair with a foot rest that sprang up when you tilted it back. I found another chocolate bar in the top drawer of Frank's desk and lobbed it at him. It was the closest thing to a happy pill that I could come up with. 'Chew on that, yeah? I need to have another look around.'

There were two remotes on the desk top. They controlled the screens on the opposite wall – a huge flat-screen TV and a security monitor. I fired up both. The monitor split into a dozen constantly shifting images, covering every approach to the chalet and every room inside. I fucked around with the remote for a bit. It was a great bit of kit. At the press of a button I could choose which camera to focus on; I could zoom in and out. I could wind the thing backwards and then forwards again at 2x, 6x, 12x and 30x speed.

I wished I could do the same thing with the screen inside my head. The distant past seemed to be less of a jigsaw, but I was still finding it almost impossible to pin down the events of the last forty-eight hours.

My journey here last night was a blur.

So was most of this morning.

How did the flatbed know we were on our way? The driver – or whoever launched the stripy pole at me – must have been told our route in advance, and had comms with an insider. And if Stefan hadn't lost it, I now knew who that was.

I pictured Mr Lover Man looking over the edge of the precipice after my wagon had taken its nosedive.

Him and Hesco giving it a huge high-five.

Frank's body.

The bubble of blood at the corner of Stefan's mouth.

Legging it downhill.

The fight in the barn.

Carrot-cruncher number two raising the muzzle of my weapon.

The dead man's click . . .

When you've got your pistol raised and a big fucker coming down an alley towards you with an AK-47, it's the worst sound in the world. But when a big and very angry Frenchman fails to blow your brains out with your own weapon, it was the best. I had no idea whether he'd pulled the trigger on purpose or by accident. I just knew it hadn't fired.

I took the Sphinx out of my waistband, put it on Frank's old-school blotter and gave my temples a rub.

The gunmetal glinted dully in the flickering light from the monitors. It had done that when Mr Lover Man had handed it to me that morning. Mr Lover Man, not his boss. He'd smiled as he did so.

I picked up the weapon and unclipped the mag. Then I ejected the round from the chamber and held its base up to the light. It didn't matter what angle I held it at: the copper percussion cap was totally unmarked. The ammunition wasn't defective. Something else was.

I removed the top slide, turned it upside down and took out the spring and the barrel. With a little help from one of Frank's platinum-sheathed Mont Blanc ballpoints I pushed out the stub that anchored the firing pin and popped it out of its housing.

Shit.

It didn't matter how many times I ran through my NSPs (normal safety precautions), I'd just see the base of the firing pin, where it came into contact with the hammer. And the big lad with the dreads would have known that. Only by dismantling the working parts could I tell that it was five millimetres too short to strike the round. These things are made of turned steel. Their tips don't just fall off, and this one hadn't. A grinder had taken it down. I'd have bet a fistful of Frank's euros on where that grinder was kept.

I thought about what might have happened if they'd been waiting for me on the hill. Mr Lover Man had probably saved my life when everything had gone to rat-shit in the barn. But he hadn't meant to. He had meant *me* to be the one squeezing the trigger and not hearing it go bang. And by then I'd have been terminally fucked.

Mr Lover Man.

Stefan's protector.

His dad's most trusted sidekick.

Someone must have found a way of getting to him. Someone higher up the food chain than Frank Timis. And there weren't many of *them*.

10

I reassembled the Sphinx, then bounced the TV from channel to channel until I found twenty-four-hour news. Every bulletin was about bad things happening in Syria, Iraq or the Crimea. Putin was bent on clawing back as much of the old empire as possible, and he wouldn't stop at Ukraine. He also seemed to be picking off his least favourite oligarchs and rivals, one by one.

The Crimea report was interrupted by a breaking story. Frank's Range Rover filled the frame, surrounded by stripy incident tape and blue and red flashing lights. I probably should have saved Stefan from having to watch this bit, but it was already too late. He stopped in mid-bite as a body bag was lifted off a gurney and slid into the back of an ambulance.

It was too early for the dead man to have been formally identified, but that didn't stop the newshounds from speculating wildly about a connection with the still unsolved murder of Saad al-Hilli, his wife and mother-in-law in a layby near Lake Annecy in 2012. Lake Annecy was spitting distance from there.

There didn't seem to be a mystery biker this time around; the prime suspect, as far as they were concerned, was a man in a Nissan X-Trail, who appeared to have suffered a fatal accident further down the mountain. Cue footage of more flashing lights and charred, mangled wreckage being hoisted on to a low-loader.

With his passport in my day sack, the police wouldn't be able to ID Frank immediately. But it wouldn't take them long. He'd kept a low profile, as far as the outside world was concerned, but you didn't do the things that Frank did without leaving some kind of trace.

And it would also be only a matter of time before the forensics people got busy with what was left of the Nissan and discovered that there was no body inside it.

I bent and sifted through the desk drawers. None of them was locked, but that didn't surprise me. Anything Frank wanted to keep to himself would be buried in the safe in the rock face behind me, somewhere offsite, or behind a series of passcodes on the razor-thin laptop he always kept within reach.

Always.

I stopped mid-sift and frowned.

He'd been tapping away on it last night. He'd turned the screen towards me, and shown me something.

Something important.

What then?

I hadn't seen it in the Range Rover.

And it wasn't here.

'Stefan . . .'

He turned.

'Your dad's laptop. Did he have it in the car?'

Another slow nod.

So where had it gone?

I riffled through a few sheets of paper in the third drawer: a fixture list for Brindisi Football Club, an out-of-date invitation to the formal opening of some distribution depot in Albertville, a glossy estate agent's brochure for a Swiss chateau on the shore of Lake Konstanz – the kind of place where if you had to ask the price you couldn't afford it – and two or three printouts of the kind of puzzles and brainteasers designed to do your head in if a stripy javelin hadn't done that already. I guessed they were what Frank did with Stefan when he wasn't reading him Dostoevsky at bedtime.

Something prevented me pushing the drawer shut.

Puzzles . . .

Brainteasers . . .

Precision . . .

Most of us kept out-of-date shit for no good reason. Frank didn't.

I needed to take another look at that invitation.

The depot was owned by a company called Adler Gesellschaft. Their logo was embossed top centre, inside the card. I rolled back my sleeve, though I didn't need to. That eagle, with its outstretched wings and talons, was becoming a regular feature in my life. I folded the card in half and slipped it into my pocket.

I left the news rolling. The infrared had kicked in on the security monitor now that darkness had fallen. I told Stefan to keep eyes on while I nosed around. Anything else that might help fill in the blanks in my head was going to pay dividends, so I started with the picture gallery. I needed to fix the images of the key players in my mental databank.

One look and I knew I'd recognize Mr Lover Man and his mate Genghis if I saw them again. I'd spent time with them both in Moscow and Mogadishu, and some other third-world shitholes as well.

I struggled to remember whether I'd ever met Frank's wife. I didn't think so. I examined every shot she starred in. Long dark hair. Perfect skin. Catwalk posture. Cheekbones you could cut yourself on. The kind of symmetry that only came with a surgeon's knife. Strikingly beautiful from a distance, but less so up close.

As always, the clue was in the eyes, and these ones didn't miss a trick. I saw ambition in them, but not affection. And, judging by the size of the diamonds and rubies she had decorated herself with, her ambition was working its magic.

The TV was telling me nothing I hadn't already heard so I switched it off. I showed Stefan the remote for the security monitor and began to run through the basic programming options. 'Look, mate, this is how you shift from camera to camera. And this is the zoom—'

He rolled his eyes and snatched it out of my hand. In case I hadn't got the message, he went on to demonstrate a whole lot of functions I'd had no idea about. I left him to it, but turned at the door. 'I'll be along the corridor. Come and get me if you see anything happening, front or back.' I gave him a grin. 'And finish that chocolate bar, eh? Or I'll eat it.'

From the contents of their cupboards and chests, one of the staff quarters had been set aside for a chef and another for a maid. The remaining two were empty, beds stripped, not even a half-used tube of toothpaste on the glass shelf above the basin.

But this time I spotted another empty Marlboro pack in the waste bin.

Whoever had vacated them wasn't expecting to come back any time soon. It had been worth the second visit, though. I now knew without a shadow of a doubt who had stayed there.

Mr Lover Man, and me.

I returned to the study. Stefan still looked like you'd expect a kid to look when his favourite BG had just shot his dad. But he was taking his security job very seriously indeed. His eyes were glued to the six key screens in which absolutely nothing was happening, and he was juggling between them like he was playing on an Xbox. I let him know I was going back upstairs.

I pressed the remote and closed the steel roller shutters in the master bedroom before switching on the lamp beside the four-poster. Mr and Mrs Timis watched me from the portrait on the wall above it as I whisked through their handcrafted drawers and wardrobes. Something in her expression left me in no doubt she didn't approve.

The very expensive contents didn't tell me much I didn't already know about Frank's personal tastes, and only one thing about what might have been happening in other areas of his life. Every single item belonged to him. I found nothing that might have been hers.

The same was true of the en-suite bathroom. A lot of Frank's man stuff, but no sign of the sort of shit women can't live without. It wasn't because she hadn't popped by for dinner last night.

She'd gone.

Was that why Stefan's face had fallen when I asked him where his mum was?

I caught sight of myself in the mirror above one of the basins. A scab had formed on my forehead, starting a couple of centimetres below my hairline and running back across my scalp. There was a smear of blood on each side. It was ugly enough to make me open the medicine cabinet, where I found shelves of Factor 60, Deep Heat, and all the things you might need to patch yourself up after a fuck-up on the *piste*.

I dampened one of Frank's designer face flannels and cleaned myself up as much as possible, then applied three butterfly strips and a dressing to the crusty bit. It would stop it going septic, and made the whole thing look a bit tidier.

I rinsed the flannel under the cold tap, wrung it out and tucked it into my bomber pocket, along with some spare dressings and sticking plasters, and a blister pack of ibuprofen, a crêpe bandage and Tubigrip for Stefan. He appeared at the door in the same instant I heard the sirens whooping up the road from the centre of town.

I flicked off the light and took Frank's triumph of Italian design and German engineering double quick down to his study. I wasn't about to stick my head out of an upstairs window to see if we had a drama on our hands. I already knew that we did.

11

I got back to his monitor in time to see four Toyota Land Cruisers screech to a halt outside the front of the chalet. GENDARMERIE was emblazoned across their bonnets and door panels and their anti-riot grilles were tilted back. It was too dark to tell what colour the carriers were, but I knew they were midnight blue, like the Kevlar assault suits of the lads in helmets who started spilling out of them.

These guys weren't just our friendly neighbourhood bobbies. I couldn't see their shoulder flashes, but I could picture them: a blue circle with an open parachute, a telescopic sight, flames and a steel karabiner.

GIGN.

A special-ops outfit bridging the gap between the police and the military. Whoever thought the French were cheese-eating surrender monkeys had never seen the Intervention Group up close. I had. We'd served together, back in the day. They specialized in anti-terrorist and hostage-rescue tasks. Which meant they were taking whatever they thought was happening here very seriously indeed.

They normally operated as twenty-man troops, and it looked like today was no exception. Four of them stayed out front, SIG 550 assault rifles in the aim. They'd have Manurhin MR73s – a 357 Magnum revolver that Dirty Harry wouldn't have sneered at – in their holsters. I didn't want to be on the receiving end of either. Or the GIAT FR-F2 sniper rifles that would have peeled off earlier, aiming for the high ground. They could throw a 7.62 round 800 metres.

While it was all very well being able to dredge up this shit, I was beginning to regret not having spent more time planning my exit routes.

The rest of the squad spread out around the sides and back. They didn't have the pass code, but that didn't seem to slow them down. A couple swung themselves up over the rear wall and took cover where I'd put Stefan, behind the Jacuzzi. So nipping out the way we'd come in was no longer an option.

Blasting through the garage doors and up the front drive in the Range Rover wasn't either.

I wondered about climbing out on to the roof and launching myself at the next-door chalet.

I'd be quicker on my own.

It would mean leaving the boy.

The GIGN would guarantee him a place of safety . . .

But I'd be fucked.

They were top of the heap when it came to hostage rescue, but wouldn't just give him a kiss and a cuddle. It'd take less than thirty seconds for the little fucker to tell them I was alive, put me in the same zone as the killing, and give them a full description.

I scanned the monitors. They confirmed what I already knew. Every option was going to end in a gangfuck.

The boss man with the megaphone certainly felt that way. He told us so in three languages. He was now inviting anyone inside the chalet to come out with their hands raised.

What about staying in? Was there somewhere we could conceal ourselves? I scrolled through the possibilities on the screen inside my head. It was finally beginning to work. But it didn't give me a solution.

Inside cupboards and under beds were strictly for sitcoms.

And the attic was the first place I'd look.

Did Frank have a panic room? I hadn't seen any sign of one.

No. Frank didn't do panic. And neither – I now realized – did his son. Most seven-year-olds would have been flapping and crying and hiding under the bed right now. He just rolled his eyes. The kid seemed to have the same part of his brain missing as his dad.

The megaphone kicked off one last time. Same message, harsher delivery. If there was anyone inside, they had three minutes to make themselves known.

I didn't want to make myself known. I never had. Not even to the postman.

As the assault team moved in, I went over to his chair and gripped him. 'There must be a way out, yeah? What would your dad do right now?'

The kid got up and limped towards the left-hand end of the photograph display. He opened the storage cupboard beneath it and reached inside.

The front door burst off its hinges at the third strike of the GIGN battering ram. The speakers in Frank's hideaway captured the moment in cinema-quality surround-sound. But even if it had been dead quiet, I doubt I would have heard the shelving unit rotate to reveal the mouth of a tunnel that had been bored into the mountain.

I took two steps towards it, then turned back to the desk and grabbed the security remote. Fuck it, this thing had more buttons and icons than an Enigma machine. I didn't know which ones to punch.

Stefan gripped my arm and tried to pull me away. I shook him off. 'The security cameras. They would have recorded us coming in, yeah?'

He nodded.

'And me going through every room.'

He nodded again.

'I need to wipe the memory.'

He treated me to something very like a smile, and more words in a single sentence than he'd given me since I'd dragged him out of the Evoque. 'You left me in charge, remember? That was my job.'

We both heard shouted orders and boots on the ground at the far end of the corridor. As we legged it across the threshold, the room was plunged into darkness and a trail of LED lights showed the way ahead. The shelving unit closed silently behind us. There was a touchpad set into the rock for a return journey, and a screen the size of an iPad, which showed an infrared image of the place we'd just left.

Apart from our footsteps, all I could hear now was the gentle whir of the ventilation system.

12

There was obviously nothing wrong with Stefan's mind, apart from it being a pint-size replica of his dad's, but his ankle stopped working again after another fifty. I picked him up and kept on going.

I soon lost track of how far we'd walked, but I didn't care. It was all about making distance, and a steadily downward slope really helped. I had no idea whether we'd emerge in Bulgari Land or out in the wild. I stopped every so often and listened for any sign of pursuit. Unless the boys in blue had found their way through Frank's secret escape hatch and changed into the world's quietest brothel-creepers, there was none.

Eventually a shiny steel door appeared out of the gloom in front of us. A spyhole glinted at head height. I peered through it into what looked like a neon-lit lock-up. I pressed the button that opened the door and moved from a spotless designer planet into the one I was more used to – the one with dirt under its finger-nails, sweat on its bollocks and oil stains on its floor.

A couple of old bicycles hung from the ceiling. The shelves that lined the walls were loaded with all sorts of shit that even real people didn't need to keep but couldn't bring themselves to throw away. I knew this was exactly how the place was meant to look; it wasn't just because Frank had forgotten to bring in the cleaners. Once the door had closed, there was no hint of what lay behind it.

A dark green Volkswagen Polo stood to one side, with French plates and an up-to-date Swiss car-toll vignette in the bottom left corner of the windscreen. Nothing too flash, but solid. This wagon was designed to stay under the radar.

There was no sign of a satnav, which suited me just fine. I'd spent the last few hours wondering where the fuck I was, and still wanted to find out how I'd got here, but I was in no doubt that I'd spent the rest of my life doing my best to remain untraceable.

The only concession to high tech was the little black plastic box on the driver's seat, which I guessed must power up the shutter that separated us from the outside world. The ignition key had been left beside it.

When I put Stefan down he made for the passenger door, but I steered him to the rear hatch and told him to curl up in the boot. 'It's safer. No one will give a scruffy fucker on his own a second glance in a wagon like this . . .' I liked the sound of that. I hoped it was true.

He got the message and curled up without complaint on what looked and smelt like an old dog blanket, beside a folded safety triangle and a clear plastic container full of spare lightbulbs. I didn't feel too bad about that. Despite the crocodiles crawling all over his kit, I knew he'd been in shittier places. I knew because I'd been there with him.

Before I closed the hatch I asked him who knew about this set-up.

'Just me and my dad.'

'Not the black guy?'

He shook his head.

I sparked up the engine, threw the Polo into gear and pressed the button on the black box. Sure enough, a green light flickered and the shutter rolled open, then closed as soon as we were through.

Immediately on my left there was a storage facility for winter grit, and a vehicle-repair yard on the right. You wouldn't have given either a second glance as you headed up or down the mountain. And if you took the heli from Geneva to the Altiport, you'd never even know that places like this existed.

I drove fifteen metres up the rutted track between them and turned right, away from the sign pointing towards 'Centre Village'. I needed to go back to pick up my day sack, but right now I had to make distance from this drama and work out what the next one would be.

I kept going until I reached Moriond – not too far from Courchevel 1850, but the kind of place that looked like you could still find a takeaway kebab instead of an over-priced three-course meal. I pulled into a parking lot outside a block of flats that was in need of a lick of paint, and turned off the engine.

Someone had smashed the only lamp in sight, so it was nice and dark here. I wound down the front windows a fraction to stop them misting up, and watched the comings and goings on the main.

First up, I wondered who the fuck had pressed the GIGN button. Even if someone had reported us gaining entry, those guys didn't bother with break-ins. They were heavy-duty. National security. So who were they after? Me? Frank's killers? Or was this only the tip of a bigger, uglier iceberg? Whatever the answer, I needed to nail it on my own terms, and not from the inside of a police interrogation room.

Now we seemed to be out of the immediate shit, I was going to focus on finding out who had leant on Mr Lover Man forcibly enough to get him to kill his boss. Because when I knew that, I'd be a step closer to neutralizing the threat to Stefan. And the threat to me.

The traffic was sporadic for the next hour or so. Family saloons, mostly, the odd tourist coach and local bus. That was OK by me. It gave me time to try to join some of the dots.

I heard Stefan give a small cough and then whisper, 'Can I come out now?'

'No.' I kept eyes on the main. 'But while you're there, you can tell me some stuff. Question one: how long had you and your dad been at the chalet?'

A couple of boy racers with Day-glo decals on their wings roared up the hill, then stood on their brakes as a GIGN Land Cruiser sped past in the opposite direction. It was four up and without blues and twos, so I guessed the sniper team had been stood down. Three more came by at intervals.

'Two days.'

Then a command unit, then nothing.

'And your BG?'

'BG?'

His voice was muffled, but it was clear he had no idea what I was talking about.

'Yeah, you know, your bodyguard . . .'

'He was always there. Except maybe once.'

'When?'

'Last night . . . While you were with my . . .'

'Dad?'

He gave the smallest of whimpers.

'Did he talk to anyone? Meet anyone? Anyone you didn't know?'

'Oh, Nick . . .' He sounded like he was in pain. 'He was my friend. I didn't *spy* on him . . .'

'My meeting with your dad, in the green room—'

'You were in there for . . . ages.'

Ages . . . So it *had* been more than a heads-up and a swift espresso.

'He was worried about something. Do you have any idea what?'

'No . . .' He let out the world's biggest sigh. 'I just knew he was . . . He thought he kept it hidden, but I knew.'

Time for a break. The whimper and the sigh told me I was pushing too hard. And it was getting cold.

I shut the windows and started the engine.

Fifteen minutes and a few hairpin bends later I was in the heart of the resort. The twin cables from the Verdons lift station stretched up the valley to my right. A female cop was directing traffic at the roundabout, but she'd gone by the time I'd repeated the circuit. I parked up in a space outside the cinema. There was no sign of any more of her Special Forces mates.

The *piste* map beneath the stationary line of bubbles told me where I was, and where I had to go. I got back in the Polo and wound my way through Courchevel's answer to Rodeo Drive, past the kind of hotels where they warm your toilet seats as well as your ski boots, on to the high ground.

I drove a hundred past Le Strato, pulled into the next layby and waited another half-hour before getting out of the wagon and circling back to my hiding place. I didn't trip over anyone en route, and everything seemed to have gone quiet at Oligarch Central.

My day sack was where I'd left it. The ATV was too. I wrenched off its registration plates and chucked them into the middle of a big clump of bushes on my way to the road. It wouldn't take for ever for someone to find and then identify Claude's Honda, but I didn't want to make it too easy. The more time passed without them being able to make the connection, the better.

I dumped the day sack in the passenger foot well of the Polo and tucked the Sphinx under my right thigh. Mr Lover Man would know it was fuck-all use, but it might stop anyone who didn't getting too close. And I could always throw it at them if the shit hit the fan.

I drove on through the one-way system, avoiding the heart of the village, and took a right towards Le Praz, past a floodlit ski jump that seemed to be its social centre even when there was no snow anywhere near it. A handful of people milled around outside a bunch of all-weather tepees that lined the base of the landing strip.

I was still searching my jumbled memory for something significant Frank might have said. It didn't get me anywhere. All I knew for sure was that I hadn't been able to save him, and he hadn't been able to save himself.

I pulled off the road and tugged the map book out of my day sack. A bunch of euro notes came with it, and fluttered into the foot well. I leant over to gather them up.

I paused, midway.

Money . . .

Mexican drug money . . .

Frank had laundered it, then fed my share into the bank in Zürich that had supplied me with my magic debit card.

I grabbed one of the Nokia bodies and slotted in a battery and a SIM card. 'Mate, I'm just getting out of the car again. But I won't be far away. Stay right where you are.'

13

I punched out what I hoped was the Swiss dialling code and my account manager's mobile number. The key to conjuring up regularly accessed data sequences was to crack on instinctively. Interrupting the process with any kind of rational thought only fucked things up. And because I never compromised my security – or anyone else's – by storing contact details, it had become second nature.

Whether I got through now would show me if my medium-to-long-term memory was salvageable, or as elusive as my grip on the recent past.

'Bonsoir.'

The voice was familiar. And it didn't give me a bollocking for calling after hours.

I rattled off a nine-figure code.

'Oui . . .'

So far, so good.

'About two years ago I received a series of payments from a Mr Frank Timis.'

'Oui.'

'Do you have any record of those payments?'

'Bien sûr.' I heard a keyboard being tapped. 'No movement for . . . eight months, then another transfer yesterday evening, from the same source.'

'What source?'

'La Banque Privée, in Albertville.'

'Address?'

I scribbled it on my arm as he gave it to me.

'Who authorizes the transactions?'

'The manager. A Monsieur Laffont.'

I was about to ring off when he asked if I'd like him to confirm the amount of the most recent payment. I said I would.

'Five hundred thousand euros.'

Fuck me. 'Any description?'

'Non.'

Of course there wasn't. Frank would have told me what it was for. He didn't need to share the job spec with anybody else.

I dismantled the phone, trod the pieces into the earth and got back into the Polo.

My immediate objective had been to get out of the resort area. Now I knew where I was going. Albertville was less than fifty Ks away. It looked large enough for us to lose ourselves in for a day or two. And it was where I would find Mr Laffont and the Adler depot.

Before sparking up the ignition, I called back over my shoulder. 'All right, Stefan? We're about to go somewhere safe.'

I got a muffled grunt in response. Maybe he believed what I'd just said as little as I did. The fact was, nowhere was completely safe, for either of us. But I couldn't just mince around. I needed to find somewhere out of the immediate firing line to hide the boy, then to track down Mr Lover Man.

The further I got down the valley, the more comfortable I began to feel, and not only because I didn't see any flashing blue lights or overly interested Range Rovers in the rear-view. We were back in the real world, where people scraped a living, shopped at discount stores and chopped their own wood.

There were no Gucci cable cars here, just columns of electricity pylons marching along beside the Isère river, through pleated-tin prefab industrial estates, cement factories and parked-up earth-moving equipment. Lights blazed from the odd car showroom. A pillar of rock rose up from between the carriageways, topped by some kind of shrine.

A big fuck-off set of white neon horns announced the presence of a Buffalo Grill, a macho version of McDonald's, to the right of the main. I'd emptied the contents of my gut up on the hill, and I was pretty sure Stefan hadn't got anything down his neck since breakfast, apart from the chocolate bar I'd given him while I went and borrowed the ATV, and the one in Frank's drawer. I pulled off at the next exit, asked him what sort of stuff he liked, and went in to order a takeaway.

The place wasn't heaving with customers, but there were enough to stop me drawing too much attention to myself, and judging by the plates in the parking area, quite a few of them were Brits. I emerged ten minutes later with burgers and chips and a couple of bottles of Coke.

I pointed the Polo further away from the main and found a floodlit communal sports facility with an AstroTurf football pitch and a basketball game in full flow, where no one would give a second glance at a scruffy guy taking time out with his lad.

I lifted him out of the boot and told him we didn't have to do the whole hugging thing, but from now on anyone looking in our direction had to pick up that vibe. 'Kids with strange men always stick out like a sore thumb. Boys with their dads pass unnoticed in places like this.'

He shut and then opened his eyes a couple of times, but he managed to stop them leaking. Then, while the local dudes rocketed around the court, dreaming of stardom, Stefan sat and looked at his dinner like it was something I'd wiped off his shoe. I thought for a moment that he was going to push it away. I suddenly remembered that Frank had kept as strict an eye on his diet as he had on his education.

'What's the problem, mate? Not enough curly kale?'

He grimaced. 'I hate curly kale.'

He took an experimental bite and got stuck in. I did too. I'd never been a big fan of acid reflux, and this stuff was exactly what I needed to combat it.

When we'd finished, I sat him in the front of the wagon and went in search of a cheap motel with several exits and no security cameras. I found one between the pitches and the train station that was just about perfect. I circled the area around it. My head hadn't been straight at the chalet, and I'd fucked up. I didn't want to make the same mistake twice.

It wasn't long before I found what I was looking for. Beside the railway track: a wooden shed where the locals came to dump their household waste, their wine bottles and empty boxes. I pulled up alongside a pile of discarded bin bags and opened the door. Three big plastic wheelie-bins with different-coloured lids stood in front of me. There was enough space between them for a small person to squeeze through.

I gave Stefan a wave and motioned for him to join me.

His expression told me he didn't know what the fuck I was up to. When he'd poked his head inside, he was none the wiser.

'ERV.'

He really thought I'd lost the plot.

'Take a good look. I'll explain later.'

I told him to get down in the foot well as we turned through the main entrance to the motel and to stay there until I gave the signal. There were about forty parking spaces and almost as many vehicles. All good. I didn't want to find myself somewhere with so few guests that the owner could provide a Photofit for every one of them.

The check-in desk was on the opposite side of a courtyard from the main block. The lad behind it had more zits on his face than brain cells between his ears, and was a lot more interested in what was on TV than he was in me. I gave him enough cash to cover two nights in a room on the ground floor and he handed over a key with one of those lumps of metal attached that are supposed to be heavy enough to stop you walking off with them by mistake. I waved my passport at him but he didn't give a shit.

I left Stefan where he was while I went and checked out our accommodation, and our surroundings. The door was on one side of an archway that led straight through the building. I pushed it open and chucked both our bags on to the double bed. A ladder led to a bunk that ran across the head of it, and a small flat-screen Samsung was mounted on the opposite wall. There was a basic en-suite with shower and toilet and a small window above the cistern.

I fastened the shutters on the window overlooking the parking lot, went out and scanned the areas back and front. Once I was satisfied that they were deserted, I smuggled Stefan out of the Polo. He didn't move a muscle when he saw where we were staying, and I gave him top marks for that. We were a long way from Louis Vuitton country.

I popped a couple of ibuprofen out of the blister pack for him, swallowed a couple myself, and replaced the makeshift bandage around his ankle with the Tubigrip. It was a bit late in the day, but would give him some support and limit the swelling. I pointed at his rucksack and told him to get ready for bed.

He removed his washbag and disappeared into the bathroom. I flicked on the TV remote and selected the news channel. There was nothing more on the body in the Range Rover or the wreckage of the Nissan, just the usual stuff about Putin trying to turn back the clock and flex his muscles in Ukraine. They showed him riding his horse, stripped to the waist, then ran through some more stock shots of the Kremlin, Red Square and St Basil's Cathedral. That took me back. I wondered if my Russian ex still dropped by GUM to do her shopping.

Stefan poked his head round the door and asked if I'd remembered his Spider-Man pyjamas. He told me his real dad wouldn't have forgotten them.

I told him we were on a mission. That you didn't wear pyjamas on a mission. Even Spider-Man pyjamas. 'And put your trainers back on. We might have to leave in a hurry.'

When Stefan had sorted himself out, he climbed carefully into the bunk and sat there cross-legged, like he was giving a yoga class. He was old beyond his years, this lad. Somalia must have kick-started it; Frank had done the rest.

I asked if he was in the mood for a bit of Dostoevsky.

The second smile of the day invaded his face. 'Will you read it to me?'

I grinned. 'I try to save *Crime and Punishment* for special occasions.'

'You're lying.'

I looked him straight in the eye. 'I'll never lie to you, mate.' I paused. There was something about his transparency and his intelligence that made it almost impossible to bullshit him. 'I just might not always tell you the truth.'

He stared straight back. 'Don't worry, Nick. No one does.'

He wasn't wrong there. But I hadn't been talking total bollocks about *Crime and Punishment*. I'd never got to the end, but I had given it a go. It was one of the books Anna had raved about. I'd left my copy in Moscow with her and our little boy, when it became blindingly obvious to us both that I wasn't the safest man in the world to be around.

14

Later, after I'd killed the lights, I lay there, still fully clothed and booted, listening for movement outside, and to Stefan breathing. I thought about when I'd dug him out from under Frank's body, and when he had locked his arms around my neck. I'd never had much time for all that emotional shit. It always fucks you up.

The springs creaked as Stefan turned over and tried to make himself comfortable. There was silence for a moment, then a whisper. 'Nick . . .'

'Yup.'

'Where will they bury my father?'

'Don't know, mate. I guess they'll fly him back home at some point.' I wasn't going to tell him Frank was sitting with a bunch of angels on a nearby cloud, watching over him. I'd spun that sort of shit once, a few years ago. It doesn't help.

'Home?'

I let his question hang in the air. I needed to quiz him about Frank, but I didn't want this conversation to continue. I'd never been an expert on home; I wished I'd never mentioned it. I should have known that the kid would be wondering where the fuck he belonged now.

I heard a train rattling past, somewhere in the distance.

'Nick . . .'

'Try and get some sleep, mate. I'm going to.'

The pipes shuddered as someone on the floor above flushed their toilet. Whoever had built this block hadn't wasted their hard-earned euros on sound insulation. I didn't have a problem with that. It meant I'd be able to hear any approach.

'Nick . . .'

'Yup.'

I couldn't blame him for wanting to fill the silence. He was a tough little fucker, but he was only going to see one thing whenever he closed his eyes.

'Do you have a son?'

I took a deep breath. 'I've never really had the time for kids.' I gave him a little chuckle. 'Anyway, I've already got my hands full looking after you.'

He thought about this for a minute or two. 'So, when you get old or die, who will run your business?'

This time my chuckle was genuine. It really was like having a mini-Frank in the room. 'My business isn't much like your dad's. And if I had a son, I think I'd want him to do something else with his life . . .'

'What?'

'Oh, I don't know. Make movies, maybe. *Toy Story, Monsters, Inc.*?' I didn't know where this shit was coming from. I just wanted to back away from the whole dad thing.

'"Infinity and beyond . . ."' His Buzz Lightyear impression was pretty good.

'Or play football.'

'I play football. After I've finished my homework.'

'For Brindisi?'

He actually giggled at that one. 'Don't be silly, Nick. I'm not old enough. But I watch them when my dad takes me . . .'

He went quiet again.

'When my dad . . . took . . . me.'

I had an idea that Frank had mentioned Italy to me when we'd talked in the green room. I'd taken my rollercoaster ride down that side of the mountain. And he'd had an Italian map in the Range Rover.

'Why Brindisi? Why not Man U, or Barcelona?'

'My dad doesn't own Man U or Barcelona. And we don't have a villa there.'

'Do you go a lot?'

'Two or three times this year.' His mood brightened again. 'I like it very much in Italy, Nick. My dad is . . . was always happy in Italy. Except the last trip.'

'The last trip?'

'Something happened the last trip that made him sad.'

'Do you know what that was?'

'A bad business. That's what he said.'

'Is that all he said?'

He went quiet again.

I didn't push him for more detail. I reckoned he'd fill the gap if he could. He seemed to be in the mood. I also figured that however keen Frank had been to have his boy follow in his footsteps, he wouldn't have given him the lowdown on every piece of shit that floated to the surface of his pond.

I swung my legs over the edge of the bed, took off my jacket and went to have a crap and throw some warm water over my eyes. I ran my hands through my hair. The face that glanced back at me from the mirror above the basin didn't seem to belong to a stranger now. And it had some colour in it.

The dressing I'd applied at the chalet was neat and high on the right side of my forehead, with only a small amount of bruising at the edges. I was never going to be confused with George Clooney in red-carpet mode, but I didn't look like I'd been on the wrong end of a cage fight either.

I gave my hands and face a squirt of soap and water, but left the scribbles on my arm. The afternoon's sweat had blurred the Adler eagle, but I didn't need that any more. And Laffont's address was easily readable.

I still felt a dull ache above my kidneys, so pulled up my T-shirt and swivelled. The outline of the fence post was clearly visible across my back, and the bruise was darkening nicely. Claude had tried pretty hard to fuck up my ribs and spine when he took me down, and though he hadn't finished the job, he deserved some credit.

I wondered whether the boys were still locked in the barn, or if their mum had given them a good bollocking and sat them on the naughty step. Claude was probably even sorrier that he hadn't shot me in the head when he discovered that I'd fucked off with one of their ATVs. I wasn't too worried about him fingering me in an ID parade, though. Our little drama had unfolded in shadow.

Stefan stayed quiet while I put my jacket back on and lay down again. I didn't think he was sleeping. I wasn't either. I had too much on my mind. Or too little. My memory of the hours leading up to the crash was still fractured. Every attempt I made to fit the pieces into some kind of recognizable pattern failed. Maybe a visit to Frank's banker would fill some of the gaps.

A face appeared out of the darkness. A woman's face. A sad, blonde face. Her lips parted. She was speaking to me. *'Trouble always finds you. Nothing's going to change that – it's the way you are.'* English words, but definitely not an English voice. A Russian accent.

Anna? I may even have said her name aloud.

I stretched out. Tried to touch her.

But she was moving away from me now. Retreating to a place I couldn't reach.

I'd switched off the TV as soon as Stefan had hit the sack, but as I let my mind drift, two words kept fighting their way to the surface. Putin . . . Ukraine . . . Putin . . . Ukraine . . . And I knew that, whether or not there was a connection between the bare-chested ex-KGB psychopath and the events on the mountain, I couldn't take any chances.

I reached for my day sack and felt around for the second Nokia, a battery and the SIM cards. As I turned the key in the door, I heard a voice from the bunk. 'Nick . . . Where are you going?'

'Just need to make a call, mate. Won't be long.'

I locked up behind me and kept the key fob in my fist. At close quarters it would do as much damage as my fucked-up Sphinx, and would be easier to explain away.

I went round the back of the accommodation block and eased through a gap in the hedge, then under the chain-link fence that surrounded the property. I crossed the stretch of turf behind it and headed towards the railway track. Once I was in the shadow of the refuse and recycling shed, I pushed the SIM and battery into the phone and sparked it up.

I tapped out an area code I had so firmly fixed in my mental filing cabinet that even a high-speed smash hadn't been able to dislodge it.

It was ten to five in the morning in Moscow, but Pasha picked up immediately.

'Mate, I need your help. Can you call me back on this cell from a secure line?'

Pasha Korovin was one of the main men on *Russia Today*, and one of the small handful of people I completely trusted. He had been Anna's editor when she was busy campaigning to make the world a better place, and knew when to keep below the radar.

I pressed the red button and waited. The Nokia's screen lit up seconds later.

Unidentified number.

I piled straight in. He didn't need small-talk. 'A couple of things. First, could you tell me if Frank Timis was on your supreme leader's shit list?'

'Frank was found dead yesterday. In the Alps.'

'I know. I was there. That's why I'm asking.'

'There have been rumours. They have never been . . . the best of friends.'

'Can you check?'

'And second?'

'Anna. Whoever killed Frank wants me dead too. So if this *is* a Putin plot, she could be in the shit as well. They might try to use her to get to me. They might just fuck her over for being in Frank's phone book. Could you warn her? Tell her to make herself and the baby safe until I can sort this out? She'll know what to do.' I didn't need to tell him no calls, texts or email, nothing traceable. I could have done that from here.

'I will go now.'

There was a click.

I was about to dismantle the Nokia and crush the bits under my heel when the railway track started to hum. The hum became a series of rhythmic clunks and a few minutes later a beam of light swept along the line.

I waited for the goods train to draw level with me, then stepped out of the shadows, swung back my arm and lobbed the phone into the first open truck that passed. If Moscow's answer to GCHQ had picked up my call, they'd soon work out that I was heading for Lyon. And if they hadn't, so what? At least it had brought a smile to my face.

15

Anna had been a journalist when I'd first met her, the kind who would stop at nothing in the pursuit of justice and truth. So when our son was born, it didn't take her long to spot that I wasn't ideal husband and dad material. Husbands and dads are supposed to keep their family secure, and I'd always been a trouble magnet.

Before I'd said goodbye the last time, we'd talked about what might happen if they came under threat when I wasn't there to shield them from the incoming fire. Frank had bought a couple of safe houses through a sequence of shell companies, which he assured us couldn't be traced.

Even I had no idea where they were. Pasha didn't either. His job was simply to let Anna know – if need be – when she had to evacuate the gated enclave on the Moscow margins that had been designed to protect them from everyone below Frank on the food chain.

Which didn't include Vladimir Vladimirovich Putin, prime minister of the Russian Federation, chairman of both United Russia and the Council of Ministers of the Union of Russia and Belarus. *A truly powerful man . . .*

As I headed back to the motel I visualized Pasha delivering the message. I knew Anna wasn't going to be impressed. She'd do what we'd agreed. Then she'd go into meltdown. I still missed her, but I was glad I wouldn't be there when that happened. One of those laser-beam stares of hers could take your bollocks off more severely than a Flechette missile.

I circled the motel lot, then went back in the way I'd come out.

I unlaced my Timberlands before I got my head down, but still kept them on.

There was a familiar creak above me. 'Nick . . .'

'Yup.'

'Have you been on a mission?'

'Only a little one. It's all good out there.'

'Did you take the gun?'

'Yup. I always keep it with me.'

Another creak.

'I've never shot anyone before.'

'Good.'

'My dad showed me how to use a pistol. In the garden at our *dacha*. You came there. Remember?'

'Sure I do.' That wasn't completely true, but I did have a vision of a high wall, woods, and a kitchen with the world's biggest and most gleaming coffee machine. 'Peredelkino, right?'

'Yes. Peredelkino. We used real bullets, but we only fired them at beer cans.'

'Rounds.'

I could almost hear the cogs whirring in his brain.

'What do you mean, *rounds*?'

'We don't call them bullets. We call them rounds.'

'Ah. R-r-rounds . . .' He rolled the *r* around in his mouth like he was tasting it. 'So my dad was shot . . . with r-r-rounds . . .'

I didn't want to rush him back to a place he was only just starting to escape from. But, fuck it, I couldn't keep tiptoeing around this thing. I hoped he'd be able to stay in mini-Frank mode for a moment or two longer.

'Did you spot anyone else up on the mountain? Apart from your BG?'

He went so quiet I couldn't even hear him breathe.

'A guy in khaki combats, maybe? With a ring? A red ring, with a silver eagle on it? An eagle with two heads?'

Eventually he spoke again. 'No. But I couldn't see much from the back seat. And I was talking to my dad. About a maths problem.'

'A maths problem?'

'Yes. He used to set me challenges. Then something happened in front of us. With a truck, I think. A big truck. My . . . my BG pulled off the road . . . and stopped the car . . . and turned in his seat . . . and . . . and . . .' He swallowed. 'And that was where you found us . . .'

I heard him trying to suppress a sob.

Anna would have been able to say something warm and cuddly, but I wasn't built like that. I just let him have a bit more silence to wrap himself in.

It seemed to work.

'Why did my BG do it, Nick? My dad didn't trust many people, but he trusted . . . *him*.'

'Mate, I honestly don't know. But I aim to find out. Starting first thing tomorrow.'

'Where will you find out?'

'I've got a couple of addresses.'

'Can I come too?'

'Better not. Your dad always wanted me to keep you safe. And you'll be safer here.'

Since neither of us was doing much sleeping, I took him through the drills instead.

16

I did it again the next morning.

We'd keep the shutters closed; it was more secure that way, and would make the place look like it was empty.

'You can have your bedside light on. Catch up on your Dostoevsky. Or turn on the TV – but no volume. If you think someone's trying to gain entry, don't mess around. Get straight out of the bathroom window and leg it. Into the hedge first, then under the fence. The gap's plenty big enough. I did it last night. How do you get to the ERV?'

His eyes lit up. 'Along the treeline, into the back-streets, up to the railway track. The ERV is the recycling shelter . . .'

This was good. I needed him to do it instinctively. I needed it to happen before he had a chance to think himself out of it.

'Where in the recycling shelter?'

'Behind the bottle bank. I don't come out for anyone except you.'

'All sorts of people will be dumping stuff there. How will you know it's me?'

'You'll knock three times, then three more, then say the code word.'

'What's the code word?'

His face fell. He looked like I'd just marked him down on his homework.

I grinned and put my hand on his shoulder. 'We haven't agreed a code word. It needs to be something only you and I know.'

He gave it some serious thought.

But I didn't have all day. 'I tell you what: who's the main guy in *Crime and Punishment*? You know, the student in the shit?'

'Raskolnikov.'

'Let's use him, yeah?'

He nodded slowly. 'What does ERV mean, Nick?'

'Emergency rendezvous, mate. It's a safe place where you and I meet that nobody else knows about.'

He was putting a brave face on it, but I could see he wasn't convinced. He gripped my arm. 'Why can't I come with you?'

I eased his hand away. 'It's a pain in the arse, but where I'm going there are no kids allowed.' It was the first excuse that sprang into my mind: my stepdad's stand-by when he was going down the local.

His lip quivered. 'How long will you be?' He was being as brave as his dad would have expected, but I knew a part of him just wanted to curl up and hope all this was going to go away.

'I'll try to be back soon. Way before last light. But if I'm not, don't worry.'

I handed him a bag of stuff I'd picked up from a nearby Spar before he woke: water, Orangina, a croissant, a ham and cheese baguette.

I pointed at the room key and told him to double-lock the door when I'd gone, flip on the bar, and not to open it to anyone except me.

'Same three knocks, then three more, then Raskolnikov?'

'Spot on.'

I hung the *Do Not Disturb* sign on the outside handle. Then I plucked three hairs from the back of my head, gobbed on my fingertips and pasted them at intervals across the gap between the leading edge of the door and the frame. If they'd been disturbed by the time I got back, it wouldn't necessarily mean that someone had lifted Stefan, but it would tell me that the thing had been opened and I needed to sort my shit out before going inside.

My first stop was a pharmacy, where I found a rack of black-plastic-framed glasses with +1 magnification. They'd give me a headache if I wore them too long, but I didn't plan to. My next was a clothes store, to buy the sort of jacket people wear when they're paying their bank manager a visit. I saw a matching blue beret on my way to the till, but I wasn't aiming to turn myself into a cartoon Frenchman, just to cover up my head wound. I selected a blue baseball cap instead. Not the one with the *Top Gun* logo on the front: it wasn't going to be that kind of party.

I picked up a Moleskine pocket-size notepad with an elastic fastener from a nearby stationery store. Writing anything down when you're on a task can really fuck things up, but I still didn't trust myself to hang on to detail that might help me sort things out. And if it was good enough for Hemingway, it was good enough for me.

The shiniest bits of Albertville had probably been thrown up a couple of decades ago, when it hosted the Winter Olympics. Until I reached the town centre, I got the impression that it had been chucked together from a random collection of trading estates.

The Banque Privée belonged to a more elegant world, and clearly had some history. I walked past it on the other side of the street, then ran through the usual anti-pursuit routines before making an approach. Known locations are always risky, and I had to assume that Mr Lover Man and his mates knew about this one. Tucked between two upmarket cafés, it was the sort of place where you didn't get through the entrance until the people inside had taken a really good look at you.

'Quoi?' A staccato voice addressed me in French from a highly polished brass grille beneath a security camera.

I tilted my head towards it and told whoever was listening that I was English, that I was here in connection with Mr Timis, and I needed to see Mr Laffont.

The front door was made from the same kind of glass as the rear windows of Frank's Range Rover. One glance at my reflection was enough to tell me why they'd hesitated to invite me in. But there was a soft buzz and it opened to my push.

The foyer was a riot of beige and gold topped off with a crystal chandelier that would have made Glen Campbell a very happy bunny. There wasn't a cashier in sight. It wasn't the kind of set-up where you dropped by to deposit your pocket money. You either transferred it electronically or delivered it in a bulletproof attaché case handcuffed to a man mountain with wraparound sun-gigs.

A blonde in a neatly tailored suit chose to ignore the slight bleep that sounded as I walked through the metal detector housed in the inside door frame. She offered me a formal welcome and indicated that I should take a seat.

I tore the first page out of my Moleskine and scribbled the number I'd given my gnome in Zürich over the phone last night. 'Please give this to Mr Laffont.'

She rotated on one stiletto heel and disappeared up a sweeping, deep-pile-carpeted staircase. The security cameras were as discreetly positioned as possible, but I knew Laffont would already be examining me closely on his monitor.

Blondie materialized again ten minutes later, so I'd obviously passed the first test. 'Monsieur Laffont is expecting you.'

I didn't ask how.

She guided me to the first-floor landing, where a pair of massive Oriental vases flanked the entrance to a suite the size of a parade ground.

Almost everything about the man who rose to greet me from behind the world's biggest mahogany desk was grey. His hair, his immaculately trimmed moustache, his suit, the eyes that glinted behind his rimless spectacles. He offered me his hand, but I wasn't sure I could reach it. Then I realized he was just waving me towards a nearby chair – the sort you only ever saw in palaces or museums.

He opened the proceedings once I'd put down my day sack and we'd both sat. 'Monsieur . . . er . . .'

I had no idea which of my names Frank had given him, or whether I wanted to tell him anyway, so I just took off my glasses and told him I was a business associate of Mr Timis and needed his help.

'Of course, Monsieur. We heard the . . . news . . . yesterday afternoon. A tragedy. His poor wife . . .'

I knew I was being tested. Back in the day, I would have told him to stop fucking about and tell me what I needed to know. But filling a Swiss bank vault with Mexican drug money had taught me that in their world the game was played by a different set of rules. 'I'm pretty sure they were separated. And I don't think she is poor. But his son is gutted.'

'Ah . . . little Bogdan. He must be . . .'

'Stefan.'

He gave an apologetic nod. 'I have only one more question, if it will not offend you.'

I told him I didn't offend easily, but I was running short of time. I chucked Frank's passport on to the desk.

He glanced at it, but wasn't to be deflected. 'Would you be so good as to tell me the connection between Monsieur Timis's country estate and your Monsieur Le Carré?'

Thank fuck he hadn't asked me this kind of stuff yesterday. There was no way I could have dredged it up. But today I remembered my first meeting with Frank, when he'd needed me to find Stefan and kill the people who had kidnapped him.

'Frank's *dacha* is in a place called Peredelkino. He liked the fact that it featured in Le Carré's novel *The Russia House*.'

At that point, Laffont treated me to something like a smile. 'Excellent. Monsieur Timis said you would be making contact in the event of . . . an accident.'

'What else did he say?'

'That he was deeply concerned about some recent business acquisitions. He didn't divulge the details, but was confident that the contents of his safe-deposit box would usefully add to the things he told you the night before last.'

I didn't want to admit that I'd lost my marbles in that 'accident' and was still struggling to remember a single one of the key elements of Frank's briefing. I needed him to share Frank's confidence in me, and to give me as much help as he could. I didn't need him to put a call through to the local nuthouse. And I wanted him to get a fucking move on.

He stood and did that James Bond trick with his cuffs, picked up a small leather wallet and motioned me towards an archway in the far corner behind his desk. It opened on to another stairwell that led down to the vault.

A steel door unsealed itself after scanning Laffont's index fingerprint and right iris, then swung shut as we moved through it. Finally we arrived in a room that belonged in the next century, not the one before last. The lighting was as understated as the furniture.

Laffont held back a heavy crimson velvet curtain, then let it fall as we entered the land of the safe deposit. They lined all three walls, floor to ceiling. He slid two keys out of the wallet and inserted them into a box at shoulder height on the right-hand side. He turned them simultaneously, clockwise, until there was a soft click. Then he extracted the drawer and placed it with reverence on the velvet-covered table under a low-hanging light at the centre of the room.

He dipped his head and retired to the antechamber. He'd know fucking well what was in there, but maintaining the illusion of detachment obviously suited him.

I lifted the lid.

First out of the box were six passports.

Three for me, with driving licences to match. Same first name, three sets of different surnames – Saunders, Savage and Browning. Three for Stefan – now Steven – each IDing him as my son. Frank knew that, in a post-Madeleine McCann world, even the sleepiest European frontier post would react badly to any attempt to smuggle a kid across a national border. And whoever had supplied these had been busy with the Photoshop. Three slightly different hair colours and styles, one with glasses, two without.

I put them to one side.

Next up was a blueprint for a container vessel commissioned by a shipping outfit called Nettuno, based on the coast of Puglia, not far from Brindisi. I unfolded it and spread it out under the light.

The maze-like structure triggered a fragment of memory, but maybe only from some time in the past when I'd had to scrutinize the layout of a building, an aircraft or a boat before a task.

There was a set of deeds for a chateau overlooking Lake Konstanz. A chateau I'd definitely seen before. In Frank's desk drawer. Now I knew it had been purchased by a Swiss-based holding company, which must have been part of Frank's web of international business enterprises.

I put them next to the blueprint and tried not to get a headache as I ran my eyes over them. He'd meant them to be seen in the context of his briefing. He hadn't intended these things to be brainteasers. But that's exactly what they were.

There was also a wad of euros and US dollars. Frank had always believed that cash said more about you than Amex ever could.

Finally, in a chamois-leather drawstring bag, a very familiar shape. Another matt black compact Sphinx, two mags and a box of fifty 9mm Parabellum rounds. It was a fancy name that some people thought meant 'prepare for war'.

At least that part of Frank's message was clear.

I only wished he'd prepared for it better himself.

17

I picked up the pistol, removed its top slide and dismantled the working parts far enough to be able to take a close look at the business end of the firing pin. It was factory fresh. I reassembled it, loaded up one of the mags and tucked it into my waistband.

I zipped up my jacket and put everything else that Frank had left me in the day sack. I deposited the weapon Mr Lover Man had doctored in the box, closed the lid and slid it back into its slot in the wall.

Laffont stood as I emerged.

'My turn to ask the questions?' I made it sound like one, but he knew it wasn't.

He gave a brisk nod and sat down again.

'The documents. Were they arranged by Frank's bodyguard? The black guy? Because, if so, they're already compromised.'

He shook his head. 'No. They had to be done at speed, and with complete confidentiality. I arranged them personally.'

'Tell me about the chateau on Lake Konstanz. His ex-wife's place?'

'That was certainly Monsieur Timis's intention.'

'And?'

'And what?'

'Is she living there now, or in Moscow?'

'I only see the invoices. Mostly for building work. But, yes, she is overseeing the renovation personally.'

'Tell me about her.'

He looked blank.

'Is she to be trusted?'

'Monsieur Timis went to great lengths to keep her happy when he was alive. Even after they—'

'Is that a yes or a no?'

He hesitated long enough to make it more 'no' than 'maybe'. Which was a fucker, because I'd been hoping she might be the safe place I needed for Stefan.

'He seems to own an Italian shipping company. Nettuno. The blueprint—'

'A recent acquisition.' His turn to interrupt. He seemed to like that. 'The due diligence was . . . rushed. I was not privy to the process.'

'I got the impression that he wasn't happy about it.' I didn't say Stefan had told me that – or that Frank might have done and I couldn't remember.

'I gather there are . . . were . . . complications.'

'What complications?'

'The kind that sometimes come with cargo . . . which has been transported from North Africa, Greece and Eastern Europe.'

'Drugs- or people-trafficking?'

'Is there a difference?' Laffont's look of distaste made me want to ask him how much he knew about the kind of businesses that had made his client Monsieur Timis his first few millions. Frank had done his best to go respectable over the last few years, but I was pretty certain all that shit was still not far beneath the surface.

Which made me think that whatever had rattled him enough to call me must be either very bad indeed or very personal.

Or maybe both.

He'd only asked for my help once before now, and that was when he'd thought he'd lost his son.

'So what happens now? Is everything on hold?'

'An audit is called for.' He paused to give his next sentence the weight he believed it deserved. 'I will take care of it personally.'

I brought out the invitation to the opening of the distribution depot and unfolded it. 'And have you ever had dealings with Adler Gesellschaft? I'm guessing it's a German company. I found this invite in Frank's desk.'

'Of course. Monsieur Timis is the majority shareholder. And it is not German. It is Swiss. The head office is in St Gallen. But the depot . . .' he pointed at the address on the card '. . . is local.'

Majority shareholder. Acquisition. Italian shipping. Swiss construction. I knew Frank had been trying to go legit; I hadn't realized how serious he was about it.

'Are there complications there too?'

His brow furrowed. 'Not as far as I know. Why do you ask?'

My eyes locked on his. 'Because one of their monster lorries forced me off the road immediately before Frank was killed.'

'Are you sure?'

'Very.' I paused. 'And you've just told me their head office in Switzerland is on his ex-wife's very smart new doorstep. That's already two coincidences too many.'

'Nettuno was his particular concern.'

'Maybe he was looking in the wrong direction.'

He shrugged. 'I have no way of telling.'

'Maybe you should be taking a long, hard look at Adler too.'

His expression said he was happy for me to do my job but not for me to tell him how to do his.

I decided it was time for us to be new best friends again. 'Thank you for the half-million euros.'

'You are welcome, Monsieur. As you know, it is the sum you agreed for looking after his son. The balance will be paid into your account when you have discovered who is responsible for Monsieur Timis's death, and why, and then . . .'

He left me to fill in the blanks.

'The balance?'

'The other half-million.' He allowed himself the smallest of smiles. I couldn't blame him. This was Albertville, for fuck's sake, not Zürich. Frank must have trusted him a lot.

I asked if I could call if anything else came up.

He extracted a wafer-thin leather wallet from somewhere among the greyness and handed me his business card. 'My private cell phone.'

'How private?'

'Very.' His eyes glinted. Fair one.

I didn't make a habit of collecting people's business cards, but I tucked this one away. Laffont clearly had access to a whole lot of shit that I might need to tap into once the due diligence kicked in.

'Monsieur Timis was most . . . insistent that I should help you. In any way possible.'

'Excellent.' I leant in towards him. 'Perhaps you can kick off by taking care of his son. I don't like leaving him on his own. It makes us both vulnerable. And I can move faster and be less visible if I go solo.'

He tried as hard as he could to disguise it, but I knew I'd caught him off balance. He looked like he'd had a red-hot poker shoved up his arse. He raised his eyebrows and gave a small cough into his delicately bunched fist while he sorted himself out. 'Alas, that will not be possible . . . Madame Laffont, she is not in the best of health . . .'

I imagined that Madame Laffont was as fit as a butcher's dog, and couldn't be bothered to get off her sunbed.

'I'm sure you and Madame Laffont would find Stefan very . . . rewarding.' It was my turn to give him the kind of smile that wasn't more than skin deep. 'And what better way to honour his father's faith in you?'

He glanced at his Patek Philippe wristwatch. 'My apologies, Monsieur. Sadly, I have another meeting scheduled for . . . five minutes ago.'

As we got to our feet and shook, I told him I needed one other thing. Could he make sure the digital record of my visit was wiped?

He responded with another dip of the head. 'You dislike being photographed, Monsieur?'

Being photographed had once been fucking close to fatal for me, and put Anna and our son severely in harm's way too. But he didn't need to know that.

I gave him some meaningful eye to eye. 'Dislike doesn't even begin to cover it, Monsieur Laffont.'

On the way out I remembered that I'd left the +1 specs on his desk. Fuck it. He could keep them.

18

I'd left the Polo near the town hall.

I read the number on Laffont's card three times on the way back to it, waited five minutes, then checked I'd got it right. This time the magic worked. But I copied it into the Moleskine once I was back behind the wheel. I'd test myself again later.

Then I went in search of a cyber café. I wanted to get the latest on the investigation into the body on the mountain. And to find out as much as I could about the lay-out of the Adler set-up. I quartered the town for half an hour without finding one, so decided to head straight for the address on the invite.

I needed to find the driver who had slammed his foot on the brake right in front of me and sent the X-Trail off-road. Then I needed to take him somewhere quiet and grip him. I'd invite him to refresh his memory of yesterday afternoon's events, and refresh mine too. He'd suddenly realize he wanted to share some information with me – starting with the name and contact details of Mr Lover Man or the fucker who'd put him up to it. It wouldn't necessarily mean we'd be completely sorted, but it would be a good place to start.

I got back on the main for a couple of Ks and retraced the route I'd taken last night. I shot past the Buffalo Grill and exited a few minutes later, crossing the river not too far from the jumble of earth-moving equipment on its bank.

I scanned the area, trying to look like a local with a purpose rather than a tourist who'd lost his way. I passed a budget furniture centre, a mega wine store and a cement factory.

The Adler depot was on the edge of the development. Three pleated-tin warehouses the size of aircraft hangars surrounded by solid metal railings topped with spikes. I joined a line of wagons parked at the edge of the road that led to its main entrance and switched off my engine.

Ahead of me, forklifts buzzed in and out of three sets of huge sliding doors, loading artics with RSJs, prefab roofing sections and stripy steel poles. Lads in white safety helmets and yellow hi-vis jackets with reflecting stripes waved their arms around and shouted useful stuff and piss-takes across the loading bays.

High-voltage cables hung from pylons that paralleled the fence on the right-hand side of the yard, en route to a relay station. The forklifts and flatbed-mounted cranes kept well clear of them, keen to avoid being on the receiving end of a bolt from the world's biggest Taser.

I watched the flatbeds come and go, checking in and out with a couple of guys in the gatehouse who sat in front of a computer monitor and operated the barrier. I guess, deep down, I was hoping that one of their registration plates might suddenly leap out at me, triggering a clearer memory of the pre-crash sequence on the mountain.

Dream on.

I waited an hour, though it was blindingly obvious I was wasting my time. Every flatbed had ADLER on its rear panel and the eagle logo on its mudguards. There was nothing to help me tell the fuckers apart.

I decided to come back later. Each unit in a delivery fleet was tracked by GPS these days, partly so Mission Control could keep the customer satisfied, partly to save fuel, and partly to stop the lads behind the wheel taking the piss or driving like idiots.

They no longer needed to stick signs on the back of their vehicles asking other road-users to ring in and deliver a hug or a bollocking: the telematics told them everything they needed to know about every millimetre of every journey. If I could break into the gatehouse and access that computer, I'd be able to ID the driver from yesterday's route.

I swung out of my parking space and drove past the depot, keeping eyes on their security system. They hadn't bothered to lash out on state-of-the-art Fort Knox laser beams. Why would they, just to stop people nicking construction kit?

I stocked up on food and drink at a local Casino mini-mart: a fistful of chocolate bars, a bag of sticky buns, a box of cold pizza slices, some bottles of Coke and water. I got back to the motel mid-afternoon, parked up a couple of streets away and staked it out from a distance, but saw nothing that made my antennae wobble. The hairs were still in place on the door of our room, so Stefan hadn't gone walkabout, and a hostile reception committee inside seemed unlikely.

I knocked three times, then another three.

'Raskolnikov.'

I only murmured our code word, but that didn't stop me feeling like a bit of a dickhead.

There was no answer. Maybe Dostoevsky had sent the boy to sleep. I couldn't blame him for that.

I ran through the whole routine again.

This time I heard movement: the squeak of bedsprings, the creak of the ladder, the uneven pad of small feet. The door opened inwards the length of the chain. One eye appeared at my waist height and looked me up and down.

I held up the bag. 'Chocolate?'

He nodded. The door closed, then opened again almost immediately and I was invited inside.

We sat on the end of the bed and dug into the pizza. Stefan had finished the stuff I'd bought earlier, so there was nothing wrong with his appetite.

'Any problems?'

He shook his head. 'You?'

I shook mine too.

'There was some shooting.'

I stopped mid-mouthful. 'Where?'

He gestured up at the TV. 'In a supermarket. In a city.'

'A French city?'

'Yes. Lyon, I think. Is that a city?'

'Yup.' I took another bite of my pizza.

'The police were there. Our police.'

'*Our* police?'

'The ones that came to my dad's chalet. The GIGN.'

This kid didn't miss a trick. I was getting used to that now. 'What happened? Do you know?'

'Two men took some hostages. They were going to explode them.'

'And?'

'The police shot them. With guns. Big guns.'

'Good.'

I got some Coke down my neck and did some more eating. This sort of shit had been happening every fucking week, ever since IS had started flying the jihad flag big-time in Syria and on Facebook. No wonder the GIGN were jumpy.

We finished the buns and each scrunched our bag into a ball and lobbed them at the waste-bin. His went in; mine didn't.

He crossed his arms and gave me a grin. 'So what happens now?'

I told him I needed to go out again later, but was going to get my head down for a couple of hours. 'You can be on stag.'

'Stig?'

'No, stag. It means lookout. Give me a kick if you hear any bad guys.'

I unzipped my jacket, adjusted the butt of the Sphinx in my waistband, lay back and shut my eyes.

19

My internal alarm clock didn't let me down, and Stefan hadn't needed to give me a kick. I splashed some water over my face and we went through the ERV drills again. The expression on his face said we didn't have to, but it made me feel better.

He didn't ask if he could come too. I knew he wanted to, but he already knew the answer. He was in mini-Frank mode now. Before, he'd been spending some time as an ordinary, vulnerable seven-year-old.

I sorted my shit out and pointed the Polo towards the nearest Géant, one of those megastores that flogs everything from condoms to brake fluid. I was going to hang on to the baseball cap to cover the head wound, but I wanted to ditch the jacket. I didn't fancy spending the next few days looking like I was on my way to a job interview.

I gathered up a sweatshirt with a hood, a pair of Levi's, a pack of dark-coloured T-shirts, and a dark brown combat jacket that had more pouches than a fisherman's waistcoat but didn't make too much of a statement. I added a box of energy bars and six half-litre bottles of water to my basket before paying cash at the till.

I spotted a phone store on the way out and bought three more bog-standard pay-as-you-go Nokias. Back in the Polo, one went into my new jacket, along with the UZI and a fistful of euros.

I arrived at the approach road forty-five minutes before last light, but there were still enough parked wagons to give me cover.

When I was sure no one was taking any interest in me, I took the Pentax binos out of the glovebox and scanned the area, starting with the gatehouse. There was only one lad manning the barrier. Maybe that meant his mate had gone home. Or maybe he'd just gone for a piss. I wouldn't move in until I was sure.

Two of the warehouses were shut and the third had wound right down. A couple of forklifts were loading the final pallets on to the one remaining flatbed. The rest had obviously been signed off.

The arc lamps that surrounded the yard sparked up before the sun had dropped below the mountains. I wasn't surprised: dusk didn't drag on in this neck of the woods. They faced inwards rather than outwards, like in the old PoW movies, which meant I'd have some shadow to work with, but they weren't going to make my job a whole lot easier.

On the other hand, if they'd come on ten minutes later I might not have immediately IDed the larger of the two figures now making their way down the flight of metal steps that ran from the top floor of the office building on the right-hand side of the complex.

Fuck the database. I didn't need to track down the truck driver now. I'd found what I was looking for.

The dreads and the sheer size of Mr Lover Man were never going to allow him to merge completely into the background, but he'd left his red and white Puffa jacket and matching trainers in the wardrobe. Today's combo was quieter.

His companion's forklift-driving days were long gone, or maybe they'd never been. His sharp suit and tie suggested he'd honed his muscles in the executive suite. He'd taken a lot of care over his facial hair too. Maybe too much. The George Michael look was alive and well in Albertville.

There was a lot of nodding but not much smiling and back-slapping when they reached the bottom of the steps. Then George got behind the wheel of an Audi Q5 with Swiss plates and Mr Lover Man climbed into a Range Rover with French ones. He might have double-tapped his boss, but he'd managed to hang on to his company car. I scribbled both registration numbers in my Moleskine.

The Audi came through the barrier first and steamed past me, its driver staring straight ahead. The Range Rover indicated right. I waited for it to make the turn, then flicked on my dipped beams, eased away from the kerb, pulled a left and followed its receding taillights.

I glanced at the fuel gauge. Unless Mr Lover Man had a hot date north of Dijon, I wasn't going to have to stop and fill the tank. I held back as far as I could. I didn't want to lose him, but I didn't want to follow him too closely either. All I needed to do was keep far enough back to be just another set of annoying headlamps in his rear-view.

After a couple of hundred metres he took the third exit on a roundabout and I let a beat-up Citroën slot itself between us. Half a K further on he suddenly swerved off the road and came to a halt alongside a row of shops, most of which appeared to have stopped trading for the day.

For a nanosecond I thought he might have pinged me, but as I overtook I saw that he wasn't paying the slightest bit of attention to his rear-view or wing mirrors: he was too busy waving his arms and having a shouting match with whoever had called his mobile. Something was pissing him off big-time. After what he'd been up to in the last forty-eight hours, he should have been on full alert. And he wasn't. He was all over the place.

I carried on past the next junction and pulled in too, as soon as I could find a place that looked like I had a good reason for doing so. I killed the Polo's lights, picked up the binos again and swivelled in my seat to get eyes on him. I could see from his body language that he still wasn't a happy bunny. The dreads were whipping left and right and the hand movements were going into overdrive. I remembered Hesco waffling into his phone on the mountainside and wondered who was on the other end of this one.

He banged his fist a couple of times on the dash and stabbed the pad in front of him with his index finger. Then he went completely still and stared straight at me.

He didn't, of course. The Pentax 10x50 magnification just made the whole thing feel up close and personal. Up close and personal enough for me to see that he was vibrating with rage and frustration.

I was starting to think this might be a good time to intercept him. I binned the binos and glanced to my right, looking for a route that would give me enough cover to get within reach of his wagon and slip into the back seat, Sphinx in the aim.

As I reached for my passenger door handle he swung back on to the road without giving the wagons behind him any warning whatsoever. They were still giving him shit with their horns when he flew past me.

I tailed him on to the main, heading south-west. He wasn't trying to evade or test a potential pursuer; he was just putting his foot down and not giving a fuck about who he pissed off in the process. He wasn't the only one: he was driving like a Frenchman.

I put mine down too, not that it made much difference. The Polo was built for low-profile escape and evasion, not high-speed pursuit.

I had no idea where he was heading. I just had to point and hope that the traffic ahead would keep him bottled up. A flurry of raindrops belted against the windscreen, blurring the taillights ahead. But it didn't stop me seeing the Range Rover bear right off the E70, following the signs to Chambéry and Aix-les-Bains. I caught up with him again as we passed a place called Myans.

He continued to push on without a hint of caution. As he slalomed between the lanes, cutting up anyone who was mad enough to get in his way, even the locals were giving him the finger. Something – or someone – was getting to him big-time.

We both slowed for the *péage* at the end of the dual carriageway south of the airport. The Range Rover zipped through an orange-lit Liber-T channel, for wagons with a remote-control beeper and owners who preferred to pay by bank transfer.

I followed him through. The Polo didn't have a beeper but, fuck it, the fine letter would arrive on one of Frank's desks at some point, and he wouldn't care. Neither did I.

Mr Lover Man didn't do one of his last-minute jinks towards Lyon, so I spent the next few K wondering what I'd do if he was aiming for the next flight out of here from the Flybe departure lounge.

As the fork in the airport slip-road approached, I still didn't have an answer. He stayed with the main and kept on going up the east shore of what the signage told me was the Lac du Bourget. Apart from anything else, it pretty much confirmed that we were close to the end of this particular journey. Mr Lover Man might have been behaving like even more of a psycho than I was right now, but it made absolutely no sense looping west at the top of the lake to get back on the road to Lyon. And if Annecy, to our north-west, was his target, he'd taken a majorly wrong turning way back.

Judging by the lighting display, Aix-les-Bains was a big old place, stretching from the water into the foothills of the Alps. The Range Rover took a right, through the centre of town. Its mixture of palatial hotels, grand government buildings and tree-lined boulevards reminded me of the millionaires' playgrounds further south, on the Mediterranean coast. It even had a floodlit casino that looked like a pink and white harem.

Mr Lover Man slowed once or twice on the way through, so I had no difficulty keeping up. His final destination turned out to be a resort hotel right on the lake. He turned through the entrance, past a big glossy hoarding that told anyone who didn't know already that Aix was a spa town; people had come here for the good of their health since Roman times.

The hotel looked like a less shiny version of MI6's London HQ at Vauxhall Cross, with a marina behind it instead of the Thames. I could see an assortment of plunge pools and water-jets through the massive expanse of plate glass that ran left of the foyer, but I didn't think that was why Mr Lover Man was here.

As I made to follow, a minibus pulled out in front of the wagon ahead of me, sideswiped two others on the way through and clipped one in the oncoming lane. I didn't stop to provide a witness statement, but by the time I reached the car park, Mr Lover Man was only a couple of strides away from the lobby.

I exited the Polo and picked up pace to get into the building before he disappeared, but I had only moved a metre or so when there was a screech of brakes on the main. I had to dive for cover as a shiny black coupé took the corner at warp speed. It screamed past the ranks of parked wagons and came to a halt on the hotel forecourt. A Maserati, with Swiss plates. The driver clearly thought he owned the fucking place.

When he threw open the door and got out, I concentrated hard. Khaki shirt and combats. I'd only seen him from the back, but there was no mistaking Hesco when his blood was up.

20

Another guy emerged from the passenger seat. Hair so closely cropped his head shone in the lights that circled the entrance. Leather jacket. Or possibly suede. Standard Eastern European issue, but sharper. Not a bomber. With lapels. Black skinny jeans.

I paused long enough to extract my UZI and scribble the Maserati registration number in the Moleskine. Then I sprinted across the parking lot towards the lobby as they both went inside.

I saw the two of them being eaten up by one of the lift doors as I entered the busy reception area. The indicators just told me they were heading upwards, not the floor.

Shit. I didn't know their names. I didn't know if any of them were even staying here.

Which left me two options.

Stake out the cars.

Or get help from an insider.

Room service, ideally. Or a maid. They knew pretty much everything that went on behind closed doors. Who the big tippers were. Who would pay big-time for 'extra pillows' – hotel code for hookers.

That way I might be able to grip all three and get this shit over with. And if I got nothing I'd wait for one of them to go for a drive.

The kitchen entrance was the place to aim for. Which meant starting with the bar or restaurant. Flickering candles and mood lighting in the windows to the right of the foyer made me think I was on the right track. The clink of glasses, then the sight of a few punters taking an after-dinner drink around the back of the building confirmed it.

I kept scanning the area for Mr Lover Man. Just because the other two had taken the lift, it didn't mean that he had. Several groups and five or six couples were sitting beneath infrared heaters slung from canvas parasols, enjoying the view of the yacht-filled marina and the moonlight shimmering on the surface of the lake. The hum of conversation and the occasional burst of laughter blended with some distant lift music and, close by, the rhythmic clicking of halyards against the forest of masts.

I skirted the tables, keeping to the shadows but giving the odd nod and smile to anyone who glanced in my direction, as you do when you're all in the same boat. I was aiming for a set of steps leading to the level below. I didn't want the first-class lounge, I needed the engine room.

The marina was lit from every available angle, but it was darker at the edge, beneath the patio I'd just come from. I rounded another corner and found what I was looking for: a couple of lads in waiter gear having a quick break by a doorway. Pots and pans clanked in the background, and some poor fucker was getting yelled at inside for overcooking the fillet or underdoing the seasoning. Whatever, it was the back entrance to the kitchen.

One of the lads pinched out the tip of his cigarette, tucked the bit he hadn't smoked into his trouser pocket, and disappeared inside. The other stayed where he was, one thumb hooked in his not-very-fancy designer belt. He took a final drag, spun the stub into the water, and ruffled the tuft of beard on his chin.

I gave him a conspiratorial grin, fished the half-empty pack of Ukrainian Marlboros out of my pocket and offered him one. He nodded his very curly and youthful head, took one, then another for later, and leant forward to give us both a light. I hated the fucking things, but a drink or a smoke has always been the quickest way of making a complete stranger your new best friend.

'Français?'

He chuckled. *'Non. Je suis d'Oman.'*

I chuckled too. 'Muscat? I love Muscat.' I'd been there with the Regiment, training the Sultan's troops, but he didn't need to know that.

'Salalah.'

I shoved out my hand and gripped his. 'Beautiful.' I took a drag on my Marlboro and did my best not to cough my guts out. 'Salalah. Beautiful. Even more beautiful than Muscat.'

I didn't have all night to swap holiday memories, but I was prepared to waste five minutes finding out whether this guy could point me straight to Mr Lover Man's door.

'Really? You have been there?'

I nodded. 'Visiting my brother. He worked for a bank. HSBC . . .'

I got the impression the word 'bank' had suddenly earned me his full attention. 'He loved Oman too. Took me all over.' I paused. 'So what brings you here?'

He shrugged, and glanced over my left shoulder. Maybe he'd spotted a boat he fancied behind me. Maybe he was about to give me a big fat lie. 'I go to college. In Lyon.' Then he sighed. 'But what brings anybody from my world to yours, Monsieur?'

'My world isn't that special, mate. Believe me. But I tell you what – maybe we could help each other out . . .'

His eyes glistened as I took out one of Frank's fifty-euro notes and slid it into his shirt pocket. 'What shifts have you done this week?'

'The usual. Starting at five, finishing at two in the morning . . .'

'In the restaurant?'

He nodded.

'Room service, sometimes?'

'Sometimes. I prefer it to the restaurant.'

'Better tips?'

Time for another fifty. His belt was leather and had a Gucci buckle, but it was probably a fake. The marks on it and the misshapen holes told me he'd got progressively thinner in the last few months, and everything else about him – including his scratched Casio watch – said that every cent counted.

'I'm looking for a guy . . .'

He recoiled. Not much, but enough to let me know he suddenly wasn't enjoying this as much as he'd thought he would.

'Don't worry. Not . . . in that way. And he isn't in trouble. He's a friend of mine. I just haven't seen him for a while. Big black guy. From Nigeria. Dreadlocks. Looks like a rapper.' I gave him another grin and held up the cigarette pack. 'Smokes these things too.'

He relaxed. 'He arrived yesterday. I like him very much. Very . . . spiritual. A true believer.'

'What's his room number?'

'His room number? His room number is . . .' His eyes glistened and his hand twitched.

Another fifty found its way out of my pocket, but before I passed it over I heard a scuffle somewhere above us. Then a shout and the sound of breaking glass. Fuck. Why always breaking glass? But not a car window this time. A wine bottle, maybe. The talking had stopped on the patio. So had the laughter. A woman screamed. We both looked up.

I couldn't see a thing until I stepped back towards the moorings. I spun the rest of my Marlboro into the water and craned my neck.

The fight wasn't outside the restaurant.

It was on one of the top-floor balconies.

Two figures had started to beat the fuck out of a third, pushing him hard against the rail. I could only see his back. But it was enough to show me I didn't need the help of my new Omani mate to find Mr Lover Man after all.

If he had been a smaller unit, it might have been more difficult to tip him over. But he didn't have a low centre of gravity. So once he'd lost his balance, there was only one way for his dreadlocks to go.

He managed to grip the rail for a moment, and bought himself a few extra seconds.

Then, arms and legs flailing, he arced into space.

21

He bounced once, on the stone balustrade that bordered the paved area above us. I heard the cracking of bone – maybe his ribs, maybe his back, maybe both – as he crashed down in a heap on the planking that lined the marina, less than four metres away.

The waiter gasped, and started to gibber. I couldn't blame him. Not everyone can deal with a twenty-stone body falling five storeys and hitting the deck beside him. Even if he had immigration papers. I batted him away. 'Go. You don't need this shit . . .'

I didn't need this shit either. I wanted this fucker alive and talking. I couldn't fuck about. If he wasn't unconscious already, he soon would be. Plus the crowd wouldn't spend all night rubber-necking from the gallery above me. They'd find their feet any second now.

I knelt by the body. I saw the waiter hanging around in the kitchen doorway, and I sensed a growing audience on the level above me, but I didn't look up: iPhones would soon be recording, and when they did, I didn't want anything visible beneath my baseball cap.

He'd landed face up. His eyes were open, but the back of his head wasn't healthy. The dreads were like snakes, swimming in a pool of blood.

Most of the damage seemed to be low down, though, so I reckoned that, with a little encouragement, he'd still be able to talk.

His left arm didn't look too clever. The chunky gold chain hung limply from his wrist. And his leg was folded back underneath him at a severely terminal angle.

I touched the pulse in his neck with my fingertip. His heart was pumping like a piston, doing everything it could to oxygenate his failing body.

I leant my ear right up close to his mouth and heard him let out a halting, pain-racked breath. His eyelids fluttered. I was pretty certain he wouldn't be able to feel anything from the chest down, so I put some pressure on his smashed-up arm.

His jaw clenched. Then his lips parted and a crimson bead rolled down his cheek from the corner of his mouth.

'Why did you kill Frank?'

He tried to suck some air into his lungs. It wasn't working. He only got enough to whisper four syllables. '*Ly . . . u . . . bo . . . va . . .*'

Four syllables that made up one word. *Lyubova*. I'd never used it myself, but I knew what it meant. *Lyubova* was the Russian word for love.

'Who wanted him dead?'

His chest quivered and his eyes closed.

They sprang open when I gripped his arm again. Gave it a twist.

'*Who?*'

'You . . . ran . . .'

'What the fuck are you talking about?'

'You . . . ran . . .'

His voice was so weak it was almost drowned in the sound of footsteps on the stairs.

Then I heard the sirens.

For the benefit of the spectators, I shook my head sadly as I got to my feet. It also gave me a couple of seconds to decide on my next move.

Hesco and his sidekick would be legging it as quickly as they could now that the gendarmes were getting closer, and so should I, if I was going to have any chance of gripping them.

I turned and walked swiftly to the far corner of the hotel, past the rear of the section housing the plunge pools. On this level all I could see through the windows to my left was cool lighting and empty massage tables.

To my right sleek yachts were hitched to a series of floating pontoons. A grass bank sloped up from the hard standing that bordered the water. Clumps of evergreens had been planted along the top of it, to provide shelter from the wind or maybe to hide the moorings from people who didn't like boats.

There was a shout as I reached the bank. I ignored it, climbed into the treeline and went left, towards where Hesco had left his wagon.

On the far side of the trees a row of hard tennis courts, surrounded by a high chain-link fence, stretched down towards the lake. A string of blue flashing lights bounced off the night sky beyond them.

As I reached the front of the hotel, two dark blue Land Cruisers screeched to a halt four hundred short of the resort entrance, and eight lads in combats leapt out. They split up almost immediately, and spread themselves across the southern flank of the complex, advancing towards the marina in pairs, weapons in the shoulder.

The Maserati had disappeared, but I kept walking until I got to the Polo. Like Hesco and his shiny-headed mate, I needed to get the fuck out of there before the GIGN established a cordon.

Two more Land Cruisers and an ambulance filled my rear-view as I headed left on the main. As they turned into the entrance behind me, I took the second right and looped back towards Albertville.

22

An hour later I passed the Buffalo Grill. Not a hint of neon. The place was deserted. That was fine by me. I'd rehydrated and got an energy bar down my neck en route, and food was so far down my list of priorities it hardly featured. My head was already filled with the events of the night.

'Ly . . . u . . . bo . . . va . . .'

Four syllables.

I let them echo through the darkness as I drove.

Four syllables meaning 'love'.

At first I'd thought he was telling me that he'd been thrown off the balcony because he had saved the boy.

Now I remembered that Lyubova was also the name of Frank's ex-wife. The one Laffont couldn't bring himself to trust.

Was Mr Lover Man saying that *she* was responsible for Frank's death?

And what the fuck did *'You . . . ran'* mean? Is that what I had done on the mountain? Or had he said, 'You . . . run'? Had he been warning me to get away from Aix? To get away from this whole gangfuck?

My head was starting to spin again, just like it had when I was chucking my guts up at 1,987 feet. I opened both front windows, breathed deeply and steadied myself.

I was sorted by the time I reached the motel. I slid the Sphinx back into my waistband and swung myself out of the wagon. A motion sensor triggered the light beside our door. All three hairs had gone missing.

I carried on through the arch and checked the bathroom window from the outside. It was firmly shut.

I went back and pushed gently on the door, but it didn't give. I went through the knocking routine, then murmured, 'Raskolnikov. . .'

Nothing.

I repeated the sequence a little more loudly.

Still no sign of life from inside.

I fired up the Polo and made for the recycling point. A goods train rattled past as I parked up. I did the whole knocking thing all over again, pulled open the door and whispered our code word. This time I got a response.

'Nick . . .'

There was a bump and a squeak and Stefan poked his head out from between the wheelie-bins. He rushed over and grabbed me, like I was some kind of lifebelt.

'Stefan . . . no . . .' I managed to prise myself loose and steered him straight into the boot of the wagon, stopping only to slide his rucksack off his shoulders.

Before I closed the hatch he handed me the room key. The big chunk of metal hung down from it, with the motel's address stamped on one side. Fuck that. I threw it into the bottle bank and drove north towards Ugine.

I didn't stop until I got to a truckers' café off the main. I pulled into a parking space alongside a white van as the first hint of dawn crept into the sky. I went inside and grabbed a salami baguette for both of us, a big frothy coffee for me and a Coke for him, then hauled him out of his hiding place and on to the passenger seat.

He immediately kicked into overdrive, in a completely impregnable combo of Russian and English.

I told him to take a deep breath, get the food and drink down his neck, then start again. Slowly.

He opened and closed his mouth a couple of times, then nodded. After three mouthfuls and one gulp of the fizz he rattled out the story of his last few hours.

I gripped his shoulder. 'Wait. Stop. First things first. Did someone try to get into the room?'

He shook his head. 'No. But I knew someone would, very soon . . .'

Either this boy had gone telepathic on me, or he'd seen something. 'The TV?'

He nodded. 'They're saying that the man who crashed didn't die. That's you, isn't it? And they're saying he stole a boy . . .'

'Any pictures?'

'Some . . .' His expression clouded. 'Of my father. And the chalet.'

'And you?'

'Not so far. But . . .'

My turn to nod. 'You're right. It's your picture next.'

If it was, I'd have to give the boy a very quick makeover. But I wasn't going to worry about that until I had to. If I tried to second-guess every possible action in theatre and out, I'd spend my whole life frozen to the spot. And right now I needed to get us into Switzerland.

I fished around in my day sack and took out the two matching UK passports in the names of Nick and Steven Saunders, each of which IDed the other as next of kin. They were both renewed recently, but someone had done a good job of making them look as though they hadn't come straight out of the printer. They even had some Eastern European stamps for places we'd both been.

I ran through them with Stefan, and asked him to rethink his memories of places he'd visited with his real dad as places he'd visited with me. We practised our names a bit. I told him he was Steven now, and I was going to call him Steve. Then I shoved them in the glovebox and pocketed another Nokia, a battery and one of the SIM cards.

I wrapped the new Sphinx, spare mag and rounds in Frank's face flannel, opened the boot and put it under the spare tyre. I slung the day sack in on top. Stefan was about to follow it on to the dog blanket but I shook my head. 'If we get stopped, that would be quite difficult to explain. Steve, mate, it's time for you to ride up front again.'

I assembled the Nokia, texted Pasha and stepped away from the wagon as his call came through.

He kicked straight off. 'I don't know for sure about Frank and the Kremlin. But the knives are out.'

'And the other thing?'

He hesitated. 'She wasn't happy, my friend. But she took your advice immediately.'

Trying not to picture the expression on Anna's face, I punched the red button and chucked the phone into the back of a random cement mixer. I didn't know where it was going and I didn't much care, as long as it was somewhere else. The Swiss federal authorities tracked every mobile signal, twenty-four/seven, from the moment you found your first relay mast, and I didn't want to be on anybody's radar while I paid Lyubova a visit in Lake Konstanz.

As we headed for the border, Stefan and I continued to build a cover story we could share.

'If anyone asks you what I do, tell them I'm a collector.'

'What do you collect, Nick?'

'I think maybe you should get used to calling me Dad.' I kept my eyes on the road. 'Safer that way.'

'What do you collect . . .' he went quiet for a moment '. . . Dad?'

'Militaria.'

'Soldier stuff?'

'Soldier stuff. Medals, helmets, swords, that sort of thing.'

'And guns?'

'Only old ones. With the firing pins removed.'

'Like the one you had in the chalet?'

I didn't answer, but my expression obviously gave me away.

'You were away for a very long time tonight, Nick—'

'You were away for a very long time tonight, Dad.'

'Whatever. I had time to think . . .'

I let the silence stretch between us as I focused on the road ahead.

'I thought about what you did with the weapon. At the desk.'

I frowned.

'I watched you take it apart.'

'You don't miss much, do you?'

'I miss my dad . . .'

'Of course you do.' That hadn't been what I meant, but it reminded me that he was still seven, not forty-seven.

'The signs keep saying Geneva. Is that where we're going?'

'We're taking a holiday together, Steve. It's not a business trip. We're not . . . collecting.'

His eyes narrowed. 'Why Switzerland?'

'It's a lovely place. Mountains. Flowers. Fresh air. All good.'

I steered him back to the cover story. I told him we'd lived in Moscow for the last few years, which was true, and would be going back to England in a couple of weeks, which wasn't.

'Where in England?'

'Have you ever been there?'

'No.'

'Then if anyone asks let's just say London.'

He gave this some thought. 'The Houses of Parliament?'

'Not exactly. I'm more at home on the other side of the river.'

'The Arsenal?'

'Close. They started south, but went north.'

'Highbury. Emirates Stadium.'

'That's the place.'

'Yes!' He pumped his fist. 'Olivier Giroud!'

It was only a thin cover story. Our relationship wouldn't stand up to any real scrutiny, but we had a connection, and it would help us look and act the part. And as we approached Border Control I'd tell him to close his eyes and pretend to stay asleep for as long as he was allowed to.

I switched on the radio when we'd run out of football waffle – which was pretty soon because I knew fuck-all about it. I surfed the airwaves for a moment before hitting a rap channel.

The drumbeat seemed to match our mood. 'This is not a drill . . .'

'Yes!' Stefan pumped his fist again. 'Pitbull is the *man*! This shit is for *real*!'

I felt myself starting to grin like an idiot. Despite Frank's best efforts to school the heir to his business empire in mathematics, new technology and classic literature, I was starting to get a handle on where the kid's heart really lay.

The sun was well and truly up by the time we approached St Julien. This was the location of the crossing closest to Geneva airport, so the volume of traffic was normally heavy enough to ensure that anyone with an up-to-date vignette would be waved through without any hassle.

Except today.

The way ahead was blocked solid a good few Ks from the frontier post. As far as I was concerned, that could mean only one thing. And even if I was wrong, it wasn't worth putting it to the test. I didn't want to leave it too late and be the only driver to reverse the fuck out of there, so I joined the queue of vehicles bailing out at the next slip-road and aimed the Polo in the opposite direction.

I told Stefan to climb on to the back seat and get his head down before pulling in at the nearest service station. Every man and his dog around here now thought a boy had been stolen. The law would be taking a close look at all the local CCTV footage they could lay their hands on, and linking Stefan, the Polo and me on film was something I wanted to avoid.

I filled the tank, dug the Sphinx out from under the spare tyre and consulted the map. The Morzine area looked like my best bet. About an hour twenty away, and within easy reach of Avoriaz. I knew you could ski backwards and forwards between France and Switzerland around there all winter without having to get out your passport, so I figured it wouldn't be that different now the snow had retreated and the Alpine flowers had taken over.

PART TWO

1

I picked up a lift map and a timetable at the Morzine station.

The most direct route to Switzerland from there was up the Vallée de la Manche and over the Col de Cou, but the whole area was hatched with hiking and biking trails. There was no way every one of them could be patrolled by border guards.

I asked the woman behind the counter if she could give me some advice. Stefan managed to conjure up one of his smiles for her, and suddenly nothing was too much trouble. I swivelled the map in her direction, pointed to the Col, and asked how long it would take to get there on foot.

She said that we could drive up to the Mines d'Or, park by the lake and walk from there. 'Ninety minutes to the top, maybe less, for you.' Then she glanced down at Stefan and pursed her lips. 'But not so good for your son, I think. Six hundred metres up.' She pointed a finger at the ceiling. 'And steep.'

I'd already come to the same conclusion. There was no lift, and no way was I going to cycle up and down that ridge with Stefan on my handlebars.

The key chairs had opened elsewhere for the summer walking season, and I'd already IDed the ones I needed two valleys further west. But I let her come up with a whole raft of other suggestions, and nodded at every one.

'So, you must have this.' She handed me a leaflet with a livid green stripe and pictures of Dad, Mum and the kids climbing rocks, riding around on mountain bikes and having a great time at the pool. 'The Portes du Soleil multi-pass.'

It gave us access to all the fun on both sides of the border, and the transport we needed to get there. It also provided the perfect place for me to hide the kid in plain sight while I came back to fetch the wagon.

'Family?'

'Sorry?'

She beamed and gestured at Stefan. 'Would you like a family pass?'

Good thinking.

I turned to him. 'Great idea, eh? Your little sister loves a swim, doesn't she?'

He didn't even blink. 'I love to swim too.'

I took the six-day option for myself, my wife and two children. It didn't cost a fortune and sent a nice cuddly message: the four of us were planning a whole lot of adventures over the course of our holiday. It wasn't just the two of us here to cross the border without being traced.

I bought some extra-strength ibuprofen and a can of anaesthetic spray for the boy at a pharmacy across the street and hoped his ankle would hold out. If it didn't, I'd have to carry him. Fuck it, I'd humped a Bergen three times his weight across the Black Mountains in sub-zero temperatures with an RSM yelling insults at me every step of the way. And the rest. This was going to be a walk in the park.

Next stop was a ski-hire shop that also flogged hiking kit when the snow had melted. I treated Stefan to some boots. They didn't have crocodiles on them, but they would give him a bit more support than his trainers. I selected a pair of anti-shock poles to help with his balance and momentum. I got a pair for myself as well. They'd help me look the part.

A pack of energy bars and a couple of water bottles from a nearby Casino went into the day sack, and after getting some painkillers down the boy's neck and giving his foot a spray we were good to go.

I drove up to Les Lindarets and found a parking space almost immediately beside a restaurant with big green parasols that backed on to the hill. The goats in the street seemed to outnumber the people and there wasn't a traffic warden in sight. This was my kind of place.

We reached the end of the village in a couple of nanoseconds and kept on going. The first of the four lifts we needed was a K and a half south-east. The valley wasn't filled with trippers, but we weren't alone. I could see a mixed bunch of enthusiasts ahead of us, from bearded tree-huggers in open-toed sandals shepherding their wives and kids uphill to manic endurance freaks with top-of-the-range everything bent on breaking land-speed records. We fitted comfortably at the lower end of the scale.

As a pair of middle-aged men in Lycra pedalled past, drenched in sweat, I showed Stefan how to get the best out of his poles. His expression made it clear he didn't think it was rocket science. To hammer the point home he set off at speed, arms pumping, with only a hint of a limp.

I told him we still had a fair distance to go, there were no prizes for getting there first, 'And if you fuck that ankle of yours again, you can get some other dickhead to give you a piggyback . . .'

He slowed as the incline steepened and was ready for a pit stop by the time we'd got halfway.

An energy bar and half a litre of water took us to the base of Les Mossettes, a four-seat chair to the ridge. When I'd done winter training here as a young squaddie we used to stand up there with a brew and watch the big-timers somersaulting down what they called the Swiss Wall. If you failed to negotiate the concave bit at the top of the slope you wouldn't see your skis again until you got back from the hospital.

When we were almost there, the Suunto told me we were 2,200 metres above sea level. I showed the read-out to Stefan. He shrugged. I guessed his room in Courchevel was almost as high.

There was a uniform waiting at the top station, but it belonged to a lift attendant. And he seemed to be paying more attention to the dudes filming themselves biking along the Col than to us. A lad on an ATV buzzed around the bare hillside below us.

On the way down into Switzerland, I realized that something

the Omani had said, when we were giving ourselves lung cancer and becoming new best mates, was still nagging away at the back of my mind. Very spiritual, he'd called Mr Lover Man.

A true believer.

I tried to remember if I'd ever seen the Nigerian with a prayer mat, and failed. 'Your BG, he's your godfather, isn't he? Does that mean you go to church together?'

The kid was gazing at the rooftops of Les Crosets, on the wooded slopes at the far side of the valley. 'We used to go when I was young. Not very often, though. Then he started going to the mosque instead.'

I didn't know whether that was important. Maybe the atmosphere of fundamentalist lunacy that was gripping Europe right now was gripping me as well. Just because he'd converted to Islam didn't necessarily mean he'd suddenly turned into Jihadi John. But I tucked the int away for future reference.

Two more lifts and not much hiking took us to Champéry, another Disney village. It was on the outer edge of the Portes du Soleil area, so our multi-pass got us into its bike park.

Stefan thought he'd died and gone to heaven when we stepped through the entrance. The whole area was heaving with *über*-cool teenagers in mud-spattered kit pulling stunts on mountain bikes. There was some kind of competition going on.

The main track was like a rollercoaster, part bare earth, part grass, in the open and running through the trees. A series of smaller circuits featured more bumps, jumps, ramps and bridges than you could bounce over in a week.

He was even happier when I bought him a full-face helmet, a pair of Ali G goggles, a T-shirt with go-faster stripes, some gloves and elbow pads. He wasn't going to get on a bike, but he'd fit in nicely. And there was no way he'd be recognized in that gear unless he collided with someone he knew.

I told him to be within reach of the finishing line every thirty minutes until the bike park closed, and I'd come and find him. Then I gave him a cheery dad-like wave and headed back the way we'd come.

There were two obvious routes to Champéry from Les Lindarets.

I chose the one via Lac Leman. It was forty Ks further but only about twenty-five minutes longer.

So two and a half hours after saying goodbye to the goats and the green parasols I was back at the bike park with a big wad of Swiss francs in my pocket and a bigger one in my day sack, telling Stefan to get a fucking move on.

We still had more than three hundred Ks to travel.

2

Stefan went quiet as we hit the main to St Gallen. I glanced at him from time to time, between keeping eyes on the rear-view and wing mirrors as well as the road ahead. His body language told me it wasn't because he'd run out of things to say: he was miserable.

It didn't take a genius to work out that any kid whose dad had been killed in front of him only forty-eight hours ago wasn't always going to be a bundle of laughs, but this was about something different.

'I guess you must be getting to know this part of Switzerland quite well by now . . .'

He turned his face to the side window and shook his head. 'I have never been here.'

'Never visited your mum's new house?'

That didn't even earn me a shake.

After a while he muttered, 'She's not my mother.'

'I know, mate. Your real mum was a friend of mine.' I hadn't forgotten that. I'd buried it somewhere in the darkness, along with a whole lot of other shit. Tracy had been a mate since my Regiment days. That was why Frank had asked me to go and dig her and Stefan out of a hole in the ground in Somalia, and why I'd been with her when she took a round and died there, trying to save her son.

I decided to take another tack. 'The woman *I* called Mum wasn't my real mum either.'

He didn't turn back towards me, but I sensed that I'd sparked his interest.

'She used to get really pissed off with me. But you know what? She looked after me too.'

The wagon ate up another K or two before he spoke again. 'Pissed off?'

'Yeah. Angry. You know. Cross.'

'Why?'

'Me and my mate Gaz . . . we used to do all sorts of stupid stuff when we were your age. Our favourite hiding place was on the roof of his block of flats – his apartment block. We sat up there and watched the world go by. One time we—'

'My father owns apartment blocks. He owns many apartment blocks.'

'Your dad was a very rich and clever guy.' I paused. 'Gaz didn't own his apartment block. The council did. But maybe I'll explain that some other time—'

'You were going to tell me why your stepmother got pissed off with you . . .'

'Pissed off . . . yeah. Very, very pissed off. We made some bombs – not real bombs, tomato sauce, you know, ketchup, in, er, plastic bags – and went up on the roof and threw them at people in the street. Hardly ever hit anyone, but we made a bit of a mess. Explosions of red all over the place.' I'd lied about the bags. We'd nicked a packet of Gaz's dad's condoms, but now wasn't the time to explain.

He did turn then, and I could see he wasn't enjoying the story as much as I'd hoped. 'Did she beat you?'

'Nah.' I tried to make light of it. I suddenly had a fairly good idea of where this was leading. 'She clipped me across the ear. She and Gaz's mum went ballistic because they didn't know we climbed up on the roof and they thought we might fall off and kill ourselves. It was a fair way down to the pavement.'

He went quiet again. He seemed to be watching the very well-behaved Swiss houses and countryside sweeping past his window, but I knew he wasn't taking much in.

'Remember all that shit, eh? It'll help the cover story. You remembering some stupid stuff your dad did back in the day.'

'My stepmother beat me.'

It was my turn to shut up. I didn't have much choice. I spent a minute or two wishing I hadn't sparked this up in the first place. I pictured him flinching when I'd raised my hand outside the chalet. I should have read the signs.

Then I told myself, Fuck it, why worry about what you can't change? 'What did she beat you for?'

He took a long, halting breath. 'I think maybe because I am not her son.'

He probably wasn't wrong about that. There was a fair chance that Stefan jumping ahead of her in the inheritance queue and being groomed to take over the business empire had also had something to do with it.

Another of my chats with Frank rose to the surface and swam towards me. On a landing strip in Malindi. We had just snatched Stefan back, first from his al-Shabaab kidnappers, then from the Georgians who were trying to use the kid as a lever against him.

I remembered Mr T leaning in towards me, eyes fixed on mine. *'My wife's name is Lyubova. It means "love". She has much of it.'*

I'd admired his optimism. Lyubova knew Frank was a world-class shagger without a doubt, but at that point he hadn't told her Stefan even existed.

'I believe she will embrace my son as her own. I hope she will forgive me. I hope that I may become the husband she deserves.'

His words still echoed in my head, even when the image of his precise, sharply chiselled features faded, and was replaced with hers. The portrait on the bedroom wall. The photographs in the green room. Those eyes. That calculating face. They now told me that forgiveness wasn't high on her list of favourite things.

I took Stefan's distress about his stepmother seriously. It sounded like Frank's embracing scenario hadn't happened. I had no idea whether he had even got close to becoming the husband she deserved. Whatever, the magic hadn't worked. Had he binned her, or had she binned him? Had he become the ex-husband she wanted to kill?

Ly . . . u . . . bo . . . va . . .

Had *she* told Mr Lover Man to pull the trigger? Had she paid him to? Was Hesco *her* fixer?

I'd already asked myself why the chateau wasn't Frank's number-one choice of bolthole as soon as he had perceived a threat. As the tarmac unrolled in front of us, all sorts of possible answers were bouncing around inside my head. They all pointed to the fact that I needed to go and grip the ex-Mrs Timis. And that she would not be laying out the welcome mat.

Stefan reached out and patted my wrist, and I suddenly became aware that I'd been holding the steering-wheel tightly enough to throttle it. I tried to give him an encouraging smile. 'Mate, I need to pay her a visit. But don't worry, I won't leave you without an ERV.'

It sounded pretty weak, even to me.

The atmosphere inside the wagon was suddenly heavy with the things that we weren't saying to each other. He was the one to cut through it.

'Nick?'

'Steve?'

'How do you know who you can trust?'

Given what had happened to his mum and his dad, he'd already had enough first-hand experience of betrayal in his life for there to be only one answer to that question: *You don't. Ever. So trust no one.* But I couldn't bring myself to say that. It wasn't my job to tell him the world was a heap of shit.

He was too switched on for me to fudge it. On the other hand, I did want him to know that there was the occasional light at the end of the tunnel. A small handful of individuals had shown me that, over the years. They hadn't helped me find God or inspired me to rush out and hug some trees, but they had probably kept me out of prison.

'It's not easy. I don't have to tell you that. There are going to be people who . . . let you down. And people who don't, however bad things get. The trouble is, you can't always tell the difference between them – because maybe there's some shit happening in their world that we don't know about . . .'

'So?' He wasn't about to let me off the hook.

'So . . . we have to understand that we don't hand out trust like chocolate bars. People have to earn it. But it's brilliant when they do.'

'It's like being a soldier, then.'

I didn't answer immediately. I'd known a good few soldiers who hadn't earned my trust. Ruperts, mostly. And a handful who had, big-time. 'When you're in the fight, you do find out pretty quickly who you can trust.'

He nodded slowly. I'd never been around a kid who took the job of decoding life's mysteries so seriously. I'd been through some gangfucks when I was his age, but I couldn't remember trying to learn from them until much later.

'We're in the fight, aren't we?'

'We are, mate.'

'And I trust you, Nick.'

I hesitated, but only for a nanosecond. 'Same.'

I sensed him giving the faintest of smiles.

He let another few Ks speed past his window. 'Nick?'

'Yup.'

'Er . . . maybe *you* could be my *actual* dad.' He paused. 'Would that work for you?'

He had tried to keep the question matter-of-fact, but failed. Even I could hear the tremble in his voice.

Since we'd exited the chalet, he'd done a really good job of convincing me, most of the time, that he was a tough little fucker. He'd grown up fast – because he'd had to. This was a wake-up call – to remind me that there was still a lonely seven-year-old kid hiding behind the armour plating.

But I couldn't piss about. I had to leave him in no doubt that extracting him from the gangfuck in Somalia and then the one on the mountain wasn't the same as doing the whole dad thing. I didn't know how to look after my own son. Some days, I didn't know how to look after myself.

'No, mate. It wouldn't work for me. And, believe me, it wouldn't work for you either.'

I gripped the wheel again, concentrating hard on the brake-lights of the wagons in front of me. I was pretty sure he was doing the same. I knew I had to choose my next words with a fuck of a lot more care than usual.

I hoped they'd come out right.

'The thing is, Stefan, I can do my best to protect you against the bad guys. It's my job. And us pretending to be father and son is part of that. But it's an act. It's a performance. In real life, I'm not your dad. In real life, your dad is dead. Me, I'm a gun for hire. And that works, when it works, *because* I can't do all that stuff dads are supposed to do. The stuff your dad did. I can only do what *I* do. I can't do the mathematical challenges. I don't have any of the things a bright guy like you needs. I don't have the skills.'

I listened to the hum of the engine. The rasp of the tyres on the tarmac. The silence inside the wagon was like the silence that fills the gap between the whoosh of an RPG launcher and the missile sending a jet of molten copper through the side of a fighting vehicle. I felt a sudden need to fill it.

'Also, I don't have a home. I have some mates, I have some contacts. I don't really have friends. A lot of the people I called my friends are dead now, so maybe it's better that way. Maybe it's . . .'

I was blabbering now.

I shut the fuck up.

When I did glance at him, I saw that he was still staring straight ahead, chewing his bottom lip between his teeth and nodding to himself. He was processing what I'd said to him, like he always did.

Eventually, he turned and looked me straight in the eye. 'So I guess that means we're both in the shit, eh, Nick?'

'Nothing new there, mate.'

3

St Gallen was a sizeable place, east of Zürich, close up against the German border. We arrived there shortly before dark o'clock. It was less than forty-five minutes, by my reckoning, from Lyubova's country pile.

Stefan's mouth fell open as I headed towards the centre. He pointed at a square in the business district where everything seemed to have been covered with red carpet, including a couple of wagons. A group of teenagers huddled together on big red banquettes, too busy texting to talk. Lights flickered on above them, suspended on wires, like baby barrage balloons.

I remembered reading something about a couple of designers winning a competition to create a public living space that looked and felt like a room where you could hang out with your mates. Fuck knew where their inspiration came from. The only rooms I'd ever seen like that had been in Iraq and Afghan, when the grenades had detonated and we'd had to scrape what was left of the inhabitants off the walls.

I drove past a big fuck-off cathedral and found a very shiny shopping mall a few blocks from the train station that advertised a cyber café and a McDonald's. I parked up on the street a couple of hundred beyond the entrance, opposite a tram stop the size of a suspension bridge.

He made to get out but I gripped him. 'No, mate. You stay here . . .'

Then I thought, Fuck it. This might go on for ever. He can't spend the rest of his life living on takeaways, staying off the radar. Even if his photograph was on the Net now, we had to get used to hiding in plain sight.

I threw on my baseball cap and jacket and guided him inside. Stefan still limped a bit, but I didn't need to carry him.

We got some Big Macs, fries and Coke down our necks and practised our father-and-son act. That was the trick. We weren't the only ones doing it. Some of the dads in the restaurant area were in jeans and T-shirts. A few others were in grey suits and looked less like they were in the mood for a Happy Meal than we did. It was after seven p.m., but they had probably only stepped away from their desks for a quick break between currency swaps.

Stefan told me that what we were eating had zero nutritional value and I told him not to talk with his mouth full. Whatever, I don't think either of us gave a shit. It filled a space.

The cyber café was on the floor above, and felt like a designer schoolroom. I paid for an hour, chose a keyboard and monitor in one corner and began by checking out the location of its most obvious competitors. I might need them later, and I never liked going back to the same place twice. Three names and addresses went into the Moleskine.

Next I ran through the budget accommodation directory. The Swiss didn't really understand the meaning of 'cheap', but there was quite a bit of choice. I got scribbling again.

On balance, I thought we'd avoid the B-and-Bs. I liked their anonymity, but preferred the idea of being able to disappear into a crowd. Top of my list was something that called itself a hostel, with four storeys and an external staircase leading to each one. It was in a stretch of open ground dotted with trees on the far side of what was apparently the oldest library in the world. I pointed at a picture of visitors in blue felt slippers admiring ancient illuminated manuscripts in display cabinets. 'What do you think? We could pop in there if we get short of reading material.'

He was still stressing about our visit to Lyubova, but he managed a weak grin.

I googled Adler Gesellschaft. Laffont had been right. Their glass and steel executive HQ was on the northern edge of town. Their manufacturing bases – which seemed to turn out everything from aircraft fuselages and wing panels to fence posts and stripy poles – were mostly in Eastern Europe and their distribution depots were scattered across the continent, but their tax returns were definitely filed in the canton of Zürich.

They weren't the kind of outfit to broadcast precise details of their ownership, but I found my way to the glossy PR section of the corporate website and discovered that the George Michael lookalike I'd spotted at the Albertville depot was IC logistics. His name was Adel Dijani, which sounded more Lebanese than Swiss to me.

I was about to leave the site when I pinged a shot of their head of security at a recent event – maybe the opening Frank had been invited to. The first thing I noticed was a flash of red and silver on his ring finger. I zoomed in on it.

A silver double-headed eagle on a red enamel background.

An Albanian eagle.

I'd definitely seen that ring before. When its owner's hand was clapping Mr Lover Man on the back. Celebrating the fact that me and a Nissan X-Trail had fallen off a cliff.

As far as I knew, this was the first time I'd been able to have a good look at Hesco's face. Sideburns that had been given a little too much love and attention. Dark, tightly curled hair. A neat white scar running down his nose that looked like someone had shoved a stiletto up his nostril and taken it out sideways.

I stared at the photograph.

He was definitely one of the two on the hill. He was definitely at the Aix marina. Had he been in the chalet? On the road before the crash? The harder I tried to remember, the less I could. That part of my recent past was still splintered and remote.

But now I had the fucker's name.

Zac Uran.

Zac Ur-an.

You . . . ran . . .

That settled it.

Mr Lover Man had known he was dying. He knew he'd been

fucked over. He had nothing to hide. He *had* given me the name of the guy who had fixed for him to kill Frank.

But Zac wasn't at the top of the food chain. If he had been, he wouldn't have been bouncing about on the hill. He wasn't simply chomping around in the pondweed though. It took more than that to drive a Maserati.

I surfed the news sites, starting with the sport and UK-based shit, as any Brit would. Then I got more local. The assassination victim in the French Alps had been formally identified as Ukrainian multi-millionaire Frank Timis. There were a number of theories about what lay behind his death. The police had released a photograph of the oligarch's son, who, sources claimed, had been abducted – possibly by the killer.

Stefan's picture had been taken from the shot I'd pinged on the wall of the green room. Everyone around him had been cropped, but you could still see the BG's hand on his shoulder.

I felt myself relax a fraction; it was at least eighteen months out of date. His features had thinned out since then. His nose seemed sharper now, his cheekbones more pronounced, his eyes darker. And a trip to the mini-market on the ground floor, followed by a session upstairs, would help me make him even more difficult to recognize.

I ran through a few of the story links and found some footage of a hillside farm I recognized. A couple of big lads in dungarees were being interviewed by a French news crew. I couldn't understand a word they were saying, but that wasn't a problem. They were so fired up that they mimed the highlights of their recent experience – the fight, the theft of the ATV – vividly enough to leave no need for subtitles.

The piece was followed by an e-fit of the fucker who had ruined their day. Apart from the stubble and the head wound – which Claude or the artist had transposed from right to left – it didn't look remotely like me. Or I hoped it didn't. The shadowy figure staring at us from the screen looked like he'd be completely at home on the Planet of the Apes.

Neither of them would have pinged Stefan, and the authorities didn't seem to have joined the dots between the gangfuck in the barn, the events further up the mountain and the chalet in Courchevel. I guessed they would at some point. I'd cross that bridge when I came to it.

Next came an update on the investigation into last night's fatality at a marina in Aix-les-Bains. The text for this one was in English. The police were looking for two men who had been seen entering the victim's suite. There was no mention of a Brit in a green Polo.

I didn't expect to find much on the Net about Lyubova Timis, and I was right. When you've had a child kidnapped and not quite ransomed, you didn't advertise your wealth and your whereabouts in *Hello!* magazine. And Frank had always done his best to keep in the shadows, even when he was up to something legal. All I learnt was that she divided her time between Russia and Switzerland, and had once been an air stewardess.

I sparked up Google Earth to see what was on file for the chateau. The shots had been taken a couple of years ago, and told a slightly different story from the estate agent's brochure: holes in the roof; a major damp problem in one wing; crumbling outbuildings; a lawn that hadn't seen a mower for a while. But it gave me a heads-up on the layout.

I also scanned the surrounding area, on the lookout for approach routes, places I could safely leave the wagon, areas of dead and open ground, and to get a more detailed sense of the overall lie of the land.

I already knew Lyubova was no pushover. Now I needed to find out how well protected she was, whether there were points of vulnerability I could exploit, whether I'd have to go in or just wait for her to come out and do a spot of shopping.

I'd have to do a recce before deciding on my next move, but this was a good place to start. I zoomed in on the road that ran along the edge of Lake Konstanz and followed it up to Kreuzlingen and beyond. Before closing down I also checked out some of the mapping and picture-postcard imagery of the Swiss shore. If I had to lift her, I'd need somewhere quiet to read the ex-Mrs Timis her horoscope.

I steered Stefan down the escalator and on to the pharmacy section in the mini-market. I bought a hand towel – I couldn't be arsed to go outside and get the one he had in his rucksack – a pair of barber's scissors and a plastic bottle of overpriced hair dye. I'd stick with the hood or the baseball cap until Claude came up with a sharper e-fit, but I needed to treat Stefan to a makeover before the police techies realized that they should fire up the age-progression software on his photograph and bring it up to date.

The toilets were on the top floor of the mall, which suited me fine. It meant that nobody bothered to go up there unless they were desperate for a leak. I locked us inside the parent-and-baby room and lifted the boy on to the mat alongside the sink.

I switched on the mood lighting and the soothing music. I could still hear the occasional footstep and waffle in the corridor outside, but no one hammered on the door, desperate for a nappy change.

The two of us had the place to ourselves for long enough to turn him into a crewcut, peroxide-blond hipster. I managed not to turn myself or my kit the same colour, and took the polythene gloves, packaging, towel and hair trimmings away with us in the pharmacy bag.

He grinned when he checked out his new look in the mirror, and I spotted him admiring his reflection in the plate-glass window by the main exit, so I knew he was pleased with the result. It was blindingly obvious that Frank had never encouraged his boy to take a walk on the wild side. To set the seal on his new relationship with the world he asked me if he could borrow thirty francs and disappeared into a record store. He emerged almost immediately, waving a Pitbull CD.

The central post office in St Gallen was across the road from the main train station. There was plenty of glass for Stefan to admire himself in there too. I found a phone booth and placed a call to Moscow. Pasha picked up after three rings.

'Mate, I've got a couple of names. Could you possibly run them through the system? The first is Zac Uran. Yup. U-R-A-N. I don't know for certain, but he wears a ring with an Albanian double eagle. He's the security chief of a construction company that Frank had a big slice of. Adler Gesellschaft. Based in St Gallen,

Switzerland. If he wasn't responsible for the death in Aix-les-Bains yesterday, he certainly had a ringside seat.

'The second is Dijani. Adel Dijani. Same outfit. Head of logistics. Sounds Lebanese to me.'

I could almost hear Pasha's pencil lead scratching its way across his notepad.

'Any news on the other thing?'

'The Crimea crisis is very complicated, Nick. I don't need to tell you this. The battle lines have been redrawn. And it is very possible that Frank found himself on the wrong side of one. And you won't be surprised to hear that the supreme leader does not like oligarchs to be confused about who is the boss.'

I didn't need a lecture on the state of the former Soviet Union, so I asked him to zero in on any possible connections between Putin, Uran and Dijani, and I'd take it from there.

Then I thanked him, and said I'd call back at some point in the next thirty-six hours.

4

The hostel was heaving with kids and mums and dads who wanted to show them a fun time without paying a fortune for it. Stefan and I went into waffle mode as we approached the front desk and did all the stuff you don't do if one of you is a kidnap victim and the other an abductor. That was stage two of hiding in plain sight.

I'd smuggled Stefan into the motel in Albertville because we were still uncomfortably close to the killing zone, but I couldn't keep doing that. Hiding in the shadows was sometimes the best way to raise people's suspicions, and the Swiss didn't like bending the rules. Someone was bound to spot the kid at some point, and even if they just thought I was trying to avoid paying in full, they'd call in the local cops.

I asked the receptionist if they had a spare ground-floor room and Stefan swung into action. 'He gets vertigo.' He gave me a cheeky schoolboy grin. 'Don't you, Dad?'

She gave him the kind of smile that Lyubova wouldn't have understood, and said we could have the last one going.

We checked in as Nick and Steven Saunders. I peeled off enough Swiss francs to cover a two-night stay and handed them over with our passports.

As she flicked through Stefan's he moved closer to the counter. 'Please don't look at the photograph. Not cool.' He pointed at me. 'I blame him.'

She was loving this. Handed his passport back and barely glanced at mine.

Our ground-floor room was a twin. The window didn't offer much of a view, but it opened fully, with a bit of encouragement, and was close enough to the nearest patch of cover to give us a chance of legging it if we got any unwelcome visitors.

'ERV, Dad?'

I ran through our escape and evasion drills. They were boring as shit, but he seemed to enjoy them. We switched off the lights, checked the all-clear and slid out over the sill. Then we hugged the wall, staying under the shadow of the fire escape, and made our way to the corner of the building. From there we paralleled the edge of the car park, the far side of the lamps that ran along it, and disappeared into the trees.

I was hoping for a shed or a lean-to or a log pile, but we did better than that. Ten paces in there was a Native American camp with a joke totem pole and three tepees that looked like they'd been built especially for not very tall seven-year-olds. They were filled with blankets and cushions.

I told him to go inside the middle one and cover himself up. It worked a treat. I knocked three times on the wicker door frame, then three more. 'Raskolnikov.'

He lifted the blanket so slowly I couldn't see it move. Checked me out with one eye. Then we looped round behind the coppice and went back to the room.

The decor wasn't quite as basic as it had been in Albertville, and the en-suite even had a bath. I told Stefan to get into it and give himself a good soak while I went off and did a bit of a recce. The swelling on his ankle had retreated but he still wasn't going to break any sprinting records.

His expression changed again as I shut the window, drew the curtains and prepared to leave. He gave me the same look he'd worn on the way there. I chose to ignore it.

'Do you know her BGs?'

He shook his head. 'They came and went.'

'How many does she have?'

'Three. Perhaps four.'

'Who else might be there? Does she have maids?'

'I only know two of her maids. One was very kind to me. Natasha. She's from Kiev.' He brightened. 'She taught me to swim. She loves to swim. I also like to swim, Nick. Very much.'

'Yup, you told me. Any others?'

His eyes narrowed. 'Rula. She wasn't kind at all.' He hesitated. 'I don't know if they came here to Switzerland.'

'Do they usually live in?'

'It's possible . . . When the girls are there, maybe.'

'Girls?'

'My two sisters. Half-sisters.'

The pink and fluffy room in the chalet. I'd wondered who that belonged to.

'They are in Moscow. Until the house is finished.'

I stuck the hair and saliva tell-tales in place before I left, in case the receptionist had been paying us more attention than she appeared to have done. I didn't plan to be away for more than a couple of hours – long enough to get my bearings in the area immediately surrounding Lyubova's hideaway – but precautions like that were never wasted.

On the way out of town I passed a bunch of dossers on a stretch of waste-ground, gathered around a flaming oil drum and sipping extra strong lager. I handed them a fistful of coins and bunged in the pharmacy bag with the empty peroxide bottle and the offcuts of Stefan's hair. I hadn't bothered to wipe down everything he'd touched in the motel and the hostel, but leaving a gift pack of his DNA lying around was asking for trouble.

The chateau commanded a chunk of high ground between St Gallen and Konstanz. It was surrounded by walls you couldn't leap over, but enough of its floodlit façade was visible through the entrance to confirm that the estate agent's brochure hadn't needed to fuck around. One wing was covered with scaffolding and tarpaulin, but it still looked like something out of a fairy tale. You'd need a really good reason not to want to live there.

I was increasingly sure that Lyubova was the reason, and not only because of what Stefan had told me. When I'd originally thought of hiding him here, I'd reckoned a telephone call and a cup of tea would crack it. Now it was high on my list of hostile environments.

I slowed as I drove past, but didn't stop immediately. Lights glowed in a number of the upstairs windows to my left. I took that as a good sign. However much you wanted to show off the place, I didn't think you'd bother to leave them on if no one was home.

There was a patch of woodland to my right, split by a formal avenue that led down towards the lake. I guessed it must once have been part of the estate. The massive trees on either side of it looked like lindens. They might not have been, but they reminded me of the things that lined the main that ran towards the Brandenburg Gate. I'd had a few beers in the bars there when I was a young soldier stationed in Berlin.

I pulled up a couple of hundred further on and walked back, hood up, keeping to the shadows on the far side of the road. The CCTV cameras fixed on each side of the main gates told me to keep my distance, and the pair of Dobermanns that banged against their wrought-iron railings sent the same message, only louder. Someone yelled at them from behind the wall and I decided it was a good moment to fuck off back to the wagon. I was never at my best with furry animals that growled and bit.

I turned left at the first opportunity and circled the plot, looking out for a vantage-point I could employ in daylight without breaking cover. Unless something else presented itself after first light, I was either going to get eyes on the rear, from the top of the hill, or climb one of the lindens and recce it from the front.

I pinpointed the Adler HQ on my way back. It was a much simpler target. The security set-up was bound to be high-end, but those guys weren't hiding from anybody. Lights blazed on every floor. Everything about the building yelled global domination. And there was a multi-storey car park on the opposite side of the street.

I drove up to the barrier and took a ticket. The Adler executives clearly put in the hours for their top-of-the-range Audis. It was well past the end of the working day, but at least half their marked spaces on the third level were still taken. I followed the arrows to the top, registering the CCTV set-up as I went, then worked my way down and out.

Stefan was channel-hopping between the rolling news and the Russian Premier League on the TV when I returned to the hostel. He hadn't legged it to the ERV to do his Sitting Bull impression, so I assumed he hadn't seen anything that put the shits up him, but I asked anyway.

He shook his head. 'More of the same.'

We watched the highlights of the Spartak Moscow game, which seemed to suit us both fine. I didn't feel like talking, and he obviously wasn't keen to ask me anything that might trigger more Lyubova stuff.

I knew he wasn't settling again when we'd switched off the lights. There was a lot of tossing and turning and sighing.

'Nick?'

I didn't answer for a bit, then gave him a drowsy, 'Early start tomorrow, mate. Best we get our heads down, eh?'

I didn't expect that to be the end of it, and it wasn't. He waited about five minutes before coming back for more.

'Was my mother beautiful?'

'Very.'

'When I was younger, I could see her when I closed my eyes. I can't do that any more. I can't really remember what she looked like.'

'Don't you have photographs?'

'No. No photographs. My father said they made him sad . . .' He hesitated. 'And my . . . his wife she said she didn't want them in the house. Maybe there were some, and she burnt them.'

He might well be right about that, for all I knew. But I doubted there were albums full of the things in the first place. Frank had had a son with Tracy, but waving happy snaps of her in a bikini at Lyubova would only have ended in tears.

Stefan took another of those deep, halting breaths that was always a sign of more bad things on the near horizon.

'Did she love me, Nick? My father said she did.'

I didn't really want to go down this road. Cutting away from the emotional shit was always safest. I'd become less able to do that since my son was born, and it wasn't good. The people who depended on me needed me to keep them safe, not to give them hugs. And keeping them safe meant doing my job, even if that sometimes involved curling up and taking the pain.

When I didn't answer immediately, he repeated his question. There was no escaping this one.

'He was right, mate. You meant everything to her.'

'Why were we in Africa?'

'She took you away on holiday. A special one. You and her. Together. But some very bad people took you both prisoner.'

That was the simplest version. And it wasn't a lie, exactly. It wasn't the whole truth either. Tracy had made the mistake of falling for the wrong guy, and he'd fucked her over big-time. She'd also made the mistake of thinking that she could do a runner with Frank's son, and that was never going to happen.

'She died too, didn't she?'

'She did, mate.'

'How?'

'She was shot, trying to protect you.' I probably wasn't doing him any favours by ramming home the idea that everyone who loved him ended up dead, but I didn't want to dress it up.

'Like my dad . . .'

I turned in my bed and propped myself up on an elbow. 'I'm pretty sure your dad's last move was to protect you. But that wasn't your fault either. He died for different reasons. More complicated reasons. And I'm trying to find out what they were. That way I keep both of us safe.'

I didn't mention my family. I'd already pretty much told him I didn't have a son.

I don't know how long it took him to finally fall asleep, but we both went quiet after that.

5

The next morning I flicked on the news as Stefan took a piss.

The latest report about the missing child began with film footage of the border guards in action at the Geneva airport crossing. Every car and every coach was being given a proper seeing-to, passengers and contents on the pavement, sniffer dogs, the lot.

I was glad I'd had second thoughts about going that route. Especially when I spotted the lads in black combat gear wielding Heckler & Koch MP5s in the background. The Einsatzgruppe TIGRIS were an elite paramilitary force. They operated in tandem with the canton police, but only on high-risk special ops, so covert that the federal authorities had only admitted to their existence nearly a decade after they'd been formed. Their PR claimed they hadn't fired a shot in more than a hundred and twenty ops. They probably thought we believed in Santa too.

First the GIGN. Now TIGRIS. What the fuck were they up to?

We hit the road before first light. I wanted to be in position before too many people – dog walkers, personal trainers, hikers, sightseers, whatever – were up and about. Even the sausage stands weren't open for business. I told Stefan we'd have breakfast later. Right now we were going to have to make do with an energy bar or two and one of my remaining bottles of water.

'Hard routine, Nick?'

'Yup, hard routine.' I aimed for the chateau, but this time followed the route alongside the water. 'How do you know about hard routine?' I didn't want to prolong the conversation, but I had to ask.

'It's what soldiers do, isn't it? When they're on ops, and don't want to light a fire or do cooking and stuff. In case they give themselves away. I read about it.'

'In Dostoevsky?'

'No!' He was wearing his serious face. 'I don't only read Dostoevsky, you know. I read all sorts. My dad said I must. He said knowledge is power. He said that I have to know my enemy.'

'I told you he was smart.' I figured Frank had been quoting from Sun Tzu's *Art of War,* not the Manic Street Preachers album or the song by Green Day. Either way, it was good advice. It was why I planned to spend however long it took scoping Lyubova's place instead of steaming straight in there.

He spent the next five Ks listening to Pitbull and grappling with the disciplines of hard routine. I left him to it. Then he turned the volume down on the CD player and sparked up again.

'You have to go to the toilet in a plastic bag, don't you, Nick? When you're on hard routine?'

'Yup. Wherever you lie up has to be left sterile.'

'Does that mean no toilet paper?'

'It means no anything. No trace of you ever being there.'

'Wow . . .' He whistled softly. 'That's *great* . . .'

This wasn't helping me get in the zone. I didn't shut him up, though; at least it was keeping his mind off the wicked stepmother.

'Nick?'

'Yup?'

'I think maybe I'd like to be a soldier . . .'

'Not a footballer?'

'I'm not joking, Nick.'

Fair one. I hadn't meant to sound like I was talking down to him. When I was a kid, I'd hated it when people did that to me. It had made me want to hit them. And sometimes I did.

'Mate, you'd make a brilliant soldier. A brilliant officer, probably. There's a whole world out there for people like you. You're clever. You're already more educated than I'll ever be. You're rich.

You can be anything you want. But right now there's a job to be done. We're closing on our target now. And I need to focus on it.'

I saw him nod at the periphery of my vision. Then he started murmuring the hard-routine mantra to himself. 'No fires, no toilet paper. And no talking . . .'

I hung a left a hundred short of where I thought the avenue of lindens began and scanned the area ahead of us for a secure place to leave the wagon. The houses along there were few and far between, and had no shortage of land around them. I turned into a designated parking area at the edge of the patch of woodland, which seemed to cater mostly for walkers and anyone who didn't want to pay the outrageous charges for a space by the lake.

There were only three other vehicles there so I pulled up between two of them, got out and had a good look around. When I was sure there was no one else around, I tucked Stefan into the boot with my day sack and gave him the torch. We were close enough to the wicked stepmother for him to be safer out of sight. And I was planning to stay in cover while I did a more detailed recce of her HQ.

We didn't bother with the Dostoevsky jokes. I fished out my binoculars, closed the hatch and headed into the trees.

The sky was blindingly blue. There was still a chill in the air, but it would be stiflingly hot later.

The whole area, as far as I could see, was deserted, apart from one dog walker to my half-right. And it didn't look like a real dog: it was one of those small, smooth-haired things that yapped a lot and belonged on the end of a cocktail stick. By the time I reached the edge of the avenue, he and his owner had found their way back to the parking area.

Staying inside the treeline, I walked up the slope towards the chateau until I found a linden whose lower branches were within reach of the ground and whose higher ones promised a combination of good cover and a wide enough field of vision.

I swung myself up into the foliage. My eyes started to leak almost immediately, and I had to stifle a sneeze. It was definitely a linden. The spores from those things could give you hay fever even if you didn't suffer from it. Its bark was smooth, but sticky with sap. As the temperature increased, that would only get worse.

I gripped my nose between my thumb and forefinger and managed to strangle another sneeze at birth. I kept the trunk between me and the target until I was about fifteen metres from the ground. Then I worked my way round and climbed high enough to see over the wall and into the chateau grounds.

I raised the binos and scanned as much of the front of the building and its surroundings as I could through the leaves. We weren't talking Buckingham Palace here, but all told, it wasn't much smaller than the south London council block I'd grown up in.

The main part of the house had four storeys. The shutters on the upstairs windows were all open but the curtains behind them were mostly closed. As the Google Earth imagery had shown me, it was flanked on each side by a two-storey wing. The one on the right was encased in a scaffolding frame, covered with blue tarpaulin. A yellow plastic telescopic chute ran from the top floor to a skip on the ground.

The Dobermanns were still mooching around outside, hoping for somebody to sink their teeth into. The two beasts that had bounced against the railings last night had been joined by a couple of mates, and they were a mean-looking gang. I couldn't see any sign of a handler.

As seven thirty approached, a guy in black combats and polo shirt appeared from the back of the house with a pile of metal bowls and a bucket. I had a really close look at his face, but it didn't trigger a memory.

The guard dogs bounded towards him and I soon saw why. He put the bowls on the ground and filled them with enough raw meat to feed a battalion. Maybe it was to stop them eating the tradesmen who appeared at the entrance during the next half-hour.

Lyubova was clearly in makeover mode. Plumbers, decorators, electricians, roofers and chippies in shiny white vans with corporate logos were waved through the electronically operated gates by another couple of uniforms.

The security people had a good poke around inside the first vehicle to come out, so it looked like they were more concerned about the contractors helping themselves to Lyubova's jewellery collection than someone or something being smuggled inside.

I swept the binos from window to window as a squad of identical blonde women in cream shirts drew back the curtains and raised the sashes to let in the morning air. It was like *Downton Abbey* on fast-forward. Lyubova hadn't made an appearance yet, but I didn't expect her to be doing much of her own housework.

Men in white overalls, hi-vis waistcoats and hard hats swarmed around the scaffolding, either looking busy but doing fuck-all or waffling into their mobile phones. I couldn't be sure at this distance, but I'd bet they had a smile on their faces. They'd know an earner when they saw one.

I was about to clamber back down and go in search of a vantage-point at the rear when the phones suddenly disappeared in unison. It was like watching a well-rehearsed troop respond to a barked instruction on a parade ground. When I lowered the binos, I saw why.

A very smartly dressed woman – cream blouse, leopard-print pencil skirt – had just emerged from the front door. She flicked her shiny black hair over her shoulder and made her way across to inspect their work. Lyubova had broken cover. It was obviously still too early for her to be flashing the diamonds and rubies, but no one was in any doubt about who was calling the shots.

She waved her arms around and gave them shit until they started doing whatever they should be doing at warp speed. Then she turned on her no doubt very expensive designer heel and went back inside.

I stayed where I was, half hoping she'd decide to take a trip into town. She wasn't about to wander into the local Spar, even if there was one, and I doubted that she'd wander about on her own, but I reckoned it might be easier to lift her outside the estate rather than in it.

I gave half a thought to the kid in the boot of my wagon, then dismissed it. The breeze off the water was still cool enough to give me goosebumps so he wouldn't be baking yet. Besides, hard routine was hard routine. He knew that. And I wasn't his nanny.

An hour later a couple more visitors arrived.

The first wagon through the gates was an Audi Q5. The second was a Maserati. They'd obviously travelled in convoy. I didn't need to check their registration numbers against the ones I had in my Moleskine. Hesco and Dijani were paying the ex-Mrs Timis a visit. And, judging by their extremely cheery greeting, they hadn't come simply to offer a grieving widow their condolences.

Mr Lover Man's message had just become very clear indeed.

After she'd ushered them inside, I focused the binos on the white vans. This time, I did bring out the Moleskine and the UZI, and scrawled the name, contact details and website address of every contractor within reach.

More minutes ticked by. When Hesco and Dijani showed no sign of leaving, I climbed down and went back to the wagon. Whatever they were discussing over coffee and biscuits, I was now absolutely certain that there was a whole lot more to Frank's death than revenge for his infidelity.

6

For the first time since we'd started doing this shit, Stefan didn't seem too happy about his morning in the boot of the wagon. I rewarded him with an extra-large takeaway sausage, a roll and a bottle of Coke, but it didn't seem to make much difference to his mood.

We sat in the parking area alongside a greasy spoon on the main back to St Gallen while I got a big frothy coffee down my neck and he ate. When one mouthful started to feel like it was going to last for ever, I gripped him. 'OK, what's the problem?'

He concentrated very hard on the next bit of sausage. 'You're hoping to leave me with her, aren't you?'

Fuck. I'd been focusing so much on keeping him in the dark that I'd let his imagination run wild. 'Mate, I told you I won't lie to you.' I put down my coffee and gently lifted his chin. It wasn't easy, but I finally got him to look me in the eye. 'There was a moment when I thought a nice Swiss chateau might be what you needed. But after you told me what you told me, and now I know more about the woman, I'd rather sell you to the circus.'

What happened next was an amazing thing to watch. It was like I'd lifted the world's heaviest Bergen off his shoulders and he'd become two feet taller. He gave me a mega candle-power smile and demolished the rest of the *wurst* in no time.

We didn't hang around long after that. I was about to go into the decorating business, and time was money in that game.

The second cyber café on my list wasn't that far from the first, but it always paid to ring the changes. Stefan cheered up a bit more when I steered him into an artists' store a few doors down and said I needed his help on a new mission. When he asked me what sort of help, I told him to wait and see.

He wrinkled his brow when I bought a plain A4 pad, two soft pencils and a rubber. Then his eyes lit up as we stopped by a display case of folding Laguiole knives with bone handles and good-sized blades. The assistant spotted us and went into over-drive. Yes, they were expensive, but the quality . . . Every man should have one . . . You never knew when they would come in useful . . . You could take them on picnics . . . You could sharpen pencils with them . . . How could I resist?

I couldn't. But not for the reasons he had in mind.

He beamed as I looped the leather sheath for mine on to my belt, and Stefan put his in his pocket.

The café was a bit more like a café this time around, so I ordered a coffee and a milkshake as well as Internet time. Me and Stefan pulled up our chairs in front of the monitor furthest from the till and I kicked off by googling the contractors' names I'd taken down at my linden lookout point.

Only two of the outfits weren't owned by Adler, and boasted about their independence. One of them went on for ever but seemed to be mostly about *konstruktion*. I chose the other. They called themselves Hochfliegend, and had the simplest logo – three thought bubbles: small, medium and large – and the simplest lettering.

'Mate, what does that mean?'

'Hochfliegend? Great Ideas.'

That explained the logo. I hoped what I'd planned turned out to be one of mine.

I pointed at the decal on the side panel of one of their Peugeot vans and handed Stefan the A4 pad and pencils. 'Draw that, will you, mate? The company name, the address, everything except the contact numbers.' I didn't need some nosy fucker ringing Head Office to complain about my driving.

He looked at me as if I'd had another blow to the head. 'This is our mission?'

'Trust me. It's important. I can't draw for shit, and I remember you being pretty good with crayons and a paintbrush. I need the thought bubbles and the lettering to be as accurate as possible.'

He shrugged and got on with it. Out came the tip of his tongue and he wedged it between his teeth. I remembered him doing that when he was younger, and Frank had sat him down in front of yet another mountain of homework.

He went wrong once or twice and had to get busy with the rubber, but came up with the goods in twenty minutes flat. It wasn't perfect, but it was a fucking sight better than I was ever going to be able to manage.

I picked up the sheet of paper and smiled. 'Brilliant, mate. I should put you on hard routine more often.' I folded it carefully, twice, and put it in my pocket. Then I motioned him towards a sofa on the other side of the room and told him to catch up on his Dostoevsky.

Next up was the search for a second-hand auto dealer. I couldn't just head for the Hochfliegend depot and borrow one of their vans. The word would go out at warp speed, and I'd be fucked as soon as I arrived at Lyubova's front gate, if not before.

I toyed with the idea of cruising around until I found a Peugeot Expert, then nicking it. But I needed to be in control of this. I didn't want to put the shits up Stefan any more than I already had done. I didn't want to get caught doing it. Or to feature on the canton police computer when I had done. Or to go to all that trouble and then discover it didn't have a plywood-lined load space.

And I didn't have all the time in the world.

Most of the traders on the site looked like they welcomed more formal business arrangements than I had in mind. I needed the sort you could find underneath the railway arches in south London, run by lads who felt the same way about cash business as I did. I selected three possible contenders and wrote down their details. If they weren't right, maybe they had a mate who was.

Finally I scanned the news.

The abductor still couldn't be named, but they were looking for an Englishman who was rumoured to be connected to the murder victim, and had been seen in the proximity of the abandoned

Range Rover. One theory was that a paedophile ring was involved.

My brain had been scrambled big-time up there, and I wasn't getting everything right, but I didn't think I'd been spotted – except by Claude the carrot-cruncher, and there was no way he'd ID me as a Brit. So someone on Hesco's side of the fence had to be feeding the investigation to make my life more difficult and theirs easier.

Mr Lover Man must have been their original source from inside Frank's camp. We'd spent quite a bit of time together, on and off, both in Moscow and Africa, so he knew I was a Brit. I wasn't sure if he had ever been given my real name. I fucking hoped not. Not just because it would put us deeper in the shit right now, but because I liked it that way.

The paedophile thing was always a good line to throw to the media. They knew it grabbed the public's attention like nothing else, and they wanted whoever had taken the kid to have nowhere to hide. But it still didn't explain who was calling the shots here, and why TIGRIS and the GIGN were out in force.

7

I visited a bunch of holes in the wall over the course of the next half-hour. My magic black debit card did the business, now I remembered what it was for, and my fingertips knew the PIN without having to consult my head. The thing had no limit, but the individual machines did.

Next I checked out the used-car-dealer options. The second of the three was ten Ks from the centre of town, with a couple of rusting diesel pumps under a sheet-metal canopy that had also seen better days.

A row of previously enjoyed but freshly polished wagons stood to one side off the forecourt. The one I needed was a three-year-old Peugeot Expert refrigerator panel van with a fair amount of mileage on the clock, a current *Autobahn* vignette and a hand-written sign taped on to the windscreen asking for SFr 7,999.

The side door was open so a potential purchaser could share the salesman's excitement about the business end of the vehicle. And I did. The interior had been fitted out with a plywood floor and walls. The insulation made these things the bike thief's wagon of choice. You could lift a top-of-the-range Ducati off the street and nobody would hear the alarm going off as you drove it away. Even from the road, it looked perfect for what I had in mind.

I cruised on past, keeping an eye out for somewhere to park. Somewhere close enough to walk back from, but far enough away to avoid linking the Polo, Stefan and the van.

'Can I come too?'

'No, mate. Best to keep you out of sight right now.'

'Not in the boot, Nick. Please. I hate it in the boot . . .'

I'd never heard him complain about anything before. I thought I might have to start gripping him again.

'I try my hardest to think about hard routine, but I can't help thinking about being trapped under my dad instead.'

The gripping idea went out the window.

I found a space outside a newsagent and gave Stefan two ten-franc notes in case he wanted to buy himself a fizzy drink and a sherbet fountain while I headed back to the used-car lot.

A blond lad who'd stood even further away from a razor than I had over the last few days emerged from the workshop, wiping the grease off his palms on the sides of his faded blue boiler suit. He had a wicked smile and spoke even better English than Stefan did. I knew within seconds that we could do business together.

I got him to fire up the Expert and drive me around the block. He told me the cooling mechanism needed some attention, which was why the price was rock bottom.

'What kind of attention?'

He grinned sheepishly as he threw it around the first corner. 'It's totally fucked.'

I told him I'd sort it.

I was no vehicle geek, but the engine did what it was supposed to when you turned the key, and the gearbox didn't seem to be about to fall apart all over the tarmac. When we made it back to the pumps he slid open the side door and invited me to take a closer look at the load space.

It was even more impressive close up. The ply on the floor was at least forty mil thick, and thirty on the walls. The previous owner had added shelves and a lockable tool chest on the passenger side, and also lined the partition, leaving a small window into the cab. I wondered whether he had lived in it.

Blondie liked the idea of SFr 7,750 cash and, yes, he did know someone who could fix me up with something very nice on the panels at short notice. 'If you have some more of these . . .' He eyed the roll of notes I'd just handed to him.

He tore a page out of a spiral-bound notepad and wrote down a name and address. 'Klaus has a very big talent. An artist, really. But not mainstream, maybe. He is like your Banksy. An anarchist.'

Perfect. Klaus sounded like he was going to be even less likely to call in the law than this lad.

We shook on the deal and both scribbled something unreadable on the registration document, which I reckoned would go straight into the bin as soon as I'd left. He wouldn't want to waste any of his valuable time with the tax people, and he knew I wouldn't either.

Almost as an afterthought, I asked if he had any degreaser or solvent he could spare. I wasn't going to use it for cleaning, but he didn't need to know that. He took me into a mechanic's Aladdin's cave at the back of the workshop and gestured at a shelf lined with plastic containers of all shapes and sizes. I examined the labels and chose the 200ml bottle with the highest diethyl ether content. It cost me another fifty.

Klaus was only about a K away, in a wriggly-tin lock-up with huge skylights on the other side of the railway tracks. He wore a T-shirt that told me to feed the world over jeans that hung off his arse and were distressed in more ways than one. The whole fuck-you look was topped off nicely by moth-eaten dreadlocks and beard, and an anarchist's attitude to physical hygiene.

He rested a roach the size of a prize-winning carrot on the edge of an ashtray that looked like a coiled dog turd. This lad was definitely not going to be in a hurry to call in the law. He slid off his stool to greet me. The air in his lock-up was sweet with cannabis fumes, but it didn't hide the fact that he badly needed a shower.

The samples of his work on display told me that he was up for almost anything from anti-capitalist graffiti slogans and X-rated cartoons to apparently uncontroversial corporate stuff. I showed him Stefan's drawing and asked if he could scale it up in blue for the side panels.

'Hochfliegend . . . I like zis.'

Klaus liked the idea of cash too. For him it was clearly a political statement. So I offered him a bonus if I could pick up the van in an hour.

He pursed his lips, raised his arms and shrugged.

I tried to lure him back to the real world. 'How long will it take?'

His eyebrows disappeared into his moth-eaten hair. 'Zis is not rocket science.' He poked a nicotine-stained finger at a battered laptop and a machine covered with multi-coloured Post-it notes in the corner. He was right. It looked like a Dalek with a letterbox in its chest.

'I will design on screen, zen print on self-adhesive vinyl. You can come back in one hour for ze decals. You can apply zem yourself. Piece of piss.'

He reached for a bruised student portfolio and fished out a handful of graphic illustrations of a dominatrix not quite dressed in PVC. 'Maybe you like vun viz a naked girl instead of sree sink bubbles? Very good for business . . .'

I massaged my chin with my hand for a moment. 'Tempting . . . But no. It's not really that kind of business.'

'If you say so, my friend. Zo I never came across a business zat didn't involve somebody getting focked.'

'You're not wrong.' I tapped the dial of my Suunto. 'And right now you've got fifty-four minutes before you have to add your name to that list.'

He gave me a snort of derision and reached for his keyboard.

I left him to it and walked back to Stefan.

The boy had his nose in a *Spider-Man* comic. He'd stocked up on fizzy apple juice and Kinder Eggs too. The foot well on his side of the wagon was filled with empty wrappers. He was really cutting loose from the curly kale. I leant in through the window. 'You know that stuff has no nutritional value . . .'

He looked up. 'Want one?' He held out his hand. The wrapper was still in place, but it wasn't egg-shaped any more.

'Last one?'

He nodded.

'Nah. You have it.' I got in behind the wheel. 'But you'd better get it down your neck before you have to drink it. We're going to the beach. You like to swim, remember?'

I knew he thought I'd totally lost it now. And maybe I had. But I'd decided he was right: he couldn't spend the rest of his life stuck in the boot of one wagon after another. It had taken a lot of courage to tell me he was having nightmares about Frank in there, and I didn't want him freaking out. Besides, today had turned into a scorcher. I didn't want him hallucinating or dying of heat exposure.

I followed the signs to Kreuzlingen until I came to a stretch of grass covered with parasols and half-naked bodies. A crescent of trees shielded it from the road on one side, and the lake on the other. An overpriced parking area and a cab rank sat close by.

The primary-school day had obviously come to an end, because the place was crawling with kids Stefan's age, their mums or nannies, and even some dads. Not many of them were reading Dostoevsky.

I fed the meter, then handed him his rucksack, fifty francs and the keys to the Polo. After a moment I added another fifty. 'This isn't all for Kinder Eggs, mate. It's for a taxi into town, to the ERV, if I'm not back before last light.' I told him to ask the driver to take him to the cathedral. It was the safest place I could think of. And if I still wasn't with him by ten tonight, he should go and ask a priest for help – because that would mean I needed one too.

He tried to keep his happy face on, but I could see he was rattled.

'Nick . . .' He did that chewing thing with his lower lip. 'What are you going to do?'

That was a fuck of a good question, and I had no idea how to answer it. Stefan might have had the IQ of a university professor and the armour plating of a born survivor, but he was still a kid. I couldn't tell him I thought his stepmother had had something to do with the murder of his dad, and had probably aimed to kill him too. I couldn't tell him that I was going to persuade her to tell me why.

And I also couldn't claim that I was about to wave a magic wand over the whole situation so we could all live happily ever after.

I gripped his shoulder. 'Listen, it's a nice sunny day. Enjoy it. Just don't talk to any bad guys. And remember, I'm only telling you this stuff because it pays to have a plan. You know that. ERV, remember?'

I walked him across the grass and fixed him up with a couple of deckchairs and a parasol near a friendly-looking woman in a sundress, who'd just treated her twin girls to the Swiss version of a Mr Whippy. I went and got one for Stefan while he laid out his towel. It was already melting when I handed it to him.

He seemed to cheer up as he took his first lick.

'Mate . . .'

He nodded, dribbling ice cream down his chin.

'You know that has—'

'Yup. Absolutely no nutritional value.' His eyes narrowed in the sunlight. 'But who gives a fuck?'

I looked for a hint of a grin on his face and couldn't find one.

I left him surrounded by very healthy-looking families. As long as you didn't spot the haunted look in his eyes, he blended in nicely. Maybe it would remind him of the things he didn't have, but there was fuck-all I could do about that.

And he wouldn't be the only kid in the world to feel like he was on the outside, looking in.

I'd been there too.

8

I took the first cab on the rank and paid off the driver when I was only a brisk walk from the Expert. Next stop was my anarchist sign painter. He'd done a great job, and even helped me press the decal to the metal, without a single air bubble. He stepped back to admire it, but I knew he felt something was missing.

'Viz tits next time, eh? Big vuns.' He cradled an imaginary pair in his open palms in case I hadn't caught his drift. He must have been on the weed again.

I nodded as I brought out his bonus. 'Without a doubt.'

He returned to his own planet as I reversed away to go in search of a DIY shed he'd aimed me at. It didn't take me long. The place was in a trading estate just off the main, and the size of an aircraft hangar, with a cash-and-carry right next door.

Even without artificial stimulants, it was decorator's heaven. A smart white overall, a hard hat, safety glasses and a yellow hi-vis waistcoat went into my trolley. Then tins of paint, brushes, white spirit, sandpaper, disposable cloths, a hammer, a set of screwdrivers, a serious-looking padlock, a box of double-barbed fence staples and a staple gun, screws and ring-shanked nails, a bag of heavy-duty cable ties and two rolls of gaffer tape.

I needed the right equipment if I had to lift Lyubova and take her into the woodland at the northern end of the lake for an in-depth conversation. And if I didn't, all well and good. Everything looked a bit squeaky clean, but it was the sort of shit that belonged in the back of any builder's van.

I rolled back the side door and loaded everything up, then climbed inside, took off my jacket and Timberlands, shrugged on the overall and rolled back its sleeves. I replaced my boots, tore open the bag of cable ties and took off the lid of the box of staples.

I visualized a diagonal cross – the shape of a prone body with arms and legs outstretched – and banged sixteen ties, two at a time, into eight key positions: wrists, ankles, knees and elbows. Then two more for the neck. The gun gave a satisfying thud as it buried them in the ply.

Maybe she'd just tell me what I needed to know over tea and biscuits. But I wasn't counting on it. And if I did have to lift her, I needed to keep her secure. The gaffer tape plus one of the cloths would take care of the mouth until I needed her to start talking.

When I'd fired in the final staple, I selected one slotted and one Phillips screwdriver, both medium, slammed the door and stepped up behind the steering-wheel. My next task was to go and find myself some extra licence plates.

I stayed on the wrong side of the tracks and drove past three or four white vans, which had either doors or windows open and looked like their owners would come back to them any minute.

Then I spotted another, streaked with grime and with a nice collection of dents, parked on the street alongside a church. It carried a German country code, so I pulled in twenty metres ahead of it, ducked down in the gap between its radiator grille and the taillights of the next vehicle and spent less than a minute removing its front plate.

Half an hour later I had five of them – two German, one Italian and two Swiss – from a variety of not very shiny vans parked well out of CCTV range. The trick was never to take both plates from the same vehicle. You could drive legally with just the rear one attached, and if the other was missing, most people assumed that it had just fallen off. Nobody in their right mind would have stolen it on its own.

The only thing you had to be careful about was not transposing

Swiss plates. The rear one had country and canton badges; the front one didn't. And they had different colours for different classes of wagon. Utility vehicles' were blue. They were cunning fuckers, the Swiss.

I pulled on the hard hat, glasses and hi-vis waistcoat. A glance in the rear-view told me they topped off my whole fancy dress costume very nicely. The Sphinx came out of my waistband and slid under my right thigh. It could almost make that part of the journey on its own.

I was within sight of the chateau by 16:30. I'd reckoned that most if not all the contractors would have gone home by then. One of them was parked about a hundred away, smoking himself to death in a layby.

I slowed as I passed the entrance and liked what I saw.

No Dobermanns on patrol, for starters. Part of me thought, Thank fuck for that, but a small warning bell also started to ring. The absence of the normal often indicated the presence of the abnormal. It was known in the trade as a combat indicator.

The Maserati and the Q5 had also left, unless someone had moved them round the back. They might have been the best of mates, but it looked like a cosy dinner with Dijani and Uran wasn't part of the deal. All good. I'd like to have got my hands on all three of them, but whatever her portrait said, she was the weakest link.

Five minutes later the gates opened automatically as the last of the vans I'd watched coming in that morning stopped to be frisked on its way out. I gave the boys in black a smile and a wave as I accelerated past them and carried straight on to the wing that was getting all the attention.

I parked behind the monster skip at the bottom of the yellow chute, alongside a gap in the tarpaulin sheeting where the ties had been left undone for easy access. I undid the front buttons of my overall, adjusted the Sphinx in my belt and transferred my shiny new knife from its sheath to the right-hand pocket. I tucked the ether into the left. Then I shrugged off the hi-vis waistcoat, exited the Expert and slipped through the gap.

The scaffolding wasn't alarmed. That was what the security team and the dogs were for. There was no obvious way into the house on the ground floor. All the shutters were closed, probably to prevent the lads doing the heavy lifting from smashing the glass. I made for the ladder that had been clamped to the horizontal poles and stepped out on to the boards. No joy there either. No breaches in the wall, no empty window frames. Just more shutters. I had to try the roof.

The platform that ran along the guttering on the top level was stacked with tiles. They weren't patching the holes: they were replacing the lot. And they still had a long way to go. There was a ten-square-metre area that was covered with battens and a water-proof membrane.

I took off the helmet and glasses and dumped them on the platform. Then I stood absolutely still, opened my mouth and listened. I'd expected the security guys to come sniffing round as soon as they spotted the fact that I wasn't coming straight back out again, but I couldn't hear any yells or footsteps on the gravel. The tarp overhead rippled in the breeze and the sun shining through gave the space below it the strange, unearthly quality of a hospital corridor.

I took out the knife, pulled it open, sliced a hole in the membrane and peeled it back far enough to scan the attic beneath. There was enough ambient light to see that it was a bit of a mess. The work-force had looked like they were taking the piss through the binos, and this confirmed it. Electricity cables snaked through randomly laid strips of insulation and heaps of sawdust, broken slates and all sorts of other builder shit that should have gone straight down the telescopic chute and into the skip.

There was no sign of cabin trunks filled with family heirlooms or contractors who'd missed the last wagon home.

I lowered myself through and went in search of a hatch that would take me down into the house. Almost immediately, I realized I could do better than that. The joists that paralleled the gable end of the wing were still open to the rooms below. I was going to be able to make entry without the creaking of a hinge or the clunk of a telescopic ladder.

I picked up a length of frayed blue nylon rope as I crept towards the gap and lowered myself on to my hands and knees half a metre short of it. Five minutes of listening satisfied me that either nobody was in the immediate vicinity or they were being even quieter than I was. I moved forwards and craned my neck far enough to check out where I was going next.

The room with no ceiling was as full of construction crap as the place I was about to leave. More cables, some with bare wires, some leading to halogen arc lamps on yellow tripods. Others that led nowhere in particular. Stacks of wood panelling that had been ripped off the walls. I slung the rope over the nearest joist and eased myself into the middle of it.

As soon as my feet touched the floorboards I stopped and listened again. Then I switched the knife to my left-hand pocket, closed my right around the pistol grip inside my overall and brought it up into the aim.

There was no carpet to deaden the sound of my footsteps, so I trod as lightly as the Timberlands allowed. I stepped to the left of each doorway I came to, did the mouth trick and cocked an ear before carrying on.

The doors themselves had been removed, so I didn't have to worry about squeaking hinges. And I wasn't silhouetted as I stepped across each threshold: I was moving towards the light, not away from it. But it still took a while. There were a lot of doorways.

The fabric of the place looked like it was in the middle of a major identity crisis. Some bits were covered with fresh gilt and moulded plaster, others seemed to be trying to throw off the bling of the past and go minimalist. There were enough pots of paint and glue and twenty-litre containers of white spirit lying around to last my anarchist mate a lifetime of artistic protest.

The builders' mess didn't seem to be confined to the wing I'd infiltrated. Four rooms further on, there was still not much sign of habitation. Then I came to the fifth, where a sheet of clear polythene had been fastened to the double door frame, separating the plaster dust and the lads responsible for it from what appeared to be the Gucci end of the house.

All the doors, hinges attached, had been leant against the wall to my right, opposite the shuttered window. Someone had obviously been busy with a blowtorch here. There was a stack of propane cylinders alongside them.

Keeping the pistol in my right hand, out came the knife again in my left. It made short work of the polythene. I waited again. No hint of movement. I seemed to be the only body fucking about with the air molecules around here. I eased through the slit I'd made, muzzle first.

Lyubova obviously didn't share Frank's enthusiasm for grey marble, but she hadn't stinted on the Afghan rugs. The one that was now beneath my feet was the blood red of a Himalayan sunset, and must have been worth a fortune. I'd seen dozens of women in Kabul sweatshops at work on pieces like this, and only drug barons and dot.com zillionaires could afford to buy them. It stretched at least ten metres from the front of the house to the huge central staircase that dominated the back, and another ten from side to side.

I moved to the nearest window. It was the first I could see through beyond the scaffolding. The shutters were open. So were the curtains. Standing far enough back to avoid being spotted from the garden, I looked towards the main entrance. I needn't have bothered. There was no one there.

The now perfectly mown lawn was as deserted as the house seemed to be. The gates were shut, but unmanned. Unless the boys in black were tiptoeing around below me, with weapons at the ready, they'd taken an early bath. Even though the water was a couple of Ks away, the boats scudding across it seemed to be within touching distance.

I turned back to the staircase. It rose from the entrance hall to a gleaming glass dome four storeys above. If the security boys were down there, they were as still as statues. Nothing moved beyond the banisters at every level.

The doors into the first Gucci room had both been thrown back. This was no building site. It was flooded with sunlight, some of which seemed to be bouncing straight off the surface of the lake. Every piece of furniture had probably been made for Napoleon personally. The mahogany gleamed and the velvet looked like it had never been touched. I couldn't see Stefan having much fun here, beatings or no beatings. It felt like a museum.

I was about to move on through when I heard a sound behind me. A creaking board. A misjudged footstep, maybe. I swivelled 180 degrees and brought up the weapon.

Nothing. Nobody. Maybe I'd imagined it.

No, I hadn't.

The same sound again.

Not a creaking board. A low groan. From somewhere overhead.

I filled my lungs with oxygen, melted back through the doorway, and raised the muzzle of the Sphinx as I raised my eyes, following the staircase.

A muffled cry echoed through the empty space.

A female cry.

Not the kind of cry you make when some fucker has broken into your home and you're desperate to alert the men you're paying to keep you safe. The kind you make when you're trying to fight your way out of the deepest of sleeps, but the nightmare won't let you go.

There was no sign of the hired help hurrying to the rescue. So, staying close to the wall, I climbed towards the cry one step at a time. I had to move around a marble bust on an ebony plinth halfway up. Fuck knew who it was. Could have been Lenin, for all I cared. Or Dostoevsky. It certainly wasn't Frank, even though he'd paid for all this.

I slowed almost to a standstill as I approached the second-floor landing, and stopped short of the corridor that ran off it. There had been no more cries, but I thought I could hear breathing. Irregular, husky rasps. Then nothing.

I didn't wait any longer. Weapon up, I spun through the first door I came to. A bedroom, nearly twice the size of the master suite in the Courchevel chalet.

Two windows ahead of me, overlooking the lake.

A three-sided, gilt-framed mirror between them, on a dressing-table lined with designer make-up containers and sparkly stuff hanging from gold stands.

A bed, built on the same scale. Covers thrown back. Head-shaped dent in the pillow on the far side of it.

So, slept in recently.

Two more windows behind it, above the tarpaulin tent that sheltered the roof I'd cut through. Separated by an enormous wardrobe with a mirror front.

Another fucking great mirror on the wall to my right, beside the half-open door to her bathroom.

Lyubova clearly liked her mirrors.

I took another step forward and caught sight of a bare foot in the one on the dressing-table. A body in a leopard-print skirt lay between the bed and the side window.

It wasn't moving.

9

I slapped the pistol back into my waistband and piled in.

When I got closer, I could see that Lyubova wasn't breathing either.

She was on her side, left arm outstretched, right hand clutching at the bare skin above her breast. Raven hair glued to the sweat on her face. A thin strand of mucus linking the lower corner of her mouth to a pool of vomit on the white sheepskin beneath her head.

I knelt beside her, swept her damp hair aside and felt for her carotid pulse. It fluttered under my fingertip. I glanced at her bedside table. An empty brown bottle, lying on its side. A glass of water, half full, with lipstick on the rim. I wasn't going to need the ether.

I hooked my index and middle fingers into her oral cavity and scooped out her tongue and another gob of grey gloop, flecked with crimson. I rolled her on to her back, put one hand on top of the other and, allowing my body to rock for maximum force, compressed the centre of her chest. Once. Twice. Three times. Then again. And again. I wanted her groggy, but I didn't want her to die on me.

I felt one of her ribs crack fairly early in the process, then another, and kept on going.

After thirty compressions I took a deep breath, squeezed her surgically enhanced nose and gripped her perfectly sculpted chin, sealed my lips over hers and tried to fill her lungs.

I caught a hint of no doubt incredibly expensive perfume from near the base of her neck, but it was no match for the acidic taste and stench of her mouth.

Somewhere in the background I could smell alcohol. Not sixteen-year-old single malt or seven-star brandy, more like raw ethanol. And that didn't strike me as something that Lyubova would go for if she had a choice.

I leant forward and gave her another blast.

She arched her back. It was almost impossible to spot, but she did arch it. Then she retched weakly. Took a breath. Exhaled. But she was still pretty much unconscious.

I shoved both my arms under her like a forklift. Carried her through to the bathroom. Held her head over the toilet and shoved my index finger down her throat as far as I could. The drug and alcohol combo she had taken – or been given – needed to come out again, and fast, before her stomach had fully digested it. She gagged and gave another low moan, but nothing much ended up in the bowl.

I needed something more heavy duty. I grabbed the toilet brush handle, reversed it, and repeated the process. This way I got in deep, and wasn't going to have her chew my finger off.

That didn't work either.

I laid her down on the tiled floor, in the recovery position. Turned on the hot tap and found a plastic beaker. Ran through her medicine cabinet for anything I could mix into a warm saline solution. It contained every upper and downer the Swiss pharmaceutical industry could provide, and a few that it probably couldn't.

The bad news was that there wasn't a grain of salt to be seen.

Or anything else that I could use to make her puke her guts out. The medics didn't like doing that sort of shit, these days. If the patient inhaled, you could fuck them up big-time. But it was a risk I was going to have to take. And Lyubova hadn't earned any special treatment.

I checked her pulse again and decided to look downstairs.

The set-up on the ground floor was pretty much the same as on the first. One side of the house was gleaming and fully functional, the other still under wraps. I glanced through another polythene screen on my way past. All I could see close up were two or three more propane cylinders. They lay at odd angles on the floor, like torpedoes.

The kitchen was on the opposite side of the entrance hall.

This was where Frank's taste and Lyubova's did gel. Acres of polished granite and state-of-the-art stainless-steel cooking equipment and an island with a sink unit. There was only one gadget missing. She had settled for a little George Clooney coffee machine instead of one the size of a nuclear reactor.

Boiling water would dissolve the salt quicker than the stuff that came out of the tap. I'd dilute the mixture with cold when I got back to the bathroom. I filled the electric kettle and pressed the on button, flooding the surrounding area with blue light.

Leaving it to bubble, I scanned the shelves above the work surface by the cooker. They were stuffed with herbs and spices and tins of smoked mussels and five kinds of pepper, but not what I was looking for. They didn't seem to go for Colman's mustard around here, and the Gucci packet of pink Himalayan rock salt was almost empty. I dived into the cupboard under the sink. Dishwasher salt would do just fine.

I reached for the bag and got another whiff of white spirit vapour. I'd been aware of the smell upstairs in the wing that was still under reconstruction, only fleetingly, though, and in an environment where I'd expect it. Maybe this smelt stronger because it didn't belong here.

As I straightened, the socket powering the kettle buzzed and flashed and popped and the blue light snapped off. I flicked the nearest wall switch and half a dozen LED bulbs in the ceiling sparked up, so only the ring circuit feeding the sockets had blown.

I emptied the dishwasher salt into a glass jug, poured the not-quite-boiling water over it and gave the concoction a stir.

Upstairs in the bedroom, Lyubova was pretty much where I'd left her, still out of it, but breathing more easily. I fixed her a saline cocktail in the plastic beaker and gave it an experimental sip. If this stuff didn't work, nothing would.

I went down on one knee and, keeping her arse on the floor, hauled her up far enough to lodge the back of her neck in the crook of my left arm. Her ribs must have been on fire, but she didn't even blink. I reached round and gripped her jaw with my left thumb and forefinger, locking her chin in the web of skin between them. Keeping her face horizontal, I pushed open her mouth and poured as much of the emetic down her throat as I could.

A fair amount of it spilt down her cheeks and some went into her nose, but most of it was on target. The result was almost immediate. Her sneezing then her gagging reflex went into overdrive. Her chest heaved and I managed to tilt her sideways before she propelled whatever she'd had for lunch across the tiles and, with any luck, a critical amount of whatever had been forced into her before I arrived. It wasn't a pretty sight, but house beautiful had been put on hold.

I poured her another slug of saline and she gave a repeat performance. Then she opened her perfectly shaped eyes. But this wasn't a Snow White moment. Her surgeon wouldn't have been pleased. She still looked like shit. And felt like a dead weight. I didn't expect her to crack into a kettlebell workout anytime soon.

She didn't seem at all surprised to see me.

She took a deep, rasping breath, swallowed painfully and tried to lick her lips. Then she spoke.

'Those . . . fucking . . . bastards . . .' Her words were slurred, but her voice was deep and husky.

'Who?'

She turned on her own this time and sprayed the porcelain once more. It took her another couple of minutes to gather her marbles. I knew exactly how she felt.

Then she managed to wrench her head back in my direction. 'Whatever that little . . . shit . . . is paying you . . .'

She closed her eyes and I felt her body slump.

I shook her like a ragdoll until she resurfaced.

'. . . I will . . . pay you . . . *double* . . . to kill them . . .'

Her eyes flashed.

'What little shit? Frank?'

'Frank?' She snorted. 'He's dead.'

'What little shit?'

Her mouth opened and closed. 'Frank's . . . *creature* . . .'

I waited. I didn't have a fuck of a lot of choice.

'Laff . . . ont . . .'

'Who did this to you?'

I knew the answer, but I needed it to come from her.

'The Albanian . . . bastard.'

'Uran?'

She summoned the energy to curl her upper lip. 'Ur-*anus* . . .' She must have been quite pleased with that one, because the sneer almost turned into a smile. 'And . . . the other . . . *asshole* . . .'

'Dijani?'

I couldn't help admiring her anger. But I didn't want her confusing me with her new best friend. I tightened my elbow and felt my left fist clench. 'You helped them to kill Frank.'

'Frank . . . deserved . . . to die.' Her dark eyes blazed. 'But they . . . are . . . *peasants* . . .'

I couldn't argue with that. And Lyubova should know: she'd made the journey from air stewardess to aristocracy in double-quick time.

She went limp on me again. I bundled a big fluffy bath towel under her head, then stood and filled the jug with cold water and emptied the whole thing over her face.

Her eyelashes fluttered and she fought to get some more oxygen into her lungs.

I knelt down and gave her a slap, leaving a livid red mark on her cheek. So her circulation wasn't completely shot.

'Where are they? Where are your peasants?'

She mumbled something I couldn't hear.

I felt for her pulse again. Her heart was now beating like a snare drum.

'Where?' I leant in closer and turned the volume up. '*Where?*'

Her eyes widened, but they were glassy now. Unfocused. Her breathing quickened.

'*WHERE?*'

Blood-flecked spittle leaked out of the corner of her mouth.

'Ad . . . ler . . .'

In the silence that followed, I knew that the interior of the chateau was no longer still. The quality of the air had changed. My eardrums registered it first. Something or someone had fucked with the molecules in our immediate environment.

I drew down the Sphinx as I got to my feet.

10

I reached the archway that led through to the bedroom and heard a crack from below us. The entrance hall, maybe. A door banging shut? No. I had a bad feeling about this.

Then a noise behind me.

The empty glass jug smashing against the tiles.

I turned to see Lyubova struggling to raise herself off the floor. Gasping. Her skirt riding up her bare thighs. One hand clutching her ribs, apparently unaware that blood was flowing freely from the other, where shards of glass were embedded in her palm.

'Mis-ter . . .'

She shook her head, trying to clear it.

'Stefan . . .'

I smelt a hint of smoke now. I glanced in the direction of the stairwell. I couldn't see any sign of it in the corridor, but it was definitely in the atmosphere.

'They . . . have . . . him . . .'

As I went back to her, Lyubova's supporting hand slipped away, leaving a streak of crimson on the tiles. She collapsed, shoulder first, on to the towel I'd shoved underneath her head, and gave a pain-racked groan.

I gripped her outstretched arm and rolled her on to her back. She was in all sorts of shit, but her eyes were open. She was relishing this.

Steering clear of the broken jug, I pushed my head right up close to hers. 'What did you say?'

It was a fucking stupid question. We both knew what she'd said. And I'd just given her the pleasure of saying it again.

'Those . . . assholes. They have . . . taken . . . the . . . boy . . .'

'You're talking shit.'

Her tongue slid out, moistened her lips, then slid back in again.

'So . . . go back . . . to . . . the beach . . . and check . . .'

I replayed my movements over the last few hours at top speed inside my head. I hadn't been followed. I was ninety-nine point nine per cent sure of that.

'Where have they taken him?'

She said nothing. Didn't even blink. Her expression told me everything she wanted me to know. *You may have saved Frank's son on the mountain. But now you're both well and truly fucked . . .*

I let her have a good look at the muzzle of the Sphinx, then pressed it against her forehead, right between her eyes.

'I said, *where*?'

The weapon meant nothing to her. She'd already been a millimetre away from terminal and, with a bit of help from a gutful of dishwasher salt and sheer determination, she'd fought her way back to consciousness. Whatever else was going to rat-shit in her life, this was her reward.

'Where?' I gripped her bicep and gave her a fucking good shake. *'Where have they taken him?'*

She wasn't going to let the grinding of her broken ribs steal her moment of triumph. 'I wouldn't tell you . . . even if I knew . . .'

A smile began to take shape on her no longer flawless features, but never made it to the finishing line.

She heard the crackle of flames at the same time as I did.

I sprang up and accelerated through the bedroom and into the corridor. Grey smoke was billowing up the stairwell from the ground floor.

I rammed the weapon back under my belt and spun back into Lyubova's bathroom. She hadn't moved.

I soaked a hand towel under the shower. Folded it into a triangle. Covered my mouth and nose with it and tied it around the back of my neck. Then gave another the same treatment. Wrapped it around my head like a *shemagh*.

I was vaguely aware of her watching me, but she'd had her moment. I didn't need her to slow me down any more than she had already.

I ran through the smoke, two steps at a time. When I was halfway down the second flight, a jet of superheated propane from one of the cylinders blasted through the polythene sheeting opposite the kitchen and enveloped the space below me. The shockwave of the explosion that followed drove all the air from my lungs, lifted me off my feet and punched me against the wall.

I lay on the cold stone steps long enough to be reminded that the bit of my back which Claude had hammered with his fence post still hurt like fuck. And that I had to get moving before the rest of the propane and white spirit accelerant ignited above me as well. This might have been designed to look like an accident, but there was no way it was. I wondered whether whatever triggered it had been on a timer or detonated remotely. The van in the layby, maybe?

I hauled myself up as the smoke thickened. The far side of the hall was an inferno. I pulled one towel further down my forehead and the other up on to my cheekbones. The heat seared the strip of unprotected skin between them.

The fire began to consume the stairway. If the cylinders kicked off on the floor above, I'd be completely fucked. There were a whole lot more of them there. When they ignited, I'd have a major bleve on my hands.

I couldn't get back to Lyubova, even if I'd wanted to.

Fuck her.

Whoever was pulling the strings was clearing up after himself. First Frank's BG. Now his ex. It was no accident that the dogs, the security crew, the maids and whoever else had pissed off. And now I had to as well, before the emergency services arrived.

I legged it up to the landing and dived through the polythene I'd sliced on my way in. I whipped off my *shemagh* and wrapped it around the nearest propane cylinder. It sizzled like bacon fat but saved my palms from being fried long enough for me to hurl it through the nearest window.

Glass and shutter disintegrated. I clambered over the sill and on to the planking. The big hole I'd made would help fan the flames, but there was fuck-all I could do about that.

The heat was suddenly fucking outrageous up there too.

The mouth of the telescopic chute was two metres to my left. The shutter one metre beyond it burst outwards. A swirling eruption of glass and splintered wood, debris and dust. But I knew worse was to come. I vaulted over the retaining scaffolding pole while I still could, raised both arms and went into the chute feet first.

It was like one of those water slides you should never make the mistake of going down on a stag weekend in Portugal, but without the jets and the chance to level out before you hit the pool. I managed to slow myself with my boots and my arse and my elbows, and hoped that I'd land on a pile of plasterboard and insulating fibre rather than metal and slate and brick and chunks of wood with nails sticking out.

It was metal and slate and brick and chunks of wood. I couldn't feel any nails. My right knee took most of the pressure of the fall, and my arse didn't enjoy the experience either. I lay in a heap for a moment, counting the seconds until the boiling liquid expansion vapour explosion took out the front of the wing and everything immediately in front of it.

I took a breath or two and tested all the bits of myself I needed most right now. Then I hauled myself out of the skip and hobbled across to the van.

Three or four more windows on the upper floors at the centre of the house burst outwards as I went, showering the ground with razor-sharp shards, which sparkled like diamonds in the evening sunlight. Lyubova would probably have liked that. I didn't look up. I needed to get out of range, double quick.

Two more went, sucking in air to feed the fire and superheat the propane.

I whipped out the Sphinx. Ripped open the driver's door. Shoved the weapon under my thigh. Rammed the key in the ignition. The engine coughed, then died, then caught. I threw the gear stick into first, floored the accelerator pedal and sprayed gravel across the tarpaulin as I took off.

No flashing lights yet. And no sudden reappearance of the Dobermanns or their handlers.

I slowed as I approached the gates and skidded to a halt between the sensors that prompted them to open for outgoing vehicles. On went the baseball cap. Now I could hear sirens. I waited for the metal railings ahead of me to shudder and swing back.

They didn't move a millimetre.

I felt my shoulder and jaw muscles clench as I willed them to release me. The entry and exit system might have been fucked by the fusing of the ring main, or whatever had sparked up the blaze. I'd have to get out and wrench the fuckers open.

The tone of the sirens changed as they drew nearer. I knew what that meant. It meant they were reaching the end of their journey. I gripped the pistol and was reaching for the Expert's door handle when the gates gave a shudder. Then another. And a gap between them began to widen.

I eased the van forward and, with the pressure wave of the bleve kicking in behind me, I was out of there.

11

My knee throbbed as I put my foot on the gas and headed away from the sirens and the flashing lights I could now glimpse through the trees to my half-right. There was no sign of the smoker in the layby.

I didn't want to get nailed for speeding, but needed to separate myself from the chateau, then get to Stefan as quickly as possible. I took the second left, hit the brake, then the third right, then left again.

After a couple of Ks I pulled off the road. I wasn't in cover, but about a hundred from the nearest house, and with a fair amount of foliage close by. I dusted myself off and peeled both decals off the side panels. Then I slid back the door and chucked them into the rear toolbox.

I dug out a screwdriver and swapped the registration plates for the first of the Swiss ones. The original set went into the toolbox too. This was turning into a weapons-grade gangfuck, but I had to grip it, not lose it. The remote drive for the chateau security cameras would be well out of reach of the fire, and the first place any halfway competent investigator would look. Moving freely right now was vital, especially if the van was pinged, and I was in the frame for what Hesco and Dijani had done there.

I put the degreaser down by the partition, then extracted myself from my overalls and bundled them in too.

I glanced in the wing mirror as I rejoined the main and pointed the van north towards the beach where I'd left Stefan. Smoke spiralled into the sky from the chateau behind me. The traffic ahead pulled into the kerb to make space for the two fire engines screaming towards us.

A white and green police wagon, four up, was hot on their heels. One glance at the black combat kit worn by the lads inside it told me they were TIGRIS. They were a long way from home – the Einsatzgruppe HQ was two hundred Ks west, near Bern – but the Zürich canton cops didn't dress like that, and they didn't have *Sécurité Internationale* splashed across their rear wings either.

I heard the rhythmic beat of rotor blades from the south, approaching from St Gallen. The heli might have been carrying a news crew or another TIGRIS team. I'd find out soon enough.

The parking area by the lake had a lot more empty spaces now, and most of the parasols had been taken down. I pulled in a fair distance from the Polo and scanned the surrounding area. Families were being shepherded towards their wagons. Nobody seemed to be there without a good reason, and I couldn't see anyone dressed for work talking urgently into a mobile.

I got eyes on Stefan's deckchairs. They were empty. That was when I really started to leak sweat, even from places I didn't know I had sweat glands. On the way, part of me had still hoped Lyubova was bluffing.

The woman in the sundress was packing up her picnic basket and yelling at her twin girls to come out of the water. They weren't paying her the slightest bit of attention. I scanned the shoreline to the left and right of them. Stefan wasn't anywhere in sight.

I climbed out of the cab and checked out the Polo, in case he'd got bored and decided to listen to his Pitbull album, or some other rap on the radio. He'd chucked his towel on to the passenger seat, but he wasn't in there with it. Nor was his rucksack.

I ran down a gangway on to the stretch of turf, then on to the sand. The sun was low in the sky now, and much of the heat had gone out of it. The place wasn't nearly as packed as it had been earlier, but bunches of locals and holidaymakers were still intent on having a good time. One or two began to point at the pillar of smoke rising into the sky behind me.

Two girls in wetsuits hopped off their windsurfers as they skimmed into the shallows. Four well-oiled teenage dudes were playing volleyball at the far end of the beach, surrounded by a small crowd of kids. Stefan wasn't one of them.

As I turned back towards the deckchairs, the mum in the sundress finally lost her patience with the twins and heaved them both out of the water. I almost collided with her as she strode back to her basket, gripping a small female wrist in each hand. She looked up, muttering something in Schweizerdeutsch, then recognized me from earlier.

'Have you seen my boy?'

Her angry-mum face was immediately replaced by her old smiley one. 'You mustn't worry. He has gone with the maid.'

'The maid? Ah . . . Natasha . . .'

'Very pretty girl.'

'Did she say where to?'

She frowned. 'She told me you would know. She said they would see you later . . .'

I nodded again and tried to react as if this was all part of our plan for the evening. I needed answers, but I didn't want her – or anybody else – to go on red alert.

She obviously wasn't buying it. 'Everything is OK, isn't it?'

'Sure. She just called.' I paused. 'Thanks for looking out for him.'

She shrugged. 'I'm a mother. That's what we do. She was way over there . . .' She pointed towards the volleyball game. 'Then he looked up from his book and spotted her. He waved and ran over. That's why I didn't worry. He was very excited.'

'He likes her. She taught him to swim.'

I tried not to let the smile slide off my face, but my chat with Stefan about trust kept ringing in my ears, and that didn't help. Next time I saw him I'd tell him the truth. You can't trust any fucker. Not even nice-looking ones who once taught you how to keep your head above the water.

'You didn't see which car they were in, did you?'

She shook her head.

'Or who she was with? Her boyfriend, maybe?'

'I think there was a man.' She gestured vaguely towards the car park.

'Big guy? Chunky? Pointy sideburns?' I traced the shape of them on my own cheeks.

'Sideburns? I think . . .' She started to look anxious again. 'I am so sorry. I don't know . . .'

I wanted to ask her more, but her finger was hovering over the panic button.

'Don't worry. It's all good.'

I turned back towards the van, leaving her to gather her gear. I'd gone about five paces when she called after me. 'Natasha . . . and your boy . . . I heard them say something about the cathedral . . .'

I glanced over my shoulder and waved. I hoped I still looked happier than I felt. The cathedral was our ERV. If he'd told her about that, he was in danger of telling her everything.

My only consolation right now was that although Stefan had drawn the thought-bubble decal he didn't know I'd bought the Peugeot. And what he didn't know, he couldn't pass on.

12

The passenger door of the Polo opened at the press of the button. The towel hadn't been left there by accident. Underneath it were the car keys and the Pitbull CD. And a cheap Nokia mobile.

I powered it up. A pay-as-you-go SIM, five bars of signal and a full battery. No numbers in the memory, but one voicemail from an unidentified source: 'You will be contacted at twenty-one hundred.' A voice like gravel. Heavily accented. Eastern European.

I'd heard it before. '*Fuck him. He got what he deserved.*' Hesco had been no more than six metres away from me. He'd been talking into a mobile phone then as well.

21:00 made sense. Just before last light.

It gave me two hours.

I pocketed the Nokia and checked out the interior of the Polo – glovebox, door compartments, boot, the lot – to make sure that we hadn't left anything behind. Now they'd pinged it, I was ditching the wagon here. It was a complete liability.

The only thing I needed was the Swiss map book. But I took the towel and the Pitbull CD as well. I left the keys in the ignition and hoped someone would nick it before the parking Gestapo hauled it on to a low-loader. It would create some more confusion. And if the bad guys had stuck a tracker underneath it, so much the better.

Back in the van, I opened the map book, laid it on the passenger seat, took a couple of deep breaths and focused.

They had him.

And now they were using him to get me.

Once that was done they would kill us both.

So I wasn't about to settle down with a Starbucks and wait for them to call. And I wasn't going to wander around the cathedral hoping that Natasha was playing happy families and the boy was telling her everything he knew about ERVs.

I had to strike first.

The security guard at the cash-and-carry tapped his watch as I came through the revolving door. I signalled that I wouldn't need more than five. He gave me a smile and held up three fingers. At least it wasn't two.

I had most of what I wanted from my earlier trip to the neighbouring DIY store, when I'd prepared for the possibility of having to lift Lyubova and take her somewhere quiet. Now I needed something more heavy-duty.

I finished my final shopping spree of the day at warp speed. Fifteen hundred metres of meat-packing-grade cling-film complete with metal wall mounting, a nice big mug and twenty-four 20cl bottles of Cherry Fanta on two shrink-wrapped trays.

I didn't go for the cans. I needed as much precision as possible, and the bottles had a nice narrow neck. I didn't take the *zuckerfrei* option either: I wanted this stuff to be as sticky and as fizzy as possible.

I had assumed I could get Lyubova to talk by securing her in my mobile fridge, opening up my clasp knife and threatening to give her some extra plastic surgery. Hesco was going to need a different approach. First I had to catch him. Then I had to get him to tell me where they were keeping Frank's boy. And what the fuck he and Dijani were up to.

To celebrate barbecue season, they had a rack of bubble-wrapped openers, the kind you fasten to the wall beside the fridge, on special offer by the till. Just what I was looking for. I threw one into my trolley. I also bought a can of WD-40.

I packed the stuff into the front end of the Expert's no longer refrigerated load space, then climbed in after it. Out came the screwdriver again. I mounted the cling-film holder and the bottle opener low down on the partition that separated it from the cab, making doubly sure they were both within easy reach of my right hand when I was kneeling. I put the degreaser and the Cherry Fanta packs underneath. I needed to be able to rip off those bottle tops with zero effort.

I padlocked all the other shit I'd bought, apart from the cloths and the mug, into the toolbox with my day sack. The only sharp objects I wanted around were the ones I had under my control. The last thing I did was give the handle, rollers and bearings of the sliding door a man-size spray of WD-40.

I checked the Nokia before turning the ignition key, even though there was no reason for there to be any further messages. It was forty-five minutes before the first deadline. I'd be within range of Adler HQ in twenty, as long as the traffic was no worse than it had been during my recce.

But I was still on a tight schedule.

13

I got to the multi-storey as the streetlights were sparking up. The Adler section on level three was less full than it had been last night, even though it was earlier in the evening.

The Maserati was parked nose out, its rear end against the wall overlooking the street, with a couple of spaces on either side of it. That suited me fine. It meant that if I drove straight in, my sliding door would be exactly where I wanted it – a metre behind his driver's door. It also meant that the Expert blocked Hesco's wagon from the CCTV camera.

I rested the Nokia on the ledge beneath the speedometer and rev counter and stayed where I was. The cab was high enough off the ground to let me see straight over the white-painted concrete parapet and into the offices across the way. From this distance I couldn't see faces with the naked eye, so I brought out the binos and focused on each illuminated window in turn, right to left.

Most of the late staff seemed to be running around in neat business suits, with the odd jacket across the back of a chair if they were really hanging loose. I spotted a pair of security guards doing their rounds but couldn't catch anyone built or dressed like Hesco. So what? It didn't have to mean he wasn't there.

If he'd binned the Maserati for the night, I would have to live with that and do whatever the next call told me to. From there, I'd wing it.

But I still had three advantages.

He'd think I was still in the Polo.

I knew what he looked like.

And I didn't think he'd yet pinged me.

If he stuck with the Maserati, I'd have a fourth. It would confirm that he was a cocky fucker, and didn't feel the need to stay out of sight.

I exited the cab and threw back the side door, taking the Nokia with me. I put the phone, face up, at the base of the partition and started to sort myself out.

First, I pulled the door almost all the way shut. It slid along its rails without a squeak. I moved my right eye up close to the two-centimetre gap and checked my field of vision. I could see the headrest of the Maserati's driver's seat, and, over its roof, the passageway that led to the lift. The stretch between the two was dead ground.

Leaving the Nokia where it was, I unrolled a metre and a half of cling-film, twisted it into a rope, then knotted it at both ends and a couple of times near the middle. I hung it on a hook to the left of the window that looked through to the front of the van.

Next, I ripped open the bag of disposable cloths and crumpled one into the mug. I poured some of the degreasing solvent over it and sealed the rim with another strip of cling-film. I peeled back the first few centimetres off the roll of gaffer tape. Then I gave each of the cable ties a vigorous tug to make sure they were secure. Lyubova would have been no pushover, but the Albanian was at least twice her size and would put up more of a fight.

The double-barbed staples were going nowhere.

The Nokia's screen flashed on as I got out. *Unknown number.* I steadied my breathing and pressed the green button.

'Yup?'

'Be at the Stadtlounge in exactly two hours.'

'The *what*?'

'The City Lounge. Bleichestrasse. In the business centre. You can't miss it, even at night. It's red.'

'I know it.'

I tried not to think of the expression on Stefan's face as we'd passed the place yesterday evening.

'Park in one of the spaces in the square. By the blocks. Do not get out of the car.'

'Put the boy on. I need to know he's alive.'

He cut the connection.

14

Hesco had the leverage and he knew it. He had me by the bollocks and could squeeze as much as he wanted. Fair one. I'd have cut the connection too. I wasn't being ordered to the City Lounge for a kiss and a cuddle. They weren't just going to hand over the kid and tell us to go and have a nice holiday somewhere warm. They were going to kill us both.

I moved to the parapet. Keeping close to the pillar, I looked across the street. I didn't have to wait more than a couple of minutes before the main entrance of the Adler building swung open. A familiar figure came down the steps and out on to the pavement. He stopped and glanced at his watch. Probably counting down the minutes until I turned up at the lounge.

For a moment I thought Hesco might be waiting for reinforcements. I hoped not. But I'd deal with it if it happened. I was pretty sure he wouldn't be picking up Stefan in full view of Adler HQ.

He clamped a cigarette between his lips. Lit it. Took a couple of drags. Then he walked five paces up the street, away from the entrance to the multi-storey, and took a couple more. Finally he launched what was left of it into the gutter and headed in my direction.

I climbed back into the Expert's load space, eased the side door into position then reached up and turned off the light. I adjusted the Sphinx in my waistband, flexed my shoulder muscles and controlled my breathing.

I unpeeled the seal on the mug and left it within close reach.

I unhooked the cling-film rope and gripped an end in each hand.

I heard the lift open, then footsteps. A figure appeared at the mouth of the passageway. Thin. Bearded.

Not Hesco.

He turned left and out of sight. A key fob cheeped. An engine fired up. A set of headlamps swept towards me. Then screeched to a halt. Judging by the height of them, they didn't belong to something low and sleek. They belonged to a chunky 4x4.

This wasn't good. The wagon completely blocked my line of sight. A Land Cruiser or a Shogun, judging by the silhouette.

If he stayed where he was, I wouldn't spot my target until he was breathing my oxygen. And my whole performance would be floodlit.

And if he was the guy Hesco had been waiting for, I was comprehensively fucked. There was no way I could exit the Expert without being seen.

He stayed where he was for another three minutes, then took off at speed. But that was all it took for Hesco to come in under the radar. I heard the squeak of boots. A shadow fell across the gap between my door and the frame.

There was another electronic chirrup, and I saw the Maserati boot open. A chunky set of shoulders moved past. Dark, tightly curled hair. An arm. A hand, carrying a suitcase. I shoved back the door and threw the cling film over his head like a skipping rope and heaved it back as my feet touched the ground.

He didn't only have one case. He had two. A smaller one in his right hand. He dropped them both and raised his fists.

When you're being garrotted, your natural instinct is to try to get both sets of fingers between your throat and whatever is about to stop you breathing. Hesco didn't do that. Only his left hand went for the cling-film. He tried to destroy one of my ribs with his right elbow, then swivelled, brought his arm up and, gripping the ignition key like a bayonet, did his best to bury the metal shank in my ear, my eye, my carotid, whatever – he didn't much care.

I turned with him, keeping him close, fending off more elbow action with my upper arm and getting another loop around his neck. He didn't just look like a Hesco barrier, he felt like one too. He'd been filled with sand. He was carrying some surplus weight, but there was no give.

I leant back into the Expert's load space, tightened the noose and clenched both knotted ends of it in my left hand. While Hesco was flailing, trying to win the gravity battle, my arse was firmly on the lip of the plywood floor, my knees bent, the soles of my Timberlands flat on the ground. I heard a clink as his key hit the concrete and my free hand found the ether-soaked cloth, whipped it out of the mug and clamped it on to his nose and mouth.

I kept it in place long enough for his head and neck to go limp, then the rest of him followed. I laid him out alongside my Fanta trays before retrieving his keys, overnight bag and briefcase, and hurling them into the van.

I closed and locked the door behind me, switched on the interior light and hooked my little finger through the keyring. Then I kicked the bags out of the way so I could reach him and stuff three-quarters of the cloth into his mouth. Keeping the rest over his nostrils, I wound gaffer tape around his head until I'd mummified him from the neck up, leaving only his nose and ears unbound. All I needed was for him to be able to hear and breathe.

I lifted his right hand. It was the first time I'd been able to admire his ring up close. Silver double-headed eagle on red enamel.

I fastened his wrists, ankles and neck with the cable ties. Once all eighteen were in place and Hesco was nicely spread-eagled, I listened at the door again, then jumped out and sifted through the Maserati's boot and glovebox. Nothing more than car shit.

I'd give him and his bags a closer look later. Right now I needed to get the fuck out of there. I had less than two hours before I should be at the meet, and had no control of what would happen when Hesco didn't show up earlier. But, fuck it, I just had to get on with what I could control. I pressed his padlock button twice and climbed into my cab.

I didn't try to beat the *Guinness Book of Records* for the time it takes to piss off out of a Swiss multi-storey car park. I needed the

CCTV to show there was nothing unusual about my journey to the exit.

When I'd checked out Google Earth at the second cyber café, I'd spotted a massive expanse of forestry at the northern end of Lake Konstanz, stretching almost as far as the German frontier. It would be quiet and dark and that was all I needed.

Lights glimmered in the windows of the converted barns and farmhouses of Chatzerüti, the hamlet at the edge of the forest. A dog barked in the distance, but no one paid me the slightest attention as I drove past. I turned on to gravel tracks and doused my headlamps as soon as I was inside the treeline. The deeper I moved into the forest the quicker it would soak up the lights.

The place was probably crawling with wildlife – wild boar for certain, and possibly the odd bear – but none of them seemed to be carrying torches.

I turned down the dashboard display as low as it would go and moved forwards slowly, keeping the headlamps off.

I hung a right after about a K, and passed a wooden hut with the shutters down and a bunch of those bench-and-table combos you find at every picnic spot in Europe. This would be a great place for a Swiss sausage and a hunk of bread at the end of a day's hiking, but last orders would have been taken well before sundown.

I kept on going another K, then pulled off the track and got out. There wasn't much more than a glow from the moon down there. I got half a litre of mineral water down my neck and listened to the night sounds. The odd rustle in the undergrowth. The call of an owl. But I wasn't about to go into David Attenborough mode. I just needed to be as sure as possible that none of them was human.

Locking the cab, I got into the back with Hesco, closing and locking the door behind me. He was still out for the count as I ran my fingers along his belt, wrists and calves. No weapon.

Then I had a good look through his clothes.

He wasn't sterile. Why would he be? He hadn't planned to spend his evening strapped to the floor of my van.

I lifted his wallet, his Adler ID and pass cards, and two mobile phones. One was a cheap Nokia with no call or text history, which must have been the twin of the one he had left on the passenger seat of the Polo. The other was an iPhone with a pass code.

I brought out my day sack and stowed all the goodies inside it. Last to go in was the iPhone, after I'd powered it down and removed its SIM card. Whoever was waiting at the City Lounge might just want to check where he was.

I unzipped his overnight bag. A couple of changes of basic kit, a spare pair of deck shoes and a washbag. So he was on his way somewhere, after he'd sorted me and the boy out, and wasn't planning to stay long.

The briefcase was more interesting. Some routine corporate shit. A bunch of keys. A Space Pen. An unloaded SIG Sauer P226. A 9mm Elite Stainless with a walnut handle. This lad really did fancy himself. It was the perfect weapon for an arsehole who drove around town in a wagon that yelled, 'Look at me!'

I also found two chrome-plated twenty-round mags and a suppressor, an Albanian passport and a Lufthansa boarding pass for tomorrow's 06:30 flight from Zürich to Naples – which explained why he had already packed. And although Brindisi was on the opposite side of the southern Italian peninsula, it made me think I was some way towards finding out why Frank had been sad there on his last trip.

The best came last: a thirteen-inch HP laptop in a neoprene sleeve.

There's no point in breaking down a door if it hasn't been locked, so I fired it up, in case it wasn't password protected. It was. I folded it shut, replaced the sleeve, put it down a safe distance from the Fanta zone.

I opened the tool chest, squeezed the bag and the briefcase inside it and put my day sack on top of them. As I replaced the padlock, Hesco gave a low moan from somewhere inside his binding, and seemed to be testing the wrist ties. I gave him a couple of kicks in the kidneys and got nothing in response, so maybe I was imagining it.

15

The ether had pretty much evaporated from the cloth and Hesco was starting to show signs of wakefulness.

I stood over him briefly before collapsing my weight to sit on his chest, driving out what little air was left in his lungs.

His immediate reaction was to try to arch his back and throw me off, but as long as the staples held, the cable ties made that impossible. I still didn't say anything. He tried sucking in through his mouth but that wasn't working. His nostrils flared with the struggle for oxygen.

I brought out my knife, unfolded the blade and slid it under the binding below his left ear. I did it slowly, so he had plenty of opportunity to feel the cold metal against his neck. It worked. He went very, very still. Maybe I was right about the scar on his nose.

Then I sliced upwards, peeled the flap of tape away from his lips, taking a strip of his designer sideburn with it, and pulled the cloth out of his mouth.

He didn't shout. He didn't swear. He took a huge, juddering breath, partly because air had never tasted so good, and partly because he'd want to oxygenate fully before trying to unseat me again.

'Zac, this isn't complicated. Where is the boy?'

The blade on his throat, a centimetre above the place where the cable ties were tautening against his Adam's apple, reminded him that silence was a bad idea.

He went the 'I don't speak English' route. I got a stream of turbo-charged Albanian waffle before he coughed up a gob full of phlegm and spat it at me with as much force as he could muster. Almost in slow motion, it smacked on to the front of my T-shirt and stuck there, like a jellyfish.

His lips opened and closed. When the words came, it was in little more than a whisper.

'Fuck *you*.'

I grabbed the first Fanta bottle that came to hand and snapped off its cap.

I balled up the cloth, rammed the whole thing back in Hesco's mouth and held my left hand over it. Then I sealed the bottle with my right thumb and gave it a good shake.

As he tried to suck in oxygen through both nostrils I pressed the neck against his upper lip and gave him as much of the foaming cherry-coloured liquid as he could snort.

16

You don't expect to drown on dry land, in the back of a panel van, but every nerve ending tells you that's what's happening. You can't see a thing. The carbonated liquid is jet-cleaning your sinuses. The sugar content is coating every membrane. This is high-octane waterboarding on wheels. And you're starting to realize there's no escape.

I removed my hand and pulled out the cloth.

Day-glo cherry was bubbling out of his nose and mouth, and maybe his eye sockets too.

'Where's the boy?'

He didn't answer immediately.

He coughed up another load of phlegm. It wasn't an act of defiance this time, though. It was an act of survival. The stuff dribbled from the corners of his lips and clung to his cheeks for a second or two, then gathered at the back of his collar.

When he found his voice, it came out as a low growl. 'Fuck you . . .' He paused to bring up a throatful of puke. 'And fuck your mother.'

I threw aside the empty bottle and reached for another, taking the top off before thumbing the opening and slamming its base down on to his skull, making the drink ready to go volcanic. As he took the pain I shoved the cloth back into his mouth, covered it with my hand, and pressed the back of his skull hard against the floor before slotting the bottleneck into position and letting it discharge.

It fizzed like a firecracker.

He jerked his head from side to side, as far as my grip and the cable ties would allow, but it didn't help him. I leant down, pushing my hands into his face. The sticky liquid sprayed over my arms and thighs of my jeans. The smell of cherry flavouring filled my nostrils.

It was pointless talking just yet. I wanted him to believe that he was going under. I wanted his sinuses to feel like they were dissolving in acid. And I wanted his imagination to do the rest.

When the last of the cherry had spilt down his cheeks and gummed up his hair, I whipped my hand off his mouth again. He tried desperately to breathe through the cloth.

I pulled it out for him, waited for him to sort himself out, then spoke very slowly. 'WHERE – IS – THE – BOY?'

'She didn't . . . find him . . . He found . . . her . . .'

'Where?'

'The beach . . . She called Lyubova . . . I picked up the phone.'

I tightened my fingers around his throat. 'Natasha? He thought she was on his side.'

'Maybe . . . she was . . . once . . . But her world . . . has changed.'

'Who changed it?'

'Putin.' He bared his teeth. 'And me . . .'

I didn't need to ask him again. I knew he wanted to tell me. It wasn't only the Maserati and the sideburns that said vanity was his big weakness.

But he also wanted to make me wait. I would, if this was the way he'd tell me where the boy was. But not for long.

'She is from the Crimea . . . so . . . in different ways . . . she is being fucked . . . by both of us.'

Through the tape, the gunk and the vomit, it looked like he was smiling.

The best way to fuck Hesco right back was by depriving him of any kind of rhythm. He'd be able to take the pain if he knew he could relax and have a nice chat straight afterwards. He'd be able to keep a grip on the passing of time. He'd know that I didn't have all night for this. And I didn't want that to happen.

'You know what? I don't give a shit who you're fucking. Unless you're fucking with me. Is Putin calling the shots? Did Putin order Frank's killing?' I couldn't help thinking of Anna and the baby. Their safety was even more important to me than Stefan's.

'Putin?' He snorted red bubbly snot. 'Putin . . . would give me . . . a medal . . . for killing Timis . . .'

'Did he order it?'

'Putin . . . has nothing to do . . . with this . . . You . . . have much more . . . to fear . . . than Putin . . .'

'Why did you throw the black guy off the balcony?'

It wasn't the question he was expecting. And it wasn't one he felt the need to block.

'He was . . . unreliable.' His voice was raw.

'Because he didn't kill the boy?'

'Because . . . he didn't obey . . .'

'And who helped you do it? Who was the guy with the suede jacket and the shiny head?'

'He . . . is a man . . . who will . . . kill you . . . if he . . . ever . . . sees you . . . again . . .'

'What about Lyubova?' I wanted to keep the questions coming. To keep his mouth working so I could get where I needed to be. 'Was she unreliable too?'

He tried to gasp in more oxygen, but the sticky stuff coating his lungs kept getting in the way. He was gurgling like a blocked drain.

'She . . . had her . . . own . . . agenda.'

'Which meant helping to set up Frank, but not sitting and watching you and your mate Dijani take over his businesses?'

Maserati or not, Hesco was the monkey. That's why he was there. But I knew he'd like me putting him up there with the organ-grinder.

'She . . . thought . . . only of . . . herself . . .'

'Not like you, eh? You're a man of vision. I can see that.'

He nodded slowly. He could see it too. Even when he was blindfolded.

'And what you're up to is bigger than Frank's BG or Lyubova could understand, eh? Big enough to get the GIGN worried. And

TIGRIS. I thought they were after me. But they're not, are they? They're looking for *you*.'

More nodding. It wasn't just sweat and sugar leaking from every pore now. It was satisfaction.

'They're looking . . . for both . . . of us . . .'

'Where is the boy?'

He made an attempt at a scoff.

I gave him a third bottle, at warp speed, and followed it with another. The spray was all over the place now. Every muscle group was in meltdown. His heels were drumming against the floor. Both hands were flexing big-time too. Trying to find something to grip. Trying to find a fixed point in a world that was going to rat-shit.

His fingernails were starting to gouge crimson tracks in his own palms.

As the drink fizz died down I dropped the bottle and let him turn his head and expel what was left in the back of his throat.

'Where is the boy?'

17

His lungs had more sticky cherry shit in them than air. The rest of it was pooled around his head, along with most of what he'd eaten and drunk in the last six hours. I reached for Fanta number five.

He reacted when he heard the clink. 'No . . . wait . . .'

I carried on going. He recoiled when he felt the cold glass against his upper lip.

'No . . .'

'Where is the boy? Come on, Zac, you're smarter than this.'

'Smarter . . . yes . . .'

'So tell me.'

'Smarter . . .'

I bent forwards again and yelled in his ear. *'FUCKING TELL ME!'*

I'd meant to shock him into a response, but it didn't work.

'Smarter . . . *smarter* . . . than *you*.'

'You think? So how come you're the one who's drowning?'

I didn't wait for an answer.

'Where's Dijani, Zac? He's in this up to his neck, isn't he?'

All I got was a long, rasping breath.

'Was he up on that mountain road, or were you in charge of sending me over the edge?'

'Me . . . I was . . . *in charge* . . .' Another happy memory. 'We had to . . . split . . . you up . . .'

'So I got a javelin through the windscreen, and Frank Timis got a double tap.'

'We should . . . have put . . . a bullet . . . in you . . . as well . . . We will . . . soon . . .'

His confidence was returning. He was back on safe ground. He could talk about this all night. Good. That was the way I wanted him to feel.

'Tell me about Italy.'

He went absolutely rigid for five seconds, then flapped around a bit, but there was no disguising it. Italy had rattled him.

'I know about the people-trafficking, the drugs . . . Is that what you fuckers are up to?'

I gripped his throat again, to help him concentrate.

'Asylum . . . seekers . . .' He tried to launch another gobbet of phlegm at me, and failed. 'Scum . . . Who cares . . . if they drown? You cannot escape . . . the judgement of . . . *Allah* . . .'

'So how do you think Allah will judge *you*? What does it say in the Quran about shagging Ukrainian maids, or mincing around in a Maserati, or profiteering, or child abduction?'

He didn't seem too concerned about any of that. 'Allah . . . will . . . welcome us . . . to Paradise.'

'Where's the boy?'

He struggled to turn his head again and clear some of the shit out of his chest. I wouldn't let him.

'WHERE – DO – YOU – HAVE – THE – *BOY*?'

He tried to suck oxygen into his lungs. He sounded more like a cement mixer than a human being.

I selected another bottle and made sure he was well aware of the clinking and shaking process. He opened his mouth again before I clamped my hand on it.

'I will . . .

'. . . take you . . .

'. . . to the boy . . .'

If he'd had a white flag, he'd have waved it. But so would I, in his position. I'd have done almost anything. Every second off the waterboard, every millimetre of distance, was an opportunity to regroup.

I told him that was all well and good, but I still needed him to convince me he meant it. I told him I wanted a sign of commitment.

'What's the password, Zac? The password for the laptop.'

'What . . . *the fuck—*'

I sat more heavily on his chest as I emptied the foaming Fanta into the mug and put it beside the door. Then I picked up the HP, tucked it under my chin, removed it from its sleeve and placed it on the floor far enough from Hesco's head to keep it away from the red liquid flood. That was easier said than done: the stuff was even dripping from the ceiling now. It stank so badly of cherry-flavoured E-numbers in here I could taste it.

I flipped open the brushed aluminium lid. 'I need something from you. I need to know that you've got skin in the game.'

'Skin?'

'Something that shows me you're serious.'

I eased the pressure long enough for him to nod, and pressed the power button. The start-up tone seemed to fill the space around us. A log-in box appeared at the centre of a screen-saver shot of a distant galaxy.

'So give me the fucking password.'

'Paradise . . .' He barely breathed it.

Still gripping his throat, I tapped in all eight letters, beginning with a capital *P*, then the return key.

The box quivered and went blank.

It didn't react well to a lower-case *p* either.

'Don't fuck with me . . .'

I tried Jannah instead. I wasn't an expert on the Quran, but a few of the most important words had stuck. And Jannah was the place all good Muslims were aiming for.

Same result.

'You . . . must go . . . through . . . the correct gate . . .' The fucker listened to my increasingly staccato tapping. He was still wanting to play.

I allowed my mind to wander for a moment.

Back to the Iraqi desert.

The land of flaming oil wells and missile emplacements and storm drains.

And endless exchanges in interrogation centres during the dark hours as we took Frank's advice and tried to get to know our enemy. There were eight gates to Jannah. The second was for those who had fought the Holy War. I was fucked if I could remember what it was called.

Then I did.

I hit the keys. *Baab.al.Jihad* . . .

More quivering.

Baab al-jihad . . .

The security software didn't like that version either. But I wasn't going to give Hesco the satisfaction of asking him for another clue.

baabal_jihad . . .

Was I going to be timed out?

baabaljihad

Bullseye.

A selfie with a palm tree and his Maserati filled the desktop, and was instantly peppered with icons.

I was in. I'd take a closer look at the contents later.

I shut down the HP and replaced the sleeve. 'So, where's the boy?'

'First, you will cut me free . . .' He strained against the cable ties.

I shook my head, not that he could see it. 'No.'

Switching off the light, I pulled back the door and emptied the mug.

When I'd retrieved the map book and the torch from the cab, I let him know that I was ready for directions. He told me to find the E41 between Schaffhausen and Winterthur, and take the Zürich exit.

I traced the route with the LED beam.

If I turned right after fifteen Ks, before we got to Berg, then left, I'd find three construction sites. Stefan was being held at the one in the middle.

'So that's where your foot soldiers will be waiting to welcome me with pickaxes and shovels and power drills and fuck knows what else.'

He shook his head. 'It will be . . . deserted . . . until seven . . . tomorrow morning. Three . . . Portakabins. One . . . security guard. Gated . . . I have . . . a key.'

Every word was still half drowned in Fanta, and he was not about to forget what he'd just been through. But I'd believe it when I saw it.

I poured him another mugful of ether, dipped the cloth in it and, as he was starting to relax, took him back to square one. I smacked it over his nose and mouth, held it in place until he went limp again, and forced three-quarters of it into his oral cavity.

I wrapped a metre of gaffer tape around his mouth and neck and, after making sure that his nostrils could still function, I picked up the map book, climbed out and slid the door shut behind me.

The night air was cool and fresh and I breathed in a couple of massive lungfuls. I realized only now that the cocktail of ether, vomit and sugary cherry had been making my head pound. No wonder Hesco was out of it.

Back in the cab, I took out Hesco's SIG, flicked on the torch again and dismantled its working parts. I didn't think it would have been anything less than fully functional, but I didn't want to risk a dead man's click at any point during the next couple of hours.

Once I was satisfied, I clipped in one of the mags, fed a round into the breech, positioned it under my thigh, and put the spare mag and the suppressor in my pocket. The Sphinx stayed where it was. The law of increasing firepower says that two pistols will defeat one, and a rifle will defeat two pistols. And no matter what he claimed, I needed all the help I could get.

Easing the van back on to the logging trail, I stopped long enough at the edge of the forest to take one more look at the map, set my sights on the E41, and put my foot down.

18

To start with, I drove with both windows down. The noise was deafening, but the cold air rushing through the cab continued to clear my head. I still couldn't dredge up any more helpful stuff that Frank might have said to me in the green room before all this shit happened, but I now knew I was making some progress.

Dijani and Uran, and whoever else hadn't yet come into view, had infiltrated a number of Frank's companies. Why bother to build your own when someone else's were already fit for purpose?

Frank had unearthed something, and didn't like it. He didn't like it so much they'd needed to kill him and his son. And then kill me too, for being there.

Lyubova had been keen to help.

Mr Lover Man had been forced to.

This still didn't feel like a little local difficulty, though. GIGN and TIGRIS were the dog's bollocks. They didn't deploy for local difficulties.

I couldn't shake the image of the iceberg out of my mind.

I wasn't about to start believing every word the man in the back said, but three of his claims stuck with me.

You have more to fear than Putin . . .

You cannot escape the judgement of Allah . . .

Allah will welcome us to Paradise . . .

And Hesco was aiming to go through the second of the eight gates – for those who fought the Holy War.

That didn't mean these fuckers were directly linked to the jihadist shit that was going down, but it felt like part of the same pattern.

And he'd gone rigid when I mentioned Italy.

I listened to the steady beat of the tyres on the motorway sections for a while, then powered up the windows and cut away from the big picture. Getting Stefan back was what the rest of tonight was about.

I took the Zürich exit off the main, carried on for fifteen Ks, hung a right, then a left and slowed as I approached the second of the three construction sites. Unless every alternate new build in the area featured the Adler eagle on its advertising, I was on target.

There were three double-decker Portakabins inside the gate. So far, so good. Only one of them was showing any illumination.

The artist's impression on the hoarding promised a nine-storey apartment block next spring, complete with indoor pool, gym, twenty-four-hour concierge and young, good-looking residents relaxing between workouts on designer settees. And more to come the following summer.

As I drove past the Portakabins, I immediately spotted two bodies. Neither was Stefan. Hesco had said one, but why should I be pissed off about that? I was sure there were more lies heading my way.

There didn't seem to be much construction going on above ground level yet, but a tower crane stood ready at the centre of the plot to swing its prefabricated sections into place. Sixty metres up, a pattern of red lights lined the boom, warning aircraft to keep their distance.

I took a right a K further on, past the third site. Only one of every ten streetlamps seemed to be connected to the grid there. My side of the road was lined with red-and-white-striped traffic cones and linked metal barriers covered with perforated orange plastic. Behind them was a freshly dug ditch, piles of cables and pipes and all the other shit required to take power and water to wherever it's needed.

A parade of light industrial units with their own forecourts, all boarded up, ran along the opposite verge. I pulled over, parked in front of one and switched off the engine. We weren't overlooked by massed ranks of inquisitive locals there. The whole area seemed to have been evacuated and earmarked for development.

About a hundred ahead, the tarmac curved to the left. I tucked the SIG underneath my jacket, shouldered the day sack and walked round the bend. Three pallets of breezeblocks stood at the front of the eighth lot I came to. I hid the sack beside the one nearest the perimeter wall and covered it with three empty cement bags. If the van had been pinged, and was no longer a safe option, I wouldn't be totally fucked.

I screwed the suppressor on to the barrel of the SIG when I got back to it. After checking Hesco's ties, I opened the toolbox and took his keys out of his briefcase. Then I climbed aboard him, sliced through the tape around his chin and uncovered his mouth.

He groaned as I pulled out the cloth and replaced it with the weapon's suppressor. I jammed it down into his mouth until he gagged. Anyone in our business would know what that meant, no matter what state they were in.

'OK. So here's what we're going to do.'

I explained that I was about to cut him loose, one set of ties at a time. I'd start with his neck, then free his arms, then his wrists. He was still mummified from the nose up, but I could see that he liked this idea a lot.

I turned the knife so that the blade bit into the plastic rather than his flesh, and sliced through it. He gasped in air like a bellows and raised his head a few centimetres off the floor.

When he'd settled, I cut through the restraints around his right bicep.

As I prepared to do the same to the ones securing that wrist, I moved the SIG to within three centimetres of the crook of his left arm, and took first pressure. Even in his weakened state, I knew he probably wouldn't be able to stop himself trying to seize the initiative the first chance he got, whatever I said.

Up came the blade again.

And so did his hand.

Before it got halfway to where he thought the side of my head would be, I squeezed the trigger. There was a sound like a fist hitting a punch-bag and a neat hole appeared in the sleeve of his jacket. The exit wound was uglier.

Instead of clawing a big chunk out of me, Hesco gave a strangulated cry and tried to hold his shattered elbow together. Blood pooled on the plywood beneath it.

'OK. This is the choice: either you stop fucking about, and let me patch up that mess, or you carry on and I'll destroy your other elbow.'

His answer didn't take long. 'Patch . . . up.'

I pulled another five metres of cling-film off the roll, twisted it into a rope, looped one end around his right wrist, tied it off and bound it tightly enough to his neck to cramp his movement, but not so tightly that he couldn't breathe. It left his undamaged elbow sticking up in the air. I tapped it with the butt of his pistol to remind him what was going to happen if he suddenly changed his mind.

I cut the ties around his left bicep and started to wrap the thing in cling-film. All I needed was for him to stop leaking so he could take me to the boy.

He wasn't enjoying this process one bit. He was finally on receive, though. I got his best behaviour as I freed his left hand, untied his right and sat him up. I taped his wrists together behind his back. It would keep them where I wanted them. And would also mean that any attempt to free himself would rip the lid off another big can of pain. I kept the cling-film noose around his neck.

When we were ready to roll, I opened the rear door, sliced off the ties that still confined his ankles and tugged him out. He shuffled his arse towards me until his legs hung over the edge of the plywood and his feet touched the ground.

Keeping the SIG trained on him, I removed the noose and cut the rest of the tape away from his head. I might have been able to control him better if I'd left it in place, but it would be a nightmare directing his every step.

He sat there blinking for a couple of beats, took in the SIG, then his eyes bored into me. His chest heaved and he gobbed another mouthful of cherry-coloured phlegm in my direction. I didn't look down to see where it landed.

'You . . . cannot imagine . . . how much pain . . . you will be in.'

'You know what? You're the one without an elbow.'

I waved him up with my left hand.

'Now, the boy.'

The SIG stayed where it was, zeroed in on his centre mass. I pocketed the second roll of gaffer tape and a fistful of cable ties, pushed the door shut and pressed the fob.

The indicators blinked, making Hesco's uncertain steps seem even more uncertain. For a moment he reminded me of a *Thunderbirds* puppet. His knees didn't seem able to carry his body weight. I thought he was going to crumble. Then he got his act together. He wasn't totally stable, but he gradually managed to lengthen his stride.

On the way to the junction, I tried to put myself in his shoes. He probably assumed that I wouldn't take his word for the number of security people standing by, and that I'd be switched on. At the same time, he'd be hoping that I'd completely focus on getting Stefan back; that I'd believe he was there; that it was about to happen; that tunnel vision might leave me exposed. And maybe I did have tunnel vision – but what else could I do to get the little fucker back?

We turned left on to the road that led to where he had said the boy was located. The streetlamps were fully operational there, but widely spaced. I slipped the pistol under my jacket as I followed him closely enough to try to camouflage the fact that he was my prisoner, yet far enough away to stay out of range of a sudden reverse kick, however much I reckoned he wouldn't have the strength to deliver it.

The traffic was light and intermittent. Two or three wagons sped past in the oncoming lane; only one came from behind us. None of them slowed as they went by.

I kept an eye out for a way into the site that wouldn't channel us straight at the security detail. There was a pedestrian door set into the hoarding fifty metres short of the vehicle entrance, but none of the keys on Hesco's ring worked their magic. We moved on to the main gate.

The floodlit strip immediately inside it reminded me of the area you couldn't step into without getting hosed down in *The Great Escape*. I told him to keep his distance while I got busy with the padlock. The third key snapped it open, and by the time it did so, we had company.

A not-quite-matching pair of lads in blue uniforms and white hard hats emerged from the ground floor of the middle Portakabin. A night stick, a torch and a two-way hung from their belts. I couldn't see anything that might go bang. The older and more hard-bitten of the two balled his fist and yelled at us. I assumed it was Schweizerdeutsch for 'What the fuck are you doing here?'

I waved my left arm and gave them some reassuring Euro-waffle. They seemed to relax when the shouty one recognized Hesco, and got anxious again when they realized he had both hands fastened behind his back. But by then we were inside and I'd replaced the padlock and brought out the SIG and used it to help explain what I wanted us all to do next.

19

I shepherded the three of them into the Portakabin. It was starkly lit and furnished, cupboards and work tables bolted to the floor, and architectural blueprints spread out on every surface. No home comforts, apart from an electric kettle and a mini fridge, not even a flat-screen TV. And no Stefan.

I instructed Hesco to take the weight off his feet. As he perched his arse sideways on a straight-backed chair, I told the guards to remove their hard hats and put them down. The younger and more nervous of the two then raised his hand and tried to wipe the sweat off his forehead. His blond hair was dark with it, and plastered to his skin.

As three more sets of headlamps swept past the site entrance, I motioned to him to sort the venetian blinds. When he'd lowered and closed them all, I chucked him eight cable ties, miming what I wanted him to do.

Struggling to tear his gaze away from the SIG, he looped one tie through another like a figure of eight and used them to fasten Shouty's wrists together behind his back.

'Tighter.' I raised the pistol and aimed it at his head.

He didn't need me to translate.

He repeated the process on Shouty's ankles, then his own.

Finally, he did the figure-of-eight trick with his own wrists. I moved behind him and pulled each tail until it bit, then sat the lads back to back and wound the tape around their chests and necks and a nearby metal table leg. Hesco decided to stand up halfway through the process. One look was all it took to remind him that his right elbow was next on my list of targets, then both knees. He sat down again.

When I'd finished, I knelt to one side of the guards. I'd seen this set-up a million times. Shouty looked like he'd been around the block, but he was all piss and wind. He wasn't going to risk taking a round for what Adler paid him; he wasn't going to go out of his way to help me either. The younger one looked like he was doing shift work to put himself through college.

Those guys were solid. The threat was going to come from somewhere else.

I focused on the kid. 'You speak English?'

He hesitated, so I let him take another long hard look down the barrel of the weapon.

'Yes.'

'What about the boy?'

His Adam's apple rose and fell, but his expression told me he didn't know what the fuck I was talking about.

I gestured at the digital clock on the wall: 01:45. 'What time did you start your shift?'

'Since forty-five *minuten* . . .'

'Is there anyone else here?'

'No.' His Adam's apple bulged. He'd have been shit at the poker table.

'So you put the call out when we arrived.' I took first pressure on the trigger. 'How long will they be?'

His throat went so dry he just croaked. 'Twenty *minuten*. No, maybe fifteen.'

I got up and walked across to Hesco.

'So where the fuck is he?'

He opened his mouth, moistened his lips with his tongue, and said nothing.

I circled the chair and tapped the handle of the weapon on his shattered elbow. His torso went into spasm but he didn't give more than a gasp.

'Where?'

He turned his head. 'I will . . . show you.'

He stood again, waited for me to nod, and made for the door. I didn't believe a word this fucker said now, but I didn't have a choice.

He still wasn't too steady on his feet, but I wasn't taking anything for granted. I followed him outside.

'How many of your guys are with him?'

'None.' He flexed his neck muscles. I hoped it hurt like fuck. 'He cannot escape.'

He headed away from the ribbon of light that ran along the front of the site and into the darkness at the heart of it. As my night vision started to kick in, I could see that the construction here had progressed further than it had appeared from the other side of the gate. The one-storey skeletons surrounding the base of the central block acted like a prefab maze for Hesco to lead me through.

Every shadow began to look like his friend. And my enemy. Or maybe that was just the way he wanted it to seem. I stayed two strides behind him, scanning the area, holding the muzzle of the SIG rock steady halfway down his spinal column. All I could hear was the crunch of sand and builder shit beneath our boots.

As we passed the footings of the crane, the silhouette of another blacked-out Portakabin emerged from the jumble of structures and heaps of building material beyond it. When we were less than ten metres away from its door I ordered Hesco to stop and go right, into the cover of a wall.

He gave a slight tilt of the head and did as he'd been told.

The wall was double-skinned, and chest high. I made him stand with his back to it, then take a step away, leaving his shoulders pressed against the breezeblock. His pinioned arms hung in the gap behind him. The pain was etched on his face.

I positioned myself two metres to his left and bent my knees so that only my eyes were above the top course. I scanned from one end of the Portakabin to the other. Long enough to know he was talking shit.

He shuffled his feet back towards the base of the wall and managed to lean away from it. 'You can free my hands now, yes?'

'I'll free your hands when you free the boy. He's not in the cabin, is he?'

'No.'

'So where?'

'Close.'

I checked the Suunto and let him go ahead of me again. By the security guard's calculation, I had twelve minutes before his reinforcements arrived. Or maybe seven.

He steered left, away from the Portakabin, towards a huge hole in the ground. It was at least fifty metres by fifty, lined with pleated metal plates. As we got closer, I saw massed ranks of steel pillars rising out of the freshly poured concrete two levels below us. Judging by the size of them, these were the foundations of the tower block.

Hesco stopped a couple of steps short of the edge of the yawning space and glanced over my shoulder. It was only fleeting, no more than a twitch, but it told me the younger guard had been spot on. Still keeping my distance from him, I looked back in the direction of the main gate. I knew he was expecting reinforcements. Now he was hoping I might think I was already under threat.

As far as I could tell, there was no one there.

I turned and concentrated on the foundations instead. I quartered the entire area and saw nothing. No underground recess large enough to hide a child. Just moisture glistening on the pale grey surface of the concrete.

Hesco was shifting uneasily from one foot to the other.

For a split second I could see that he was torn between letting me know how much smarter he was than me, and carrying on with his charade. Then I caught sight of something beyond him, wedged behind the pleated tin at the corner of the pit. I walked over. Bent down. Lifted it out of the crack between earth and metal.

A paperback book.

I peered at the jacket. The artwork and the lettering took fucking ages to come into focus in the gloom, even though I'd been certain about what this was from the moment I'd spotted it.

The script was Cyrillic.

But I knew what it said.

Dostoevsky.

Crime and Punishment.

I took it across to Hesco.

He ignored me. He was now staring openly towards the gate. We could both hear a wagon travelling along the main, at speed.

He took a step forward and dropped his gaze to the base of the nearest steel pillar before finally giving me eye to eye. He was very pleased with himself indeed. 'I told you . . . he couldn't escape.'

I was the first to look away. I didn't want to see his triumphant expression for a nanosecond longer than I had to. And I didn't want him to have the satisfaction of knowing he'd got to me.

I tried not to picture the kid being dumped in there.

Watching the first load of liquid concrete spilling down the chute.

Realizing what was about to happen.

Had he tried to climb one of the pillars? Had he felt his grip loosening as the grey stuff sucked at the crocodiles on his trainers? Then his knees?

No. They'd have drugged him. Or killed him first.

I dropped the book, lifted the SIG and gave him two double taps. In the head, and into his chest as he went down.

20

I transferred the SIG to the front of my jeans and ran through my options as I melted back into the prefab maze. I couldn't go out the way we'd come in, and I certainly wasn't going to climb the crane. I had no idea whether there was an exit at the rear of the site, but I reckoned that was the only route I could take. And, fuck it, this wasn't Stalag Luft III.

I stopped by the Portakabin I'd recced earlier and remained absolutely still until I'd listened, ears pricked and mouth open, for signs of Hesco's cavalry. The shouting had stopped. Now they'd be moving into the development. If they spotted Hesco they might slow down to check him out, but I wasn't counting on it.

A couple of torches flicked on and pierced the night, and I caught a glimpse of a shiny bald head as they headed towards Stefan's grave and Hesco. A shiny bald head that belonged to a man who would kill me if he ever saw me again. I guessed he'd be even more enthusiastic about that idea when he spotted his mate's body.

A couple more beams sparked up on the far side of the pit. I didn't wait for them to join forces again and head my way. I ducked around the back of the cabin and, treading as lightly as possible, legged it in the opposite direction.

There was plenty of stuff to lose myself in there. Piles of external wall panels, stacks of piping in all shapes and sizes, pallets loaded with brick and stone, RSJs, lintels, pre-assembled balcony sections

– everything was arranged with Teutonic precision, and provided me with as much cover as I could use.

A squad of forklifts and cement mixers on wheels stood to attention along the rear fence. I transferred the weapon from the front of my jeans to the back and sprinted across to a track-mounted mini-digger, one of three parked at the corner of the site. I climbed on to the driver's seat and swung myself up on to its roof.

I heard a shout.

A suppressed round striking steel.

The whine of a ricochet.

I didn't look back.

I launched myself at the top of the hoarding, clambered over it and slid, feet first, toecaps scrabbling, down the other side.

I landed on a raised bank and drew down the SIG again as I scanned the ground in front of me. I was at the edge of some kind of orchard. Ten metres in I was surrounded by branches full of the world's biggest cherries, as geometrically organized as the contents of the construction site I'd just left. I didn't hang around to admire them. The torch beams and staccato exchanges just inside the hoarding told me loud and clear that I had to get the fuck out of there.

I sprinted a hundred and fifty further, keeping as close as possible to the trunks of the trees. The sky was increasingly overcast, but I didn't want to risk being silhouetted in the gap between the rows. Then I went down on my belt buckle, crawled swiftly left through the long grass until I was under the neighbouring canopy, and got back on my feet. I repeated the process at thirty-metre intervals until I arrived at the far end of the plot.

Beyond it stood a huge open-sided barn where they sorted the fruit before sending it to the Fanta factory. Hesco would have felt right at home there. I glanced over my shoulder as soon as I was in its shadow. The torch beams were still sweeping through the foliage and across the ground two hundred behind me.

I skirted the back of the building, ran through another neat yard and out on to the road. None of Claude's Swiss cousins suddenly appeared out of the darkness to hammer me with a fence post on the way.

I hung a right and a left, then did the same again. I didn't have all night for evasive action, but I needed to approach the van from a safe distance.

The parade of boarded-up industrial units came into view. I came level with the three-pallet forecourt and went in at a crouch. The cement bags between the breezeblocks and the wall hadn't been touched. I retrieved my day sack and, hugging the front wall of the unit, scanned the stretch of tarmac on either side of the Expert.

I was tempted to bin the thing and just stay on foot, but I needed to make distance double quick.

The road was deserted as far as the junction. That was no guarantee Hesco's crew wouldn't have a surprise in store, but if I waited there too long the torchbearers from the orchard would catch up and fuck me over anyway.

I got as close as I could to the front of the vehicle without showing myself in open ground, then crossed the pavement, keeping low. I paused beside the radiator grille to do a quick one-eighty behind me, then got behind the wheel. Keeping my speed down and using just gears to keep the brake-lights off, I didn't put the headlamps on until I'd turned four or five corners. Then I put my foot down.

I followed signs towards Zürich. It seemed as good a place as any to head for to sort my shit out and decide on my next move.

I looped back on to the *Autobahn* and drove towards it for forty minutes. I felt I should be thinking more clearly now – but my mind was whirring.

I flipped open the Pitbull case one-handed and fed the CD into the player. Maybe I could clear my head with some angry music. I pressed the eject button before I'd heard three chords.

This wasn't going to work.

All I could hear was Stefan yelling, 'Pitbull is the *man*! This shit is for *real*!'

All I could see was him pumping his fist.

All I could feel was that I'd been given the world's most important task – to look after a man's son – and I'd failed.

21

Fuck this. I needed to get a grip.

As fingers of light began to scrape across the sky I pulled into a service station and topped up the tank with diesel. I also bought a five-litre container and filled it with unleaded.

I threw two boxes of matches, an energy bar, a couple of cans of Monster and a two-litre bottle of water into my shopping basket, then ordered a strong black coffee, a bread roll and a sausage the size of a fire hose to go. I parked up between two artics and took a bite. It had absolutely no nutritional value, but who gives a fuck?

I necked half the water before switching on Hesco's HP.

The photograph of the Maserati kicked in as soon as I'd typed in the password, and was then overlaid by file and document icons, some with Russian labels, some with English. My first objective was to find out how many of them had been downloaded from Frank's laptop. Every time I looked at the thing I pictured him turning his screen towards me in the green room, and showing me something that came close to sending him into meltdown.

I double-clicked on each of the top row, then a random selection, and got nowhere. Every single one had its own access code. I don't know what I expected, but I probably should have guessed that nothing Hesco volunteered would ever come for free.

I tried his calendar, hoping it might give me a lead on Dijani's whereabouts over the next few days, but that was also locked.

Even the name of the second gate of Paradise failed to work its magic. I let my mind wander back to the Iraq prison and managed to remember the names of four or five others.

baabassalaat
baabassadaqah
baabalhajj
baabarrayyaan

None of them let me in.

There was another gate whose name I could never get my head around. But it was an eight-word sequence, and was reserved for those who hugged trees and were big on forgiveness, so that wasn't going to be one of his favourites.

I powered down again and slid the thing back into its sleeve. I needed a computer geek to sort it out for me, and I wasn't going to find one here.

I tried to gain access to Hesco's iPhone. The second gate didn't sort it. Nor did any of the others I could remember.

I slotted a SIM card and battery into one of the Nokias and texted Moscow instead. Pasha called back when I had the brew halfway to my lips. I put the cup down on the dash and thumbed the green button.

'OK. The first thing you need to know: the president had no love for Frank, but there's no evidence to suggest that Dijani and Uran work for the Kremlin.'

So Zac hadn't been talking bollocks about that, at least. If a solid Putin connection didn't surface in the next couple of days, I'd tell Pasha to give Anna the all-clear. Maybe she'd start liking me again when she and Nicholai were back in Moscow.

'Who *do* they work for?'

'Good question. You were right about Dijani. The Lebanese bit, anyway. Once-strong affiliations with the Saudi political elite. Educated in America. MIT. But no criminal connections, as far as we know. Until four months ago.'

'What happened four months ago?'

'He chose Uran as his security chief.'

'And Uran isn't a completely law-abiding citizen?'

'To put it mildly. Born in Lushnja. One of three brothers.'

I knew about Lushnja. It made Palermo look like Pleasantville. 'Albanian Mafia?'

'Albanian Mafia. Into everything. Prostitution. People-trafficking. Drug-trafficking. Brutal. Even Cosa Nostra are scared of them.'

'Zac was on his way to Naples. So that's where I'm going. Do you have people on the ground there?'

'No. But I have a good contact. He writes mostly for *Il Diavolo* – tough, investigative stuff – but does the occasional piece for us. Luca. Luca Cazale. We Skyped this morning. He's been on the trafficking story since the Balkan wars. It's out of control.'

'Sounds like Luca could use some good news. Tell him Zac is staying in Switzerland, after all.'

There was a silence at Pasha's end of the line.

'How long for?'

'For good. His jet-setting days are over.' I paused long enough for Pasha to take on board what I'd just said. 'Mate, could you keep digging for stuff about Frank's southern European business network? And about Dijani? He's the key to this thing. He keeps turning up in all the wrong places. I'd also like everything you can get me on the other Uran brothers. Including imagery. Zac seems to think I'm not on their Christmas-card list.'

'They're Muslims, my friend. They don't send Christmas cards.'

'It's a Brit expression. A joke. Kind of.'

'Ah.' He wasn't laughing.

Nor was I. There wasn't much to laugh about.

'Do me a favour, will you? Get hold of Luca. Tell him I'll be in touch, and soon.'

'So you can share your English jokes with him?'

'Something like that.'

I cut the call. Then I dialled the number Laffont had given me. I didn't care how early it was. Frank had paid him a fortune, and he'd reversed away from Stefan at warp speed. It was time for him to get the fuck out of bed and step up.

It rang eight times before his recorded voice invited me in three languages to leave a message.

I didn't.

I took the Nokia into the back of the van, cut the SIM into slivers that were small enough to swallow and smashed the rest of it to bits with my hammer.

The coffee and Monster had done nothing to fight the fatigue. I couldn't afford to mess up. I needed to get my head down. Even an hour would be better than nothing. I curled up in the far corner; the only bit that wasn't completely soaked with blood or Fanta.

'Nick . . .'

'Stefan?'

I heard my own voice echo in the load space.

'Maybe you could be my *actual* dad . . . Would that work for you?'

'Go to sleep, mate. I am.'

I wasn't, though. I was caught in a place where the dead walked and talked.

'Hard routine, Nick . . .'

'This shit is for real . . .'

Did he say that, or was it me?

Fuck . . .

My head was pounding like a jackhammer. My back was on fire.

I'd had the night sweats before. It was just part of the shit I had to live with.

But I'd never had a problem snatching twenty minutes of oblivion to recoup and regroup.

Wherever.

Whenever.

It made no difference.

Halfway up an Arctic ice wall.

At the edge of a *wadi*.

In the tropical rainforest, with humidity so severe you didn't know if you were breathing or drowning.

I'd done it with artillery fire overhead. With the wind chill blackening my cheeks and freezing my bollocks off.

So why not now?

Instead of tossing and turning and speaking aloud to the ghost of a half-Ukrainian seven-year-old.

Maybe it was the coffee and Monster cocktail.

It wasn't.

Thin grey light spilt through the partition window. I cranked myself up and rubbed my eyes, then slid open the door and went back to the driver's seat. My forehead was sticky with grease, sweat and Fanta.

I tried to swallow, but my throat was coated with sandpaper.

I scrabbled around for the water bottle, first on the seat and then in the foot well. I found it underneath my feet, crumpled but intact. I unscrewed the cap and took five or six mouthfuls, then splashed my hands and face. I pulled a small towel out of my day sack and dried myself.

Stefan's towel.

What the fuck did it matter? He wasn't going to need it again.

I took a long, slow breath, then another, and wiped more water over my face. My eyes stopped stinging.

I gave the final Monster a good shake, pulled back the ring a fraction and gunned it before it sprayed everywhere. I could almost feel the caffeine blasting its way into my bloodstream as I fired the van up and moved off. Troop drivers in Afghan were restricted to two cans of this stuff a day because it made them so hyper.

The boy might be dead but I wasn't. And I planned to keep it that way.

Nothing had changed.

Find out what's happening. Stop it. Kill it. Do whatever's necessary to get me out of this shit now I'm the only one left.

22

I steered around the northern edge of Zürich.

The Üetliberg – the eight-hundred-metre mountain on its western flank – seemed a good place to aim for. Densely wooded and crisscrossed with hiking trails, which turned into toboggan runs in the winter, it was easily accessible and had plenty of cover. And a small train station connected it directly to the centre of town.

A viewing tower and a bunch of platforms overlooked the city, catering for people admiring the spires and the bridges at its centre, and the lake beyond it. They wouldn't be looking the other way. So as long as I stayed clear of early-morning cyclists, sightseers and bearded tree-huggers in socks and open-toed sandals, I should be sorted.

I found a secluded spot at the far side of the hill, off the road, on the lower slopes, and replaced the SIG with the Sphinx in my waistband. Once I was certain that I didn't have any spectators, I dug Hesco's bags out of the toolbox and opened them over the Fanta-soaked wooden floor. The huge pool of crimson that had gathered around his head had also been sucked up by the plywood, but it wasn't yet dry.

I pulled Stefan's towel out of my day sack and added it to the pile, along with the Moleskine. I hadn't needed to scribble in it for a while now, and I'd never liked it as much as they claimed Hemingway did. The deeds to the chateau, the Adler invite, Hesco's passport and his Adler pass went on too.

I'd toyed with the idea of trying to use it to access the St Gallen HQ and have a look around, but now reckoned that the risk outweighed the potential reward. I glanced at the boarding pass for the Naples flight and wondered whether Dijani would be on the plane. Then I crumpled it into a ball and chucked it on as well.

I hesitated before binning Stefan's passports. Fuck knew why. He wasn't going anywhere, thanks to me.

Before I stepped out into the open again, I pulled the last two disposable cloths out of their bag. Then I removed the vehicle's fuel cap and rammed them down the spout, leaving a nice long tail.

I slit the front seats with my knife and soaked their stuffing and the cloth bung with unleaded, then emptied the jerry-can all over the contents of the load space.

Finally, I threw a lighted match through the cab window and the sliding door, ignited the cloth, and legged it. It was burning front and back as I disappeared into the trees. Mr Molotov would have been proud of me. The diesel wasn't going to explode when the flames reached into the tank, but the heat it generated would be intense. It would finish the job very nicely.

By the time I'd got halfway up the hill, black smoke was billowing up through the canopy. I hooked my thumbs through the straps of the day sack and carried on walking.

The sirens began to kick in as I crossed the crest and the cityscape spread out below me. I didn't bother with the train. There were only two an hour and I wasn't in the mood to hang around and be pinged.

As I stretched my legs on the downward path, I assembled the components of another Nokia and punched out Laffont's number. As before. Eight rings, then his recorded voice in three languages. Maybe he was being guarded about an unknown number.

I called him again half an hour later, before I hit the outskirts. With the same result.

So I called Adler HQ in St Gallen instead. The receptionist on the main switchboard picked up immediately. I asked if I could talk to Mr Dijani. I had no idea how I was going to play things if I got through, but it didn't come to that.

'I'm sorry, sir. Mr Dijani is currently away on business. He won't be returning until the middle of next week.' She had one of those voices that made whatever she said sound like I'd just won the lottery.

'Ah, he's already left, has he? I was hoping to catch him before we get together in Italy . . .'

'If you'd like to leave your name and number, sir, I'd be very happy to pass on your message.'

I believed her. The happiness was coming off her in waves.

'Don't worry. I'll ring him on his mobile.'

I thanked her and she thanked me, and she very much hoped I'd enjoy the rest of my day.

Obliging was obviously her default position. But I was glad I hadn't pushed too hard. I hadn't wanted my call to be memorable for the wrong reasons. She hadn't confirmed Dijani's whereabouts, but she'd done the next best thing when I mentioned Italy. She hadn't reacted at all.

I dismantled the phone and lobbed the bits into the first stretch of deep water I came to, the canal that ran past the main train station.

I didn't have to hunt around for a cyber café here. I headed straight along the river Limmat to the one in Uraniastrasse which boasted fine food and fast Internet. It was surrounded by the solid architecture that must have been all the rage in this part of town during the nineteenth century, but had gone for the vibe of an airport departure lounge. It must have been a cool place to be, though: a bunch of very shiny, raked Harley Davidsons were parked nearby, alongside an underground car park that looked like Hitler's bunker.

I bought a frothy coffee and the Swiss version of a sticky bun, then selected a monitor at the end of a row with my back to a wall the colour of Hesco's favourite brand of Fanta. I ate and sipped and played catch-up on the news channel.

There had been another jihadist gangfuck, not in Lyon this time, in Marseille. A nightclub. Hostages. The GIGN had sorted it, but with five civilian casualties.

An Italian security expert was being given some serious shit for warning anyone who would listen that Italy – the cradle of global Christianity – would be the next on the extremist hit list. It wasn't just the people-traffickers who had worked out that Sicily was only a hundred and seventy Ks north of Libya.

The French police had enlisted the support of Interpol in their search for the killer of Ukrainian billionaire Frank Timis and his missing son. A lad in a quilted jacket waffled into a big fat microphone outside the gates of Lyubova's smouldering chateau as the police and fire crews did urgent stuff behind him. He was doing his best to report the next chapter of the unfolding family drama with the seriousness it deserved, but his eyes shone with excitement. Stories like this didn't come by every day on the shores of Lake Konstanz.

As a body bag on a gurney was wheeled towards the back of a waiting ambulance, he told us that Mrs Timis had not been seen since before the fire. Was it a tragic accident? The suicide of a grief-stricken widow? Or was there a more sinister link to the murder on the mountain?

The report ended with a close-up of a black and grey circle with a very pissed-off tiger at its centre, the badge on the police combat gear. And one more question: did the presence of TIGRIS mean they suspected a terrorist involvement? No member of the elite SF team was available for comment.

The shot of Stefan aged about five with Mr Lover Man's disembodied hand on his shoulder filled the screen. It had gone viral, and already prompted 439 separate sightings, seventeen of which were in Bangkok.

The kid might be trying to elbow his way into my nightmares, but this made him seem a whole lot further away.

The bad news was that if the mum on the beach had time to catch this story between trips to the ice-cream van, she might put two and two together and make five. And since we'd been right up close, in daylight, the next e-fit had every chance of looking like me.

I ran through the flights to Naples from Zürich and Geneva, but decided it made no sense heading into Mafia country without checking what Laffont had found out about Nettuno first.

I clicked on the cross-box, finished my brew and stepped outside.

I assembled another Nokia as I walked down to the river. At this rate I was going to keep the Finnish economy on the rails singlehanded.

This time he answered.

We hadn't agreed an ID code, so I just said two words. 'Russia House.'

He didn't reply immediately, but I could hear his breathing.

Then: 'Peredelkino.'

'I need some information. The shipping line. Frank's Italian villa. In Brindisi.'

'I . . . need your help.' It must have cost the grey man a fuck of a lot to admit that. Which meant he was severely rattled. The smooth-talking arrogance he'd displayed at our meeting had gone. 'I've found something.'

'What?'

'One of the vessels . . .'

'Give me a name.'

'I need to see you.'

'From Libya?'

'No. From the east . . . From Odessa. I can't say more now. I need to see you.'

'Are you safe?'

'I am where we met.'

'With security?'

'Yes.'

'Then get Mrs Laffont to join you, and stay there.'

I told him to switch off his cell phone and take out the battery and SIM card until five o'clock this evening. I'd contact him after that with instructions.

I unzipped my day sack and took out the blueprint Frank had left for me in his Albertville safe-deposit box. It was about as useful to me as a corporate balance sheet – filled with a mass of detail that you needed a different kind of brain to understand.

When I'd first seen it, I'd thought he was drawing my attention to Nettuno and the trafficking. Now it sounded like something more focused. What the fuck had he said to me? What was so important about this boat? He never did anything without a very good reason.

The more closely I examined the maze of interlocking blue lines, the more it did my head in. Only one thing was now clear to me: the name of the container vessel was *Minerva*.

I wasn't the world's leading expert on Roman mythology, but I knew that she was the goddess of all sorts of shit.

Including war.

23

I went in search of a bike shop. I needed a new helmet. I found a full-face job that could have doubled as an Apollo re-entry shield.

When I got back to Hitler's bunker, the Harleys were still on parade outside, tipped over to the left. Some had their steering locks on, some didn't. Zürich had to be one of the top ten places on the planet where rich men could congregate to show off their toys. Outside the US, only retired accountants and dentists seem able to fork out for one of these machines. Once the mortgage is paid and the kids have left home, forget the fact you've only ever ridden a moped, let's get a Harley, why not? No wonder so many fifty-year-old European widows collected early on the life insurance.

I wasn't after the newest, shiniest model in the range, but the oldest. It didn't take long to find it. The Electra Glide had seen quite a few summers. Old guys favour them because both their seats are like armchairs. You can cruise for miles with your legs stretched out.

This one's saddles had seen a lot of arse wear in their time, and gave mine a warm welcome. The chrome work was the metallic version of distinguished grey. There was only one bit of it that mattered to me: the ignition switch on the tank, immediately above the petrol cap. Engraved on its personalized cover were the words *Live to Ride, Ride to Live*.

Strangely, the ignition key wasn't the ignition key on the older Harleys, which was why this one was my getaway vehicle of choice. All it did was free the ignition switch.

I pulled out my UZI and eased its tip beneath the lip of the cover, to engage the lug that locked it in position when you turned the key. I didn't care if I broke off the lug. I didn't even care if I broke off the switch. I could still fire it up by jamming the pen into the well and giving it a turn.

I found the lug, then pushed and shoved with both hands until it gave way. I turned on the ignition and hit the starter switch on the right side of the handgrip. 1700 ccs of throbbing manhood was immediately drowned out by the radio speakers on each side of the pillion behind me, banging out some classical violin.

I pulled in the clutch, kicked it into first, and headed for the open road.

I had almost reached Annecy by five. I took the exit off the main to the next rest area and stopped the Harley at the end of the row of parking spaces. There was a queue for the toilet, but that wasn't what I was there for.

I took off my shiny new helmet, put it down on a picnic table, and rang Laffont's number. It went straight to voicemail. I checked the Suunto: 17:03. Precision was supposed to be this lad's middle name, but maybe he was losing his grip. When I'd called him from Zürich, his voice had been vibrating with tension.

I gave him ten minutes before trying again. I didn't mind that. It gave me a chance to have another look at the map and run through the options for a meet. Two or three places to the north-west of Albertville seemed promising. Out-of-the-way places he could come to with his security people that had a variety of routes in and out. Places where I'd have time to arrive first and recce the RV point.

If he had a better suggestion, I'd listen. As long as it wasn't on his doorstep. I'd got away with that once, and once was enough.

When he failed to pick up at both my next two attempts, it looked like I no longer had a choice. After I'd passed the truck stop near Ugine where I'd pulled in with Stefan, I stopped and punched the redial button one more time. Immediate voicemail. Not good. It was more than an hour since he should have powered up his mobile.

I swung back on to the road and carried straight on until I reached the outskirts of Albertville. The early-evening sky was the kind of blue you only see on the holiday ads, which made the plume of smoke rising from the old town difficult to miss. And the two police wagons blocking the street fifty away from the entrance to the Banque Privée pretty much confirmed that my meeting with Laffont had been cancelled.

I turned back to the nearest parking spot and joined the crowd of rubberneckers outside the cordon. The buildings on either side of Laffont's HQ had been evacuated, and three fire crews were doing their best to stop the flames that were leaping out of every window from spreading.

Water jets played up and down the frontage, mostly turning to steam as they touched the superheated walls. A lad in full urban disaster kit was poised to jump off the top of his ladder as soon as he could get close enough. But, unless the fire started above ground level and the bank staff had found a way of sealing themselves into the basement vault, I doubted he'd be bringing anyone out.

I wasn't the only biker in the audience, so keeping my helmet on wasn't an issue. From behind the safety of the visor, I scanned the surrounding area for anyone I recognized, and anyone whose only reason for being there was to check on the results of the explosion they had triggered.

It took me a while, but I spotted one of each. The guy I'd pinged as the potential arsonist hadn't given himself away by his behaviour. I spotted him because I'd seen him before. Shiny head. Sharp lapels. Getting out of a Maserati outside the front of the hotel in Aix-les-Bains about half an hour before Mr Lover Man took his dive off the balcony. And then again at the Adler construction site last night.

He was in the mix on the far side of the blaze, where another couple of wagons were keeping onlookers at bay.

I was scanning the place for a route through to him when I saw Laffont's assistant about fifteen away, to my half-right. She wasn't as crisply tailored as she had been when she showed me to his office, but she wasn't smouldering at the edges either. She glanced towards me, but there was no hint of recognition on her face. That was partly down to the helmet, and partly because she was obviously completely shell-shocked.

I didn't approach her. I waited for her to decide that she'd seen enough, and extricated herself from the growing crowd. Then I peeled off too, and followed her at a discreet distance. It wasn't difficult. There were plenty of people weaving their way towards the place we'd just left. They only had eyes for the drama behind us. She was going against the flow, staring straight ahead.

She crossed the road, away from where I'd left the Harley, and took the next right. I had no idea where she might be aiming for, and I'm not sure she had either. She was doing a pretty good impression of an automaton. After a couple more turns she went into a café and sat down. I gave her some time to settle, and myself some time to make sure she hadn't been tailed, then followed her inside.

I removed my helmet as I went through the door, walked up to her table and sat down. She looked straight through me for a moment, then finally showed a spark of recognition.

Her lips moved, almost by remote control. 'He was waiting for you to call. Then he . . . I . . .'

Keeping eye-to-eye and my voice low, I leant forward. Tears gathered on her mascara, toppled off and rolled down her cheeks. 'He was definitely in there?'

She grabbed my arm and threatened to squeeze the life out of it. She nodded and tears jumped from her cheeks on to the tablecloth. 'He let me leave early. Stomach pains . . . I might have . . . I was only two minutes away when I heard the explosion . . .'

She removed her hand and reached for a paper napkin as the waitress appeared, so I ordered two frothy coffees and let her sort herself out a bit before speaking again.

'When I called him this morning, he was really worried. He'd found out something. Did he tell you what it was?'

Her eyebrows headed north. As if. 'Monsieur Laffont . . . He shared very little. But I know he was . . . investigating . . . Monsieur Timis's Italian shipping company.'

'A container vessel, maybe? *Minerva*?'

She nodded again, more slowly this time, but with increasing conviction. '*Minerva*.'

Another tear gathered and dropped.

'It wasn't an accident, was it, Monsieur?'

'No.' There was no point in bullshitting her. 'So tomorrow you need to go and talk to the police. And right now, you need to go somewhere safe . . .'

'My boyfriend?'

I told her to stay right there and call him. Get him to pick her up. And not to mention me to the police unless she really had to.

'Oh, one more thing. Do you know the address of Frank Timis's house near Brindisi?'

'Of course. I processed the paperwork.' She gave me the details. 'In fact, it is closer to a place called Ostuni . . .'

I didn't wait for the coffee to arrive. Maybe her boyfriend would get there in time to enjoy it.

I paid at the bar on my way out.

PART THREE

1

I ditched the weapons and the Laguiole knife before I got anywhere near the outskirts of Milan, dumped the Harley in the middle of town and swapped the helmet for my baseball cap.

I had bought a clean set of clothes in Albertville, from boxers outwards, so I didn't look like I'd been living on the streets for a month. I changed before catching a cab to Malpensa airport and arrived in the departures hall of Terminal 2 just before three in the morning. The first available flight to Naples wasn't until 09:40.

Since there wasn't a single chair in sight, I found a cubicle in the toilets. I hung my day sack on the back of the door, lowered my arse on to the plastic seat and unfolded the *Minerva* blueprint yet again. I spread it on my knees, hoping it would trigger any kind of memory of my briefing with Frank. Had he told me why the fuck it was so important? Had he let me know where it was going to dock and when?

I could picture him talking to me, and pointing at something. I could see his lips moving, but I hadn't a clue what he was saying. It was like watching a silent film, or having him under surveillance from across the street without any sound coming through my earpiece.

I decided to get my head down. With my shoulder wedged in the corner of the partition and a guy banging around with a mop outside, I'd had better nights. But I'd done nine hours on the bike since leaving Zürich, and I didn't fancy another nine.

I cranked myself up at 06:00. My eyeballs and tongue felt like sandpaper, and my back and neck ached. I banged some euros into a wall-mounted chew-ball dispenser and gave my teeth a clean, then filled a basin with cold water, splashed my face with it and felt halfway human again.

I couldn't see or feel any swelling on my head, so I peeled off the dressing and took a closer look. The wound still wasn't pretty, but it wasn't going to leak any more blood unless someone gave it another hammering. Until that happened, the baseball cap was all I needed.

As the departures hall swung into action I bought a plane ticket and found a copy of *Il Diavolo* on one of the newsstands. I flicked through it over a brew and four or five slices of pizza, followed by a marmalade *brioche*.

Luca Cazale had two major pieces in this edition. The first explored the Mafia's role in the people-trafficking business. Swarms of refugees – from Ukraine, Syria, North Africa and as far off as Indonesia and the Philippines – handed over everything they had to be lifted out of their own local gangfucks, and were then left pretty much to fend for themselves.

The Italian government had kicked off Operation Mare Nostrum – their attempt to rescue the victims from drowning in international waters – in late 2013, but had had to cut it back the following year. It had been costing them nine million euros a month. I could only guess what kind of cash the traffickers were making.

Luca's second article was on the Islamic State doing shit in Mosul and Syria. I'd kept a close watch on the Middle East since getting fucked over in Iraq during the First Gulf War, and this guy really delivered. His mugshot said he wasn't going to take any prisoners, and his journalism kept the promise.

I called his office from a payphone, mentioned Pasha's name, and fixed a meet.

2

Despite the cloud cover, Vesuvius, the volcano that fucked up Pompeii, dominated the skyline to the south-west as we came in to land. Nothing was spilling out of it right now, but it still looked angry.

There was only ten metres of tarmac between the bottom of the aircraft steps and the terminal, but it was enough to raise some sweat. The temperature must have been thirty plus, and the humidity was outrageous.

Inside, the Aeroporto di Napoli Capodichino couldn't seem to make up its mind whether it wanted to be a designer boutique and sushi franchise or a bus station. But, being Italian, it didn't give a shit. I liked that.

I helped myself to a fistful of leaflets at the hotel reservation desk in the arrivals hall and circled the twenty I thought Dijani would be most likely to stay in. They were all on or near the waterfront. I started calling them in alphabetical order from the nearest payphone. It was a long shot, but still worth a try.

The Continental was first on my list. It seemed suitably grand and had a commanding view of the castle and the western side of the bay. Whatever, the receptionist didn't recognize his name.

By the time I'd had the same response from the next fourteen on my list, I was flagging. Number sixteen was the Paradiso. Another negative. Maybe Dijani didn't feel the same way about the afterlife as Hesco had. The seventeenth was the Romeo. I tapped in the number and repeated my request. By now I sounded like a recorded message.

'I'm extremely sorry, sir. You've missed him. Mr Dijani *was* staying with us last night. He checked out earlier this morning.'

'You don't know where he went, do you?'

She was even more apologetic. 'I'm afraid we can't share that kind of information, sir . . .'

It wasn't the best I could hope for, but it wasn't the worst either. It told me I was on target. It also told me that the clock was ticking on whatever these fuckers had planned.

I took the shuttle to the car-hire area and was handed the keys to a white Seat Leon twenty minutes later. It had just two hundred Ks on the clock and was so factory fresh that some of the interior was still coated with plastic wrapping.

Keeping my Nick Savage passport and driving licence, and a bundle of euros in my jacket, I put the rest of my cash and Nick Browning's ID in a plastic bag under the spare tyre in the bottom of the boot, then replaced the lining. I got behind the wheel, opened Frank's map at the large-scale grid of Naples and aimed for the city centre.

I navigated my way to a two-storey underground car park in the Via Shelley where there was loads of neon and twenty-four-hour security, and none of the wagons looked like they'd been recently looted. I slid Hesco's laptop under the driver's seat, pocketed the binos, left the day sack in the boot and stuck a couple of hairs across the crack when I'd closed it.

Luca didn't want me to show up at the *Il Diavolo* office, and I wasn't about to argue with that. Given the kind of hard-nosed journalism they were known for, it was bound to be a target. He'd asked me to come to the back of a mate's mattress store on the Via Annunziata instead. Unless he was just short of sleep, it meant he was already on high alert. He'd fixed for us to meet at 19:30, which gave me about six and a half hours to kill.

My plan was to familiarize myself with the lie of the land around the RV, recce the Romeo, then head for the docks. I'd kick off by checking the unloading bays for Nettuno containers and try to bring myself up to speed with the latest rumours on the people-smuggling circuit.

I'd bounced around on the cobblestones on the drive in. Now I was on foot I realized they were everywhere, in all shapes and sizes. Either the town planners were in the quarry Mafia's pocket, or they believed you couldn't have too much of a good thing.

The merchants along the Via Annunziata seemed to feel the same way about budget bedding and kids' clothes and toys. Every single shop sold one or the other. And the magic was clearly working. The pavements were crammed with people. Wagons were double-parked up one side, leaving zero tolerance for the one-way traffic. I made a mental note to keep the Seat where it was. A quick getaway would be out of the question here.

One of the things I loved about the Italians was that they never changed their style for anybody. Apart from the massive yellow and grey façade of the local church, the whole street needed a power spray, and a pile of rotting rubbish had spilt across the pavement opposite, but nobody seemed to care.

Luca's mate's store was thirty beyond the overflowing wheeliebins on the right-hand side. I wandered past, looking in most of the windows, as you do when you're hoping to pick up a nice bargain to take home. A good few doorways and open-fronted workshops provided cover for both concealment and surveillance.

I didn't stay long. It made no sense drawing attention to myself. I headed to the Romeo via a choggy shop in the back-streets where I replenished my stock of previously enjoyed Nokias.

The hotel was a shiny glass-and-steel monster about eight blocks from where I'd left the Seat. It looked like it had made the journey from another planet and come in to land beside the hydrofoil pier. I could see why Dijani fancied it. It had great views across the harbour and the water, and was so stylish it made your bollocks ache.

Hoping that my jeans and jacket would be mistaken for shabby chic and my six-day growth for designer stubble, I strolled inside. I kept the baseball cap on. The wound on my head was still livid enough to put people off their lunch, and that made it an identifying feature.

I headed straight for the lift. I wasn't in the mood for see-thru table football or a visit to the screening room and the virtual golf driving range. As I was being propelled soundlessly to the restaurant and bar on the ninth floor, I heard Frank's voice again: *'Italian design, German hydraulics . . .'* His favourite combo. I just wished his elevator chat didn't keep drowning out the other stuff he must have told me. I knew he had a place near Brindisi. Had he mentioned Naples?

It was the maître d's pleasure to guide me to the corner table on the roof terrace. He showed no disappointment when I ordered a club sandwich and Diet Coke instead of Beluga caviar and Stolichnaya. He was too chilled for that. Or maybe he wasn't on commission and didn't give a shit.

I got some designer water and crusty bread down my neck as I waited for my order, and gave the binos some exercise. I could see a fair distance along the main, which fringed the port, but pointed them at Vesuvius first because that's what everyone else in the world must do. The cloud had lifted a fraction. The mixture of heat haze and pollution softened its outline and turned the buildings that surrounded its lower slopes to gold.

When I'd finished the token sightseeing I adjusted the focal length and zeroed in on each of the quays that lined the seafront. There was no shortage of Maersk and ZIM and Christian Salvesen container ships, and plenty of passenger liners closer to me. On my second sweep, I spotted a lone Nettuno cargo vessel in the distance.

My club sandwich and Coke arrived, and between mouthfuls, I scanned the fence that separated the main from the outer parts of the dock. There were any number of ways through it, where either the chain-link had surrendered to time and repeated attacks by the salt spray, or simply been ripped apart by whoever wanted to get in and out without troubling the security detail.

I left a pile of cash on the table when I'd finished most of the sandwich and all the Coke, including the ice and slice of lemon.

When I stopped on my way through the foyer to ask Reception if my old mate Adel was around, I got the same answer I'd been given on the phone.

I summoned up my biggest shit-eating grin. 'He told me he'd be here quite often over the summer. He'll be back any day now, right?'

The guy behind the desk was as warm and friendly as TripAdvisor could have wished for, but he wasn't about to give me access to the future plans of the Romeo's elite guest list either.

It was time for me to rejoin Planet Earth.

I crossed Via Cristoforo Colombo and turned left. It didn't take long to move from the Gucci end of town to where the real people hung out. A few were wrapped in minging old blankets, sleeping bags and sheets of cardboard up against the wire. A bunch of others sheltered in the lee of one of the storage depots. The woman running the flower stall close by didn't give them a second glance. She'd seen it all before.

I remembered having a chat with a lad in the 82nd Airborne who'd once been a Los Angeles street cop in South Central. He told me that crimes whose victims were hookers or crack addicts or hopheads – or simply below the breadline – were classified as NHI. No Humans Involved. These sad fuckers would come under that heading for sure.

I didn't expect any of them to have come in off the boats from Africa or Eastern Europe. The asylum seekers would either be locked up in an immigration facility, or legging it north as fast and invisibly as they possibly could. But maybe they could tell me if *Minerva* rang any bells, or if anything unusual had been happening around there.

I stopped by the second group of dossers I came to and asked if any of them spoke English. A few five-euro notes brought forward a young guy with zits, bad hair and a piercing who nodded a lot and said, '*Si, si, si . . .*' but his version of English turned out to be nowhere near the same as mine. Whatever had come out of the bottle he was clutching was probably to blame.

A few of his mates clustered around me, but only because they liked the look of the euros. They stank of piss and none of them had anything useful to say in any language.

I backed off and carried on past a row of warehouses and several stacks of empty containers, until I reached where the real security began – five-metre-high railings topped with razor wire, which separated nosy fuckers like me from the working parts.

I paralleled it as far as the boat I'd spotted from the Romeo, with 'NETTUNO' painted across its side. When I was near enough to be able to read the lettering on its arse end as well, I could see it wasn't *Minerva*. This one was *Juno*. But I decided to get as close as I could and try to grab a word with one of the crew.

Juno was moored beneath three cranes mounted on a giant mobile gantry. There was a lot of very energetic unloading going on. I couldn't believe how many containers you could fit on one of those things. So it took a while for me to grab anybody's attention. And even when I did, I was given the finger the first two times.

Ten minutes later another couple of guys came down the gangway. They were younger and bouncier than the ones who'd exited earlier. Judging by their banter, they seemed to be more in the mood for a chat. I gave them a wave and they wandered over to my stretch of railing.

'*Parliamo inglese?*' It was pretty much the only Italian I knew.

One of them shrugged his shoulders and looked embarrassed but the other nodded. 'Sure. Who doesn't?' His accent carried more than a hint of American. Maybe he'd spent some time with the US Navy, or watched a load of Hollywood movies.

'I'm on the lookout for a mate of mine who's working on one of your boats.'

'Ships.'

'What?'

'We call them ships.'

Fair one. I remembered telling Stefan we called bullets rounds. 'Whatever. Not *Juno. Minerva*.'

His eyes lit up. 'Lucky guy. She's, like, *awesome*. Not massive, like some of those Maersk monsters, but the newest ship in the fleet. Word is she's on her way back from the Bosphorus, along with *Diana* and *Vesta*.' He grinned. 'Kind of funny naming container vessels after Roman goddesses, don't you think? I mean, they're cool, but you wouldn't call them beautiful.'

'Will she park right here?' I indicated *Juno*'s slot.

He shook his head. 'Anything from the east goes east. Brindisi, I guess. Bari, maybe. Head Office would tell you.'

I was staying well away from there. For now, anyway. I needed to keep my powder dry.

I thanked him and turned to leave.

'It's "berth", by the way.' He couldn't resist correcting me again. 'She doesn't park, she berths.'

I went back through the first available hole in the chain-link fence and took a wide loop to the parking garage, running through the usual anti-surveillance drills en route. The hairs were still in place on the Seat so I picked up my day sack and headed for the RV with Luca.

3

I walked up the steps to the yellow church's entrance. They gave me a vantage-point diagonally opposite my target. I scanned the length of the street while appearing to concentrate hard on the laminated cards that introduced tourists to the history of the basilica and the paediatric hospital that were part of the complex. Back in the day there'd been an orphanage too.

I gave it ten minutes. No one seemed to be paying me too much attention, or bending over backwards to avoid looking at me at all.

A young couple was pointing at stuff in the window of Luca's mate's store and I joined them as they went inside. I spent some more time trying to decide which pillow to go for, then made my selection and took it to the till. As soon as the lad behind the counter heard my voice, he motioned me towards the back office.

I caught a stream of turbocharged Italian when I was still a couple of paces away from the door. The room was filled, floor to ceiling, with ledgers and fabric samples, some on wire hangers, some just piled on whichever work surface was nearest. A guy in his late thirties with tortoise-shell glasses on the top of his head sat facing me, waffling into a mobile.

Luca's dark hair was longer than it had been when his *Il Diavolo* mugshot was taken. It was almost shoulder-length. He wore a brown moleskin jacket, immaculate jeans and a crisp white shirt. His feet were up on the only desk, and a laptop open on his knees.

There was no air-con in here, and not much air, but he looked like he never broke sweat.

I had, big-time. I took off the baseball cap and wiped a small river of it off my forehead.

He waved me towards one of the two remaining chairs without pausing for breath. After a lot of *ciao*s and one or two *bello*s he pressed the red button, slid the laptop and the phone on to the table beside him and swung his feet to the floor.

'You must be Nico.'

He sprang up, gave me the world's warmest handshake and clapped me on the shoulder. Close up, his cheekbones and chin looked like they'd been carved out of granite, then polished, and his piercing blue eyes missed nothing. 'All clear?'

'Yup.' I nodded. 'I stopped by the church to make sure.'

'Ah, yes. The Santissima Annunziata. Did you see the infamous *ruota*?'

'The revolving basket in the wall? I just read about it. Is that shit for real?'

'Sure. Desperate mothers used to put their babies in it. The nuns plucked them out once they were inside, washed them, labelled them, baptized them. And saved their souls, of course.'

'Where I come from, they just dumped kids they didn't want in carrier bags or wheelie-bins and did a runner.'

He chuckled, not knowing that I was speaking from personal experience. 'They had to close it down when people started forcing their unwanted teenagers into the basket as well.'

There had been plenty of times when the woman I called Mum must have wanted to do that with me.

'But enough social history. Pasha . . .' He held out both hands, palms up. 'Pasha says the most *terrible* things about you.'

'Pasha is a *very* smart guy.'

'And Anna is your . . . partner?'

'You know her?'

'I worked with her in Libya. Brilliant journalist. Incredible woman.'

I wasn't expecting that. I probably should have done. The Middle East connection. Their world was a small one.

'And *che bella* . . .' His eyes sparkled. '*Very* beautiful, of course. You know, she always reminds me of the blonde one in Abba.'

'Me too.' I hesitated. 'We're not . . . together any more. Still mates, but . . . you know how it is . . .'

He nodded. 'I know how it is.'

He did, too. I could tell by the look in his eyes.

He cleared a pile of fabric samples off an electric hob and fixed us both an espresso. As he completed the ritual and handed me one in a small thick glass with a metal base and handle, we talked about the people-trafficking drama.

I took a sip of my coffee. 'I read your Mafia piece.'

'The Sicilians have been making a fortune out of this shit since the Third Balkan War. And the Georgians, and the Russians – from Moscow and St Petersburg. The Albanians, too. They are all over here.'

'Do they have a subscription to *Il Diavolo*? They must *love* you.'

He smiled ironically and chewed at the corner of his lower lip. 'It's true to say that I'm not very popular with some of these guys. And having seen Pasha's latest email, it seems that you're not either.' He rotated his laptop in my direction, lowered his glasses on to his nose, tapped the keyboard and brought up a series of photographs. None of them was posed. They all looked like they'd been snatched through car windows or from darkened doorways.

And they all featured two men, one of whom I recognized immediately. Shiny head. Sharply tailored suede jacket. Black skinny jeans. I hadn't been near enough to admire his snakeskin cowboy boots when I'd seen him getting out of Hesco's wagon at Aix-les-Bains. Or advancing towards me at the Adler construction site. Or rubbernecking outside what was left of Laffont's bank yesterday night. But I was now.

I glanced up from the screen. 'Do you have names?'

'Of course.' He pointed a finger at the bald guy. 'Meet Elvis Uran.' Then the other one. 'And his kid brother, Rexho.'

I took a closer look at Rexho. He was a hairier, bearded version of the fucker I'd dropped beside the concrete pit. Same eyes and nose. No stiletto scar, but a badly burned neck instead.

And they both shared Hesco's taste in rings.

'I was told they want to kill me.'

'Then I'm very glad that we are keeping in the shadows, Nico. These men are from Lushnja. And the Lushnja Mafia are the worst of the worst.'

I thought about what the Omani waiter had said about Mr Lover Man being a true believer. Hesco telling me that Allah had given the thumbs-up to drowning the refugees, and using jihad in his password. 'They're Muslims, right?'

Luca shrugged. 'Along with more than half their fellow countrymen. Why do you ask?'

'These arseholes may not be wandering around with detonators in their trainers, but they're starting to smell like Islamic State to me. And everywhere I've been lately, IS fans have been up to some kind of shit. It's going to happen here sooner or later.'

He wasn't about to disagree. 'They look at us, and what do they see? A lot of Cs. Italy is the cradle of Christianity, corruption and crime. Our Twitter feeds think it's all a joke: hostile militants will be beaten by our bureaucracy and our traffic. But you're right. They're already coming in with the migrants from North Africa and Syria. We're the perfect target. And so are you.'

'What else do you know about the Urans?'

'There is a third brother—'

'Not any more there isn't.'

'Ah. I'm beginning to understand why you are also not welcome in the home of this family. Pasha and I are examining them more closely. For now, all that I can tell you is that they are experts in trafficking – drugs and girls and children and people who have nowhere to go.' His eyes narrowed. 'And they are experts in vengeance.'

I gestured at the photographs. 'Have these two been seen here?'

'I have asked around – including my police contacts – and there have been no sightings in Naples. But someone looking very like Rexho has been spotted in Brindisi.'

'This place have Wi-Fi?'

He nodded.

I pressed the Google button on his laptop and scrolled down the Adler site until I reached the photographs of the depot opening. I zeroed in on the head of logistics and pressed the zoom button. 'Pasha is already on the case, but could you add this guy to the list of people we need to . . . examine? I think he's their boss. His name is Adel Dijani.'

'What do we know right now?'

'Not a lot. Lebanese. Educated in America. MIT. Strong affiliations with the Saudi political elite, but not with any extremist groups. As far as we can tell. On the other hand, he hired Zac Uran as his security chief.'

Luca knocked back his espresso. 'Better luck next time, eh?'

'I think he'll want to keep it in the family.'

Up went the glasses again. 'You make him sound like an Italian.'

'Mate, I need to know what's driving this fucker. If he smells clean, maybe there's another connection with the dark side. Through someone close to him, maybe.' I caught the look on Luca's face. 'Oh, fuck. You don't need me to tell you this shit . . .'

'Apology accepted.'

'He was at the Romeo last night. And I'm pretty sure he's also on his way east, if he's not there already.'

'So, where does this take us?'

It was time to give him the headlines.

I told him about Frank's killing. The stuff I'd found in his desk at the chalet. Laffont and the safe-deposit box. Adler and Nettuno. Mr Lover Man's high dive from the balcony. The fire at Lyubova's place. The explosion at the bank in Albertville . . . Finally, I heard myself mention Stefan's name.

'The boy who was abducted?'

I shook my head. 'The fuckers killed him, Luca. They drowned him in a sea of concrete.'

Luca showed the normal signs of revulsion that people have when a kid is killed but there wasn't any time for that.

'I thought there was a Putin connection at one point. That maybe this was all part of his plan to cut the oligarchs down to size. But I was wrong. Putin has sown the seed for a lot of this shit by fucking up Ukraine, and he won't be mourning Frank. But Dijani and the Urans never were his people. They need Frank's companies – but not for people- or drug-trafficking.

'As you say, the Mafia have been doing all that perfectly happily since the Balkans imploded in the nineties. They don't need any help from Nettuno. So Dijani and his team must have a different agenda. And if I sort that shit out, I can sort my own shit out along with it.'

I got the rest of the coffee down my neck and put the glass to one side. 'Mate, could one of your people locate a container boat for me? With auto ID software, maybe?' I took out the blueprint and draped it across the desk top. I'd fucked around with it so many times now that it was starting to go at the folds. 'It's on its way from Odessa, according to Frank's banker, and a Nettuno crewman says it's somewhere between the Bosphorus and Puglia. It's called *Minerva*.'

'Ah, Minerva . . . The virgin goddess of wisdom, medicine and poetry.' Luca grimaced. 'But her name conjures up a certain sadness in the southern Italian heart. You know about the Martyrs of Otranto?'

I shook my head.

'August the fourteenth 1480. Eight hundred and thirteen inhabitants of the city were slaughtered by the Ottoman invaders on the Hill of Minerva. Supposedly for refusing to convert to Islam.' He paused. 'What is the significance of this vessel?'

'I'm still working on that. Frank was really worried about it. Laffont was too—' I stopped in my tracks. Another piece of the jigsaw had fallen into place. Frank hadn't just left me the blueprint to find in the safe-deposit box. He'd also talked specifically about *Minerva* in the green room, the night before he was killed.

I pictured him rotating his laptop screen, the way Luca had done. And this time I saw what was on it.

Instead of grainy shots of Albanian mobsters, he'd shown me detailed multi-coloured specs of a variety of different vessels. Vivid blues, greens, reds and yellows, representing the configur-ation of containers in the load space.

I'd been amazed by how many of those lumps of metal you

could fit in the hold, and how many more you could put on the deck without tipping the whole thing over.

He said I'd missed the point. The vein above his temple had started to pulsate. I wasn't *looking* properly. He'd tapped the images of *Minerva*. *'Look again . . .'*

He hardly ever raised his voice. I could still feel his frustration now. But it wasn't a patch on mine. Once again, the harder I tried to remember what it was that he'd spotted, the further our exchange swam out of reach.

'Nico?'

I wrenched myself back into the present. Luca was wearing the kind of expression you save for people who have really lost the plot. 'Sorry. I won't bore you with the details, but I got a bang on the head when this whole thing kicked off a few days ago, and some stuff got buried. I think a bit of it has just shaken itself loose.'

I picked up my day sack and extracted Hesco's HP. 'There's something else I could really use your help with. I took this off the third of the Uran brothers. Maybe the answer's in it.'

Luca reached across and powered it up.

'I have the pass code: *baab al jihad*. Lower case. No gaps.'

His smile returned. 'The second of the eight gates to Jannah. If only it were always this easy to find your way into Paradise . . .'

'The problem is, it doesn't work for the individual files. I've already tried all the other gates I could remember, and hit a brick wall every time.'

He picked an icon at random and tried to open it.

'Have you got a tame geek who could crack them? Quite a few seem to have been downloaded from Frank's laptop. I think we should start with those.'

I watched his fingers dance across the keys and his frown deepen as he ran through five or six different strategies and none of them worked. Eventually he shut the thing down. 'If we can't do it at the office, there *is* a guy I know.'

I handed him Hesco's iPhone. 'Maybe he can have a crack at this too. I've tried the second gate. And a few of the others. Got me nowhere.'

As he put Hesco's gear in his shoulder bag, alongside his own, the door opened. The lad who'd been behind the till poked his head through and made the sort of noises you make when you want to fuck off home. They're the same in any language.

I checked the Suunto. We'd passed last light. 'How many ways out of here?'

'Two. Front and back. That's one of the reasons we're here. And the boy tells me he's padlocked the roller shutters at the front.'

I asked him when he thought he might have some answers about *Minerva* and Hesco's data.

'Perhaps tomorrow evening. More probably the day after. If the vessel isn't registered on the Automatic Identification System, it won't be easy. And the computer?' He sighed. 'We live in hope.'

'Fair one. But I need to go east. That's where it's heading. I can't just hang around at the Romeo's virtual driving range all day.'

In fact I couldn't hang around at it for thirty seconds. I'd never picked up a golf club in my life. Except when I'd nicked some kind of iron from a sports shop in Peckham when I was a kid. I only managed to fence it for 25p. I hadn't realized you needed the whole set.

He nodded. 'Ring me at the office. If I'm not there, your call will be forwarded.'

All the lights were now off in the store apart from the ones in the rear corridor. At the end of it I could see a door with a push bar to enable a swift exit if there was some kind of health and safety drama.

I gripped Luca before he opened it. 'What happens outside?'

He turned. 'An alleyway. Then the street.'

'Lit or unlit?'

'Unlit.'

'And how often have you used this place before?'

He shrugged. 'Three or four times, perhaps. But not regularly.'

So, we weren't as deep in what Luca called the shadows as he believed.

'OK, I'll go now, and turn left. If there's anyone out there, I'd rather they followed me than fucked you over and took the laptop.

You call a cab, and tell the driver to run you around for half an hour before taking you to wherever you need to go.'

I peeled off a note and handed it to the boy. 'Tell him it would be best for him to wait another twenty before leaving.'

The kid seemed well pleased.

I gave him a grin. 'Yup, you *should* be smiling. A euro per minute beats the shit out of the minimum wage where I come from.'

4

I didn't aim to go straight back to the car. Not because I was in the mood for sightseeing: I just needed to check whether Luca had been followed from his office. He was clearly well able to take care of himself, but maybe his anti-surveillance skills weren't as highly developed as mine.

As soon as I emerged from the mouth of the alley, two guys with shiny heads turned away from me and got very busy ordering pizza at the takeaway on the opposite side of the street. Too busy. I'd seen their faces clearly enough to be sure that neither was Elvis. Now I was about to find out whether they were run-of-the-mill Neapolitan muggers or something a bit more switched on.

By the time I'd moved half a K to the west, and travelled twice the distance in the process, I knew they weren't just out for a good time. No one orders pizza, then doesn't wait to collect it. Or turns three corners to walk back on themselves. Unless they're stupid Brit tourists holding their map upside down.

But was Luca their real target, or were they after me?

I was moving west, a few hundred north of the Romeo. The sea about a K to my left, the rest of the town sloping up to some kind of castle on the hill in front of me. I lengthened my stride so that I could increase my speed without breaking into a run. The gap between us stayed the same.

I slid my UZI out of my pocket, held it in my right hand and twisted out the nib. I thought about turning towards the docks and taking them down there, or going the Gucci route and holing up in the Romeo, but they'd already thought of that. One of my pursuers was waffling urgently into a mobile phone, and when I glanced left at the next junction, so was a guy on a moped, moving purposefully up the cross street towards me.

I tightened my grip on the UZI and kept aiming for the high ground.

Thirty ahead and to my half-right was a steep flight of stone steps, which looked like they curved up to a church. As I reached them, the clouds obliterated the moon. That suited me fine. I climbed them two at a time, mostly staying in the shadow of the high wall to my right. They seemed to go on for ever.

The moped's engine shrieked in protest as its rider throttled up and sped further along the street I'd just left. I heard footsteps below me. I gulped in a couple of lungfuls of warm, damp Neapolitan air and quickened my pace. It felt like a storm was coming.

I reached the stretch of level paving that led to the church door and thought about taking them on there, but only for a nano-second. I legged it past, aiming for the next set of steps. I could still hear movement below, and the odd curse. I hoped the fuckers were leaking. I was. I felt sweat prickle at the base of my spine and the back of my neck.

I was level with the tops of the fourth or fifth tier of buildings now, and could see streetlamps above me, and the occasional sweep of vehicle headlights. I was closing on the upper road.

The balustrade that bordered the steps was lower on this flight. I glanced swiftly over each side of it in case there was an opportunity for an early exit.

There wasn't.

Just a sheer drop.

Nothing to grab on to.

Nothing to break a fall.

I spotted a point a hundred or so to my left where one corner of the flat roof of a massive yellow block of flats edged close to the parapet. Close enough for me to jump.

I kept low as I approached the road. When I got to it I didn't bother to stop, listen and look. What was the point? I already knew I had two behind me, and at least one in front.

I bounded out on to the pavement and went immediately left, staying in the crouch, shoulder almost brushing the wall. It gave me good cover from the steps; less good from the streetlights. But why worry about what you can't change?

Three-quarters of the way to my target, the night was torn apart by the world's biggest lightning bolt, followed by a crash of thunder loud enough to drown the sound of the moped careering along the tarmac towards me. As soon as the rumble retreated, I heard it big-time. Fuck crouching. I went into Usain Bolt mode, fast and straight. If those lads were carrying, they were going to do more damage to the stonework at this range than they would to me.

Fifteen metres from the corner of the roof, the rain began. Not just a gentle shower, an Italian monsoon. Clear air one second, torrential the next. Moped man mounted the pavement five metres away and rode straight at me. I stood my ground, then jinked right and left and he lost it on the kerb. The engine whined as the tyres lost traction and the bike dropped with a clatter, trapping his left leg beneath it.

His mates appeared at the top of the steps as I took a pace towards him. The climb had slowed them down, but they weren't going to hang about long enough for me to give this lad a smack and ask him what the fuck they were up to.

They were ten away when I leapt on to the wall.

The distance to my landing zone was further than I'd anticipated. I hate it when that happens. I barely had time to steady myself before pressing the launch button, but I was in the air long enough to wonder what the fuck would happen if I landed on the wet tiles that edged it instead of the flat red asphalt-coated expanse I was aiming for.

I soon found out.

I buried the UZI into the roofing felt and hung on, but the tiles were slippery as shit, and seemed determined to take me down. My arse was hanging in space. I didn't even want to think about the distance between my flailing legs and the ground. It wasn't as big a drop as it had been when I was trying not to follow the Nissan off the edge of the mountain, but it was far enough to be a one-way trip.

The only solid thing I might be able to grab hold of was a galvanized-tin chimney cowl with four legs and a lid the shape of a pyramid. But it was a metre out of my reach.

The asphalt coating was like heavy-duty sandpaper. I scrabbled for a grip on it but all I got in return was a set of bleeding fingernails. Apart from the UZI, the only thing keeping me up there was the slight ridge beneath my elbows, where the tiles began, and the friction of my jacket sleeves.

The rain was part curse, part blessing. It was drowning me, but it was also drowning the noise I was making. And though it was making my life difficult from the waist down, the weight of my wet clothes helped to glue my arms and torso to the rooftop.

I balled my hands into fists, wedged my elbows more firmly against the far side of the ridge and levered the top half of my body upwards until I was able to raise my right knee high enough to give it some purchase too. Then I used it to push myself forwards until, at full stretch, I could close my left hand around the nearest leg of the cowl.

I wasn't dry, but I was almost home.

That was when one of the takeaway pizza team joined me.

He'd misjudged his jump too, but had me to hold on to.

He landed on my arse and right leg and I felt his chin dig into my lower back. He grabbed at my jacket to stop himself sliding back over the edge.

I tightened my grip on the cowl, but it wasn't designed for this kind of shit, and snapped off its mounting. Which meant that if I didn't do something fast, we were both fucked.

I managed to bring my right heel up quickly enough to hook it over the ridge as well as my knee. As my body rotated ninety degrees anticlockwise, I lifted my left elbow and drove it back as hard as I could into whatever bit of him was in its arc of fire.

I couldn't see a fucking thing, but I felt it connect with the side of his head, like a ball hammer on an eggshell.

He didn't make a sound. He didn't loosen his hold on my jacket either. He tightened it instead. I could feel him trying to wedge his hands beneath me, trying to grip my thighs in a bear hug.

I slid sideways and back and felt the weight of him and his swinging legs taking me down. I twisted my left shoulder upwards and my head on to the asphalt and managed to bury my fingers in his hair – so it was Mr Moped, not one of his shiny-headed mates – and clamped them strongly enough to be able to bang his face against the tiles.

Another bolt of lightning confirmed that I'd already smashed his cheekbone into the roof of his mouth and taken some of his eye socket with it. He didn't look happy.

I felt his grip slacken, so I did it again.

And again.

And one more time, for luck.

Then I realized that my hand in his hair was pretty much the only thing that was keeping him there. So I let go, pulled myself up with the UZI and rolled the rest of me into a secure position half a metre from the point he'd just disappeared. I didn't hear him bounce off anything on the way down. Just the noise of a big sack of shit hitting some very wet ground.

I hauled myself up, dug out the UZI and stayed in the crouch for a moment, listening for any other sign of imminent threat above the driving rain, and looking back at the parapet I'd leapt from. One set of head and shoulders was silhouetted against the street-lamps. The other – along with arms, legs and body – was poised on the top of the wall.

As more lightning split the sky, I saw him measure the gap, then look down and not like what he saw.

I needed to build on that.

They both had blades, but neither was showing anything that might go bang. So I got to my feet and made it clear that I was armed and ready.

A stream of oncoming headlights appeared from further up the road, and seemed to convince the boys that they were on the wrong end of the risk-and-reward spectrum. They pocketed the blades. Going back to pick up those pizzas was suddenly a much safer option.

The one on the wall dropped on to the pavement and his mate picked up the moped and off they went.

I turned and scanned my immediate surroundings. Apart from three other cowls there was a matching skylight, which probably crowned a stairwell. I didn't bother looking. I could tell from there that it was fixed. It wouldn't give me access unless I dived through the glass.

To my immediate left was another L-shaped roof, five metres lower than mine, surrounded by a waist-high wall and three horizontal rails, which suggested that the residents came up there on a fairly regular basis, and therefore that the structure like a garden shed at the apex might provide the route in and out.

I got down on my very wet belt buckle and went over the edge feet first, slowing my descent as much as possible with toecaps and sleeves and fingers and my fistful of UZI until I had to let go. I landed more or less upright and legged it round the corner.

The shed wasn't a way in. It was half glazed and filled with deckchairs; somewhere for people to sit and enjoy the view, or shelter from the rain. But behind it there was an access point with a sloping roof. And a door that had been very firmly locked and bolted, top and bottom, from the inside.

A sixth sense made me glance back through the rain-lashed windows towards the road. Now that I was five metres below my original landing zone, I no longer had a clear line of sight to the stretch of wall I'd jumped from. But I could tell that the headlamps the other side of it were stationary. And the lights on top of the two wagons now standing there were flashing, and blue.

Which explained why the remaining two-thirds of the takeaway team had fucked off, instead of waiting to see what I was going to do next.

A pair of mega-powerful torch beams sparked up and bounced across the level above me. Then they shifted ten metres to the right and began to quarter the one I was on.

5

A white stink vent stood proud of the rail at the far corner of the building. Keeping the access point between me and the torch beams, I moved towards it and looked down.

The rigid plastic pipe ran vertically down the side of the four-storey building, disappearing into the wall beside each of three unlit balconies on the way. I gave the top of it an experimental shove, which was enough to show me that the metal retaining brackets wouldn't guarantee me a safe trip to the ground.

But it would be strongly bedded at every joint and, fuck it, I didn't have a choice.

I couldn't go back.

I couldn't take the stairs.

I pocketed the UZI and slid between the top and middle rails. Closing my fingers around the bottom one, I lowered myself as far down the wall as I could. Paused for a moment to slow my breathing and blink the rainwater out of my eyes. Grabbed the pipe with my left hand and wedged the toe of my left boot between it and the wall, just above the fixing.

The pipe immediately bowed outwards, but the bracket held steady enough for me to complete the journey to the uppermost balcony. One glance through the window confirmed that nobody was home, so as soon as my feet were on firm stone I stepped back into the arched recess. It didn't give me much shelter from the storm, but it allowed me to stay out of sight of anyone who might be above me, looking down, or below me, looking up.

Still facing the glass, my back to the handrail, I tilted my head up and, with infinite slowness, leant outwards from the waist until I could scan the length of the parapet, from the stink pipe to the opposite corner of the block.

I thought I saw movement up there, and ducked back under cover.

But when I looked again, I realized it was simply my vision being blurred by the falling water.

I repeated the process, one hand gripping the outer strut of the balcony rail, the other the pipe, toes scrabbling for purchase on the masonry, and managed to reach the next balcony down without separating myself or the pipe from the wall.

A light sprang on as soon as I stepped on to the handrail of balcony number three. I didn't wait to see who had just come into the room, or how many. One call to the *carabinieri* was all it would take to really fuck up my night.

For the second time in the last hour I had to make a move without being able to check in advance where I was going. I renewed my grip on the pipe with my left hand, placed the tip of my left boot against the rendering on the far side of it, slid my right hand behind it, and walked two paces further down the wall.

I would have been fully visible to anyone stepping out on to the platform I'd just vacated but, again, the virgin goddess of weather stopped that happening.

Two more paces.

Then two more.

Although the fixings weren't firm there either, the lack of leverage between the joints worked in my favour, and I was able to drop the last couple of metres to the gravel forecourt.

Much as I liked the idea of the takeaway team consoling themselves over their pizzas, I figured they'd be working their way round to intercept me on the downward path, or possibly to come and pick up what was left of their mate.

The moped was strictly a solo machine, so I reckoned I'd got there a fuck of a lot quicker than they'd be able to. But that didn't mean I could piss about. I dodged and wove my way through the warren of passageways and cul-de-sacs that linked the blocks to the main, passing a surprising number of people who didn't seem to want to kill me, and were also sorry they'd forgotten to bring an umbrella.

I twisted as much water as I could out of my jacket and hung it on the passenger seat of the hire car before feeding the ticket machine at the parking garage a day's worth of euros.

I slotted a SIM card and a battery into my last Nokia as soon as I'd gone through the barrier and punched in Luca's office number as I drove.

'*Pronto . . .*'

'I was pinged coming out of the alley.'

'Pinged?'

'Spotted. Then followed. Fuck knows who they were. Two youngish bald guys, and a hairier one with a moped. Ring any bells?'

He gave it some thought. 'I've seen a couple of bald guys in the street outside the office . . . yes . . . and the moped. I thought they were just stealing handbags.'

'I think there's more to it than that. Mafia, probably. Your mate's mattress shop is obviously a known location. So don't go there again. Unless you want your kids in the orphans' basket.'

'I don't have any kids.'

'The same goes for your sister's kids.'

'I get the message.'

'You OK, mate?'

'Sure. But thanks for the warning.'

'I'll call you.'

I pressed the red button and threw the phone out of the window as soon as I hit the flyover out of town. All the arrows pointed to Brindisi, and not just the ones on the *autostrada*. Rexho Uran had been spotted there. Hesco had gone very still when I mentioned Italy.

Frank was killed on the road to Turin.

His boy had been wearing Città di Brindisi football strip.

They'd been to their villa three times this year.

A bad business, Nick . . . A bad business . . .

Minerva was on its way there from Odessa, via Istanbul.

And I was now almost certain that wherever *Minerva* was, Dijani and the Uran brothers would be too.

If a stripy pole and a downhill rollercoaster hadn't rattled my brain, maybe I'd have made this journey earlier. But I was where I was, and still alive. That was all that mattered.

If I put my foot down, I reckoned I could be at the port before first light.

6

The rain started to ease when I was halfway to Bari. By the time I veered south, with the dark waters of the Adriatic on my left, it had stopped. I opened all the windows. The wind noise was outrageous, but it would blast some of the dampness out of my kit. I'd tried turning up the heater when I left Naples, but all it did was fog the windscreen and fill the Seat with steam.

I passed the sign to Brindisi airport, then another to the football stadium, and focused hard on following directions to the port, partly because that was where I needed to go, and partly so I could ignore the kid in the blue and white Città di Brindisi strip who was suddenly sitting beside me.

But Stefan couldn't be ignored. I should have learnt that fucking ages ago.

'Nick . . .'

I tried to lose myself in the noise of the wagon's tyres against the untreated scars in the road surface. Once you left the toll road, the tarmac went to rat-shit around here. Maybe the Ferrari owners stuck to the *autostrada*, or the west-coast Riviera.

It didn't work.

'Nick . . .'

I wanted to tell him to fuck off, but I couldn't quite bring myself to do that. I didn't know why. Normally I had no problem letting people know when I'd had enough of them. Even ghosts.

'I like it very much in Italy, Nick. My dad is . . . was . . . always happy in Italy. Except the last trip . . .'

'Mate, I'm pretty sure I'm about to find out why. It's a bit late for you, but I need to get myself out of this shit and find the fuckers who killed you and your dad at the same time. Not all bad, eh?'

That was my voice. Inside my head.

Or not.

Maybe I said it out loud. Who cared?

He seemed to like what he heard, though. He turned and gave me a slow smile. *'Know your enemy, Nick. Know your enemy . . .'*

And then he disappeared.

But his words still hung in the air.

Know your enemy . . .

He wasn't wrong. Sun Tzu hadn't been either. And I found myself thinking that if Frank had taken his own advice we wouldn't have been in this shit in the first place.

7

I hit the town centre and carried on going, bearing left wherever I could, and took the first exit off a roundabout, which pointed me towards something that called itself the Sant' Apollinare quay.

I passed what had once been a public park but had morphed into a migrant camp. Families in rags stood round the kind of pop-up tents you see at Glastonbury, or makeshift structures cobbled together from wood, wriggly tin and blue plastic tarpaulins. The human nightmare was shrouded in a haze of woodsmoke as they tried to cook whatever the charities had given them. And these were the lucky ones. The only ones laughing were some of the kids in the swing and slide enclosure.

The only light source on the road down to the quay's entrance was the massive sign to its left, which announced that this was the place to be if you wanted a ferry to or from Greece.

I parked fifty metres short of it and walked up to the gate. Another sign on each pillar told me there was a strong chance my wagon might end up in the water if I wasn't paying attention. And that wasn't the only reason to fuck off out of there. Yet more signs warned me that the complex was crawling with police and Customs officials, and that I was approaching SECURITY LEVEL 1.

Before I had a second to wonder what that meant, a guard with a big nightstick and an even bigger gut emerged from his hut and stationed himself on the other side of it. I had my answer. There was only one of him.

He gave me the once-over with his torch, and it didn't feel like the warmest of welcomes. I didn't have a problem with that. The quay was deserted, and the pictogram above my head made it pretty clear that, even when it wasn't, it catered for cars and pedestrians only. I raised my hand to let him know that I'd come to the wrong place, and wasn't going to climb over the fence and shake up his pasta dinner.

The next exit off the roundabout looked more promising: Turkey, Greece and Albania. And the road was lined with containers, stacked two and three high. The lighting was more generous here, but there were still plenty of nice, comfortable shadows to get lost in.

A big brown panel welcomed me in five languages, but everything else in the main access zone to this part of the docks yelled, *'Fuck off!'* Men in uniform carried pistols on the hip, automatic number-plate recognition cameras clocked every vehicle on entry, and if you drove your wagon off the quay, the water was even deeper than it had been at SECURITY LEVEL 1.

I kept my distance and swung the wheel towards the terminal building instead. It promised coffee and a restaurant for anyone going to Greece or Albania. I guessed that the Turks had to bring their own.

A couple of lads in an MPV pulled up in front of a row of artics and container-lorries, opened their boot and started to hang out a display of blue and white football gear for sale. It wasn't yet 04:30. They were obviously keen to make the most of the early trade. A white Fiat stopped alongside them. The blue stripe across its door panels said SECURPOL PUGLIA and the lettering on its windscreen – ISTITUTO DI VIGILANZA – reinforced the message. But these guys were obviously old mates who shared a bit of banter every morning.

I cruised the length of the parking area, scanning my surroundings for another route into the docks. A covered conveyor, mounted on pylons, dominated the skyline in front of me. It took grain or gravel or cement or whatever to the quay from a storage facility across the dual carriageway that bordered the complex. Some of the pylons had rungs from top to bottom, to allow maintenance engineers access to the working parts. If all else failed I'd climb one and get inside that way.

I turned on to the dual carriageway. The conveyor ran alongside me for a couple of hundred, on a gradual downward slope, then took a sharp left to the loading bays.

From what I could see in the wash of my headlamps the chain-link security fence beneath it was a whole lot more secure than the one I'd wandered through in Naples. It was reinforced every so often with prefab concrete panels, and there wasn't a hole or a tear in sight. But after another two hundred it seemed to come to an abrupt halt by some kind of currency-exchange kiosk, which wasn't as eager for business as the lads in the MPV.

I parked up further along the road and grabbed my binos. After I'd checked in front and behind for approaching vehicles, I put on my jacket. It was wet and cold and heavier than I needed it to be, but the less skin I had on display, the better. I chucked the day sack in the boot, locked the wagon and crossed the central barrier.

The turning beside the kiosk was a dead end, and I wasn't wrong about the fence. It stopped at the top of a bank, covered with bushes and scrub, which ran steeply down to a train line. The track emerged from a tunnel to my right and paralleled the road to my left. A spur curving towards the dockside was still under construction.

The open ground between it and the water was only illuminated by the ambient glow from the main cargo quays to my half-right, the world's biggest gantry to my half-left, and the lamps running along the top of the conveyor that divided this side of the port from the heavily manned access point.

The railway was sporadically lit as well, but once I'd crossed it there would be plenty of cover. Earth from the freshly dug cutting had been piled up on the far side of the conveyor. A pair of king-size mobile hoppers towered above stacks of sleepers and lengths of track waiting to be laid.

There were endless stretches of that orange plastic netting too; the stuff that's meant to warn you about a big hole in the ground, then does fuck-all to stop you falling into it.

I always felt safer when I'd had the opportunity to do a close target recce, but I was here now, the sky had already turned a couple of shades paler than it had been when I got there, and if *Minerva* had arrived at its parking space, it wouldn't just sit and wait for me to come aboard.

Fuck berthing: I liked parking.

8

The soles of my Timberlands were clogged with soil as soon as I'd taken a couple of steps down the slope, and I slithered most of the rest of the way, grabbing the odd branch to steady myself. My plan was to start looking at the far end of the port, and work back through the forest of cranes and gantries until I was as close as possible to the sector patrolled by the police and the Vigilanza.

Union regs or punishing overtime rates meant that the place wasn't exactly crowded. I spotted a bit of movement on the decks of three or four of the boats, and not much on the machinery above them.

There was no sign of *Minerva* on the quays closest to the harbour mouth. *Diana* was safely parked on the fourth one I came to, pointy end out towards the water. When I got nearer, I could see *Vesta* immediately in front of it. They were both piled high with cargo. Two containers had been lifted straight on to flatbed artics. A third was in the process of being lowered into position.

I couldn't stand by the gangplank this time round, waving at random crew members and pretending I was there to meet a mate before first light. I stayed out of sight, in the shadow of a gantry.

As the leading artic pulled away from me towards the port entrance, the darkness beyond the overhead conveyor was suddenly ripped apart by blue flashing lights and sirens. The truck driver put his foot down. I didn't hang about either. I legged it away from the metalwork, aiming to keep the moving container between me and the approaching *carabinieri* as I crossed the open ground.

When I was still thirty away from the railway line, the driver spun his wheel into opposite lock. The cab veered back towards me, headlamps blazing. I kept on running. I didn't have a choice. And I already had a feeling that the driver was about to lose control.

The forward momentum of his load and the tightness of his turn forced all three sets of left-hand tyres at the back end of the trailer off the road surface. The front end started to lift as well. He tried to correct, brakes shrieking, but it wasn't going to happen. The vehicle whipped across the tarmac, like a cut snake. Then it began to roll on to its side.

There was a thunderous crash and the scream of tortured metal. A shower of sparks five metres high and twenty long. Now the fucking thing was coming at me, wheels spinning, looking to churn me up. And the main beams were showing me my escape route.

I swerved left, away from it. Legged it past a stack of sleepers and across the railway track. I was a couple of metres up the bank and zigzagging through the bushes when the blue flashing lights reached the crippled artic. I didn't stop to watch. I wanted to make maximum use of the diversion, and of the denser foliage ahead of me. I could work my way behind it and slip out at the end of the fence, as long as there wasn't another police detachment aiming to pen me in from the road.

I turned and scanned the disaster area as soon as I was in cover.

The wagons were Iveco VM 90s. And the lads in blue were GIS. The Gruppo di Intervento Speciale were close mates with the Regiment, and they didn't fuck about. They weren't there to hand out speeding tickets.

They hadn't seen me.

And it soon became obvious that seeing me wasn't why they were there.

Four of them, in goggles and helmets, leapt out of the lead vehicle as it crunched to a halt. Two stood back, weapons in the aim. Two piled in to try to crank open the doors of the container. Fuck knew what they thought was in there.

The other five VMs hurtled straight past, then peeled off in sequence towards the place I'd just been. They stopped ten short of the arse end of *Diana,* boxing in whoever might have been thinking of doing a runner from the two RIBs I could now see bouncing in from the sea.

More lads in goggles and helmets debussed, weapons at the ready, and converged on the artics that hadn't yet left the quay. Both drivers climbed down and made it clear that they weren't looking for trouble. The third container was still hanging from its crane. The doors of the second, sitting on the flatbed, were thrown open.

They were facing away from me, so it was a while before I saw what was inside. First out were a whole lot of packing cases. The GIS lined up and passed them down the chain. When the guys at the end of it had built a fair-sized stack, I heard a shout.

Up came the weapons again. Ten minutes later, about twenty hunched figures had spilt out and were clustered beside them, wondering what the fuck had just happened, and who had betrayed them. These lads weren't going to be staying in the park.

I glanced back at the artic on its side. The driver had managed to kick his way out through the smashed windscreen and was being told to lie flat on the ground in front of it, hands behind his neck. The uniforms at the back were still trying to lever open the container. There was a lot of shouting and waving of hands and weapons, and then a fucking great bang did the job for them.

Whatever had triggered it, the back and the side blew out and its contents sprayed across the hard standing like shrapnel. I couldn't see how many of the GIS team survived the blast, and I wasn't going to stick around and count.

The road was still clear as I made my way back to the Seat, but by the time I turned the key in the ignition, three vehicles had stopped beside the fence to enjoy the drama. I pulled away, heading south. I needed to put some distance between myself and the action on the quay.

I also wanted to check out the coastline for somewhere a container boat might park up without too much fuss. Because the more I thought about the shit that had just happened behind me, the more it felt like a diversion.

If something doesn't feel right, it normally isn't.

I put myself in my enemy's shoes.

They were planning to bring something in under the radar.

They couldn't afford to be compromised.

Palermo and Naples were People-trafficking Central, so the main terminals in the south-west quadrant were bound to be the first port of call for anyone on their trail.

Brindisi was quieter, but still dealt in huge-volume cargo. It was less than two days by sea from Istanbul, and only 130 Ks from Albania. Anyone within reach of a Google button knew that.

So what would I have done in Dijani's position?

I pressed the replay button for the screen inside my head, and watched the first artic doing its thing all over again.

The driver might have been a loose cannon, or a lad with a very guilty conscience, but he hadn't needed to take off like a rocket, snaking right, then left. He must have known he'd roll it.

And then the explosion.

No ruptured fuel tank, ignited by a rogue spark. A perfectly choreographed performance, guaranteed to create maximum impact.

Hesco had pretty much confirmed that they'd been feeding int about me and Stefan to the GIGN and TIGRIS, to take the heat off them and make my life more difficult. So supplying the GIS with a rumour of a load of illegals hitting town at dark o'clock fitted the pattern.

Parking two boats somewhere visible, each with a big manifest, then putting on a bit of a show for them, ending with a fireworks display, would guarantee their attention.

You didn't do that just for the fun of it. You did it so the emergency services would have their hands full for the next twenty-four hours – and boat number three could slip in somewhere quiet and unnoticed, and do whatever it needed to do.

And you couldn't time a detonation with such precision without eyes on the target.

So I hadn't been the only infiltrator.

Some other fucker had been there, binos raised, thumb on the detonator button. Rexho Uran had been sighted in Brindisi. Now I knew why.

9

I turned off the main as soon as I could and joined the coast road in the direction of Otranto. I found myself a coffee and drank it in the wagon as I did the usual with the first Nokia out of the day sack.

While I waited for Luca to pick up, I ran a finger down the map. There seemed to be three or four locations with either inlets or harbours, but since I was working on 1:200,000 scale I wouldn't know for sure until I had eyes on every nip and tuck.

'Pronto . . .'

One word was enough to tell me I wasn't the only fucker who'd been up all night. He sounded like shit.

I filled him in on the Brindisi experience. 'You mentioned your police contacts. The GIS were there in force, minutes after *Vesta* and *Diana* began to unload. No way was it just a lucky break. Someone wanted an audience. It smells to me like a tip-off. Could you do some digging?'

'Sure.'

He hadn't yet had any luck tracking *Minerva*. Maritime law demanded that the Automatic Identification System had to be fitted to every vessel in international waters that weighed in at a gross tonnage of three hundred or more. If the AIS was switched on, pretty much anyone with access to the Internet could pinpoint its location in real time. If it wasn't, the tracking process became a lot more complicated.

And it wasn't.

But Luca had put the word out to his sources in Çanakkale and Patras and asked them to get straight on to him if *Minerva* or any other inbound Nettuno vessels were sighted.

The body who jumped on me in Naples had been found at the bottom of the apartment block and taken to the local mortuary. He was a small-time Sicilian enforcer and nobody gave a fuck. The other members of the pizza takeaway team hadn't come forward to help the *carabinieri* with their enquiries, but a couple of shiny heads had threatened the *Diavolo* staff when they'd arrived at the office that morning, so it sounded like last night's shit *had* been about trying to close Luca down, not me.

'Anything on Dijani?'

'We haven't located him yet, but I have people checking the best hotels near where you are now, and some of the not so good ones too. We looked closely at his past, and couldn't find anything to get excited about. Then we followed your advice . . .'

'Funny.' Even with a dodgy signal and a voice like gravel in a concrete mixer, I could tell he was taking the piss.

'We checked out his father. Some questionable business deals, but that's all. Then his uncle. An imam, but not radical—'

'I don't have all fucking day, Luca. How many uncles has he got?'

'Three only. The second owns racehorses. At first glance, the youngest, Asif, seemed to have disappeared without trace. Then we discovered that he had changed his name to Abdul Azeem, Servant of the Mighty. And Abdul Azeem was very close to Imad Mughniyah. He was also assassinated by Mossad. Also in Syria. Also in 2008.'

Imad Mughniyah had been Hezbollah's international psychopath-in-chief, and made Osama bin Laden look like a very cuddly bunny. He was blown to bits in Damascus after a party to celebrate the anniversary of the Iranian Revolution. The CIA designed an explosive device in one of their facilities in North Carolina. The Mossad hid the thing in the spare tyre of a wagon parked near his Pajero and detonated it as he walked by. It couldn't have happened to a nicer guy.

'So, Nico, you are a genius. We would never have discovered this connection without your help.'

'Mate, stick around. We'll make an investigator of you yet. How's your computer geek shaping up?'

'Nothing so far. But he's only had the laptop and the iPhone for three hours. Call me later. This afternoon.'

We swapped *ciaos* and I dismantled and binned the Nokia.

I got back into the Seat and took some nice deep breaths. Then I realized I'd hammered the steering-wheel a couple of times with my fist.

Imad Mughniyah.

Fuck.

He'd masterminded the bombing of the US Embassy in Beirut in '83 and the Israeli Embassy in Buenos Aires in '92. Total body count: more than a hundred. I'd been in Dhahran when his people blew off the front of the Khobar Towers apartment block in '96, killing nineteen USAF pilots and staff. They'd sifted through the debris on plastic sheets laid out across the forecourt.

We reckoned Mughniyah was also responsible for the torture and death of the CIA's Lebanon station chief in '84, and the training and supply of the Shiite militias who fucked up Allied troops in Iraq seven or eight years ago.

And those were just the highlights.

So, I no longer felt like I was wandering around in the dark. But if the George Michael lookalike was even a part-time member of the Mughniyah fan club, this was not going to be a good day out.

I had about ninety Ks of ground to recce, so it took me nearly three hours to confirm that you couldn't hide anything larger than an eighteen-metre gin palace at any point along the way. A cargo vessel would stick out like a dog's bollocks. It would also be impossible to unload a single container.

Otranto itself had a big fuck-off marina, filled with boats and masts and rigging and all that shit, but no way could a merchant ship fit in. The castle and loads of the buildings beside it looked like they'd been there since the Ottomans had had the place under siege. The seafront was heaving with locals and tourists.

I only stayed long enough to get a sense of the place, and where

I'd launch an attack on it if I was in that kind of mood. August 14 was a few weeks away, but I couldn't bin the idea that Dijani, nephew of Abdul Azeem, Servant of the Mighty, was about to open up another can of martyrs. And if he had the same liking for iconic targets as Al Qaeda, maybe this was the place to do it.

10

I spent the next few hours combing the coastline around the tip of the peninsula – the heel of the Italian boot – and the west side of it, taking in Leuca, Gallipoli and Porto Cesareo en route. Yesterday's clouds had done a runner, so I could see further in the bright sunlight, and my progress was quicker. But Taranto was the only place large enough to do the job, and *Minerva* wasn't there either.

I got back to the port of Brindisi by mid-afternoon. The road that ran alongside the fence at the top of the bank had been sealed off with barriers and stripy tape, and the GIS were still out in force. Another couple of Iveco VM 90s loomed in my rear-view and sped past me as I hung a left into the parking area.

The football-gear traders in the MPV had packed up and gone. Everybody in the immediate vicinity of the terminal building was doing their best to behave like nothing much was happening, but you could feel the tension in the air.

I joined a small crowd that had gathered by the rail overlooking the main entrance to the docks. The Nettuno quay was a fair distance away, but we were high enough here to have a grandstand view of the continuing drama around it.

Coastguard patrol boats were tied up at each end of *Diana* and *Vesta*, and the dock crew were busy hoisting containers off their decks. As we watched, another group of refugees was extracted from one that had recently been unbolted, and shepherded to a waiting coach. I reckoned at least seventy per cent of their cargo was still aboard. At this rate, the process was going to take all night and most of tomorrow.

A mobile crane and a low-loader were being moved into position beside the overturned chassis of the artic. What was left of its metal coffin lay where I'd last seen it that morning, skin peeled back like a sardine tin, at the centre of a tight cordon, with the bomb squad sifting through the wreckage. A lot of uniforms were bouncing around nearby, so they must have completed scanning the thing for secondary devices.

A row of Iveco VM 90s stood in the shadow of the gantry, and I spotted the UNHCR and Médecins Sans Frontières logos on a couple of other vehicles parked nearby.

The terminal ticket office only dealt with passenger ferries, but I managed to find an admin guy with nothing much to do who thought that a couple of twenty-euro notes – even slightly damp ones – might well give me access to the cargo schedules.

After quite a bit of tapping and frowning he said he could find no trace of *Minerva* being booked into Brindisi during the next two months. I handed him another twenty and asked if he could check the timetable for Bari and the other Italian ports as well, and he gave me the same answer.

Checking out the coastline to the north was next on my agenda. Frank's villa was only a minor detour. Dijani would have to assume it was high on my list of known locations, so I didn't expect him to have set up shop there and be waiting for me to come and give him the Hesco treatment. But I needed to check the place out, if only to cross it off my list.

I slowed before the turning, hung a right on the opposite side of the road, and parked outside a sleepy-looking garden centre.

There were fresh tyre marks on the track through the trees that led up to the entrance to the villa, but no wagons parked in the driveway. A big *In Vendita* sign had been hammered into the grass beside the locked gates.

The villa wasn't as grand as the Courchevel chalet, but who cared? It was right in the middle of an olive grove, with a view up to the hill town of Ostuni behind it, and down to the Adriatic in front. I wasn't surprised that Frank had been happy there. Until that last visit.

Every shutter that I could see was closed. The garden swing creaked as it moved in the breeze. I didn't feel the need to hang around. This must have been where we were heading when Frank was killed, but there was no reason it would be bursting with clues about the location of the boat I was looking for.

As soon as I was a safe distance away I stopped again and pulled out the blueprint, willing it to give up its secret, willing Frank to tell me all over again what he must have told me in the green room.

If he'd known where and when *Minerva* was going to park, if he'd known what cargo it was carrying, I was sure he'd have said.

Maybe he did.

Maybe he had.

But all I could hear was his frustration. *'Look again . . .'*

And all I knew was what the pantomime at Brindisi told me: that if *Minerva* hadn't already arrived, it would do so inside the next twelve to eighteen hours, while the GIS were so busy fucking about with *Vesta* and *Diana* and the exploding container that they wouldn't be paying any attention to what might be happening elsewhere.

I was about to fold the blueprint and put it back in the day sack when Frank finally lost his cool with me. *'Look again. Look at the hold. Then look below . . .'*

I knew fuck-all about boats, but I'd had to gain access to one or two of them, and knew how they worked. The basic objective was to keep load space to a maximum. I traced the outline of the engine room. Then the cabins. Then the hold.

This time, I *did* look below the hold. And I noticed something. A row of boxes sitting just above the keel. I'd previously thought they must be containers. Now they looked like compartments.

I glanced at the Suunto and sparked up another choggy Nokia.

Luca sounded even worse than he had that morning.

'Mate, I think I've spotted something. On the blueprint. There's a bunch of compartments under the hold. So whatever they've got in there is something they want to keep well hidden.'

'My source in the *carabinieri* says you were right about Brindisi. They did get a tip-off. Two of them got hit by the explosion. One dead, one critical. And they won't finish unloading *Vesta* and *Diana* until tomorrow night.'

He went quiet on me for a moment.

'Nico . . .'

I suddenly realized it was tension in his voice, not tiredness. And it wasn't about the Brindisi gangfuck.

'Mate, what's up?'

'The laptop . . .' I heard him gulp, then the chink of glass. Another espresso had just bitten the dust. 'Bad news. Very bad news. My man has been able to access three files so far. Nothing about *Minerva*. But one of them contains a detailed breakdown of Frank Timis's property portfolio . . .'

I was still shit at remembering the twenty-four hours that had led up to me being thrown off the French mountain road, but I knew exactly what Luca was going to say next.

'Oh, fuck. *Fuck.* The safe houses . . .'

'It wasn't one of our big priorities so, to begin with, I only looked through the list with half an eye. Frank owned a lot of places, all over the world. Mostly for business or investment purposes.

'Then we found a more personal file. A *dacha* in Peredelkino. A chalet in Courchevel. A villa outside Ostuni. Apartments in New York and London. And two others, in Ukraine. Not luxurious. Not expensive. At the end of a chain of shell companies, camouflaging ownership, I saw Anna's name.'

'Those fuckers are supposed to be so secure even I don't know where they are.'

'I called Pasha immediately. He phoned her, got no answer. Then he sent one of his local guys to check both places as quickly as possible . . .'

He hesitated.

'She and the boy have gone.'

11

My pulse rate barely altered during a contact, or even when I was tabbing across high ground in hostile territory. But my heart was doing its best to fight its way out of my ribcage right now. I opened my mouth, slowed my breathing and gripped myself.

'OK. He say anything else? He have any idea where they might be?'

'He will leave no stone unturned, you know that.' Luca was trying to sound as upbeat as possible, but I could tell he was in pieces. 'He'll be asking everyone in the surrounding area for . . .'

He kept talking, but I stopped listening.

I needed to focus.

Dijani would have had Frank's laptop within hours of his death. If they'd cracked the password and taken her and the baby before I picked up Hesco, that fucker would have told me. He'd have used them to save his own skin.

Maybe Luca's geek was a magician, and Dijani's guys were still scratching their heads and failing to gain access to Frank's files.

Maybe they hadn't taken them.

Maybe Mr Lover Man hadn't given them her name, or told them Anna and Nicholai were my weak point.

Maybe Anna had found a different bolthole.

But 'maybe' wasn't good enough.

I had to work on the assumption that whichever safe house

Anna had chosen had stopped being safe at least seventy-two hours ago.

'Where were they? The safe houses.'

'One east of Ternopil. One south of Vinnitsa.'

That made sense. It was Frank's home turf.

'Will you go there, Nico?'

'No.' I felt my head shake, as if that was helping. 'Dijani will know where they are. And *Minerva* is still my best chance of finding *him*.'

My mission had changed. My target hadn't.

'We heard she left Patras four hours ago.'

It was 17:42 now. I got my brain in gear on some numbers. They would frame my actions between now and first light tomorrow. And doing the sums was a good way to avoid thinking about the shit Anna and our son might be in.

Patras was 330 nautical miles from Brindisi, give or take.

Minerva was fresh off the slipway, so should be able to do at least twenty-two knots fully loaded, more if not.

Which meant I had between eight and fourteen hours to locate the fucker.

'OK, listen in. They won't drop anchor offshore at the height of the trafficking season. The coastguards would be all over it. And it's not booked into any of the main Italian terminals. I've covered every fucking centimetre of the coast between Brindisi and Taranto, and there's nowhere it could get into without drawing attention to itself. So I'm going north. I'm starting with Monopoli. You know it?'

'I've never been there.'

'Can you Google it?'

I could hear him tapping at his keyboard. He gave me a running commentary as he scrolled down the imagery. 'Old town . . . beach . . . swimmers . . . more swimmers . . . ancient wall . . . parasols . . . swimming-pool . . . map . . . *trulli* . . . No, that must be a shot of Alberobello . . .'

I didn't know what the fuck he was talking about.

'. . . church . . . more parasols . . . fish . . . Pippa Middleton at a wedding . . . fishing boats . . . no cargo ships yet . . . more Pippa—'

I was about to tell him to shut the fuck up about Pippa Middleton when he got excited about a big ship – a tanker or a container vessel – and a crane.

'But only one photograph.'

I told him I didn't give a shit: one was good enough for me.

'Nico . . . I . . . Anna . . .'

'Luca, no need, mate. Really.'

At times like this, you have to cut people away. I needed him switched on. I didn't want him to take up time or get emotional.

'But I still need your help. I'm not going to bin this mobile. Call or text if you get any updates about Anna, Dijani, the Urans, *Minerva*, or any other shit I need to know. And if I find the fucking thing, I'll call you.'

I powered down and shoved the mobile into my jeans. If I got tracked down, so what? At least I would be one step closer to Dijani.

I just needed it to be on my terms, not his. I had to be in control of what happened next.

This wasn't just about me any more.

12

A short avenue of cypresses led up to the Monopoli graveyard. Its whitewashed outer walls and the two sets of columns on either side of a heavily barred entrance made it look like a barracks built to withstand a full-scale infantry attack. I passed it on my way to the headland immediately to the south-east of the old town.

I skirted a couple of small sandy bays filled with locals and tourists enjoying the late-afternoon sun, and parked up on the far side of a pizza restaurant that looked like it had seen better days. I bought a litre of mineral water and a slice of something that had been pattern-bombed with cheese, tomato and *peperoni*, and started on it as I walked out to the nearest spit.

I found a place among the rocks that gave me cover, swallowed the last bit of crust and got some liquid down my neck before bringing out the binos. The map had delivered on its promise of a good, uninterrupted view of my target.

This wasn't the playground of the super-rich, so the water wasn't stuffed with jet skis and luxury yachts and perma-tans. Two or three teams of rowers were working up a sweat close to the opposite shore and there was the odd swimmer and marker buoy, but that was it.

From this angle, Monopoli looked like a fantasy travel poster – a combo of blindingly white and light brown buildings, framed by the deep blue-green of the sea and the paler blue of the sky. As I scanned the place left to right, my view was dominated by the cathedral, a pair of massive old factory chimneys, another huge church and a neat little fortress that guarded the harbour mouth.

Then the thing I was really here for: the stone dock that Luca had Googled. It doubled as a breakwater and had two cargo vessels parked up alongside it. Neither of them had 'NETTUNO' painted across their flank, but there was room for a third, and maybe even a fourth.

There was no sign of a gantry or any kind of storage facility, but two smart yellow tower cranes and a third hoist, half their size, mounted on caterpillar tracks, stood against the back wall, ready to swing into action.

I lowered the binos and ran them along the surviving segment of the ancient fortifications. Part of it had been converted into what looked like a boutique hotel, with white parasols lining the battlements. I checked out the balconies in case Dijani and the Uran brothers were using it as their operating base. They were both deserted. A couple of lads with bellies overhanging their shorts gutted octopi in a rock pool beneath them.

A circular cannon emplacement jutted out between the hotel and the fortress. A red-and-white-striped mini-lighthouse and what looked like a Second World War bunker stood at the end of the quay a hundred to its right.

I moved across to the other side of the spit. A lone fishing boat was chugging out to sea. A couple of passenger ferries steamed along the horizon, heading for Bari, I guessed, or maybe further north. There wasn't a single container in sight.

I wandered back to the Seat, wrapped the passports, IDs and money in a plastic bag, pocketed the torch and left the day sack in the boot. The bag went under a rock at the edge of a patch of scrub twenty paces from where I'd parked. Then I took the boardwalk around the edge of the first bay.

I was crossing the outcrop that separated it from the second when the Nokia vibrated in my pocket.

'Nico, we have traced Dijani's hotel bookings for last night, tonight and tomorrow. All five star. All paid in advance. In six different locations: Otranto, Brindisi, Bari, Ancona, Ravenna and Venezia.'

'Pretty much every major port on the Adriatic.'
'Correct.'
'Not Monopoli?'
'Not Monopoli.'
'Has he checked into any of them?'
'Not so far.'
'So he's fucking about.'
'Looks like it.'
'I'm sticking with Plan A. Unless you get a firm sighting of either Dijani or the boat somewhere else.' I didn't have a choice. There was no way I could keep rocketing up and down the coast in the hope that I might get lucky. And this place ticked all the boxes.

I slipped off my jacket and hooked it over my shoulder as I joined a random group of punters coming off the beach. I nodded and smiled at a succession of complete strangers whenever I needed to look like someone whose top priority was to find a nice place for a beer.

The walkway beneath the hotel balconies was completely in shadow now. Even the octopus fishermen had pissed off. I stayed with the crowd and turned right, down a paved street that ran along the town side of the old wall.

Every so often cars and slow-moving delivery vehicles crept up behind us, but mostly they were too polite to tell us to get the fuck out of their way.

I ducked into a shop that advertised everything from holiday rentals to Internet access on the door and grabbed a couple of maps – a large-scale street plan of the old town and one of the whole city.

Immediately past the boutique hotel there was a small piazza with parking on each side. The road narrowed again by an apartment block shrouded in scaffolding and tarpaulin sheets, which all looked like they belonged in a different century. A series of poles jutted out from the uprights at forty-five degrees, five metres above the pavement. They supported an awning of timber planks designed to protect people passing below from falling masonry or falling workmen.

The road forked left into another maze of alleys. I carried on right, towards the harbour.

I could see a load of moorings through an archway ahead of me. The fortress that stood beside it seemed a good place to recce what – if I was right about *Minerva* – would become the heart of the action. It was hosting an exhibition of local painting and sculpture and didn't shut its doors until 21:00, so I followed a young Brit couple up through the cool, dimly lit interior.

None of us bothered much with the artwork.

As soon as I reached the top of the stone ramp on to the battlements, I knew it was the perfect vantage-point. I was one of a dozen or so visitors there to admire the three-sixty-degree view. There were five pairs of binos on display, so I fitted right in. As far as I could tell, none of them belonged to the Albanian Mafia.

This time I began by looking out to sea. Three more fishing boats, and a liquefied natural gas tanker on the skyline. I swept my Pentax anti-clockwise until I hit the first of the vessels at the cargo quay, then the second.

I was looking for three things.

An access route to that section of the port.

Possible locations for Dijani's forward operating base.

And any sign of him and the Urans.

Apart from the two uniforms by the gated entrance, there was nobody around.

I quartered the area around their glass-fronted kiosk.

A brand new security fence both sides of the gate.

A roundabout opposite.

Then two apartment blocks, maybe more.

I followed the fence left. It ran along the top of a high stone wall, which dropped into the water. I followed it right, to where it was set into the sea defences that backed on to the quay. Where metal met stone I could see a pile of those huge concrete cubes they dumped on the seaward side to create a barrier against the waves.

All I was missing was any visible proof that I'd made the right call by being there.

What if I'd ticked the wrong boxes? As the possibility of a terminal fuck-up filled my head, I lowered the binos and gave myself a mental slapping. Nobody ever said this shit was easy.

There was no formula for guaranteed success – you just had to work with what you had – but right now I really, really wished there was.

I took a couple of deep breaths and wiped the binos on my shirt.

My next focal point was the boatyard in the shadow of the factory chimneys. Boats in the water. Boats on trolleys and in cradles and on stilts all over the hard standing. Bits of boat lying around on the ground, and in the darkened doorways of wriggly-tin workshops. Loads of chaos. Loads of cover. Definitely worth a closer look too.

Further left, about a hundred from the fortress, there was a wide concrete slipway at the inner, most sheltered edge of the harbour. It ran down towards a pontoon, which bordered a stretch of water where the rowing boats tied up. And that was when I saw Elvis Uran for the fourth time in six days.

He'd binned the suede jacket with the sharp lapels but stuck with the black satin shirt, skinny black jeans and snakeskin boots. He looked like he was planning to star in the remake of *The Magnificent Seven*.

I didn't see his face at first, just the top of his freshly polished head. He was leaning over the edge of the pontoon and, judging by his body language, giving a set of instructions to a guy in one of the rowing boats. As soon as he stood up and stepped back on to the quay, I wasn't in any doubt. He had one of those don't-fuck-with-me walks that was never designed to help him blend in.

Elvis skirted the edge of the slipway and swaggered off through an arched passage that provided a shortcut into the centre of the old town. He was silhouetted briefly against the sunlight on the street beyond it, but long enough to show me that he was going left.

I put on my jacket and tucked the binos into a side pocket as I moved back down through the fortress.

The large-scale map told me that my best chance of catching up with the Albanian was to avoid the harbour route and go left, then first right as soon as I was outside.

I couldn't sprint through those paved streets: it wasn't that kind of place. But I had to move fast. I was fucked if Elvis took either of the turnings towards the main square, which had six exits, or the museum, which had seven.

By the time the Via Orazio Comes had become the Via Barbacana I'd spotted the back of three very shiny heads, but not the one I was after. I jinked past the cathedral, sweat now falling from my forehead, and found myself at the edge of a more modern, tree-lined piazza. I glanced at the queue of people waiting to buy ice cream at a place called Café Roma, and saw Elvis coming out of it with two brightly coloured scoops balanced on a cornet.

13

I slowed down and gulped some air.

He wouldn't have seen me at Aix or at the construction site between St Gallen and Zürich where I'd dumped his brother. I'd worn a full-face motorbike helmet outside Laffont's bank in Albertville. And if Mr Lover Man had given Dijani and the Urans the world's most accurate description of me, it would have been all over the Internet. So I reckoned Elvis wouldn't ping me unless I made it obvious I was on him.

Keeping the back of his body in view every step of the way, but not risking eye to eye, I walked over to the newspaper kiosk opposite the café and bought a packet of gum, then spent a few minutes checking out the magazine selection – long enough for him to cross the square and take the street that led over the railway track to the cemetery and the main routes out of town.

He didn't look right or left, just slowed when the red lights flashed, the bells began to ring and the barriers went down at the level crossing for an approaching train.

I looked into a flower-shop window, keeping eyes on his reflection. I needed an excuse to delay my arrival at the level crossing, and an obvious reason for being there.

A goods train rattled past. The barriers came up again when I was still twenty away and Elvis strode across the track with a small cluster of locals, who then split up at the main. The side wall of the graveyard ran for a couple of hundred along the left side of the road. There was a field of long grass and wild flowers to its right.

He turned half-left into the cypress avenue that led to the grand entrance. I half expected him then to go right and right again and end up coming back towards me – the sort of thing I'd done last night in Naples to check if I really was being followed by the low-budget Mafia.

He went left and was unsighted along the far boundary. I followed, hugging the rendering as I got to the corner. There was no road here, just a rough path snaking through bushes and trees.

The path wasn't well trodden enough to make my presence on it a happy coincidence. So I had no choice but to hang back. He was soon halfway along it, beneath a couple of hefty branches that overhung one of the buildings immediately inside the plot. When he got to the end of it, he became unsighted again. I got one foot in front of the other as fast as I could to get him back into view.

I eased up as I came within reach of the track that ran behind the city of the dead. When I got there, I sneaked a glance in both directions. No sign of Elvis to my right, at the back of the plot. Then I heard voices and saw movement in a rusty metal and timber barn a hundred along the track to my left. I stepped back into the bushes and kept eyes on the yard in front of it.

As far as I could make out, there were three of them in there, and a blue Fiat three-ton truck. I pulled out the binos. All I could see was one shiny head and two shadowy figures. Then an engine sparked up. But not the truck. Something inside the barn. A grinding of gears, then the whisper and whoosh of hydraulics.

I bent low and crossed the track into another patch of waste-land. Trees and spiky bushes gave me cover three-quarters of the distance to my target. The noise gave me the opportunity to move in closer. I got down on my belt buckle and crawled the rest of the way, pumping with my knees and elbows in the cover of the rough meadow grass and rampant weeds. Thank fuck it hadn't rained there in a while. I had some dust to contend with, but no mud.

The yard was surrounded by a breezeblock wall that had been

whitewashed sometime in the previous century. It was about chest high and topped off with a rusty metal railing. As I drew nearer, the pitch of the engine changed and a small mobile crane rumbled out of the barn and came to a standstill with a hiss of air brakes.

The lad in the cab extended and contracted its hoist, rotated it one-eighty, then repeated the whole performance. He wasn't wearing L plates, so he must have been testing the machine as much as his own skills.

Elvis and his mate on the ground clapped their hands. They seemed to be enjoying the show. And neither of the others looked remotely like George Michael.

The driver reversed back under the wriggly-tin roof and everything shut down.

I heard voices again. Banter. Even a laugh or two.

Elvis came out of the yard and began to retrace his steps down the track. The other two stayed inside with the vehicle. I lay flat by the base of the wall until he had passed. Then I ran at a crouch to the rear of the barn, paralleling him as far as the turning, and followed him back the way we had come.

This time Elvis hung a left before the railway. I stayed on the opposite side of the road as he skirted a massive walled area, part sunken olive grove, part lemon orchard.

The shadows were lengthening. The sky was darkening. Streetlights flickered on. But I didn't plan to lift him. Not yet, anyway. You don't snatch the monkey when you're hoping he'll lead you to the organ-grinder.

He took a right past a building site, which I realized was the back of Monopoli Hospital, and disappeared into a pedestrian tunnel beneath the track in front of it.

When I got there, it was empty, except for faded splashes of graffiti and three low-wattage lamps. I broke into a run and sweat soon stuck my jeans to my legs like it was trying to stop me moving. I caught a glimpse of Elvis as I climbed out on the far side. He was heading towards the factory chimneys, but before he got to them he quickened his pace and hung a right.

I followed him into a street with a bunch of small-time marine workshops on one side and the boatyard I'd seen from the fortress straight ahead. The gates were shut and there were no lights visible inside. I hung back while he brought some keys out of his skinny jeans, opened it and locked up behind him. He melted into the darkness.

Staying in the shadows, I moved closer to the iron bars. There was a fair amount of ambient light reflecting across the surface of the harbour. I could see a two-storey admin building immediately to my left, firmly shut, and a ribbon of clear concrete curving around behind it.

The rest of the hard standing was filled with a fuck of a lot of boats on stilts, in the process of having their hulls cleaned or their propellers serviced or whatever you do when you lift these things out of the water. Every centimetre of space beneath them was covered with engine parts, chunks of timber and bits of rope. Health and Safety would have loved this place.

I didn't think you could get to the main cargo quay from there, but you'd be able to keep it under close observation, for sure. Was this Dijani's forward operating base, or just a vantage-point?

Keeping close to the wall, I stopped, opened my mouth and did the listening trick. All I could hear was the lapping of waves and the metallic clink of whatever boats have in their rigging. I gripped a vertical bar of the gate with each hand and wedged the toe of my boot on the central rail. Then I pulled myself up high enough to be able to grab a couple of the spikes on top and managed to haul myself over them without spearing my bollocks or making it creak or clang.

I dropped almost silently to the ground, listened again, and scanned the area ahead of me for the shape, shine, shadow, silhouette, spacing and movement that indicated the presence of a body in a world of inanimate objects.

Nothing.

I edged across to the first of the boats on stilts, three metres to my half-right, and ducked under it. Keeping low and steering clear of the shit that littered the ground beneath my feet, I worked my way towards the centre of the yard.

After five or six paces I spotted a nice heavy wrench that had been left beside a bunch of dismantled engine parts. I stooped and picked it up, getting a waft of diesel fuel at the same time. I gripped its handle and moved on.

An open-fronted workshop to my left.

The cranes on the cargo quay to my right, like dinosaur skeletons, reaching into the night sky.

Just one vessel tied up between them now. The lamps on the stone wall behind it cast a weak, sulphur-yellow glow, but even at this distance it was enough to backlight the masts and keels and oil drums and a couple of abandoned fridges that separated me from the harbour.

And the big-wheeled gantry that they obviously used to heave all this shit in and out of the water.

And the body standing next to it, stock still, binos glued to his eyes, focused on the open sea.

14

Elvis's all-black kit blended in nicely with the surrounding stanchions and metalwork, but his polished head stood out like a white Belisha beacon. I took two steps closer and heard his voice. A low murmur.

At first I thought he was talking to a mate I hadn't seen. The lad in denim on the rowing boat, maybe.

Then I realized he had a mobile or a two-way stuck to his ear, and was communicating with someone off-site. Hidden away in the centre of town, maybe? Or on a container ship that I couldn't yet see?

Keeping the gantry upright between us, I moved forward again. I couldn't understand a word he was saying, but I could feel the electricity in the exchange. When I glanced through the harbour mouth, I saw why. A set of ship's lights glinted just this side of the horizon. There'd been nothing out there an hour ago, so it was heading this way.

Elvis banged the off button and rammed the phone into his back pocket, then raised his binos again.

I knelt slowly and took a good look around beneath the hulls. The gantry was surrounded by boats on stilts. A couple of parked cars occupied the space it would reverse into whenever it swung into action. I plotted a route round to the far side of it, which would give me cover until I was almost within reach of him. He still wasn't moving.

I couldn't see anyone else.

Smacking the wrench between his shoulder blades would take him down. If he didn't know where Anna and the baby were, he'd know where I could find Dijani.

I stepped out from under the hulls as soon as the nearest wagon was between him and me. Still bent at the knees and waist, I remained beneath the roofline as I skirted round the back of them. I was now directly behind Elvis.

I straightened.

The lapping of the waves was louder there, and the metallic rattling in the breeze. Loud enough to camouflage the sound of my approach.

I steadied my breathing as the lights of the boat got closer.

Keeping my weight on the balls of my feet and my eyes between his shoulders, I stole along his side of the dock.

Elvis was shorter than me, trimmer and more toned than Hesco had been. When I was two paces away from him, close enough to smell his aftershave, the wrench raised, a sixth sense alerted him to my presence.

He dropped his binos, swivelled, dipped and took a sideways step towards me. He drove his left shoulder into my chest as I brought down the wrench, only catching him a glancing blow.

He swayed back, eyes flashing, then dipped his right hand into his jeans and brought out a stiletto. At the press of a button, out slid a six-inch blade.

He came at me, left elbow raised, arm bent, knife at the ready. I swung the wrench again, aiming at his wrist. He stepped away, stooped and gathered a small boat anchor on a broken chain and swung it at me, like he was on the set of *Gladiator*. He connected with the peak of my baseball cap, sweeping it off, and nearly taking my head with it.

I charged into him, aiming the wrench at his knife hand, but he swept the anchor round and knocked it across the hard standing.

I scrambled across the concrete, my eyes focused on the wrench, not worried about what was behind me. I just wanted the weapon.

I could hear him closing in as I gripped the shaft with both hands and heaved the fucking thing in a circle behind me.

As I turned I saw the jaws make contact with his leg and heard the crunch of metal on bone. He screamed and let go of the chain. The anchor crashed into one of the boats and he collapsed on top of me. Fuck knew where his knife was.

All I could do was wrap my left arm around the back of his neck and force his face against my chest, my right hand searching frantically for my UZI.

He was still screaming, but it wasn't just pain. I could feel the force of his anger rattling my chest. His hands came into view. And the blade. I turned to the left, trying to get on top of him, trying to take control. Then his free hand grabbed a fistful of my hair and I knew what he wanted to do. He wanted to hold his target still while he plunged in the stiletto.

I gripped the pen and slammed the point of it down on to his head.

At first it sounded like I was trying to puncture a table top. I felt the third blow fracture his skull. And the fifth penetrate the bone plate.

As soon as I'd buried the bit I wasn't holding in his cerebral cavity, I gave it a couple of twists and turns and his body went limp.

I rolled him off me, sat up and took long, deep breaths.

Fuck, I'd wanted him alive.

I removed his mobile from the back pocket of his skinny jeans and his keys from the right-hand front one. I let him keep his ring.

I found a bit of frayed cord, tied it around his neck and fastened it to the chunk of metal he'd tried to finish me with. Then I wrenched the UZI out of his head and wiped it on his shirt. As blood started to leak from the hole, I heaved the whole package over the edge of the dock. The bottom half of his left calf bobbed along the concrete as if it was only attached with string.

I picked up my baseball cap and the stiletto, retracting the blade while I checked he was now out of sight.

I could see the lights of the ship getting closer. And the glow from the bridge – faint, but strong enough and high enough to show that it wasn't carrying a full load.

More importantly, I could see its silhouette. It was the same as the one on the blueprint.

15

The third key I tried unlocked the boatyard gate. I didn't go straight to the cargo quay. *Minerva* was still some distance out to sea, and I wanted to make sure everything and everyone was in place before I gained entry.

When I'd put some distance between me and Elvis, I powered up his phone. Of course the fucking thing was locked. It didn't matter. I now knew for sure where I'd find Dijani. That fucker was going to live just long enough to tell me where Anna and the baby were.

I walked round to the slipway beside the stretch of water where the fishing boats were parked, past the pontoon I'd spotted Elvis on before the sun went down. The only light filtered from the windows of the apartments and houses at the edge of that part of the harbour, which made it a great place for couples to walk hand in hand and teenagers to sit cross-legged on the paving stones, roll their own cigarettes and pass round cans of beer.

Minerva's lights glistened across the water as I passed the rowing boats and lobbed his phone into the harbour.

A very shiny white powerboat was tied up further along the quay. Unless they'd decided to shut every hatch and suffocate themselves in the heat, no one was aboard. The lettering on its back end told me it belonged to a charter company, so the guys who'd hired it might have been enjoying a nice dinner somewhere in town before coming back to get their heads down. A bunch of people were sitting, drinking, eating and fucking about on the boats at each end of it.

The mini-lighthouse was dark. Maybe it was no longer needed. Maybe it just couldn't be arsed. I circled the bunker beyond it: four-metre-wide, domed structure, with thick, blast-proof walls and four horizontal apertures that provided a one-eighty-degree view of the sea, *Minerva* and the cargo quay.

A couple was getting to know each other better on one of the huge breakwater cubes on the far side of it. Fuck 'em, they could get on with whatever they wanted. I was staying where I was.

The woman saw the pervert in the shadows first. She pushed the guy off so they could straighten their clothes and head back the way I'd just come. There was no one else around.

I brought out my binos. They hadn't enjoyed their collision with the boatyard concrete, but they still did what they were supposed to do.

The Suunto told me it was after midnight. I reckoned *Minerva* was forty-five minutes to an hour away. Once I'd adjusted the focus I could see a big white 'N' illuminated by the lights on its hull.

I tapped out Luca's number on the Nokia and waited while the call was transferred.

I kept it crisp. 'It's on its way now.'

He did too. 'So am I.'

But neither of us cut the line. We both knew the question I had to ask next, even though his silence had already given me the answer.

'Anna?'

He sounded less like a strangling victim now, but I could still hear his pain. 'Not yet. But Pasha is in Vinnitsa. He'll call me as soon as . . .'

I put the phone down on the concrete bench beside me and continued to watch *Minerva,* checking that the thing was still getting bigger and brighter.

The whole place didn't exactly spring to life as the boat drew nearer, but a row of overhead lights sparked up so I could see some signs of activity. The mobile crane moved into position at the seaward end of the quay. An empty minibus stopped right next to it, I assumed to lift off the crew.

A second set of headlamps swept towards the entrance and the gates swung open again. A three-ton truck with a canvas cover over the load space joined the party. I couldn't immediately ID make or colour. I guessed Fiat and blue.

The driver nosy-parked, jumped down from the cab and opened up the back. Then he found a bollard to sit on and started to smoke his way through a pack of cigarettes. He must have left his mate at the barn. He didn't show the slightest interest in the minibus.

A tug appeared from the direction of the boatyard and steered into the waves. The one remaining cargo vessel was moored with its pointy end facing the exit, and the one that had left earlier had been too, so I expected to see *Minerva* towed in and put through a one-eighty-degree turn before parking up. Particularly if it was planning a quick getaway.

An hour later it was in position, 'NETTUNO' emblazoned across its flank, *Minerva* on its tail. There were no containers visible at deck level. The three-tonner was now completely obscured by the ship's hull, but I could see about ten crew members being ferried away in the minibus, and a gleaming BMW SUV taking its place. The SUV's windows were tinted, but there was no mistaking the George Michael lookalike who swung open the passenger door. Unless it really was George Michael.

And, judging by the beard and the burn on his neck, Rexho Uran had been doing the driving.

16

I pocketed the Pentax and filled my lungs as I walked back past the still unoccupied powerboat. Most of the others had closed down for the night as well. The Nokia went into the water between them with hardly a splash.

I didn't continue round the inner harbour this time; it was pretty much deserted. I went left through the archway by the fortress and right along the street where I'd tried to intercept Elvis. It made no sense drawing attention to myself any earlier than I had to. After a couple more rights and a left I was on course for the road that took me past the chimneys.

Up close, I could see that the apartment blocks opposite the entrance to the cargo quay were still under construction. I went left again so that I could circle around the back of the development and climb on to the breakwater via the beach without having to go anywhere near the gates. I'd avoid most of the streetlamps too.

As soon as I was in the shadow of the shell of the third building, I flicked on my torch, unfolded the blueprint of *Minerva* and fixed the boat's external and internal layout in my head.

It took me the best part of an hour to reach my target and clamber over the piles of totally randomly spaced and angled cubes. There was enough ambient light to allow me to spot the difference between the concrete platforms and the crevices between them, but it was still slow going.

I stayed as close as possible to the seaward side of the wall until

I reached the far end of it, then moved down closer to the water. That way I could use the cubes at the top of the pile as cover. Once I'd rounded the tip I went down on my belly and manoeuvred myself into a vertical space that afforded a view of the quay without the need to raise my head above the parapet.

The overhead lights had been switched off. The mobile crane was now parked about five metres away and the three-tonner had disappeared, so whatever Dijani had taken so much trouble to bring in had obviously been hoisted out of *Minerva* and gone with it.

The BMW hadn't moved, and a slightly battered Land Cruiser sat alongside it.

I reckoned that meant Dijani would have at least a four-man back-up. More if there were still crew aboard. I couldn't see anybody on the quay, the gangway, or on stag on the deck, so I crept along the back wall and took up position in the shadow of the crane. I had a better view of each of the possible areas of compromise now, and they were still all clear. Maybe they were too busy doing sailor stuff to pay any attention to me.

Back in the real world, the odds were strongly against me. But, fuck it, I'd come for Dijani, and this was my best chance of catching him. I couldn't lurk there all night in the hope that he'd wander down the gangway at some point and introduce himself. I had to go aboard and get stuck in. And the stern hawser seemed like a good place to start. It was further away from me than the pointy end, but lower, and most of the windows on the bridge faced forward.

There were no portholes below the deck rail, so I crossed the quay and pretty much hugged the hull as I went for it. Unless one of the team leant over the thing and looked straight down, or suddenly decided to poke their head over the gangway, I wouldn't be pinged. That was what I told myself, anyway. If any headlamps approached from the entrance gate, I was in the shit.

The rope was almost the same circumference as my grip. I reached up and closed my fingers around it, then began to haul myself up.

You always feel exposed when you're suspended six metres above the water. The trick is not to think about it. I zeroed in on the place I was aiming for, three more metres above my head. I clenched the rope between my knees and ankles and pressed on, hand over hand, until I was able to grab the lower rim of the hawsehole.

I raised my head far enough to take a look around the rear deck before easing my shoulders through it. A guy in denim was leaning on the seaward rail. I wouldn't have been able to tell whether he was Elvis's mate in the rowing boat even if he'd been looking in my direction.

He had unfolded the bipod of his SAW and placed it at his feet. He must have been told to keep it out of sight. Even in southern Italy, 5.56mm Squad Automatic Weapons tend to attract the wrong kind of attention.

He tapped a cigarette out of its pack and lit up. Unless he was interrupted, or was one of those compulsive smokers who take a couple of puffs, then send the rest cartwheeling into the sea, I reckoned I had three minutes before he was fully functional again.

I wasn't sure that I could haul myself aboard, cross the deck and drop him before he turned his weapon on me or raised the alarm. But a SAW was definitely more lawful than a stiletto and an UZI pen. And there was really only one way of finding out.

My main enemies were my noise and his peripheral vision. When I saw him glancing anxiously to his left after lighting up, I realized he was more worried about getting a bollocking from his boss than he was about keeping watch in case their diversion hadn't worked and the GIS rolled on to the quay.

I decided to go for it.

I reached in and grabbed the rope just short of the noose that had been looped over the bollard. My target glanced to his left for the second time in as many drags, and sucked in another lungful. His body language told me he was so wired he was smoking at warp speed.

The sea breeze had kicked in, and got busy rattling whatever hadn't been tied down. A burst of laughter and chanting carried across the water from one of the streets near the fortress. My target leant further over the rail and scanned that side of the harbour, trying to ID where the noise was coming from. Or maybe he just wished he was having as good a time as they were.

I pulled my upper body through the hole, brought up my knees, then my feet and, keeping in the shadow of the bulwark, got my boots on the deck. Staying beneath the rail, I brought out Elvis's blade and circled around behind him. The closer I got, the more of his toxic Eastern European tobacco I was sharing.

I focused on the back of his head as I ran the last few metres towards him. Nothing else mattered. I couldn't even hear my own movement.

I gripped the blade in my right fist, my thumb over the top of the handle to prevent my sweat-covered palm sliding down it once I got the thing working. I wasn't going to fuck up like I had with Elvis. I was going to get straight in, get it done and move on.

One pace left.

He finally realized someone was behind him, but it was too late. He didn't have time to turn. I was already climbing aboard him, my legs scissoring, my left hand flying in front of his face and slamming against his mouth.

I pulled him back with my arm, my knees and calves locked around his waist. He struggled to stay upright, but it wasn't happening. I started to take him down with me, keeping his body on top of mine as I braced my back for a hard landing. Keeping my head up, I clamped his mouth even harder to keep him quiet when it happened.

I hit the deck.

A split second later he landed on top of me.

Fighting for breath, I arched my back to push up and present his chest as I punched the blade into him again and again, wherever I could make contact.

Under my palm, I felt him trying to scream.

He jerked and twisted, desperate to anticipate the next stab and avoid it. But I kept them deliberately erratic.

The point of the stiletto hit a rib and juddered until it found flesh that yielded. I forced it down again, into the side of his chest now, then switched back to the top again, trying to get it into his heart.

I didn't care where it hit. I just wanted him dead.

He jerked again, less violently. I kept on going, fuck knew how often, until he finally stopped.

I didn't waste time trying to catch my breath. I heaved him off immediately. I wanted him out of the way before he leaked too heavily.

I dragged him back to where I'd first seen him and checked if he had more ammo for the SAW. He didn't, so I bundled him over the handrail. If there was a splash, I didn't hear it.

17

I picked up the SAW and extended its butt. It was a Western infantry weapon, probably lifted from Coalition troops in Afghan or Iraq. You could belt-feed these things, but this one had a regular thirty-round M4 assault rifle mag. I released it and pushed against the rounds. My finger pressed them down a little more than a full mag would have let me. It didn't really matter: it was full enough.

I pulled back the cocking handle. It was loose, which meant the working parts were to the rear. I reloaded the mag, threw the sling over my left shoulder, folded the bipod in below the barrel. Clamped my right hand on the pistol grip and my elbow on the butt, leaving my left arm free. The thing was now ready to fire three-to-five-round controlled bursts, and so was I.

I edged around the base of the bridge superstructure. The laughter and chanting were closer now, and a few wolf whistles for the ladies as the group of rowdies spilt through the arch by the fortress. Perfect. As far as I was concerned, they couldn't have timed it better.

The starboard wing stretched over my head. I opened the door in the bulkhead immediately to my left. It swung out on freshly oiled hinges. I stopped and listened, then stepped over the cockpit. Pulled it shut and stopped again. The heat from reprocessed air was the first thing I noticed, then the low but continuous hum of engines somewhere underfoot.

A metal ladder led up to the sleeping and eating quarters, and finally the ship's command centre. Or down to the engine room. I heard a clang somewhere below deck, but nothing more.

I raised the barrel of the SAW and followed it, as carefully and quietly as possible, first into the bunk room, then the canteen on the level above. The doors to both were ajar, and both areas showed signs of recent use. But nobody was in them now.

The door at the top was shut.

These things were made of steel and firmly sealed, so I didn't expect to be able to cup my ear to it and hear stuff inside. There was a porthole the diameter of a football at head height. I peered through it.

My field of vision was a long way short of panoramic, but I saw a head to my half-left, silhouetted in the glow of the instruments on the console that stretched across the centre of the bridge. I gave it five. No one else came into view.

Keeping the sling taut against my shoulder, I levelled the muzzle of the weapon and curled my right index finger around the trigger. Then I turned the door handle so slowly even I couldn't see it moving, and pushed it open a fraction of a centimetre.

As soon as the seal was broken I heard voices.

More talk. Mostly Italian, as far as I could tell.

I was catching quick bursts of incoming radio traffic.

I waited for a response.

Got one.

A terse acknowledgement. Then the squeak of an arse shifting position on a very new seat.

I stayed where I was, listening for further sound or movement.

There was a bit more chat. I could still only hear one guy speaking at this end.

I pushed the door open.

The radio operator had his elbows on the console, and was clutching a microphone stalk. He seemed to be concentrating very hard on the monitor in front of him.

There were still no other bodies in sight.

He didn't move a muscle as I stepped over the threshold. I went forward, weapon in the aim, eyes mostly on the back of his head, but flicking from side to side, in case of a threat from the wings. The angle of my approach meant that I wouldn't have an unrestricted view into either of them until I was almost on top of him.

I stopped a couple of paces away from my target. 'Where's Dijani?'

He swivelled one-eighty in his chair and stared straight at me, completely unfazed.

For a beat, neither of us moved.

His unnatural stillness should have told me that he'd been aware of my presence all along. And when I spotted the two red dots zeroed on my chest, I knew he was not alone.

I kept the SAW rock solid on his centre mass as two figures emerged silently from the shadows on each side of me. I kept my voice low and slow. 'Drop your weapons, or I'll kill this man.'

Two more appeared from behind them.

I caught a glimpse of the George Michael lookalike to my right, in my peripheral vision.

'Go ahead. It will make no difference. There are many gates to Jannah.'

Dijani's voice was smooth and cultured, and I believed him. But I didn't lower the weapon.

If I squeezed off a burst, I could probably drop three. On the other hand, there was a strong chance that they would take me down. Or that my rounds bouncing off a bulkhead would do it for them.

If the lad on the chair was worried, he didn't show it. You can pull that kind of stunt if you're a fully paid-up member of the Paradise Club.

The two with the laser sights positioned themselves at each end of the console – and on the far side of it, so there was no chance of me getting too close, or of them dropping each other as well as dropping me. The red dots stayed pretty much in the same position on my jacket.

Dijani and the fourth man, who I guessed must be Rexho, stayed where they were, outside my immediate arc of fire.

'I planned a slow death for you. But I'd be happy to make it a quick one if you prefer . . .'

I didn't need more than a nanosecond to think about it. Slow would be a lot better. I'd never been afraid to take the pain, and as long as I was alive, there was a chance I could keep Anna and our boy alive too.

I lowered the weapon to the deck.

'Now kick it away.'

I gave it a nudge with the toe of my right Timberland. I didn't want to make it too easy for them.

'Further.'

Another nudge.

'Now extend your arms in front of you, cross your wrists, take one pace back and turn forty-five degrees to your left.'

I did what I was told.

The radio operator picked up the SAW and disappeared somewhere to my right. The laser sight at the left end of the console moved into the centre. Rexho came out of the wing I was now facing with plasticuffs at the ready. He slipped them over my wrists and tightened them until my hands throbbed.

The burn scar on Rexho's neck wasn't pretty. Neither was the gleam in his eye. He showed no sign of losing it with me yet. I wondered how long that would last.

He stepped back again, out of my reach.

The laser sight to the right moved alongside his mate. The red dots travelled down my torso, lingered for a moment over my bollocks, then settled on my kneecaps.

'Now raise your hands above your head.' Dijani was still doing the talking.

Rexho went behind me and ran the tips of his fingers around my waist and chest and under my arms. Then my legs, from ankles to groin. And emptied my pockets.

The binos, torch, maps, blueprint and a small wad of euros were soon sitting by the radio operator's mic.

The stiletto came last.

I still couldn't see him, but I could hear the blade snap out of the handle. Then I felt cold steel, first against my throat, then up my right nostril, about as far as it could go.

Keeping it in place, he moved round in front of me again.

Those eyes burnt into mine. The melted skin on his neck seemed to glow and pulsate.

A teardrop gathered on my lid and rolled down my cheek as my sinus got a metallic massage. I couldn't help it. He liked that.

He also liked the fact that I didn't know whether he was going to shove the blade into my brain, or take it out of the side of my nose, as a tribute to the brother I'd left in Switzerland.

Finally, Rexho simply removed it, and ran a finger not at all gently along the scab left by the stripy projectile that had been launched at me through the windscreen of the Nissan.

He seemed a bit disappointed by what he saw.

'You?'

He nodded, then pointed at the centre of my forehead. 'I wanted here.'

Dijani stayed on the far side of the console, but now moved close enough for me to see his face. His grey suit was immaculate. He didn't have a hair out of place. But just for a moment his eyes also burnt with something raw and explosive.

When he spoke again, his voice was even, and his expression didn't shift a millimetre. 'It took a very long time for my men to persuade Anna to give us your name, Nick Stone . . .'

My blood turned to ice. I'd never understood that phrase before. I did now.

18

'Where are they? Can I see them?'

Just being with them would be one step closer to getting them out.

'My people found her in Vinnitsa, Nick. They hurt her. Quite badly, I'm told. They had to. We knew Frank had called you in. The bodyguard supplied us with your first name, and hers, and a rough description of you both. But he proved difficult to trust, and we knew so little about you. We needed *her* to tell us who you were, and to help us find you.

'Sadly, she wasn't keen to do so.'

He sighed. But not with regret.

'They may have fucked her. I don't know for certain. I didn't question them too closely.'

His brown eyes glistened.

I shifted my viewpoint and stared out of the front window at the skeleton of the mobile crane.

'She remained silent, though. For days. I have the impression that she once loved you . . . very, *very* much . . .'

He let the silence lengthen before moving in for the kill.

'It was only when they began to damage her child that she began to tell us the things we wanted to know.'

He paused.

'*Your* child too, of course . . .'

I lowered my arms. Felt my fists clench. I couldn't help it. I also wanted to test the tightness of the cuffs.

I lifted my right boot no more than a millimetre. Maybe I was going to take a step forward.

The laser sight closest to Dijani took first pressure.

I stayed just where I was.

'We know very many things about you now, Nick. Interesting things. We know you were in the Special Air Service. We know you fought in Iraq. And Afghanistan. We know what you did there. And what you did in Somalia. And Libya.

'We know you killed many of our brothers in these places. Many soldiers of Allah. We know what you have done in Switzerland. And what you have done here. Now you will pay the price for all these things.'

'Whatever.' I kept my voice as level as possible.

'But I need to see Anna and the boy first.'

'Of course.' He gestured towards Rexho. 'Give him back his torch. We must not keep them in the dark.'

He picked up the blueprint and turned back to me. 'Frank Timis took a great interest in this ship. If he hadn't, it's possible that he might still be alive today, and that none of this would have happened.'

Rexho handed me the torch and spun me back towards the door. At the top of the ladder he told me to turn and climb down backwards. He didn't want me to jump on top of him and take him down. But I would have belly-crawled all the way on broken glass if it meant getting to Anna and our son.

One step closer. If we're all breathing, we're all winning.

He led the way. The plasticuffs weren't making things easy for me. The two triggers followed. I could see that they were itching to fuck me up. The front one waved his muzzle at me whenever I slowed or looked set to deviate, and the red dot danced across my chest. But I wasn't going anywhere, not yet.

Rexho reached the bottom rung. A gust of cooler air brushed past me as he opened the door into the hold and the hum got a little louder.

19

The hold wasn't completely empty. Two layers of containers were tethered to the racks below deck level, but no one seemed to care about them. They aimed me at an open hatch between the furthest two.

There was a bit more space down there, and the laser sights kept their distance, from me and from each other.

I followed Rexho down through the hatch. Another ladder, and the hum turned into a throb. I knew from the blueprint that we were as far into the bowels of the ship as it was possible to go, but the sudden cold and the dim lighting could have told me that on their own.

A line of low-wattage bulkhead lamps led down the entire length of the passageway. Each had a door beside it, with a centrally mounted, four-spoke wheel that rotated to engage and release the locking mechanism.

I was experiencing at first hand the place that had got Frank worried. When I saw the lead lining on the half-open door at the pointy end of the ship, I was worried too. And I couldn't see any sign of a vent.

'No vents, Nick . . .'

The key phrases from his briefing in Courchevel finally filled my head. *'And the lead can only mean two things. You know this. They need to store something in there that they don't wish to be traced. Or something that requires a radiation shield . . .'*

But that shit was for another day. All that mattered now was that if Anna and Nicholai were being held on the boat this was where they would be.

Rexho stepped behind the heavy steel panel so that he could pull it fully open and leave me room to enter the pitch-black compartment.

There was no movement from inside, no voices.

'Anna!'

Nothing.

I launched myself forward, grabbed the barrel of the SAW in my plasticuffed hands, and wrenched it to one side. I thought the guy holding it might loosen his grip to prevent himself being pulled down.

He didn't. Three rounds kicked off into the door, echoing down the hold, as he hung on tight and nosedived towards the deck and took me with him. My back hit the metal, and now my head did too – hard enough to stop me bouncing straight back up.

I lay there for long enough to see a red dot on my chest.

But he didn't fire.

Keeping the dot in position, he stepped back and left Rexho room to kneel by me.

The stiletto went back up my nose.

And took the side exit.

Blood spurted across my cheek and into my right eye and mouth as the pain catapulted itself around my head. And Rexho's hand closed over my throat.

I felt his sour breath on my skin.

I knew he was itching to squeeze the life out of me.

I balled my fists and prepared to swivel and twist and bring them up and—

He said one word: 'Don't.'

But he didn't tighten his grip.

He got to his feet.

I couldn't see anything now. My eyes were gummed up with blood, and my face felt as big as a beach ball. The pain pulsated with my heartbeat.

He stepped over the coaming, then gripped my arms and

dragged me into the darkness. There was a metallic echo as the thing clanked shut.

It wasn't the only echo in my head. Hesco's words had forced their way in there too. '*You . . . cannot imagine . . . how much pain . . . you will be in . . .*'

20

I turned and leant my head against the lead and closed my eyes.

'Nick . . .'

Voices.

'Nick . . .'

Women's voices. One of them sounds . . . Russian . . .

'You stupid little—'

Not that one. That's my mate Gaz's mum. I'd know her anywhere. She'd caught us throwing condoms full of tomato sauce off the roof of his block of flats . . .

Fuck, my head hurt. I wanted to try to stop the warm capillary bleeding that was flowing down my neck, but there wasn't any point.

Even when you can't see in a confined space, you know if you're not alone.

I was not alone.

'Anna? Nicholai?'

I flicked on my torch and played the beam across the side wall, across the ceiling ten centimetres above me, along the floor. The space was four metres long and three wide. I took my time scanning it, because I was in no hurry to find what I was now certain I was going to find.

She sat there looking at me. Wedged into the far corner, her back against the wall, her legs stretched out in front of her. She was clutching a bundle to her chest.

She was wearing a black jumpsuit with a wide embroidered sash around her waist. It had always been one of my favourites, but I wasn't sure I'd ever told her that. A grey fleece too, unzipped. And trainers.

Nicholai was in a check shirt and jeans I'd bought for him at GUM when he wasn't even crawling. Anna had taken the piss out of me relentlessly for getting an outfit that was about fifty-three sizes too large. I guess I must have been thinking about a time when we'd go hiking and do boy stuff together.

There were smudges of blood on our little boy's clothes. It had leaked from the places her fingernails used to be.

There was a lot of bruising and grazing on her face. But Anna still looked like the blonde one from Abba. She still looked beautiful.

I didn't think she had died in that position. The fuckers had propped her up like a ventriloquist's dummy.

I felt a flood of bile burn the back of my throat as I knelt beside her. I managed to swallow it back as I brushed her cheek with my fingertips. I leant forward to kiss her forehead. She was cold and tasted of salt and my blood.

Dijani had said they'd threatened to damage Nicholai.

I couldn't bring myself to turn him over at first. Then I did. His face looked . . . peaceful.

I picked him up and wrapped him in my arms; tucked his head between my shoulder and my cheek. It was a while before I realized I was rocking backwards and forwards.

I didn't need to do that.

He was already asleep.

I gave him back to his mother.

How long had they been there?

It would have been dark.

So dark.

He'd have been frightened.

She was hurting.

She'd have known that they'd run out of oxygen at some point.

An adult breathes in just short of two cubic metres of pure oxygen per day.

The air we inhale is about twenty per cent oxygen.

The air we exhale is about fifteen per cent . . .

I knew I was trying to lose myself in another sum.

It wasn't working.

She'd have taken him in her arms and told him not to be afraid. That she was here for him. That she loved him. And his dad would be here soon.

She'd have sung to him. She always did that when he woke in the dark hours of the night.

I wondered whether she had smothered Nicholai before he started hurting too.

I hoped so.

21

The bile wasn't the only thing that burnt in me.

Rage did too.

The kind that starts low down in your belly and fills every fibre of your being.

It can fuck you up badly. I'd seen that happen all too often. It can breathe all your available oxygen, and make you do stupid shit.

But if you point it in the right direction, it can give you fuel when it's most needed.

I leant forward again, untied Anna's embroidered sash, and shoved it against my face in an attempt to stop the blood flow. And, maybe, to smell her for the last time.

I touched her cheek again. Told her and Nicholai I was going to get us all out of here, then kill the fuckers that had done this.

I hung the sash around my neck and went back to where the rounds had hit the door. They hadn't made much of a dent in the steel, but had buried themselves in the lead coating. I worked the top one backwards and forwards until it came loose. Then I shoved my finger into the hole and tried to peel it back. If I could get beneath the skin at the centre of the panel, maybe I could access the reverse side of the rotating lock.

If not, they'd be back for me soon, now they'd had their laugh. I'd be waiting. Just like infantry who run out of ammo while the enemy are still attacking. They take off their helmets and get ready to batter the fuckers to death, or get killed trying.

The lead didn't move a millimetre.

I undid my belt, raised the buckle and tried with the prong instead. At the fifth or sixth attempt, I started to get somewhere.

After an hour of hard graft with the prong and the buckle frame I'd managed to make some progress. I was starting to drip with sweat, but I'd opened up about a twelve-centimetre gash in the lining and the longer it became, the easier it was to apply the leverage I needed to open it further.

I wiped the sweat and blood off my face with the end of Anna's sash, and carried on. At least the flow had almost stopped.

I was doing some thinking too. Thinking about what Dijani could have brought here, and where he might have brought it from. Odessa was where *Minerva*'s voyage had begun.

A WMD?

I didn't think so. Putin's people kept a close watch on those.

But you could still help yourself to bits that glowed from the rusting hulks in the submarine pens on the Arctic coast.

After another hour, I'd got to the place I was aiming for. I could see four concave bolts, which must have anchored the wheel mounting. And fuck-all else.

What had I been expecting? A rotating head like the ones that helped you gain access to a toilet cubicle?

I wiped my hands on the front of my jeans and took a deep breath.

Then I heard a noise directly behind my metalwork, and a series of clicks as the locks disengaged. I stood, a chunk of lead in each hand, ready to slam them into the first face I saw and then keep going until they were down or I was.

Deep breaths, ready to go for it.

Finally, the door swung open.

The first figure I saw was in black kit, head to toe, with 'CARABINIERI' written in gold across his chest, and a badge on his left sleeve: the GIS's version of the Regiment's winged dagger. He didn't enter, just stepped back into the passageway, leaving room for Luca to come into my cell, his torch burning a hole in the darkness.

He took one look at me, then at the bodies in the corner.

He didn't ask the question. He already knew the answer.

He just gritted his teeth, gripped my shoulder briefly and beckoned me outside.

'Nico—'

'Don't.' I put a finger to my lips.

More GIS moved aside as Luca followed me back along the passageway and up through the hatch into the hold. I didn't stop until I'd walked down the gangway and was in among the flashing lights on the quay.

I scanned the immediate area – unsuccessfully – for the BMW and the Land Cruiser.

Then I was ready to listen.

The GIS had stormed in twenty minutes ago, too late to nail Dijani and Rexho, but soon enough to persuade the two guys guarding the hold to hand over their weapons.

'SAWs? Laser sights?'

Luca shrugged. 'Maybe. These things all look the same to me.'

The hatch had been open, so they hadn't wasted time searching the containers.

I gestured towards the entrance gate. 'Did security see them lift anything off the boat?'

'Yes.' He frowned. 'They said it looked like a coffin.'

'Mate, when they get the bodies to the hospital, ask the pathologist to test for radiation poisoning. I don't think that's what killed them, but the lead is down there for a reason.'

'*You* can ask.'

He pointed to what was left of my face and I realized he could hardly speak. He was drowning in the pain I was doing my best to cut away from.

'No. You got a car here?'

He pointed at a mid-size Alfa Romeo a short distance beyond the ring of VM 90s, and handed me the fob.

'A spare phone?'

He sorted me there too.

'And a weapon?'

I knew from his expression that he would have if he could have.

The coffin confirmed my suspicions about the activity in the barn. The graveyard must be where they'd hidden what they'd taken off the boat. And now the GIS were on his doorstep instead of messing about in Brindisi, I reckoned Dijani would be forced to change his plans and lift it out again before first light.

'One more thing. Ask Pasha if they've got any recent thefts of uranium from the Soviet navy on record. From a decommissioned sub, maybe. Murmansk is full of that kind of shit. Over to you, mate.'

22

I left him to it and fired up the Alfa. I turned right off the roundabout, paralleling the beach in the opposite direction to the graveyard. I doubted that Dijani had a big enough team to have eyes on the cargo quay, but it wouldn't do any harm to make it look like I was heading for Bari before doubling back.

I parked in one of the residential streets between the hospital and the cypress avenue, skirted the roundabout and followed the path up the edge of the cemetery that I'd taken earlier.

The mobile crane was in position at the rear, engine running and hoist fully extended. The three-tonner was next to it. I could see movement in each cab. And two silhouettes on the ground, waiting to be lifted over the wall.

I went back to the most easily climbable of the trees and swung myself inside, on to the roof of the nearest building. They weren't short of cypresses in here too. In the thin moonlight they cast long shadows across the shiny white graves and crosses, and the maze of stone and marble buildings that housed the dead. As my breathing got heavier my split nostril started to make a rasping noise. The skin flapped and kicked off the pain once more. Fuck it, I'd get it sorted later.

It really was like a separate city, with its own paved streets, squares, monuments and glass-fronted chapels of all shapes and sizes.

I spotted more movement fifty to my half-right. I didn't have time to fuck about. I grabbed the edge of the parapet and lowered myself to the ground.

Like almost everywhere else I'd seen in Italy, this place was a mixture of shiny new, classic old, under construction and falling apart. Keeping in the shadows, I made the most of the cover provided by rows of headstones. A light flickered somewhere to my left. It wasn't a torch beam, though. It was one of those little electric candles that someone had left running on an altar.

Something else glinted by a mound of freshly dug earth. When I got closer, I found a shovel that hadn't been gathered at the end of the day and returned to the storeroom.

I picked it up and looped round towards what turned out to be a not-quite-derelict family mausoleum.

The stone facing had flaked away and the roof was crumbling. The door must have fallen off a while back. It had been replaced by a random selection of boards nailed to a rickety frame. That too had been moved aside to allow access. I couldn't see much of the interior except for a bunch of memorial plaques and a big hole in the ground.

I heard voices coming from inside – not very happy ones – and saw the silhouette of a body climbing out of it. When he reached the threshold, the figure turned and issued a string of instructions to whoever was still in the pit. It sounded like they were doing the heavy lifting. The boss man had swapped his sharp grey suit for jeans and a fleece, but he still didn't want to get his hands dirty. A couple of thick undertakers' straps lay coiled at his feet.

I scanned the area around us. Nobody else seemed to be coming to help. Rubble was moved. A tarpaulin pulled off. Dijani was still calling the shots. He still had his back to me.

I was no more than five paces from him now. I gripped the shaft of the shovel with both hands, raised it across my right shoulder like an axe, and swung the edge of the blade as hard as I could at the side of his neck. It wasn't the sharpest tool in the box, so I didn't take his head clean off. It stayed attached to his body long enough to tumble forwards into the pit with him.

I followed him in. Dijani landed on top of the one on the left. The one on the right was tangled up in the tarp they'd used to cover the coffin. I rotated the shaft so the shovel blade pointed downwards and chopped it deep into the place where his neck joined his torso. I felt his collarbone shatter and saw blood spurt from the wound. He still managed to hook my ankles with his good arm and sweep my feet from under me.

As my arse hit the ground he raised the same hand – not to hit me, but to try and stem the flow from his shoulder.

It wasn't going to happen.

I kicked him backwards and focused on his mate.

The guy was lying alongside the coffin, still trying to shift the weight of the boss man off his chest. His eyes widened as I turned and raised the shovel once more, like I was about to dig myself a hole.

He raised both hands in surrender.

Fuck that.

I brought the blade down on his bulging Adam's apple.

I glanced across at the other guy. He'd failed to locate and seal the soggy end of his carotid artery between his thumb and forefinger, and was bleeding out. Even if he'd succeeded, there wouldn't have been enough oxygen feeding his brain.

I frisked them both for weapons. No joy there. And even in the darkness, I could see that neither of them was Rexho Uran.

I grabbed Dijani by the ear. That was all it took to remove his head from his shoulders. I held it up for a moment, thinking I might feel some satisfaction. But I felt nothing. Nothing at all.

Then I chucked it into the pit and climbed out of the ruins of the suddenly rather overcrowded mausoleum.

23

I heard two or three sets of footsteps approaching and saw some more of those red dots dancing among the headstones. I hung a rapid left and legged it back to what I could now see was a small family memorial chapel. I heaved myself on to the roof and out.

As I swung down from the tree branch, I heard more footsteps at the back, and another engine sparking up.

I hit the keypad of Luca's spare mobile as soon as I'd crossed the main and was fifty from the Alfa. 'Mate, get the GIS to the cemetery *now*. Dijani is dead. There are still at least four of the fuckers, in a blue Fiat three-tonner, and a hoist. They're trying to move the shit they brought in.'

'You still think uranium?'

'Tell GIS to get a fucking move on and we'll find out.'

I'd just pressed the fob and seen the Alfa's lights flash when I heard the shriek of tyres behind me. I jumped into the driver's seat and slammed the ignition button as the rear-view filled with light.

I swung the wheel hard left, flicked the Alfa's headlamps on to main beam and did a screaming U-turn. Tyres smoking, I throttled up, straight into the path of the oncoming wagon.

He lost his nerve first. He hadn't taken his helmet off and got ready to fight.

He swerved right and bounced off a line of parked cars. I glanced left as I sped past. A BMW SUV. Rexho wrestling with the wheel.

The darkness ahead of me was filled with blues and twos. I glanced behind to see the SUV doing half a doughnut, steadying itself then coming after me.

A spider's web of cracks appeared in the top corner of the Alfa's rear screen as I went left, and the round exited through the window just behind the passenger headrest.

Another shrieked through, punching a hole the size of a fist in the centre of the glass and burying itself in the dash.

I floored the accelerator pedal on the approach to the level crossing. The lights flashed and the barrier started to lower when I was ten away. I kept going.

The paintwork on Luca's roof took some punishment, and his suspension didn't take bumping over the railway track at speed too well, but the SUV came off worse. It managed to get under the first barrier without losing everything above the bonnet, but hit the second head-on.

I put some distance between us as Rexho smashed the entire structure off its mounting and went into a ninety-degree skid. He added another two parked cars to his scorecard, sorted himself, and was thirty behind me when I took the next left, along the remains of the old city wall.

This was the highest-risk stretch for me.

I couldn't step on the gas.

It was too narrow to dodge and weave.

And if my plan was going to work, I needed him to be close enough not to be able to take evasive action.

His headlamps started to fill my rear-view again as I passed the shop where I'd bought the maps and then the boutique hotel. I careered through the small square overlooking the water.

Every parking space was taken.

I reckoned the SUV's fucked-up radiator grille was ten behind me as the scaffolding-covered apartment block loomed ahead.

I took a round in the right shoulder as I hit the throttle again but I still had enough control to swing the wheel left and take out the last two upright poles.

For a heartbeat, fuck-all happened.

Then the timber planks began to cascade off their supports and a few hundred tubes of heavy metal and sheets of tarp crashed down to fill the space between the front of the building and the harbour wall.

I hit the brakes as soon as I was a safe distance away. I got out, but didn't walk back. I just needed to make sure all that shit had landed on Rexho's head.

It had.

The front of the SUV had been flattened. The roof was half the height it had been two minutes ago.

But when the last pole and plank had fallen and the dust had started to clear, I saw movement behind what was left of the windscreen.

I scrambled over the debris and peered through the driver's window.

Rexho turned his very bloody head towards me. His mouth opened and closed like a goldfish, but no sound came out.

It would take a squad of firemen and cutting equipment to extract him. And the chances were that he'd be dead before they arrived.

But I didn't want to leave anything to chance.

I took off Anna's sash, reached inside, looped it twice around his throat, and pulled it tight.

He probably thought he was being fast-tracked to Paradise. I hoped he'd end up somewhere he could carry on feeling the pain.

As shutters started to open further down the street and across the square, I slid back behind the wheel of Luca's slightly bruised Alfa, draped the sash back around my shoulders, and drove away. Keeping a memento wouldn't bring them back. But I knew that any time I looked at it I was now going to feel a little bit better.

EPILOGUE

They stitched my nostril and sorted the rest of the damage at the hospital a little later that morning, a couple of floors above the pathology lab where Anna and Nicholai had been taken.

Luca was very understanding about the damage to his wagon, and keen to bring me up to speed on the GIS. They'd picked up the coffin. The rods of depleted uranium 235 inside it *had* come from a decommissioned Oscar-11 Class sub. Its ID code had been stamped into the casing.

Three rods was enough to make a very big dirty bomb, irrespective of whether they detonated it in Otranto or in St Peter's Square. No wonder the GIGN, TIGRIS and the GIS had been going ballistic for Dijani and his crew.

Anna and Nicholai did show signs of radiation poisoning, but not at a critical level. He hadn't been able to meet my eye when he told me that.

The last three members of Dijani's cell were in custody. One of them seemed to be keen to trade in his passport to Paradise for a place in their witness-protection scheme. He wasn't telling them everything, but had fed them one or two details.

He'd confirmed that Rome was in their sights.

They'd been tempted by the idea of reminding the world about Gedik Ahmed's great victory in Otranto in 1480, but St Peter's was a more iconic target. The cradle of Christianity. And since the Pope continued to ignore his security advisers and walk among the infidel, they had been confident of success.

I liked Luca a lot, and not just because he'd saved my life. But I found him tough to be around. The sharply chiselled crusading journo I'd met in the mattress shop had been replaced by a whipped dog. He still couldn't hide the things I was trying to bury. So I wasn't sorry to see him go.

I retrieved my day sack from where I'd hidden it, sparked up the Seat and drove towards the cemetery. Luca had told me that a couple of graves had already been selected for Anna and Nicholai, complete with all the nice shiny marble one could wish for. It was the city's gift to them, and to me.

I stopped halfway down the cypress avenue, and looked at the slightly weird motif on the stark white panels each side of the entrance: a couple of crossed bones and the Grim Reaper's scythe.

I hadn't gone down to see their bodies in the hospital. I wasn't going to visit their grave sites now. I had the sash, and that would do me.

My mantra had always been: Why worry about what you can't change? If I said it often enough, I might start to believe it.

ABOUT THE AUTHOR

From the day he was found in a carrier bag on the steps of Guy's Hospital in London, **Andy McNab** has led an extraordinary life.

As a teenage delinquent, Andy McNab kicked against society. As a young soldier, he waged war against the IRA in the streets and fields of South Armagh. As a member of 22 SAS, he was at the centre of covert operations for nine years, on five continents. During the Gulf War he commanded Bravo Two Zero, a patrol that, in the words of his commanding officer, 'will remain in regimental history for ever'. Awarded both the Distinguished Conduct Medal (DCM) and Military Medal (MM) during his military career, McNab was the British Army's most highly decorated serving soldier when he finally left the SAS.

Since then Andy McNab has become one of the world's best-selling writers, drawing on his insider knowledge and experience. As well as three non-fiction bestsellers – including *Bravo Two Zero,* the bestselling British work of military history – he is the author of the bestselling Nick Stone thrillers. He has also written a number of books for children.

Besides his writing work, he lectures to security and intelligence agencies in both the USA and the UK, works in the film industry advising Hollywood on everything from covert procedure to training civilian actors to act like soldiers, and he continues to be a spokesperson and fundraiser for both military and literacy charities.

www.andymcnab.co.uk